Paolo Bacigalupi is a Hugo and Nebula Award Winner. His YA novel, *Ship Breaker*, was shortlisted for the National Book Award. He lives in Colorado with his wife and son.

THE DOUBT FACTORY

Paolo Bacigalupi

ATOM

ATOM

First published in the United States in 2014 by Little, Brown and Company
First published in Great Britain in 2016 by Atom

1 3 5 7 9 10 8 6 4 2

Copyright © 2014 by Paolo Bacigalupi

The moral right of the author has been asserted.

A CIP catalogue record for this book
is available from the British Library.

ISBN 978-0-349-00256-9 (paperback)
ISBN 978-0-349-00255-2 (eBook)

Printed and bound in Great Britain by
Clays Ltd, St Ives plc

Papers used by Atom are from well-managed forests
and other responsible sources.

MIX

For Anjula

PROLOGUE

HE'D BEEN WATCHING HER FOR a long time. Watching how she moved through the still waters of her life. Watching the friends and family who surrounded her. It was like watching a bright tropical fish in an aquarium, bounded on all sides, safe inside the confines. Unaware of the glass walls.

He could watch her sitting at a coffee shop, intent on something in her e-book reader, drinking the same skinny latte that she always ordered. He knew her street, and he knew her home. He knew her class schedule. Calculus and AP Chem, Honors English. A 3.9 GPA, because some asshole bio teacher had knocked off her perfect score over a triviality of how she formatted her lab notes.

Smart girl.

Sharp girl.

And yet completely unaware.

It wasn't her fault. All the fish in her tank were the same.

All of them swimming in perfectly controlled waters, bare millimeters from another world that was hostile to them entirely.

Moses Cruz felt like he'd been watching all of them forever. But Alix Banks he could watch in that aquarium and hours could pass. Fund-raising events, field hockey tournaments, vacations to Saint Barts and Aspen. It was a safe and quiet world she lived in, and she—just like a beautiful neon tetra in a tropical tank—had no idea she was being watched.

All of her people were like that. Just a bunch of pretty fish in love with themselves and how beautiful they were, in love with their little aquarium castles. All of them thinking that they ran the world. None of them realizing that only a thin pane of glass separated them from disaster.

And here he was, standing outside, holding a hammer.

PART 1

PART 1

ALIX WAS SITTING IN AP CHEM when she saw him.

She'd been gazing out the window, letting her eyes wander over the perfectly manicured grounds of Seitz Academy's academic quad, and as soon as she saw him standing outside, she had the feeling she knew him.

Familiar.

That was how she put it later, talking to the cops. He'd seemed familiar. Like someone's older brother, the one you only glimpsed when he was back from college. Or else the sib whom Seitz wouldn't let in because of "behavioral match issues." The one who didn't attend the school but showed up with Mommy and Daddy at the Seitz Annual Auction anyway because sis was Seitz Material even though he wasn't. The resentful lone wolf who leaned against the back wall, texting his friends about how fucked up it was that he was stuck killing the night watching his parents get sloppy drunk while they bid on vacations to Saint Martin and find-yourself-in-middle-age pottery classes at Lena Chisolm's studio/gallery.

Familiar.

Like her tongue running the line of her teeth. Never seen, but still, known.

He was standing outside, staring up at the science building.

Ms. Liss (never Mrs. and definitely not Miss—Ms. with the *z*, right?) was passing back AP Chem lab reports. Easy A's. Even when Liss was putting on the pressure, she never pushed hard enough, so Alix had let the activity of the class fade into the background: students in their lab coats beside their personal sinks and burners, the rustle of papers, Ms. Liss droning on about top-tier colleges (which was code for the Ivy Leagues) and how no one was getting anywhere if they didn't challenge themselves—and Alix thinking that no one was getting anywhere anytime soon.

Suspended animation was how she thought of it some-times. She was just another student in a cohort of students being groomed and sculpted and prepped for the future. She sometimes imagined them all floating in liquid suspension, rows and rows in holding tanks, all of them drifting. Seitz-approved skirts and blazers billowing. School ties drifting with the currents. Hair tangling across blank faces, bubbles rising from silent lips. Tangles and bubbles. Waiting for someone to say that they were finished.

Other times, she thought of it as being prepped for a race

that they were never quite allowed to run. Each Seitz student set up and poised, runners on their starting blocks, ready to take over the world—as soon as their control-freak parents decided to let them get their hands on their trust funds. But no one ever gave them the gun, so they all waited and partied and studied and tested and added extracurriculars like volunteering at the battered women's shelter in Hartford so they could have "meaningful" material for their college-entrance essays.

And then she caught sight of him—that loner marooned on Seitz's emerald lawns—and everything changed.

For a second, when she first spied him, Alix was almost convinced that she'd conjured him. He was so weirdly recognizable to her that it seemed like he could only have emerged from her own mind. A good-looking black guy in a trench coat. Short little dreadlocks, or maybe cornrows—it was hard to tell from this distance—but cool-looking whatever it was. A little bit gangsta…and he was so unsettlingly *familiar* to her. Like some kind of music star, some guy out of the Black Eyed Peas who looked better than Will.i.am. Not an Akon, not a Kanye. They were too clean-cut.…But still, somebody famous.

The more Alix studied him, the more he appeared out of place. He was just standing there, staring up at the science building. Maybe he was lost? Like his sister had been kidnapped and dragged to one of the whitest schools on the East Coast, and he was here to break her out.

Well, the school wasn't *all* white, but pretty close. Alix could think of maybe six kids who were actually black, and two of them were adopted. Of course, there was a solid helping of Asians and Indians because there were so many Wall Street quants who sent their kids to the school, but they were, as one of Alix's friends put it, "the other white meat." Which said all you really needed to know about Seitz. If you were Ivy-bound, and headed for money and power, Seitz Academy found that it could hit its diversity targets easily.

But there was that black guy standing outside, looking in. Cool. Old-school aviator shades. Army jacket kind of trench. Looking like he could stand out on the grass all day long, watching Alix and her classmates.

Was he a new student? It was hard to guess his age from this distance, but she thought he could be the right age for a senior.

Just then, Mr. Mulroy came into view, striding with purpose.

From the man's attitude, Alix could tell the Seitz headmaster didn't think the black guy belonged on his lawn. Mulroy moved into the stranger's space. Alix could see the man's lips moving, telling the stranger he wasn't at the right school.

Move along.

Mulroy pointed off campus, his body language loaded with authority—arm out and rigid, finger pointing—ordering the intruder back wherever he'd come from, back to wherever black kids came from when they weren't here on a scholarship or given a pass via Nigerian oil money into Seitz's manicured world.

Mulroy made another sharp gesture of authority. Alix

had seen him do the same with new students who he nailed smoking. She'd watched them cringe and gather up their backpacks as the headmaster herded them into Weller House's admin offices for their sentencing. Mulroy was used to making rebellious rich kids believe he was in charge. He was good at it.

The black guy was still staring up at the school, nodding as if he were paying attention to the headmaster's words. But he wasn't moving to go at all. Mulroy said something else.

The stranger glanced over, taking in the man for the first time. Tall, Alix realized. He was at least as tall as the headmaster—

The stranger buried a fist into Mulroy's gut.

Mulroy doubled over.

What the—?

Alix pressed against the glass, staring, trying to make sense of what she'd just witnessed. Had she really just seen Mulroy get *punched*? It had been so fast, and yet there the headmaster was, clutching his gut and gagging, looking like he was trying to throw up. The black guy was bracing him up now, patting the headmaster on the back. Patting him like a baby. Soothing.

The headmaster sank to his knees. The stranger gently let the headmaster down and laid the man on the grass.

Mulroy rolled onto his back, still clutching his belly. The stranger crouched beside him, seeming to say something as he laid his hand on the older man's chest.

"Holy shit," Alix whispered. Gaining her senses, she

turned to the rest of the class. "Someone just beat the shit out of Mr. Mulroy!"

Everyone rushed for the windows. The intruder had straightened. He looked up at them as everyone crowded against the glass for a view. A strange, isolated figure standing over the laid-out body of his victim. They all stared down at him, and he stared back. A frozen moment, everyone taking stock of one another—and then the guy smiled, and his smile was radiant.

He didn't seem bothered at all that the headmaster was sprawled at his feet, nor that he had the entire class as witnesses. He looked completely at home.

Still smiling, the stranger gave them a lazy salute and strode off. He didn't even bother to run.

Mulroy was trying to get up, but he was having a hard time of it. Alix was dimly aware of Ms. Liss calling security, using the hotline number they were supposed to use if there was ever a campus shooter. Her voice kept cracking.

"We should help him!" someone said, and everyone made a rush for the door. But Liss shouted at them all to get back to their seats, and then she was back on the phone, trying to give instructions to security. "He's right outside Widener Hall!" she was saying over and over again.

The guy who had hit Mulroy had already ambled out of sight. All that was left were Mulroy lying in the grass and Alix trying to make sense of what she'd witnessed.

It had been utterly unlike any school fight she'd ever seen. Nothing like the silly strutting matches where two dudebros started shouting at each other, and then maybe pushed each other a little, and then maybe danced around playing as if they were serious—with neither of them doing much—until maybe, finally, the shame and gathering spectator pressure forced them to throw an actual punch.

Those fights almost immediately ended up as a tangle on the floor, with a couple of red-faced guys squirming and grunting and swearing, tearing at each other's clothes and trying out their wrestling holds and not doing much damage one way or the other, except that the school ended up having discussions about conflict resolution for a week.

This had been different, though. No warnings and no threats. The black guy had just turned and put his fist into Mulroy's gut, and Mulroy was done. No second round, nothing. The boy—the more she thought about it, the more Alix thought he really was student age—had just destroyed Mulroy.

Ms. Liss was still speaking urgently into the phone, but now Alix spied the school's security team dashing across the quad from Weller House. Too late, of course. They'd probably been eating doughnuts and watching *South Park* reruns behind their desks when Liss's call came in.

Cynthia Yang was leaning over Alix's shoulder, watching the slow-moving campus cops.

"If there's ever a school shooting, we're toast." Cynthia snorted. "Look at that reaction time."

"Seriously," Emil chimed in. "My dad's security could get here faster, and they're across town."

11

Emil's dad was some kind of diplomat. He was always reminding people how important his dad was, which was seriously annoying, but Alix had to admit Emil was right. She'd seen that security detail once when they'd partied at Emil's summer house in the Hamptons, and those guys had definitely been more on top of it than Seitz Academy's rent-a-cops.

The campus cops finally made it to Mulroy. He was on his feet now, though bent over and gasping, and he shook off their help. Alix didn't need to hear the words to know what Mulroy was saying as he pointed off campus. *"Go get the guy who beat the hell out of me!"* Or something like that.

From where Alix was standing, she knew they'd fail. The puncher was long gone.

■ ■ ■

A few hours later Alix heard from Cynthia that, sure enough, they hadn't found the guy. He'd just evaporated.

"Poof!" Cynthia said. "Like smoke."

"Like smoke," Alix echoed.

"I heard he was from the low-income housing over on the east side," Sophie said.

"I heard he's an escaped convict," Tyler said, plopping down beside them. "Some kind of ax murderer."

They all kept chattering and speculating, but Alix wasn't paying attention. She couldn't stop playing the incident over in her head. A shattering of Seitz's model perfection that wasn't supposed to happen, like a bum crapping in the reflecting pool near her father's offices in DC, or a runway model with lipstick smeared across her face in a jagged red slash.

As soon as the rent-a-cops had started questioning the students, descriptions of the intruder had started falling apart: He was tall, he was short, he had dreads, he had braids. Someone said he had a rainbow knitted Rasta beret, someone else said he had a gold-and-diamond grill—it quickly turned into a strange jumble of conflicting stereotypes that had nothing to do with the guy Alix had seen.

For Alix, he remained fixed in her mind, unchanged by the shifting stories of her peers. He stayed with her through Honors English and then followed her out to the track. And even though she ran until her lungs were fire and her legs were rubber, she couldn't shake the image of him.

She could play the entire event back in her mind as if in slow motion. She could still see the stranger's green army trench billowing around him as he squatted beside the head-master. She could still see the guy laying his hand on Mulroy's chest, soothing him.

She could see him looking up at the class. She could see him smile.

And the memory of his smile started her running again, pushing against her pounding heart and her ragged breath and her aching legs. Pushing against the memory of the stranger, because she could swear that when he looked up, he hadn't cared about all the AP Chem students crowding around and staring from the windows. He hadn't been looking at any of them.

He'd been staring directly at her.

He'd been smiling at *her*.

And she still couldn't shake the feeling that she'd seen him before. Familiar and frightening at the same time. Like the smell of an electrical storm looming on the horizon, ozone and moisture and winds and promise, swirling down after a long time dry.

2

AT DINNER, ALIX'S YOUNGER BROTHER, Jonah, wouldn't quit talking about the strange event. "He completely pounded Mulroy. It was like some kind of MMA takedown."

"You weren't even there," Alix said. "He just hit him, and Mulroy keeled over."

"One hit, though, right?" Jonah mimed a punch that almost knocked his water glass off the table. He caught it just in time. "Epic!"

"Jonah," Mom said. "Please?"

Mom had put candles on the table and laid out a tablecloth. Dinner was supposed to be a family ritual, the entire Banks clan gathered and undistracted for a whole half hour, instead of grabbing something out of the fridge and separating into different rooms to play on iPads and computers or watch TV.

Mom had been on a kick for family time lately, but she

15

was fighting an uphill battle. Dad had once again brought his tablet to the table, *just to reply to one quick emergency e-mail*, he said, and so everyone was engaged in the conversation while he claimed to listen: Alix, Jonah, their mother, and half of Mr. Banks, workaholic extraordinaire.

For Mom, it counted as a win; Alix's mother took what she could get, when she could get it.

Alix's friend Cynthia was always asking what made the relationship work considering that Alix's father was never paying attention and her mother always seemed a little isolated in the project of raising her family. Alix had never really thought about it until that moment. It was just the way things were. Dad worked in public relations and made the money for the family. Mom did Pilates and book clubs and fund-raisers, and tried to gather everyone together for meals. They mostly got along. It wasn't like in Sophie's house, where you could practically hear her mom and dad chewing glass every time they said anything to each other.

"Nobody caught the guy," Alix said. "He just walked away. They called security, and the police and Mr. Mulroy went out looking for him." She took a bite of Caesar salad. "Nothing."

"I don't like the town around there," her mother said. "They should have security at the gates."

"The town around there?" Alix rolled her eyes. "Why don't you just say you don't trust *those people*, Mom?"

"That's not what I said," Mom said. "Strangers shouldn't just be able to wander onto campus. They should have a guard at the gate, at least."

"Fortress Seitz," Jonah said, pushing a crouton onto his fork with a finger. "Maybe we can put in gun turrets, too. Then we can feel really secure. Put up some barbwire, right? Fifty cals and barbwire. Oh wait, don't we call that prison?"

Mom gave him a sharp look. "Don't be smart. That's not what we're talking about. Seitz is hardly a prison, no matter how much you pretend."

"You only say that because you don't have to go," Jonah said.

Mom gave him an exasperated look. "Someone just walked onto campus and assaulted the headmaster. I'd think even you'd admit there's a problem. What if that had been a student? Don't you think that's a problem, at least?"

"I'm definitely bummed I missed it," Jonah said. "I'd pay money to see Mulroy take one in the gut."

"Jonah!"

Alix stifled a laugh. Doctors described Jonah as having poor impulse control, which basically meant that Jonah's entire world was a series of decisions that balanced precariously on the razor's edge of clever vs. stupid.

Stupid normally won out.

Which meant that since he started attending Seitz, it was Alix's job to keep an eye on him. When she'd protested that playing nursemaid for her younger brother wasn't her idea of a good time, Mom hadn't even yelled; she'd just sighed in resignation.

"I know it's not fair, Alix, but we can't always be there... and Jonah..." She sighed. "It's not his fault."

17

"Yeah, yeah. It's his nature, just like the scorpion and the frog."

Alix's nature was just the opposite. She knew the difference between clever and stupid, and didn't feel any need to dive across the line. So, as long as Mom was doing Pilates and fund-raisers and book clubs, and Dad was down in the city or seeing clients in DC, Alix was in charge of keeping an eye on the little nutball.

"We could punch him for charity," Jonah was saying. "Like those old-time dunk tanks. Big fund-raising thing. Thousand dollars a pop." He mimed punches. "Bam! Bam! Bam! Slug Mulroy and feed the homeless. I bet even Alix would donate to that," he said. "It would make her early-decision application look good."

"There aren't any homeless in Haverport," Alix said. "We put them on a bus to New York."

"So save the whales! Who cares, as long as we get to punch Mulroy."

"I don't think assault is a joke," Mom said.

They went back and forth like they always did, with Mom taking it seriously, trying to persuade Jonah to stop being "troublesome," and Jonah taking the opportunity to poke at her, saying just the right thing to annoy her again and again.

Alix tuned them out. When she played the attack back in her own mind, it made her feel a little nauseated. It had been a completely normal, boring day. She could still see Mulroy walking over to the guy, thinking that he was in charge,

18

thinking he knew what was up. Mulroy and Alix had been fooled by the spring sunshine. They'd been living inside a bubble that they'd thought was real.

And then this guy turned up at school, and the bubble popped.

"It was weird," Alix said. "Right after he punched Mulroy, the guy held Mulroy up so he didn't fall over. He was gentle about it. It almost looked tender, the way he laid him in the grass."

"Tender?" her mother said, her voice rising. "A tender assault?"

Alix rolled her eyes. "Cut it out, Mom. I'm not Jonah. I'm just saying it was weird."

But it really had looked tender, in the end. So slow and careful and gentle as he laid the man down. *Tender.* Alix knew the power of words. Dad had drilled it into her enough as a kid. Words were specific, with fine shadings and colors. You chose them to paint exactly the picture you wanted in another person's mind.

Tender.

She hadn't chosen the word accidentally. The only other word she could think of that might have described the moment was *apologetic*. Like the stranger had actually been sorry he'd beaten Mulroy up. But that didn't match with what had happened. No one *accidentally* shoved a fist into another person's stomach.

Oh, gee, sorry about that. I didn't see your belly there....

19

Dad had been reading on his tablet, half listening, half working. Now he broke in as he kept tapping on his tablet. "The school is going to hire an extra security detail. They have the young man's face from the security cameras—"

"They probably got a thousand pics," Jonah said.

Dad went on undeterred. "—police have him identified. He should be found soon."

"He's identified?" Alix asked, interested. "They already know who he is? Is he famous or something? Is he from around here?" *He looked so familiar.*

"Hardly," her father said. "He's just a vandal they've been looking for."

"How'd you find that out?"

"I called the school," her father said, barely looking up. "Mr. Mulroy, despite his terrible skills at self-defense, is a very efficient administrator."

"I'll bet he's getting a lot of calls right now," Mom said. "I wouldn't be surprised if some parents pull their children."

"There's extra security?" Alix asked. "Do they think he'll come back?"

"It seems unlikely." Dad finished his salad and set it aside. "But better safe than sorry."

"Yeah," said Jonah. "If we aren't careful, we'll come into school and the whole place will be tagged."

"I didn't say he was a spray-painter," Dad said. "I said he was a vandal."

"Like he breaks windows and things?"

"Don't get any ideas," Mom interjected.

"What did I do?" Jonah looked wounded.

"You sounded like you wanted to start a fan club," Alix said.

"You know, sometimes a question is just an innocent question," Jonah groused.

"Not with your track record, young man," Mom said as she cleared the salad dishes.

Dad was ignoring the interplay, still tapping out e-mails on his tablet.

"Mr. Mulroy didn't know what other things the young man had been up to. All he knew was that he'd been associated with extensive vandalism incidents."

"So does the vandal have a name?" Alix asked.

Dad looked up at her, frowning, suddenly serious.

Alix stopped short, surprised. It was the first time he'd really looked at her all night. Normally, Dad was Mr. Multitasker, thinking about other things, working out puzzles with his job, only half there. It was a joke among all of them that you sometimes had to ask him a question three times before he even heard you. But now he was looking at Alix full force.

When Dad focused, he really focused.

"What?" Alix asked, feeling defensive. "What did I say?"

"No."

"No, what?"

"No, he doesn't have a name."

"Nice. Ghost in the machine," Jonah said, as usual

completely unaware of the way the energy in the dining room had changed. "The man with no name." He made a funny ghost noise to go with it. *"Woooo."*

Dad didn't even look over at Jonah. He was still looking at her, and she felt suddenly as if she was picking her way through a conversation that had become more important than she'd expected. Like the time Jonah had joked about seeing Kala Spelling's mom having coffee with Mr. Underwood, the European History teacher.

"So…" Alix hesitated. "If they don't know his name… then how do they know who they're looking for? I thought you said he was identified."

"He has a track record," Dad said.

"But you don't know his name?"

"He has a nickname," Dad said finally. "Something he marks his work with."

"And it's…"

"2.0."

"That's my GPA!" Jonah said.

"In your dreams," Alix retorted. To her father, she said, "What's the name supposed to mean?"

"If anyone knew, I'm sure they would have caught him already."

■ ■ ■

Alix couldn't sleep. The strange day and conversations hung with her. Finally she got up and turned on her computer.

Jonah wasn't allowed to have a computer in his room, but Mom and Dad trusted her not to do "anything inappropriate," as Mom put it, without actually meeting Alix's eyes when she said it. So Sophie and Denise had spent a year jokingly warning her not to do "Anything Inappropriate" with her computer in her room.

She opened a browser and ran a search for *2.0*.

She found Wikipedia entries. A lot of entries for Web 2.0, Health 2.0, Creative Commons, and the Apache Software Foundation came up. There were fistfuls of computer listings, actually. Software companies released new versions all the time, tracked by their release numbers: .09 beta, 1.2 release, 2.0. The Chrome browser she was using now had a release number, too, except it was something like 33.0.

2.0…

She tried image searching and scrolled idly through the pictures that came back. Lots of corporate logos, antiseptic and staid, even as they tried to claim that they were doing something new. Gov 2.0, City 2.0, and—*seriously?*—even a Dad 2.0. Apparently everything was 2.0. Even Dad could get a new version. Alix tried to imagine what a "Dad 2.0" would look like, but all that came to mind were paunchy old dudes wearing hipster plaids and skinny jeans while swaggering around in Snuglis—

An image caught Alix's eye. She scrolled back up. She'd almost missed it, but it was different from the others.

A spray-paint tag on the side of a smokestack. Instead of the carefully designed corporate brands with *2.0*s affixed as an afterthought, this was *2.0* as red scrawl spray. From the image, it looked like it was maybe at an oil refinery. And the graffiti was high up, almost impossibly high. The image was a little blurry, shot with someone's phone, but the *2.0* was starkly legible. In the foreground, dark and sooty pipes ran this way and that, linking grimy holding tanks in an industrial tangle. Against that dark foreground, the number was like a beacon, rising high above the pipes and steam.

2.0. Bright and red and defiant.

Alix clicked through to the site, hoping for more images or an explanation, but the site the image came from was just a website for street graffiti from around the world. Random people uploading their random exploits. Among all the other art, the one that she'd found wasn't particularly compelling. It wasn't complex or wildly colorful. It wasn't clever or strange or thought-provoking. Except for its location, it was an unremarkable tag. Not like a Banksy, for example. Over the winter, Cynthia had become obsessed with Banksy because he'd been in the news again. She'd persuaded Alix to catch the train down to the city for the day to go on a treasure hunt for the guerrilla street art. They'd spent the day canvassing New York, digging up every instance they could find where the street artist had left his mark.

Alix kept scanning images, focused in the way she normally focused on Calc prep. Half an hour later she found one more picture with the *2.0* tag, this time on the side of what looked like a metal-sided warehouse. The picture looked like it had been snapped from beyond barbwire, but when she clicked through, there wasn't any information on this one, either. Just a big metal building in some place that looked like it might have been a desert, judging from the yellow dirt around it.

2.0…

A new version of…something.

Alix kept scrolling, but those were the only images that seemed relevant to 2.0 and vandalism, and even those didn't carry any real information. She went back to the smokestack picture and studied it again.

The graffiti was ridiculously high up on the smokestack. Impossible for anyone to miss. A red scrawled challenge. An arrogant mark. A statement, standing out like a beacon above the soot and industrial grime of the refinery.

2.0.

Something new.

3

WHEN ALIX PULLED HER RED MINI into Seitz's parking
lot the next day, she found herself being challenged by a cop,
who allowed her to park only after he saw Jonah's and her
school uniforms.

"Use the spaces on the far side of the lot," he said.

"What the hell?" Alix muttered as she maneuvered the
MINI through the clogged parking area, avoiding students
and other cars searching for spaces. She found an empty slot
and parked.

"Is there some kind of event happening?" Jonah wondered as students and people from off the street streamed
past.

"Guess we're going to find out."

Alix grabbed her schoolbag and climbed out of the car.
Standing beside her MINI, she scanned the crowd around
the Seitz main gate. Maybe someone famous was coming to

tour the school. Seitz students and teachers, along with town bystanders, clogged all the sidewalks and approaches to the grounds.

Alix caught sight of Derek and Cynthia in the throng. "Come on," she said to Jonah. "And stick close, for once."

She pushed into the crowd, bumping and nudging through, wedging herself between students and bystanders. Up ahead, she spied yellow crime-scene tape and heard someone shouting for everyone to "move back, move back."

Broken glimpses through the crush of the crowd showed the flashing red lights of an ambulance. Alix's heart beat faster.

I hope someone isn't hurt was her first thought. Followed quickly by *I hope it's not someone I know.*

Pushing through the crowd was slow. She was fighting against the tide, she realized. People were gradually being herded back behind the low perimeter wall that ringed Seitz's grounds. She finally managed to squeeze through the press to where she could get a view and was relieved to see there wasn't anyone lying dead. There was a fire truck parked beside the ambulance, and a couple of firemen in heavy Day-Glo coats sitting on the steps of the fire truck.

How bad can it be if the firemen are drinking coffee?

She craned her neck and caught another glimpse of yellow crime-scene tape being stretched to push the crowd farther back. Beyond the tape, though, all she could see were the fire truck and ambulance parked on the quad, and, of course, Widener Hall, with its four stories of classroom windows, all looking down on the Seitz grounds like rows of empty eyes.

27

"What's going on?" Jonah grabbed her shoulder and jumped, yanking on her in the process and earning them both dirty looks as he jostled the bystanders around them. "I can't see!"

Alix shrugged his hand off her shoulder. "I don't think anybody knows." She stood on tiptoe again. Now she spied a bunch of cops standing at the doors to Widener.

What the—?

It looked like they were in some kind of hazmat gear.

Maybe something broke in the labs. Some kind of spill.

"Alix!" Derek and Cynthia were elbowing through the crowd to join them. "Did you just get here?"

"Yeah. Do you know what's going on?"

"Everyone's clueless," Derek said as he squeezed into Alix's personal space. He shifted apologetically, trying to give her room, and bumped into her again as Cynthia plowed through to them as well.

"They've had us locked out for the last twenty minutes," she said breathlessly. "The fire truck got here just before you did. The guys in the bodysuits, too."

Alix noticed that Jonah was getting antsy, looking for a chance to slip away. She barely snagged him by his book bag and dragged him back as he tried to make an escape. "Nice try, bro."

"Come on, Alix," Jonah whined as she got a firm grip on his arm. "I just wanted to see if anyone was dead in the ambulance."

My brother, ghoul in training, Alix thought.

But Jonah's mention of bodies mirrored her own suppressed worry. The whole thing was too weird, and now that Jonah had said it out loud, it made her own anxiety suddenly feel more real as well. As if he'd invoked something that had to happen now that he'd said it.

It had happened to her friend Anna Lenay that way. She'd lost her mother and father in a small-plane accident when they were sophomores. Before her parents left, Anna had joked with her dad that he was probably going to crash the plane. It was the last thing she'd said to them before they took off for Martha's Vineyard, and Alix had been there to hear it.

One of the guys in the hazmat suits jogged over to the crowd. He was sweating when he pulled off his hood. He spoke to an officer who looked like he was in charge, and then the police were telling everyone to step back even farther.

"Maybe it's a bomb," Jonah said.

"You better hope not," Alix replied darkly.

They'd had a bomb scare in the fall. The faculty and students had been cleared off the entire campus, dorms, faculty housing, science and humanities buildings, the pool house, everything, while K9 units went over the grounds. No one had been caught for it, and Alix had never said anything out loud, but she privately suspected Jonah had been behind the scare. It was the kind of thing her brother would do. The kid had serious impulse-control problems.

Luckily, Jonah hadn't even been suspected. He'd covered his tracks, at least. Alix wondered if he'd been disappointed. It was at least possible that he'd been trying to get himself caught so he wouldn't have to attend Seitz, but she never asked.

The cops kept pushing everyone farther back, and the crowd got tighter as a result. Alix was shoved up against Jonah and Cynthia and Derek. Some of the really little kids were starting to freak out. Older ones were talking on their cell phones, giving a blow-by-blow of what was happening, or else texting and posting photos online as it all went down.

Alix was starting to feel claustrophobic. The crush and shift of the crowd were overwhelming.

"We need everyone to step back, please! Behind the yellow tape! All the way back!"

The jostling increased. A truck rumbled through the crowd with the word SWAT on the side.

"Worse and worse," Cynthia said.

"You think there are hostages?" Derek wondered.

"Yeah. SWAT got a call about a crew of free radicals holding a bunch of innocent alkanes prisoner in the chem lab," Cynthia said.

In the crush, Alix couldn't turn to respond. She was sweltering in her school blazer. Seitz school uniforms were uncomfortable enough as it was, and now in the unseasonably warm spring sunshine, packed in the crowd, the layers of clothing were becoming unbearable.

A news crew showed up. A camerawoman and blow-dried-hair guy with a microphone went from person to person, asking questions. The camerawoman was gesturing for the guy to move into a better position. Everyone watched the SWAT police get out of their armored truck. They started pulling equipment and setting it up on the grass.

"Bomb squad," someone said.

It looked that way to Alix as well. The cops all had heavily padded protective garments. The SWAT guys were skulking around the edges of Widener, carrying assault rifles, and now the guys in heavy bodysuits were lumbering up the steps of the building. The SWAT guys pressed themselves up against the brick on either side of the doors. Riot helmets and body armor. It looked like the movies: cops all around the doors, ready to bust in and start blasting away at the bad guys.

The shout of "*Clear!*" echoed distantly.

Derek was standing right behind Alix, leaning over her shoulder, cheek close, his breath hot on her ear.

"Watch this," he said. "It should be good."

Alix froze.

That's not Derek.

Alix tried to turn in the constricting crowd. She barely managed to twist, and when she did, she gasped. The black guy from yesterday was right there, smiling slightly. Mirror aviator sunglasses reflected her own surprised expression back at her.

"Nice to see you again, Alix."

He looked completely different. His head was shaved smooth now, and he was wearing an expensive sports coat over a button-down shirt. TAG Heuer wristwatch. But it wasn't just the change of hair and clothing. Everything about him was different. The style of him was different. The guy yesterday had been loose, carefree—cool in that *I don't give a damn about all of you* sort of way. Hip-hop cool. But the way this guy held himself, the first thing that popped into Alix's mind was *cop*. Or even more: *Secret Service*. Like the cold men who had observed from the alcoves the time Dad had been invited to a dinner for the president's reelection campaign.

But still, this was definitely the same guy who had punched Mulroy. She was sure of it. He was an inch away, and he looked completely different, but he was the same guy.

"How do you know my name?"

"You're going to miss the show if you keep looking at me," he said. And then he smiled and raised his sunglasses, showing dark, flashing eyes. Alix felt like she'd been hit by a train. Definitely the same guy. The same blaze of wildness and laughter. The same frightening promise.

His eyes flicked toward the school. "You'll like this, Alix," he said. "This is for you."

Another preparatory call echoed up from the SWAT team members arrayed around Widener Hall's doorway, and then the air shivered as their explosives went off. A booming rush rolled over the crowd and left everyone murmuring. Alix jerked her gaze back to the school. Smoke was billowing up from around the doorway.

Widener's doors had been blown wide, and then...

Nothing.

Everyone waited with bated breath, expecting whatever they were supposed to expect when SWAT blew open a door in the movies. Gunfire. Dragons. A nuclear apocalypse... Something, at least.

Instead, there was silence.

The SWAT team dashed inside, assault rifles pointed ahead, ready to fire.

"Wait for it," the stranger whispered in her ear. His hands were on her shoulders, lightly holding her, keeping her looking at the events unfolding.

Wait for what? Alix wanted to ask.

She wanted to turn around and see him fully, ask him who the hell he thought he was—

A dull thud echoed from Widener Hall.

Alix gasped as blood splattered up against the windows.

It was a massacre. There was so much blood that it looked like every single SWAT guy had been run through a blender and splattered on the windows.

Shrieks of shock and terror rose up from the crowd, and suddenly everyone was trying to get away. Alix tried to run, but the stranger's fingers dug into her shoulders, holding her in place. His lips pressed against her ear.

"Don't panic!" he whispered. "Read! You see it, right?"

And even as everyone was shoving and pulling back and screaming about all the blood, Alix did see. Right there in the windows, a message inscribed in red, now dripping down.

Suddenly all the SWAT guys who had disappeared into

33

the building came barreling back out, shouting and hollering, wordless and panicked, their rifles held carelessly, stumbling down the front steps in their heavy armor.

Behind them, a seething wave of snowy motion erupted from the doors, a tumbling rush pouring out in a river. White fur, twisting-clawing-thrashing bodies, a tidal wave exploding through the open doors and cascading down the school steps.

"*No way!*" Jonah exclaimed from somewhere in the crowd, delighted.

Rats.

Thousands and thousands and thousands of rats, gushing out of the building and down the steps. More and more of them coming every second. They swarmed the cops and the SWAT team. They surged across the lawns. They scattered every which way. The people watching up front tried to run, but everyone was too jammed together. People were scrambling up on Seitz's wall. Police were standing in the middle of the rodent horde, kicking and shaking the rats that ran up their legs. The TV crew was balanced up on the wall, recording the whole weird thing.

Alix caught a glimpse of Jonah laughing and pointing at how all the cops were running, and then everyone was running and shoving and fleeing as the rats came scrambling through. Someone smashed into Alix and she stumbled, barely catching herself before she fell. A white furry streak bolted past, followed by another and another.

Alix spun, trying to find the guy who'd been standing right behind her, but the stranger was gone. Lost in the scrum. Gone entirely except for the rats and the word that he'd left dripping in red paint from the windows of the science building:

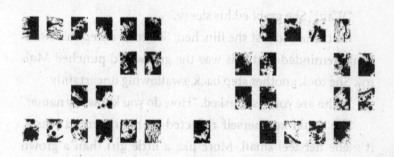

Alix dodged another surge of rats coming her way and scanned the crowd, frantically trying to spot the stranger again.

There!

He was striding away, moving confidently through the chaos. The same careless, arrogant stride she'd seen after he'd punched Mulroy.

He could be dangerous. You shouldn't—oh, fuck it.

Alix went after him.

Behind her, she thought she heard Jonah shout, but she kept her eyes on the stranger, fighting to keep him in sight as people fled in every direction.

Later, she couldn't even really say why she went after

him. She was angry, sure. Pissed that he was so smug and that he thought he could just come up on her like that. She did it because she was angry; that was what she told herself later.

She caught up to him as he was pulling open the rear door to a black town car.

"Wait!" She grabbed his sleeve.

He turned so fast she flinched. She took a step back, suddenly reminded that this was the guy who'd punched Mulroy. She took another step back, swallowing uncertainly.

"Who are you?" she asked. "How do you know my name?"

She could see herself reflected in his mirrored lenses. It made her feel small. More like a little girl than a grown woman: brown hair French-braided, Seitz school uniform with its prim blazer and skirt. *He's tall*, she thought inanely.

"You want to know who I am?" he asked, and there was so much sadness in the words that she was struck nearly speechless. She felt even more horribly aware of her school uniform. It was as if she was looking at someone who had seen the entire world. Not like she'd seen Paris or Barcelona on vacation, but more like the Bastille or the slums of India. And here she was, in all her naïveté, trying to grab hold of that. It took all her will to press him again.

"What's all this about?" she asked. "What's 2.0?"

The guy's expression was so different that she almost wondered if she'd grabbed the wrong black guy in the crowd. It reminded her of how Cynthia complained about people not being able to tell her and Alice Kim apart. Improbably,

Alix heard Cynthia's voice in her head—*Alice is Korean, for Christ's sake.*

"You've got questions now, don't you?" he said, and abruptly the heavy sadness disappeared and the brilliant smile was back. The same boisterous, knowing smile that she'd seen twice before.

A new explosion went off, right among the parked cars. Alix ducked instinctively. Smoke enveloped her, wild and thick and yellow, hiding everything from sight. Suddenly the stranger grabbed her. Hard and tight.

"Hey!" Alix tried to knee him in the balls, but he must have turned away because all she hit was thigh. She struggled against him for another second, then changed tactics and let herself be pulled close.

She bit him.

She heard a satisfying yelp of pain, but to her surprise the stranger didn't let go. Instead, he spun her around and wrapped his strong arms around her, pulling her into a tighter embrace.

"Should have known you'd have some bite to you," he murmured in her ear.

The amusement and play were back in his voice.

"You want to see how much bite I've got?" she asked. She tried to twist free again, but he was ready for her now. He had her pinned against his chest. She rested, gathering strength. Looking for a chance to hurt him again.

The stranger chuckled. His breath was hot on her cheek. "How about we call a little truce?"

"Why? So we can go for coffee?" If she threw her head back fast, she could hit his face with the back of her skull. She might crush his nose if she was lucky.

"You want to know what this is all about?"

Alix stilled, suddenly alert.

"Are you going to tell me?"

The smoke was thick around them. Alix could hear cops shouting and people running, but all of it was distant. She and the stranger were in a bubble of smoke, separate from everything around them.

She was suddenly acutely aware of how closely he held her. She could feel the rise and fall of his chest as he panted, the exertion she'd put him through. He was holding her so tightly she could feel his heart beating.

"What's this all about?" she asked.

"Ask your father."

"*What?*"

"Ask your father. He's the one who knows all the secrets." He shoved her away abruptly.

Alix spun to pursue, but he was lost in the smoke. Everything was shadow forms.

By the time the smoke cleared, he was gone, as if he'd blown away in the wind.

38

4

ALIX SAT ON SEITZ'S LOW perimeter wall, trying to get her shaking hands to be still.

Derek and Cynthia and Jonah were all missing, lost in the running crowds. She was pretty sure Derek and Cynthia would find their way back to where she was, but she suspected Jonah had seized the opportunity to escape and wouldn't be back home before dinner.

Alix was almost glad for the moment alone. It gave her a chance to try to wrap her head around what had happened. Behind her, Widener Hall was being gone over by the police and bomb squad, and now Animal Control had shown up as well. Every so often, another clot of rats burped out of Widener's main doors and made a break for freedom, dashing across sunny lawns for wherever the hell white rats went when they pulled a jailbreak.

2.0's four-story tagging job continued to drip proudly down Widener Hall's windows.

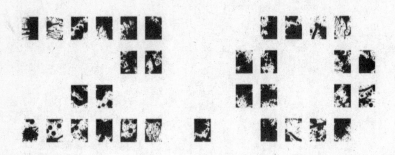

I should tell the cops, Alix thought, but that thought was followed immediately by another.

What are you going to say? That some creeper just left you a four-story love note? That he knows your dad? That you're involved in this, somehow?

That would go over well.

Her thoughts were interrupted by Derek and Cynthia's return. "There you are!" Cynthia said breathlessly. "We've been looking everywhere!"

"You look terrible," Derek said. "Are you okay?"

"Why?"

"Have you seen yourself?"

Alix looked down. She was dismayed to find that her blazer's shoulder and pocket were torn. "I didn't realize." She patted her hair. Her French braid was undone as well. She was a total mess. "It had to have happened—"

When you were busy wrestling with your tall, dark stranger.

"I—" She stopped, feeling flustered, teetering on the edge of blurting out what had just happened to her. "I lost Jonah," she said spontaneously. "We got caught in the crowd, and I lost him. I think he ditched."

"Again? Seriously?" Derek asked. "That kid should have been expelled last semester."

Cynthia elbowed him in the ribs.

"Ow. What?" Derek asked.

"We'll help you look for him," Cynthia said.

Alix felt guilty for the deception, but now that the lie was out, she couldn't think of a good way to undo it, and she wasn't sure she wanted to.

It's better this way, she told herself as they started patrolling the grounds for signs of her delinquent brother. Once she had events sorted out in her mind, then maybe she'd discuss it with people. But not yet. Everything was still too weird: the vandalism of the school; the stranger—2.0 or whatever his name was—approaching her; the fact that he knew her name. She needed time to think through what she wanted to say— and whom she wanted to say it to.

Dad was always lamenting that his clients didn't call him for advice before they started opening their mouths in the news. When Alix had been in junior high, she used to sit and watch TV with him and rate CEOs' and politicians' announcements in the wake of scandals.

Dad had a scoring system that went from Teflon (trouble would slide right off) to Self-Immolation (lighting yourself on fire for the entertainment of the public). Sometimes he also awarded Just-Add-Gasoline points for those who were really determined to double down on their own stupid.

It had just been silly fun for Alix at the time, a way to spend quality time with her father on something they both found interesting. But now the lessons of those scoring sessions felt uncomfortably relevant. If this was going to turn into news—and it was looking more and more like it would—she had to think everything through. The last thing she needed was to run around blabbing that the merry prankster who had just destroyed Widener Hall had something to do with her and her family.

"Ask your father," he'd said.

"You'll like this, Alix."

"This is for you."

This had all the hallmarks of a Just-Add-Gasoline moment.

Across the grounds, SWAT guys were marching out of Widener Hall. Alix blinked, startled. "Are they carrying paintball guns?"

Derek started to laugh in disbelief. "I think they're Super Soakers."

Whatever they were, they were toys, for sure. Plastic and shiny and primary-school colorful: red and green and yellow and blue, and all of them dripping bright red paint.

Cynthia pulled out her cell phone and started snapping shots. "Check out the color contrast!" She laughed.

The news crew clearly had the same idea. The camerawoman was dashing over to capture the image of the SWAT guys in their black paramilitary uniforms with their oh-so-serious bulletproof vests and riot helmets—and their arms full of cheerful toy guns.

Alix couldn't stifle her own laughter. She half expected the SWAT guys to suddenly break into a song-and-dance routine. Some kind of plein air musical show with waltzing SWAT guys and candy-colored guns for props.

Maybe this was what 2.0 wanted to show me, she thought as more and more people started snapping pictures. If it was, it was actually kind of...sweet.

He grabbed you, Alix reminded herself. *He's dangerous.*

So how come he didn't hurt you? You bit him hard enough.

It was strange, when she thought about it. She'd hurt him for sure, and he hadn't done anything in return. Given the way he'd punched Mulroy, she was certain he could have done almost anything he'd wanted to pay her back. But all he'd done was pull her close and whisper in her ear.

Maybe he liked her.

Get a grip, Alix, she thought.

"He'll turn up," Derek said.

"What?" Alix turned, confused.

Derek gave her a funny look. "Quit freaking," he said. "Jonah always turns up."

"Oh. Right," Alix said, covering for herself. "Mom's going to freak, though."

"That kid would already be feral if it wasn't for you," Cynthia said. "Your mom should be grateful."

Sophie came over, interrupting them. "Are you guys walking home, too?"

"No." Alix looked at her with surprise. "I've got a car."

"No, you don't. You've got a car behind yellow tape." Sophie pointed. "The whole parking lot is locked down. They're sniffing all the cars with dogs."

"But that's where they told us to park!" Alix protested.

They hurried over to the lot, and, sure enough, squads of police were going from car to car, running mirrors under all the undercarriages, while German shepherds barked and sniffed and lunged against their leashes.

"How long are they going to be at it?"

"Until they find the people responsible, I guess," Cynthia said.

"Or all the coke in the school," Derek suggested.

"Is it even legal to search like that?" Alix wondered.

"Good thing you stopped dealing," Cynthia cracked.

"Like anyone's hiding anything in their cars." Sophie stared up at the blue sky. "It's too hot to walk."

Alix watched the search continue from car to car. It looked like the German shepherds had a thing for German automobiles. Every time they came up on an Audi or Mercedes, they went nuts. "This is going to take forever." She dialed home. Her mom's and dad's phones both went to voice mail.

"No answer?" Derek asked knowingly.

Alix made a face. "They're always hammering on me to pick up immediately when they call. But when I call..."

"I think in the old days they used to call us latchkey children," Cynthia said. "Now it's more like voice-mail children."

Alix considered texting, then blew it off. *Let them find out on their own about the school.*

"I told you we were walking," Sophie said smugly. They all shouldered their bags and headed out. Alix glanced back at her MINI longingly.

Cynthia caught the direction of her gaze. "So close, and yet so far." She laughed.

"I parked right where they told me," Alix complained again.

"And I'm sure Big Brother appreciates your obedience."

"You think we'll have school tomorrow?" Derek asked. He was gazing back at the vandalized science building. The red shape of the 2.0 tag was amazingly clear now that they were standing farther away from it.

"You worried about the Calc test?" Cynthia asked.

"Actually, I was wondering how much rat poop they're going to have to clean up. That was a hell of a lot of rats."

"What do you think the '2.0' means?" Cynthia wondered.

Alix shrugged, pretending nonchalance. "Who knows? My dad says it's just some guy who likes to vandalize things."

"I don't know," Cynthia said doubtfully. "That's an awful lot of trouble to go to just to paint some windows."

"And to set up all that equipment," Derek added. "That guy had to be in there half the night aiming all those water guns and then filling them with paint and then setting up some kind of system to make them shoot like that."

"And don't forget the rats," Cynthia said. "That's a hell of a lot of work to go to if it doesn't mean anything."

"I don't care what it means," Sophie said. "I'm just glad to have a free day. I'm not ready for the Calc test."

"Free days, all around," Cynthia declared. "At least we can thank 2.0 for that."

"Says the one person who doesn't actually need an extra day to prep," Derek said.

"Don't blame me for being efficient. Every time I see you 'studying,' you're napping in the back of the library."

"That was only once, and it was because I stayed up all night trying to beat your curve," Derek said.

Cynthia smirked. "You sound frustrated."

"He's not used to being second math nerd," Alix said.

"He probably shouldn't sleep so much, then."

"It was one time!" Derek protested. "And I wasn't asleep for more than ten minutes."

"But you were snoring," Sophie said. "I've got a recording."

"It was one time."

"It was kind of sweet," Cynthia said. "I didn't know someone could harmonize his own snoring like that."

Derek gave up. "You know what? I'm just saying it would

have been nice to see you flounder for a semester or two before you started kicking my butt."

Everyone laughed at that. When Cynthia had come to Seitz at the beginning of the year, she'd entered into the college-prep environment with an aplomb that had left Alix writhing with envy. It would have been easy to hate the new girl for her brilliance—except that Cynthia had also turned out to be almost ridiculously considerate. The girl liked helping her fellow students in a way that was rare in Seitz's übercompetitive-but-pretending-not-to-be environment, and she'd become Alix's secret study weapon on more than one occasion. But still, most new students did at least have the common decency to flounder for a semester or two before they settled into the Seitz curriculum.

They continued trudging across town, headed for the leafy neighborhoods on the far side of town where property lots got larger and houses stepped farther and farther back from the road.

The sun was hot. Alix could feel herself starting to sweat. They all peeled off their blazers, but it didn't help much. Derek was dripping by the time he separated for his own home, and everyone else wasn't in much better shape. Annoyingly, Cynthia was barely sheened.

"See? You're unnatural," Derek complained as he departed up the cobblestone drive to his house. "You don't even sweat."

Cynthia laughed. "I don't sweat Calc, that's for sure."

"He likes you," Sophie said when he was gone. "You shouldn't rub it in so much."

"He needs it," Cynthia said. "If he spent half as much time studying as he does *talking* about studying, he'd be kicking my ass."

The girls continued to Alix's house, where she was surprised to find Dad working, talking on his cell.

"—tell Owens that we've already been down that road. Widening the test population is a dead end—"

He turned and waved at Alix, and smiled at Cynthia and Sophie, then cupped his hand over the phone. "What are you girls doing home?"

"Long story," Alix said as she tossed her blazer over the back of a kitchen stool.

She was about to tell him more, but he was already back to his phone conversation and absently waving her off. "That's what George is trying to tell you! The Kimball-Geier numbers don't add up...." He headed back into his office.

"Voice-mail children," Sophie said. "Leave a message and description of your crisis, and we'll get back to you as soon as we're done ruling the universe."

"He's probably been on his phone all morning," Alix said, trying not to feel annoyed and neglected as Dad pushed his office door halfway shut. She caught a glimpse of George Saamsi, her father's business partner, through the doorway gap. His feet were kicked up on the desk as he typed away on a little Sony laptop. He smiled at Alix and waved.

Alix had known George for most of her life, an extra-familial uncle who attended birthdays and holidays with steady reliability. George had what he termed a "robust" belly, and his head was almost completely bald, but he made up for the lack of hair with a thick salt-and-pepper beard that made him look a little like Santa Claus. The addition of gold-rimmed spectacles didn't do much to dispel the illusion.

Alix went over to the office and closed the door the rest of way, then went and got Diet Cokes out of the fridge while Cynthia found glasses and filled them with ice from the ice-maker. Alix poured, watching the foam rise and froth. She pressed the cold glass to her cheek.

"So who's Santa Claus?" Cynthia asked as she took a sip.

Alix and Sophie cracked up. Alix tried to shush her. "It's just George. He works with my dad."

"I want to stick a corncob pipe in his mouth," Cynthia said.

"That's what I thought, too, the first time I saw him," Sophie said.

"Sophie had a crush on him when we were in eighth grade," Alix explained.

"Ew! I did not!" Sophie punched her arm, but she was laughing as she protested.

Cynthia was laughing, too. "He's, um, *furry*." Which sent them into more suppressed fits of laughter.

Alix made frantic shushing sounds. "Let's go outside," she said. "I don't want to bother them."

She led her friends out back by the pool. They dragged their aching feet out of school uniform–approved shoes and peeled off kneesocks.

"We should have brought swimsuits," Cynthia commented as she rubbed her calves where the kneesocks had dug in. She was staring longingly at the cool waters of the pool.

"We could go out to the beach this weekend," Sophie suggested. "It's hot enough."

"We could go now if the cops didn't have our cars impounded," Alix said.

"They better not mess up the paint on mine—" Sophie broke off as her phone rang. She checked the caller. "Shit. It's my mom. I bet she finally heard about the school."

"Voice-mail her," Alix suggested. "Strike a blow for our generation."

Sophie grinned, but she answered anyway. Sure enough, as soon as she took the call, Alix could hear Sophie's mom start haranguing her. Sophie made a face as she hung up.

"Jeez," she said. "It's like she thinks this is Sandy Hook all over again." She frowned thoughtfully at the phone. "I probably shouldn't have ignored her first three calls."

Alix and Cynthia cracked up. With a smirk, Sophie headed out, leaving just the two of them. "I'll bet everyone's parents are freaking by tonight," Cynthia observed as she lay back on a lounge chair.

"Yours won't be?"

"Are you kidding?" she said with her eyes closed. "They're going to kill me for not coming straight home." She made a face. "This 2.0 thing is going to make my life miserable. Next thing I know, they're going to want to ship me to Finland."

"Are you serious?"

"Best schools in the world, my dad keeps saying. Free, too. And no school shootings."

"This wasn't a shooting," Alix protested. She was surprised to find that she felt oddly defensive about the way Cynthia characterized the morning.

Cynthia glanced over. "So what was it, smart girl?"

"A prank?"

"A prank that destroyed the science building."

"It didn't blow it up."

"No." Cynthia turned serious. "But I'd say it was a little more than a prank."

Alix was about to answer, but she was interrupted by her father's voice rising from his office. He didn't normally sound angry, but now his voice rose and fell in sharp bursts.

"Wow," Cynthia said. "He sounds ticked off."

"Work," Alix said. "I guess it's intense."

"I don't think I've ever talked to him," Cynthia said.

"I'll introduce you—" Her father's rising voice interrupted, and Alix grimaced. "Some other time."

"Yeah." Cynthia made a face. "Definitely."

Alix felt a little embarrassed. She'd had Cynthia over to the house only a few times since they'd become friends, and here Dad was, going berserk.

"He's not normally like this."

"Don't worry about it. You should see my dad when work's going badly for him. He mopes around the house and snaps at everyone, and then we all have to act like he's still the little emperor that he was back when he was a kid in Shanghai. That's the problem with only kids from China. They've got all these relatives, and there's only one kid for them to focus on. Makes them totally spoiled."

"But you're an only child," Alix pointed out.

Cynthia made a face of mock horror. "But I'm a girl! I could never be a little emperor."

Once again, Alix's father's voice interrupted them. Alix sighed. Cynthia rolled her eyes. "Seriously. Don't worry about it."

Alix was reminded again of why she liked Cynthia. Most of the other girls at school would have listened to her father and then turned it into some kind of gossip, but Cynthia wasn't interested in those games at all.

Alix's mother called Cynthia "wonderfully mature," which sounded suspiciously like "good role model" to Alix. She would have never invited Cynthia over again just for that, except Cynthia had heard the same note of approval in Mom's voice and turned it into a joke. Then she invited Alix out for a "Wonderfully Mature" evening of getting drunk in a bar with a couple of fake IDs that she'd scammed off someone.

Alix's father's voice got louder, then launched into a tirade that was impossible to ignore.

Cynthia glanced again toward the office window. "What's he do, anyway?"

"He's a product consultant."

Cynthia looked confused. Alix explained. "It's sort of a

fancy name for a PR flack. Public relations. Press releases. That kind of thing."

"Oh. Sure," Cynthia said. "Like for Coke or something?"

"For lots of companies. He's not allowed to say who."

"Is that, like, company policy?"

"Well," Alix said with a laugh, "since it's his company, it's his policy. He started out working for Hill and Knowlton, but now he's got his own company. Banks Strategy Partners. BSP." Alix couldn't help but feel a little proud of him. "When he started, it was just him and George. Now they've got offices in New York and DC, and he's got more than a hundred people working for him."

"Yeah. I guessed it was pretty successful," Cynthia said, eyeing Alix's house and pool and the grounds beyond.

Alix flushed, suddenly embarrassed at the mention of money.

"Well," she said, "he works hard."

She shut up, not sure what else she wanted to say or why she suddenly felt embarrassed. It wasn't like they were the richest people in Haverport. They weren't rolling in it. It wasn't like they were some hedge fund family or anything like that. Sure, they weren't poor—Mom and Dad reminded her and Jonah of that whenever they tried to pull a poor-me-I'm-so-deprived complaint. This was normally followed by a reminder to Alix that although they'd pay for her college, they didn't believe in people who didn't build their own lives. Which was really code to say that they weren't going to let Alix turn into one of those Seitz alums who went off to "find herself" in the Med and wound up drinking absinthe and doing lines of coke on the back of a yacht off the coast of Barcelona.... Alix's family had money, sure, but it felt a little lame for Cynthia to bring it up.

"I mean, I guess it's a lot, but he works a ton. I mean, he's hardly here most of the week...." She trailed off, trying not to show how uncomfortable she felt.

Cynthia read her loud and clear, and immediately back-tracked. "I didn't say he—" Cynthia broke off. "Sorry. I guess I'm still getting used to this place. Seitz is..."

"Prison?" Alix cracked, trying to change the subject.

"Weird. About money. And status. I don't know. Before I moved here..." She trailed off. "It was different, that's all. My dad was the richest person in town. People noticed." She shrugged. "And you couldn't really hide it, I guess. Anyway, we just talk about money in my family. It's a Chinese thing. I didn't mean to..." She threw up her hands and grinned help-lessly. "Never mind. Whatever."

"Your dad does something in tech, right?"

"Yeah. It's this dot-com thing. I don't get most of it. I guess Google uses whatever he does. Some kind of data mining."

Cynthia was fairly private about what her family life was like. She'd said her mom and dad were real first-generation Chinese, fresh off the boat, and their English wasn't that good, so it would be pointless and weird for Alix to meet them. But it did make Alix curious.

Alix's dad's voice rose again. It was odd to have him in the house in the middle of the day. Normally, he worked in the city, or down in DC and came home on weekends. Everything felt surreal today. Alix could still remember the stranger pulling her close, whispering in her ear....

"What am I supposed to ask Dad?" Alix muttered.

Cynthia glanced over, surprised. "What did you just say?"

Alix flinched, not realizing she'd spoken out loud. Part of her still wanted to keep what had happened between her and the stranger to herself.

He'd pulled her close and spoken to her. Said the whole prank was for her. And then the smoke had enveloped them, and he'd disappeared.

When she thought about it, it was kind of romantic, in a hot stalker kind of way.

You are one fucked-up bitch, Alix thought.

"What are you talking about?" Cynthia pressed, curious now.

Alix shrugged. "It's nothing."

Cynthia was too smart to be fooled. "Riiiight."

"Okay." Alix leaned closer and lowered her voice. "But you can't tell anyone."

"I won't."

"Swear it."

Cynthia looked exasperated. "I pinkie-swear it. Come on, Alix. Give."

"I still don't..." She shook her head. "I don't know. I'm still not sure what I should do. I want to think about it, still."

"About…?" Cynthia was clearly dying for the details.

"You remember the guy who slugged Mr. Mulroy yesterday?"

"Yeah."

Alix took a breath. "He talked to me."

Cynthia gave a funny squeak of shock. "*Talked* to you? When? How?"

"Right when he splattered Widener Hall. He was in the crowd with us."

"You've got to be kidding. I would have seen him."

"He wasn't dressed like before. He looked more like a cop. He was right behind me. He was whispering in my ear. He had me by the shoulders and he was whispering in my ear."

"He *touched* you?"

"What?" Alix laughed nervously. "No! Not like that. He was just holding my shoulders." *Holding them so hard that I can still feel his fingers.* "It wasn't creepy," Alix said, not sure whom she was trying to convince.

"You weren't scared?"

"No."

"You can't be serious."

But it was true. In the moment, she really hadn't been scared. She'd been mad at the guy for screwing with her head. But when he walked away, she'd followed him. If she'd been afraid, she definitely wouldn't have done that.

So why weren't you afraid?

Looking at it from the outside, of course it was scary. Some stranger coming up and grabbing her. The way he'd materialized behind her and then come in so close. His breath warm as he spoke in her ear.

Confident.

In control.

Watch this. This is for you.

Telling her to watch, to see what he had in store. He'd been closer to her than anyone except Toby Welles when she'd had him up in her room and her mother had left for another Pilates class.

Except this guy had been a total stranger.

So why hadn't she tried to get away? Or push him off? Why hadn't she done any of the things she'd learned in the self-defense classes that Dad had made her take in eighth grade? Even later, when they'd fought in the smoke, she realized she could have fought harder. She could have screamed for help.

But she hadn't.

"He wasn't creeping on me," Alix said slowly. "It wasn't like when Alan tries to get a peek up your skirt, or gives you the eye at lunch. It didn't feel like he was creeping on me. He was just talking."

And looking at me. And holding me.

Alix was suddenly afraid that she was blushing and that Cynthia might read her thoughts.

"He knew my name," Alix said.

"What?" Cynthia looked even more horrified. "How would he know that?"

"I don't know."

Cynthia threw up her hands in exasperation. "I'm sorry, girl. That's some weird shit. You're deep in stalker territory."

"I know, I know." Alix shook her head. "But the weird thing was that he wasn't acting stalker-y. He just told me to watch the prank." She deliberately left out the part where she'd chased after him and he'd grabbed her and she'd bitten him. That just complicated the whole story.

"He told you to watch it? You mean, while he felt you up?"

"I told you, it wasn't like that!"

"If a stranger knew my name and grabbed me, I'd have crippled him. Why haven't you called the cops?"

"He said it was for me."

"*What?*"

"The thing with the paint and rats and everything...he said it was for me. Right before it happened."

"For you, how? Like a big snuggly stalker present?"

"I don't know. I asked him what he meant, and he told me to ask my dad."

"Your *dad*? Ew. Now your guy sounds incest-y, too. Seriously, girl. Call the cops. They don't have any leads on this guy. You could probably help."

"Yeah. I know. I should." Alix swirled the ice in her drink, avoiding looking over at Cynthia.

Cynthia sighed. "But you're not going to, are you?"

5

ALIX DIDN'T WANT TO ADMIT it in front of Cynthia, but the more she thought about it, the more she realized she was considering not telling anyone at all.

Cynthia seemed to be reading her mind. "He *assaulted* Mr. Mulroy," Cynthia reminded her. "You do remember that, don't you?"

"So? What am I supposed to say?" Alix playacted the way it would go if she went public. "Um, like, so, there's this guy? And, like, I think he's stalking me?" Alix made a face of annoyance. "It'll look like I'm trying to get attention. People will make something out of it. I don't need that. Next thing you know, I'll be a joke on TV."

"You're making excuses."

"I am not!"

"Are you hot for him?" Cynthia accused suddenly.

"What? Ew!" Alix socked Cynthia's arm. "No!"

"So why aren't you at least telling your dad?"

"I don't know....I guess I don't want to make a big thing out of this. Maybe if he'd put my name up there instead of that stupid 2.0 stuff, then maybe I'd say something. Seriously, I don't need the hassle."

"So what's he want with your dad? He said something about your dad, right?"

"How should I know?",

Cynthia let out an exasperated breath. "What'd the stalker say?"

"I don't remember too much," Alix lied. "It was all happening so fast." Cynthia kept glaring at her. Alix relented. "Okay, okay. I think I asked him what all this prank stuff meant—you know, why he was doing this stuff, and he said, 'Ask your father.' That was it, I swear. I think he was making some kind of joke."

"Like a 'your mother' thing?"

"I don't know. Maybe. Something like that."

"You think maybe he was serious?" Cynthia prodded.

"How would I know?"

"You could...you know..." Cynthia jerked her head toward the window where Dad was still having his loud conversation. "Ask your dad if he knows anything that would clear it up...."

"He's busy," Alix said.

Cynthia rolled her eyes. "Oh, yeah. Totally busy. He wouldn't have any time to talk to his teenage daughter about some creep who's stalking her."

"He wasn't stalking."

Cynthia gave her another hard look.

"Okay, okay. Lay off, Tiger Mom." Alix made a face. "I'll do it." She started to get up, then sat back down again. "Tonight."

"Gah!" Cynthia threw up her hands. "I can't stand the suspense. Promise to tell me what he says, at least."

"I promise."

"I'm serious, Alix. Don't do some kind of bad-boy romance thing on me, girl. Stalker crushes are so last year."

It was like Cynthia had climbed inside her head and was reading every single guilty thought almost before Alix thought it. "The guy's a total stranger," Alix said. "I'm not hot for him."

"No? The big, strong, black stranger? Sooo hot." Cynthia pretended to fan herself and fluttered her eyelashes. "Sooooooo hot."

"It's not like that!" Under Cynthia's judging gaze, Alix finally conceded. "Okay, okay. I'll talk to my dad. Tonight. I promise."

"Fine. Good." Cynthia's phone beeped with a text message. She checked it and frowned. "I've got to get home. My mom's freaking."

She dialed and pressed the phone to her ear. "Ma? *Mei-you.* Everything's fine. *Shi. Shi. Shi. Wo zai* Alix *jia. Buzhidao.* Some kind of weird prank. *Wo zenme zhidao?*"

She rolled her eyes at Alix and made a circling motion with her finger beside her ear. Crazy mom. "*Haole.* I'm coming home now."

She climbed out of the lounge chair and started pulling on her socks and shoes. "Sorry. She's totally flipping."

Alix was secretly relieved to have Cynthia getting off her back, but as Alix let her out the door, Cynthia stopped and turned to Alix again. "You'll ask your dad, right?"

Alix tried to look obedient. "Yes, I will."

"Seriously, Alix. This isn't like you. This is the kind of thing Denise or Sophie would do. At least talk to your dad about this. Don't turn into some kind of weird thrill seeker on me. I don't do the whole good-girl-turns-rebel cliché."

Alix saluted. "Okay, Tiger Mom. Will do."

Cynthia laughed and made her hands into claws as Alix pushed her outside. "*Rawr!*" she said. Alix closed the door on her. The door clicked.

Alix leaned against it and sighed with relief.

It was great that she and Cynthia listened to the same music and liked to rave and that Cynthia was always free to go out for coffee or talk about Jane Austen. But sometimes she could be freakishly overbearing, as if she was trying to prove that she could be more adult—

"Talk to your dad about the stalker!" Cynthia's voice filtered through the door.

Alix winced. "I heard you already!"

Even though she'd shut Cynthia outside, the girl's admonishments refused to go away. Tiger Mom had done her job, apparently, and managed to get Alix's conscience involved.

With a sigh of frustration, Alix went to her father's office door and knocked. Inside, the talking stopped.

"Come in!"

Hesitantly, she pushed the door open. "Dad?"

Dad looked a little annoyed to be interrupted, but he at least made the effort to smile. "What is it, Alix?"

"Can I talk to you?"

He glanced over at George. "We're sort of in the middle of something. Is it important?"

"Yeah." She hesitated, trying to decide how much she really wanted to push. "I mean, well, I don't know."

Smooth, Alix. Real smooth.

Dad smiled at George. "Could you give us a second?"

"Sure." George got up. "Take all the time you need. I was feeling parched anyway." He squeezed past, patting her on the shoulder as he left. "Good to see you, Alix."

"Yeah. You too."

"Well?" Dad asked.

Alix settled gingerly into George's still-warm chair. The office was large; it had been expanded when Dad did the renovation so that he could work one day a week at home.

"What's going on?" Dad asked. "Why aren't you at school? Are you okay?"

"Yeah. I'm fine." She paused. "I don't know. Something weird happened at school today, and... I wanted to talk about it."

"Something bad?"

"No. Yes." She shrugged. "I don't know. There was a prank at school. I left a voice mail."

Dad frowned. "I've been on calls all day. Something happened?"

As Alix outlined the events, Dad's face turned more and more serious. She found herself avoiding the real reason for going into his office, but, finally, she couldn't talk around it anymore. "So..." She hesitated and then blurted out, "The guy who did it talked to me."

It took a second to register, but when it did, Dad's response was just as bad as she'd expected it to be.

"What?" He looked shocked. "What do you mean, he talked to you? How did he talk to you? When?"

Alix found herself rushing to explain. "He snuck up on me. He sort of whispered in my ear—"

"He touched you?"

"No! It wasn't like that! Why does everyone think that's what happened? He didn't do anything like that. He just said I should watch the prank. And..." There was no way to minimize it, and Alix knew it would sound terrible as soon as she said it.

"He knew my name."

Dad's expression went from surprise and concern to the intense look that she saw only when he was solving a serious work problem. She'd seen it when he talked about having to fire someone or when a client was being difficult or when there was a PR crisis. He was suddenly totally focused on Alix, and his voice was dead serious.

"Tell me everything, Alix. Everything you can remember."

And she did. She told him about the prank and how the stranger had looked totally different from the day before. She told him how the guy, whom she was starting more and more to think of as 2.0, had whispered in her ear and how he'd told her to ask her dad what was going on.

"He wanted you to talk to me?" Dad looked puzzled.

"That's what he said."

"But he went after you."

Alix could see anger rising on her father's face. She rushed to explain. "He didn't do anything to me, though."

"He did, actually." Dad's voice was rising. "He targeted you. Some lunatic activist is targeting my daughter."

"He didn't look like an activist."

"Not every activist douses himself with patchouli and dreads his hair, Alix. Let me lay this out for you. This is serious. He knows your name. He knows where you go to school. He probably knows where you live. He just told you he's after me, but what he didn't say is that he probably knows Jonah and your mother and all your friends."

"He said I should ask you what all this was about. Why did he say that?"

"There are a million possibilities." Dad's brow furrowed as he considered. "With the rats, it could be some animal rights activist who doesn't like the lab-testing one of my clients does. It might be some religious fanatic who doesn't like stem cell research. I do government work. It could be anti-nuclear...." He stood up and went to the door. "George! I want a security detail here at the house, ASAP. Alix and Jonah will need someone to take them to and from school."

George didn't even blink at the weird request.

"Williams and Crowe?"

"Yes. Definitely. Get them. I don't want to have to waste time bringing people up to speed."

George pulled out his cell and started dialing. His Santa Claus features no longer appeared calm or jolly. He looked as dead serious as her father.

"Who's he calling?" Alix asked, feeling unmoored as the two men went to work on the problem.

"A security firm I've worked with in the past," Dad said. "They're the best."

"Dad!" Alix said. "I don't need security. Nobody's trying to hurt me."

"You don't know that." Dad started ticking off points on his fingers. "This is someone who has already assaulted the headmaster. Someone who has managed to bypass all the security at your school. Someone who has the technical skill and willingness to use explosives. Someone who is obviously methodical, and who is clearly targeting us. Just because you don't feel like you're at risk doesn't mean you're safe. I don't want to give him an opportunity to take you."

"You think I'm going to be *kidnapped*?"

"If I knew, Alix, I wouldn't be worried. But that's the point, isn't it? If someone takes you, what can I do? The world isn't a safe place. Everyone's a crazy, these days. Radicals come in a dozen different stripes, and they all think the ends justify the means. Maybe I can get you back, maybe I can pay enough to make someone set you free, maybe I can beg for them to let you go alive, but if someone takes you, it will mean that that's all I'm doing: begging. I won't let you get hurt—" He stopped short. "Where's Jonah?"

"I—" Alix's heart gave a flip of worry as she realized that she didn't know. "He ditched me at school," she said. "I was trying to keep track of him, but you know how he is...." She stopped talking. Dad was staring at her. Alix felt suddenly, coldly, afraid.

"Did he leave on his own?" Dad asked. "Or did someone take him?"

"I don't know—"

"You were distracted," Dad accused.

The stranger leaning close, his hands gripping my shoulders, whispering in my ear to watch the prank. To see what happened next. The rats coming out, pouring down the stairs, all of them spreading out over the lawns like a fluffy carpet...

Oh God. What have I done?

"When the guy talked to me," Alix admitted miserably, "I lost Jonah right after."

"Dammit!" Dad exploded. "George! I want Crowe's people here, now! They've got Jonah! And call Romero at the FBI. Tell him that it's not just pranks now."

Now?

"You know who these people are?" Alix asked, but Dad ignored her.

"You shouldn't leave the house," George was saying.

"If they wanted me, they would have already come after me." Dad was pacing back and forth. "Goddammit! Why didn't I see this? Why didn't *you* see this?"

"Nobody—"

"Never mind. Get me Romero. They've gone over the line. I want the security here, *now*! Find my son."

George was dialing furiously on his mobile even as he was nodding. Dad was picking up his own phone, pushing the button that would give him an encrypted line out. He'd had the line installed when he started doing work for the Department of Energy, and Alix had always thought it was sort of overly dramatic that PR would need that much secrecy, but now...

"Dad, I—" She stopped short as her father looked up from the phone at her. He looked so sad and angry and frightened that she couldn't get any words out. She'd never seen him like this. He'd always seemed so *together*. Mom sometimes lost it about things, but Dad never lost it.

"I'm sorry," she whispered, but he wasn't paying attention to her anymore. He was talking into the phone.

"Priority code. Alpha. Alpha. Five. Nine. Zero. Tango. Zulu. Eight. Victor. Nine. Two. Alpha." Pause. "Affirm." Another pause, then:

"This is Simon Banks. My son has been kidnapped."

6

THE HOUSE WAS FULL OF people. There were guys from
the FBI, plus some other agency that Alix was starting to suspect was Secret Service, plus the private security people from
Williams & Crowe. Two clean-cut guys were going through
the whole house and the grounds outside, scouting for whatever it was that security people scouted for after it was too
late to do anything, and more people were on their cells, talking to different law enforcement agencies, and coming in and
out of the house on mysterious errands.

Alix sat alone and miserable, watching her world fall
apart.

A slim woman in a black pantsuit came over and intro-
duced herself. "Hi, Alix, I'm Lisa Price. I've been assigned
to you."

"Are you my bodyguard?" Alix asked, feeling dull and lost
in the mess and horror of it all.

Lisa smiled gently. "Something like that. We're all here to protect you. I understand you have a description of the man who took your brother?"

"I already told, like, fifty people."

"Why don't you go over it again with me."

So Alix did. Lisa kept asking her more questions: Who was standing next to Jonah? And who had been standing with her? And then what happened?

Going over it again was like ripping open a wound. Everything she told Lisa just reminded her that she'd lost track of Jonah, and it had happened because she'd been obsessed with chasing after her stalker.

This was her fault. She'd let her own brother get kidnapped. Alix wanted to vomit.

"Do you remember anything else?"

Alix shook her head. "I don't know. I can't...I can't tell anymore."

She'd been asked so many times that the events in her head were starting to seem fixed and unchanging. She wasn't sure if any of the details were real memories or if her brain was just making things up now because she wanted so badly to fill in the blanks for the investigators.

Lisa must have seen something in Alix's face, because the woman reached over to touch her hand.

"Hey, Alix. Don't worry. I'm just trying to understand who I need to be looking out for. Do you have photos of your friends, too? I need to know about you. If I'm going to be protecting you, I need to know who to consider a threat and who to pay more attention to."

"You mean you can beat up my enemies?" Alix almost managed to smile.

Lisa smiled kindly. "Only if they try to beat you up first."

The door burst open.

"Mr. Banks!" a huge guy in a suit called out. "Mr. Banks!" His voice was followed by a higher, familiar voice that made Alix's heart pound with relief.

"Let me go!"

Jonah was being dragged in by the security guys.

"Leggo of me, you goons!"

Dad ran over and the guys let Jonah go. Dad scooped him up. "Oh my God. Oh my God."

Alix didn't even realize that she'd run over, too, leaping to Jonah so fast she hadn't felt herself doing it. She grabbed him and hugged him.

"Let go of me!" Jonah kept saying. "What's going on? What's with the goons? Of course I'm okay! I'm fine! Let *go*, will you?"

Finally, they let him wriggle free.

"You ran away!" Alix accused him. "You just took off! Do you know how worried I was? Do you know—"

She broke off, because all of a sudden she was crying, all the fear and relief and anger pouring out of her. "You ran away!"

Jonah was looking at her like she was crazy. "But that's what I do."

71

They both looked at each other, and then Alix started to laugh and cry at the same time. She grabbed him and pulled him close, hugging him and wishing that she could hug him harder still. "Yeah. Sure, bro. That's what you do. We should've known."

■ ■ ■

By the time everyone had cleared out, it was dark. The FBI people had gone, along with local police and the Secret Service people Dad had summoned through his secure line.

When Alix asked him about the Secret Service, he just said that some of the people he worked with had clout. When Alix pressed, he gave her an exasperated look and said that there were certain things he wasn't legally allowed to discuss, which dead-ended the conversation and left Alix feeling somewhat awestruck at how important Dad's clients actually were.

Now the only people left were family. They had all gathered around the granite island in the kitchen. Mom was home. She'd given Alix chamomile tea, and Jonah was eating ice cream because no one was in the mood to make him eat something normal. Dad had gotten a beer from the fridge and was drinking it out of the bottle, which Mom almost never let him do.

At last, they were the only people left.

Well, the only people in the house, Alix amended.

The Williams & Crowe "specialists" had disappeared into

the woodwork. Some were in a van across the street. More were in the backyard. Lisa had been relieved by a blond guy named Terek. Terek was outside now, smoking a cigarette and watching the street.

Alix got the impression that there were other Williams & Crowe people lurking around the area as well. She couldn't decide if that made her feel safer or more afraid. Like her family was huddled inside the house, afraid of the dark, hoping these "specialists" would protect them from...something. Something big and malicious.

With fangs.

Like one of the monsters in Jonah's Xbox games that would jump out and kill when you were least expecting it.

Alix sipped her chamomile and stared at her family's reflection in the kitchen windows. She shivered.

Normally she liked the kitchen. Mom had redesigned it a few years ago, and Dad had gotten *Architectural Digest* to cover it. There'd been a lot of fuss about hand-forged fixtures and how she'd blended natural textures like bamboo with industrial textures like steel and concrete to make a space that felt both modern and warmly inviting, but Alix's favorite change had been how Mom had gotten rid of the eastern wall and turned most of it into glass to let in morning light. Every morning, the kitchen and breakfast nook were bathed in sunshine.

Now, though, the glass reflected their own tense forms, and it was impossible to know who was standing outside. The glass wall that had once made Alix feel so happy suddenly made her feel vulnerable. What was there to stop someone from just taking a hammer and smashing it?

"So how long do we have the goons?" Jonah asked, scooping ice cream.

Dad gave him a sharp look. "They're not goons, and you'll speak about them with respect. They aren't here because they want to be; they're here because I've asked them. They're here to protect you and Alix, and they'll be here until we understand who this group is and why they're targeting Alix."

"She should be flattered," Jonah said. "She scares off all the guys at school."

Alix smacked him on the arm. "I do not."

"Chad Dennison's scared witless of you. None of the guys will even go near you now."

Mom frowned at Alix. "What did you do to Chad?"

"Nothing he didn't deserve."

"Alix, I play tennis with his mother."

Jonah snorted. "Don't worry. He won't *ever* mention it to her."

What a brat. Alix couldn't believe she'd actually been worried about him a few hours ago.

"How do you know all these people?" Alix asked her father, waving toward where Terek was posted outside the front door.

"Williams and Crowe? Some of my clients use them."

"Use them…"

"One of their specialties is executive protection."

"And executive protection is…"

74

"Bodyguarding," Jonah said. "They're mercenaries, Alix. Duh."

"Mercenaries?" Alix asked, shocked. "You know mercenaries?"

Dad snorted laughter. "Jonah's being melodramatic. Some of my clients have investments in places where there is very little or no law enforcement. They need to protect oil platforms from pirates off the coast of Africa, or else they need to keep their CEOs from being kidnapped in Kazakhstan, or they've got factories that need security in places like Mexico. And, yes, I suppose that all sounds exciting, but to be honest, it doesn't have much to do with me at all. Mostly, I'm just lucky that all those companies need PR expertise as much as they need companies like Williams and Crowe. It means that when my family is threatened, I have experienced people who I can call."

"Dial-a-Merc," Jonah enthused. "Cool."

Dad shared a look of affectionate exasperation with Alix. "In any case, we're lucky that we know them, because I don't know what we'd do if we had to rely just on local law enforcement."

Alix couldn't help but think of the slow response of the rent-a-cops on Seitz's campus. "So how long will they be with us?" she asked.

"I doubt it will be too long," Dad said. "We're following up leads from the school. Now that we know there's a connection between that event and you and a couple of other vandalism attempts, the police are more likely to make progress. With the FBI helping, I'm sure a pattern will turn up."

"So they've done other things that you know about?"

Dad and Mom exchanged glances, looking pained. "We didn't want to worry you," she said. "The boy who was stalking you has done things to some of your father's clients as well."

"I didn't think it had anything to do with us," Dad said, looking embarrassed. "I was wrong."

"So what does it have to do with us?"

Dad shook his head, looking both baffled and angry. "I wish I knew. They stole the rats from a lab that specializes in human-safety testing. The most likely explanation is that they're animal rights activists of some kind."

"Fur kills," Jonah intoned seriously as he reached for the container of Coconut Almond Fudge Chip. "Also, PETA girls are hot."

"Jonah," Mom said warningly.

"What? I'm just saying that adult-content filters don't work if you search on PETA."

"Don't antagonize your mother," Dad said, but Alix could see a slight smile on his face. It made the night suddenly feel normal again: Jonah being a pain, and Mom and Dad trying to get him to settle down. Alix was surprised how much of a relief it was. If she didn't look at her reflection in the kitchen window, and think about the dark outside that she couldn't see, she could almost pretend the last couple of days hadn't happened.

Jonah finished scraping out the ice-cream container. "So are these bodyguards going to, like, come to school with us and stuff?" he asked.

Alix smirked, suddenly seeing the upside. "You'll never be able to cut school now."

Jonah glared. "Shut up, Alix. I'll bet you can't drive, either."

"Dad?" Alix looked over at him, suddenly feeling her freedom and privacy being stripped away. "I can't drive? Seriously?"

"It's just for a little while. You'll be taken to school and picked up, and we'll have a specialist in the school as well."

"You mean they're going to be with us every minute of the day?"

"This isn't a game, Alix."

"How do we know that?" Alix protested. "Maybe it's nothing. Jonah came home just fine. If they'd wanted him, they could have grabbed him for sure. Maybe this is all nothing!"

But even as she said it, she knew it wasn't true. Whoever 2.0 was, and whatever he wanted, he was serious. And he was still out there. As Cynthia had pointed out, he'd gone to a whole lot of trouble if it was for no reason at all.

So what was the reason?

Ask your father, 2.0 had said, but Dad seemed almost as confused as everyone else. Dad was supposed to know, and he didn't.

Alix stared at her reflection in the glass, hating that somewhere out there 2.0 was plotting and that she couldn't see what was coming.

7

"SHOULDN'T YOU BE ASLEEP?" TANK asked.

Moses looked up from the video feed at the skinny brown boy standing next to him. Black ringlets framed the kid's face, and a welding mask was perched atop his head. In one hand he was holding an acetylene torch, and in the other he had a tangle of soldering wire. The boy was so slight that the nickname he'd given himself always felt like a sick joke to Moses, but if the kid wanted to be a Tank, then Moses would make him a Tank.

"Shouldn't *you* be asleep?" Moses said. "I had you working all night."

"Still too much adrenaline," Tank said. He pulled out his ever-present inhaler, took a puff, held his breath, and then let it out slowly.

"You doing okay?" Moses asked.

"Better than some days, anyway."

"You should rest."

Tank nodded in agreement but still didn't move. He eyed the high-def video streaming in.

"Is that her?"

Moses glanced over at the video streams. Tiled views of a hypermodern house. Curved rooflines and iron struts and high balconies.

Alix Banks and her friends were lying out beside a pool in the backyard.

"I wanted to see how she reacted," Moses said.

"And?"

"They bitched a lot about their cars being searched."

Tank shook his head mournfully. "Nothing shakes these people, does it?"

Moses grinned. "We're just getting started."

"The prank went good, though, right? It did what you wanted?"

"Yeah, it was tight. You did good." Moses patted Tank's shoulder. "You wired that up. You're like Michelangelo, except with squirt guns and electric pumps."

A smile ghosted across Tank's features at the compliment. "So now what?"

"I don't already got you doing enough?" Moses laughed.

"Metalwork." Tank shrugged. "It's not complicated."

Moses leaned back and stretched. "Well, right now I'm going to watch and see how they all adjust. See how our old friend Simon Banks reacts. Maybe poke at our girl Alix a little more and see if she does something interesting. I kind of want to see how that father-daughter relationship holds up now that our girl's got some questions in her head. Once we see how everyone reacts, then we'll pick our next play."

Moses went back to watching the feed. Tank didn't move.

Moses looked up. "What?"

Tank shrugged. "You watch her a lot."

"That's the job," Moses said.

"Long as you're watching her for biz, and not 'cause you're getting all wrapped up in the target."

Moses made a face of irritation. "I'm the one who picked the target."

"I'm just sayin', you're spending a lot of time looking at a girl."

Moses glanced back to the video feeds and the girls beside the pool. The one called Sophie had left, but Alix and Cynthia were still there. "I'm detail-oriented."

"Detail-oriented on tight blouses," Tank said.

Moses glared. Tank was smart enough to back off. "Sorry," he muttered, and dropped his welding mask over his face.

Instant defense. The kid clamming up, putting up his walls. Moses almost felt bad that he'd made Tank close up like that.

You're better than what he had before, Moses reminded himself.

Tank said something else, muffled by the mask. Moses assumed it was another apology.

Kook wandered into the computer lab. She was drinking

something the color of luminescent slime and loaded with stimulants as she got ready for another coding session. Her electric-blue hair stuck out in wild directions, tousled from sleep. As she passed, a wave of sweet herb, seemingly embedded in her skin, wafted over Moses and Tank.

"Morning," she mumbled as she stepped over power cables and plug splitters.

"It's afternoon."

"It's morning in the Philippines," Kook said. "That's all I care about." She plopped down in front of the computer gear they'd set up for her work.

Tank said something else from behind his mask.

"What's that?" Moses asked.

Tank pushed up his defense. "I said I'm going to need more money." He gestured vaguely toward where they'd set up his workshop, waving his wire and torch. "I'm almost out of iron."

Moses nodded sourly. They were starting to burn through money now, all of it going faster as pieces fell into place. He needed to plan another cash run soon. Someplace nice and far away that wouldn't cause any disruptions in the surveillance that they knew was always there, circling overhead, gazing down from cameras in streets, peering over the shoulders of convenience store clerks, and watching from traffic cams, evaluating them all as they moved under suspicious eyes.

First Rule: You're always watched.
Second Rule: See rule one.

"How's the coding going?" he called to Kook.

"Fuckers think they're smarter than me," she answered. She was bringing flatscreens to life, twenty-nine-inch monsters casting an ethereal glow across her features, blue and green and red glitter on her eyebrow and nose piercings. A solid wall of monitors ringed her, four huge workstations, filled with tiny windows, strings of code, rotating street views from security cams, the pulsing equalizer beat of her music. Below her desk, open motherboards and fans hummed and glowed, a spiderweb of chips and backup hard drives.

Kook stuffed in her earbuds and started typing. More task windows opened. Dozens of windows now, long cascades of computer code flowing past under Kook's command. Her pausing and reading and then going on, comparing chunks, some of it regular computer code—C++, Java, and ancient COBOL—other parts in compiled binary. Kook read it all, immersed in the language of machines. The four blazing monitors around her cast a glow like the flare of a nuclear explosion on her features. She sucked the green slime drink through a straw and rubbed her eyes and stared into the rivers of code. "Fuckers think they know shit," she muttered.

"You think you can be ready in time?" Moses pressed.

"What?" She pulled her earbuds out.

"Are you going to be ready?"

"Just got to surf the wave." She toasted Moses with her toxic drink. "It'll take me right to shore."

Tank snorted. "Yeah, Kook, you keep on surfing, girl. Let us know when you ride that wave in from crazy."

"Beat it, Tank. I'm not stoned enough to ignore you, and that's all that's keeping me from feeding you to Adam's rats."

Unlike with Moses, Tank didn't seem to be bothered at all by Kook's threats. With Moses, a wrong word turned Tank cautious. With Kook, he never flinched.

"That reminds me," Tank said. "We're going to need more rat food. Adam's complaining about it."

"So Adam can put it on the list," Moses said absently. "He can get it when he's getting the party supplies."

Tank shook his head vigorously. "If you let Adam do it, he'll buy them gourmet cheese. I thought you said we were supposed to be watching money. Adam will buy them some big wheel of English aged cheddar, and he'll have us all eating dog food."

"Okay, okay. I'll talk to him." He tried to turn back to the streaming video, but Tank still wasn't leaving.

"Is there something else?"

"I just think you should stop looking at her all the time," Tank said.

"I think you should mind your own business," Moses said, but to his surprise, Tank didn't back down. The boy's brow furrowed. He hunched in on himself, but he pressed on anyway.

"You almost screwed up when you cloned the key card."

"How was I supposed to know the headmaster was just going to come after me like that?"

"How were you supposed to know?" Kook glanced over. "Your uncle would have called that sloppy."

"You didn't hear what that man said to me," Moses protested.

"Still put the wrong kind of heat on us," Kook said.

"I got the man's keys cloned, didn't I?"

Kook was looking at him now, more seriously. "Sure you did. In the most public and obvious way. It made you stand out. It probably put your face on some camera. And it made you look like a thug. You're not a thug, and you made yourself look like one."

"It's the target," Tank said stubbornly. "She's got him all screwed up."

Moses shot him another look. "She does not."

Before the argument could continue, Adam came into the computer lab. He was wearing a sports coat and slacks, his hair still wet from the shower. "Do I look rich or what?" He turned in a circle, looking pleased with himself, then stopped when he saw the expressions on everyone else's faces.

"What did I do?"

"What makes you think everything's about you?" Kook asked.

"Because I'm a narcissist?"

Kook snorted. "I'll give you that." She jerked her head toward Moses. "We're talking about Wonderboy getting wrapped up in the target."

Adam blew out his breath. "Yeah. That was sloppy with the headmaster."

"He let her bite him, too," Tank said glumly.

"Are you serious?" Kook looked interested. "You should probably get a rabies shot."

"Don't be nasty," Moses said. "She doesn't have rabies."

Kook snorted and went back to her coding. "And there you have it. He's wrapped up in her."

"Girls are trouble," Adam warned. "I try to tell you that."

"I'm fine," Moses said.

"If you say so. Now, do I look okay to go out in public or not?" He stood straight, grinning, waiting for the approving inspection.

"You really are a narcissist," Kook said.

"I'm a good-looking narcissist," Adam shot back.

"You look perfect," Moses said. "No one will notice you—" He broke off. A white rat was poking its nose out from the pocket of Adam's jacket. "Uh…" Moses pointed. "Are you planning on taking that with you?"

Adam frowned as he plucked the rat from his pocket. "I could've sworn I locked them all up."

"That's the beginning of a horror flick, I think," Tank said. "Rats getting out. Eating people in their sleep."

Adam laughed and made kissy faces at the rat. "This little guy? Nah. He wouldn't dare touch me until my body was cold."

"They're rats," Kook said as she started typing code. "They eat the ears off babies."

"Really?" Adam regarded his pet with interest. "I thought it was ferrets that did that."

"They're all rodents. They're going to take over the fuck-ing world," Kook said.

"If I were a mouse, I'd live in the walls," Tank said. "No one would ever find me."

"Don't sell yourself short, little guy," Adam said. "If you were a mouse, you'd build a better cat trap. Fuckers would never know what hit them."

The images on the camera feeds changed abruptly. Moses leaned forward, suddenly interested.

"Hey there, looks like our friends are finally waking up."

Cop cars were arriving. A lot of them. Official vehicles starting to gather. Chevy SUVs. A Lincoln town car. Moses zoomed in and started snapping license plates, capturing faces of people as they emerged. Storing images, all of them coming fast and furious now. Lots of activity. More than he would have expected. He'd expected some reaction, sure, but this looked more like straight-up panic.

"What do you make of this?" Moses asked. He pointed at an SUV as it pulled up in front of the Bankses' house and more people emerged.

Tank peered over Moses's shoulder. "Williams and Crowe, for sure. Recognize them anywhere."

Adam pressed in for a look. "Hello, old friends."

Kook got up from her workstation to join them. Everyone peered at the screen and the ants' nest of activity swarming around the Banks household. "Damn. That's a lot of heat," Kook muttered.

"More than I expected," Moses agreed.

"We screw something up?"

"Don't know, but it looks like we kicked the ant pile, whatever's happening."

"They're freaking," Tank observed. "For sure, they're freaking."

"Some of those guys look like feds," Adam said.

"We might need to speed things up," Moses said. "If the FBI is getting in on this, everything gets more serious."

"Or else slow down," Adam suggested.

"This was bound to happen sometime," Kook said. "We've got to be on some watch list already, and you know it. NSA, FBI. Big data has got to have something on us by now."

"If they had something on us, we'd already be caught," Moses said.

"Does this mean we need to be worried?" Adam asked. "Should we think about pulling back?"

Should we? Moses turned the question over in his mind. Thinking of all the work they'd done, all the setup. Everything.

We've been careful. I've been careful.

Except it wasn't totally true. He'd been careful all the way until he'd let that private school stuffed shirt throw him off his game. Even if he denied it out loud, inside he knew it had been a mistake. He could have stolen the guy's key card anywhere. Waited until he was off campus. But against all reason, Moses had been driven to go onto the campus itself.

Sloppy. His uncle would have shouted at him that he was sloppy.

So why'd you do it?

Moses shoved down the question. What was done was done. He focused on the activity. Was this something he needed to be worried about? Had he made a bigger mistake that he couldn't see? Did he have a blind spot?

"No," Moses said finally. "There's still no way they could have any idea what we're up to." He studied all the people going in and out of the house, figuring the angles. "I sure wouldn't mind being able to hear what they're up to inside, though."

"I told you we should have bugged it right from the start," Kook said.

"And that would have gone real sweet if the little brother messed with the Xbox and found us peeking in before we were ready."

"You think it's worth the risk now?"

"I don't think we've got a choice. With Williams and Crowe on the scene, we need to be inside their heads. No more of this outside-looking-in stuff."

Kook pinched her lip. "With Williams and Crowe on the scene, it's going to be harder to bug."

"We can do it, though, right?"

Kook gave him an annoyed glance. "Of course we can do it. Who do you think you're talking to? We'll have eyes inside before you blink."

Tank was nodding in agreement. "They got tons of gear in there we can piggyback."

"So let's do it," Moses said. "I want to know what they're

thinking before they think it. Information is power. I want to make sure we've got more information than they do."

Kook studied the activity boiling around the house. "Kind of fun to see old Simon Banks guessing and in the dark."

"It's going to be even more fun once we're inside his head." Moses clapped his hands. "Okay. Let's get some eyes and ears inside that house."

"No problem, boss." Tank slammed down his helmet shield and headed off.

Kook waved to Adam. "We're going to put some more things on the shopping list," she said.

They started conferring while Moses lingered at the monitors, watching the Banks household scramble.

What's got you so spooked? Sure, we're poking at you, but you look like you're prepping for the zombie apocalypse. What's got you so riled up?

It didn't matter, he decided. The plan would keep rolling. This time, he knew more than Simon Banks did.

Knowledge was power, and information was control. And for the first time in his life, Moses Cruz had more of both than Simon Banks.

You can call in all the guns and favors you like, Moses thought. *It still won't save you when I bring down the hammer.*

8

ALIX LAY IN HER BED UNDER moonlight, trying to make sense of the strange new world she inhabited.

If she pulled back the curtains, she could make out the surveillance van parked on the street. Somewhere, there were others, too. All of them waiting for…what? An attack? A kidnapping?

It felt so melodramatic to think that anything was wrong at all. The street looked so safe. Graceful oaks. Broad swaths of manicured lawns and gardens. A few lights still glowed at the entrances to various homes, marking pathways up to arched doorways. Peaceful.

And yet a stranger was out there and, if Dad was to be believed, maybe something bigger. Maybe a whole group bent on kidnapping her or Jonah. People who wanted to use the two of them to get to Dad.

It was like the stories she heard that came from places like Bangkok or Mexico. When Alix went to Cancun for winter vacation, she remembered being warned that Mexico was dangerous. When she went online, it was full of reports of people who had been kidnapped and ended up in shallow graves. Even Guillermo del Toro's father had been kidnapped, and del Toro was a movie director. The guy had done Hollywood movies, and because of that, people had targeted his family for kidnapping and ransom. Alix remembered thinking that things like that happened in Mexico but didn't happen here.

Except now maybe they did.

She got out of bed and padded downstairs. She was wearing a long T-shirt that she liked to sleep in. The day had been hot, but now everything had cooled off. Her skin turned to gooseflesh as she tiptoed down the stairs.

2:12 flashed on the stove clock, green light casting across the kitchen.

She slipped into Dad's office, not even sure what she was looking for.

Ask your father.

This was absurd. She could practically see Jonah mocking her for being a silly girl. She sat down in her dad's chair. Touched the trackpad on his computer. The screen flickered alive, showing a password challenge.

There was another computer in the den, which Jonah was allowed to use, out where Mom and Dad could look over his shoulder and make sure he wasn't surfing for porn. This computer was Dad's. She wasn't supposed to be here. Just touching the keys felt like an invasion.

Alix felt a chill of self-consciousness and glanced toward the windows. The night was so dark outside. The house felt dark, too.

A scuffling came from the kitchen.

Was someone inside the house?

Alix held her breath, suddenly afraid. The scuffling came again.

The light of the computer screen with its password challenge bathed her, and Alix suddenly felt very exposed. There was only one light on in the entire house, and it was right beside her, and she wasn't wearing anything except an XXL T-shirt. She wished she'd put on sweats at least before she came downstairs.

She glanced at the windows to the backyard and tugged her T-shirt down over her thighs. Williams & Crowe was supposed to be out there. *Are they looking in?*

She eased out of the chair. It creaked as she came off the seat. She realized she was still holding her breath and tried to make herself breathe silently. Was she being stupid? Was she just imagining the sound?

If 2.0 was in the house, he'd know she was there because of the light from the computer. He'd know right where she was.

Get a grip, Alix. There's no one here. Security would have caught him. They're supposed to be watching.

Alix slipped to the edge of the study door, straining to

hear over the pounding of her heart. The refrigerator started to hum. The computer monitor went back to sleep, plunging her into darkness. Blinded, Alix froze. She blinked her eyes, trying to force them to adjust, listening for more movement in the kitchen. Still nothing.

Nothing at all.

Feeling stupid and crazy, but unwilling to let her caution go, Alix eased out from behind the study door. She peered into the kitchen. Now that her eyes had adjusted, the light from the stove clock gave a dim view of the room. Tiles and stainless steel surfaces. Smooth bamboo floors. The Sub-Zero fridge against the clean modern lines of the granite countertops.

Nothing.

She listened, but she couldn't hear anything.

You idiot. You were imagining it.

A shadow moved behind her and Alix spun around. Her breath caught.

He was right there, looking through the glass door.

Hands to the glass as he peered inside. Shadow and eyes, looking in, seeking. Then pausing.

Alix tugged her shirt down again, trying to make herself disappear. To hide. She froze as his gaze swept across her and held.

They stared at each other. She felt pinned by his gaze. His expression was solemn.

Don't panic don't panic don't panic.

Suddenly he smiled. He held his finger to his lips. *Shhh.*

The message was unmistakable. *Shhh. Let's keep a secret.* And then, absurdly, another motion: one hand atop the other, forming a *T*.

Time-out.

Seriously?

He made the motion again, smiling. Time-out.

No. Suddenly Alix knew exactly what he was saying.

Truce.

The thing he'd suggested when he'd caught her in the smoke.

How about we call a little truce?

Unbelievable.

Alix knew she should scream. She should call the cops. She should turn on all the lights. However he'd gotten past Williams & Crowe, all it would take was one loud scream to bring them down on him.

But something about his demeanor held her. The rakish confidence. The lack of shame or fear. She'd busted him, and he didn't even have the grace to act embarrassed. Instead, he was smiling at her and signaling for a truce, as if they were playing some game of tag or hide-and-seek. Grinning at her like it was all a big game and he'd just happened to be caught.

Alix walked over to the door and stared at him through the glass. He was dressed entirely in black. He barely stood out against the night beyond. He pointed at the door lock.

Alix shook her head, but she couldn't help smiling at the guy's chutzpah.

"No," she mouthed.

He just quirked an eyebrow and made the *T* again with his hands. His lips said *truce*.

Suddenly her heart was pounding.

I'm insane.

She flicked the lock and stepped back. He reached over to slide the door open. Alix was suddenly horribly aware of decisions she couldn't take back. She retreated behind the granite island.

2.0 eased inside.

"Truce," he said.

Alix nodded. "Truce."

They regarded each other warily. It was as if they were both mindful of crossing a solemn boundary, a line that turned out to be more important than they'd realized.

Alix cleared her throat. "How did you get past our security guys?"

"Oh, you know. Williams and Crowe..." He peered back outside, seeming to check on something. "They got systems. It makes them predictable."

"And you're not."

"Try not to be." He was gazing around the kitchen, taking everything in. "You're kind of a surprise, yourself."

"Because I let you in?"

"Dumb move for such a smart girl."

"I could scream. I'll bet Williams and Crowe have a system for that."

"Bet they do." His eyes locked with hers. "You won't, though."

"No."

Alix realized her heart was still pounding. Everything about the moment felt electric. She had an almost over-whelming urge to come around the island. To walk up to him—

"You need to go," she said abruptly. "I need you to leave."

Before I do something even more stupid.

"Did you hear me?" she asked.

He didn't respond. Just ran his hand across the granite countertop. "You talk to your father?" he asked. "You ask him what this is all about?"

"He doesn't know. He said you're an animal rights activist."

He smiled slightly. "Surprised he didn't just go straight for terrorist. It's a better PR smear these days."

"My dad doesn't smear people."

"For free."

"What?"

" 'My dad doesn't smear people for free.' That's what you should have said. He smears plenty of people, but he doesn't do it unless it's worth money to him."

"I don't know who you think—"

"You don't have any idea what your dad does, do you?" His tone had sharpened and become accusatory. "You don't know where this nice house comes from. You don't know how many bodies you've got buried in the basement. You don't have any idea where all your money comes from."

"I want you to leave."

96

"So scream."

She glared at him. "Why are you going after my family?"

"You really haven't figured it out?" He laughed. "I mean, I knew your old man was good at PR, but I didn't think he'd even lie to his own daughter."

Alix felt her anger rising. "Cut the mind games. If you've got something to say, say it. No more of your Mr. Mysterious bullshit. Just say it."

He turned serious. "That how you want to play it?"

"Yeah," she said, glaring. "That's how I want to play it."

"Okay." He blew out his breath. "This is payback, Alix. Everything that's coming down on your dad is payback for everything he's ever done to all the people he's ever done it to."

"So what do I have to do with that? I haven't done anything."

"Yeah. That's true." He was nodding in agreement, staring down at the surface of the counter that separated them, looking almost guilty. "You're just the wrong person in the right place at the right time." He looked up. "Then again, none of us get to choose the right place, do we? We just get what we get, and sometimes it turns out we're just collateral damage."

There was a long pause as they both studied each other.

"I think our truce is over," Alix said finally.

All the play had gone out of his expression as well. "Maybe we never had one," he said.

He was out the door and enveloped in darkness before she could decide if she should scream or not.

9

"YOU'VE GOT A BODYGUARD?" Cynthia asked Alix, disbelieving.

Alix nodded her head tiredly. "Yeah."

Seitz had reopened, and life had returned to a strange semblance of normal, except that Animal Control was still roaming the campus in pursuit of white lab rats; the science building still showed evidence that 2.0 had been there, despite the best efforts of the custodial staff; and Alix's dreams were haunted by the merry prankster, whom she was pretty sure she was at war with. Even though she couldn't quite bring herself to hate him. Even though he seemed hellbent on doing something horrible to her.

Maybe I have Stockholm syndrome, she thought.

She'd spent the last couple of days wrestling with the question of whether she could tell anyone at all that she'd let 2.0 into her house (her house!) and concluded that her own Teflon reputation as the responsible child of the family wouldn't survive it.

She did mention that she thought she'd seen someone lurking in the backyard. That was enough to send Williams & Crowe into a new tizzy of paranoia that had also resulted in a new home lockdown policy, as well as the every-waking-minute bodyguard situation that now plagued her life.

Cynthia listened to Alix's woes as she ate french fries, complained that she was going to break out if she ate any more oily things, and then ate another fry.

"You're making up that thing about the bodyguard," Cynthia accused as she eyed another greasy stick of potato.

"I wish," Alix said. "Check out the teachers' table."

Cynthia craned her neck. "I don't—wait, that blond lady? She doesn't look like much of a bodyguard."

And she didn't. That was what Dad had said made Lisa perfect. She was a stealth pit bull, he'd claimed. No one would see her coming. All the guys in school might check out Lisa's tight butt, but nobody would guess she was dangerous. In Alix's mind, Lisa wasn't so much a stealth pit bull as a Death Barbie, and, unfortunately, Death Barbie seemed mostly bent on screwing with Alix's daily life.

The woman was perky and clean-cut, with straight, bobbed blond hair and a freckled pixie face. She could have been a cute substitute teacher. If Alix had run into Lisa at a Starbucks, she would never have guessed that the lady also happened to be carrying a 9mm handgun. Alix idly wondered if the school had guessed, either. She suspected not.

Seitz had rules, after all. The administrators might let Lisa stalk her on campus, but they'd probably shit bricks if they knew Death Barbie was packing heat.

"She's really guarding you?" Cynthia asked. "How come she's sitting so far away?"

"She doesn't have to be very close to shoot someone, I guess."

"She's got a *gun*?"

Alix smirked, feeling weirdly proud of the knowledge, even as she felt annoyed at being stalked everywhere. "Yeah. I saw it. She's got it in that cute little Indian-print purse." Alix tried to remember what Jonah had said about the gun when Lisa showed it to him, along with the telescoping baton she carried, and her zip cuffs and her Mace and her Taser....

"A Glock," Alix said. "She's carrying a Glock. And a lot of bullets. Like, seventeen shots or something insane like that."

Death Barbie was sitting at the teachers' table, looking like no one in particular. Eating a salad and talking pleasantly to Ms. Liss, not giving a single clue that she had enough firepower on her to turn the dining hall into national news.

"She's definitely subtle," Cynthia said as she gave up on her fries and shoved the tray away. "Ugh. I can't eat any more of these. They make me feel gross."

"You want my bread?"

Cynthia made a face. "God, no. I can't stand the smell of that stuff."

"Seriously? I thought everybody liked fresh-baked bread."

"Fresh-baked is the worst. I hate that smell." Cynthia

wrinkled her nose. "There's a bakery near my house. I smell it at four AM whenever the wind's blowing our way. It's like being smothered in yeast."

"Ew. Seriously?"

"Yeah." Cynthia gave a self-conscious laugh. "I think it's some housewife who got a hobby and then it took off. Now it's killing property values. I swear I'm going to buy nose plugs." She changed the subject. "Oh, look, your bodyguard is watching you."

"Yeah?" Alix glanced over her shoulder, but Lisa had already looked away. Death Barbie was subtle, that was for sure. If Alix hadn't known about Lisa, she would have blown off the woman easily. Just another teacher, maybe a sub, anything except a "security specialist" from Williams & Crowe.

All through the first half of the day, Lisa never really came close to Alix. She was just… around. Watching. Eyeing everybody and everything. Even now it was happening. She could see it happening if Alix watched long enough. Lisa was talking to Liss, but the bodyguard wasn't looking at Liss. Lisa's eyes kept moving across the dining hall, scanning. She wasn't looking at Alix; she barely ever looked at Alix. She was always looking at everyone else—all the people around Alix. All the people who came close.

"Well," Cynthia said, trying to make the best of it. "At least you know your dad loves you."

"Yeah, well, it was really Jonah who started all of this. Dad freaked out because Jonah disappeared. His one and only son." Alix made a face.

Cynthia gave her a hard look. "That's a load, and you know it. If you'd been the missing one, you know he would have been a thousand times crazier about trying to protect you. His only daughter?" Cynthia laughed. "My dad would have gone nuts."

"My dad never goes nuts," Alix said.

But it actually had been kind of amazing to see how ferocious he'd been about protecting her. Alix had always loved her dad, but it took something like this to see how much he loved her, and Jonah, too. It sounded cheesy, but she could tell. She just wished that the sudden infusion of parental love wasn't manifesting as a Death Barbie always looking over her shoulder.

Cynthia said, "Well, this will at least keep your stalker away."

At Cynthia's comment, Alix was reminded once again of her night encounter with 2.0. The guy staring in through the glass, smiling. "I guess...." Alix trailed off. She didn't want to lie to Cynthia, but she also didn't want to tell her about her second encounter. Cynthia had hassled her enough the first time around. Alix didn't need another dose of Tiger Mom, but something in her voice must have tipped Cynthia off, because her friend looked up sharply.

"What?" Cynthia asked. "What is it this time?"

Alix smiled sheepishly.

"Give it up, girl," Cynthia pressed.

"Oh." Alix made herself laugh. "It's...nothing. Just"—she leaned forward and lowered her voice—"I talked to him again."

"What?"

Cynthia's voice was almost a squawk. Everyone around them startled and turned to stare. Alix made shushing motions as Death Barbie's gaze whipped around.

"Will you quiet down?" Alix whispered.

Cynthia leaned close. "You've got a stalker, and you want me to quiet down?" Cynthia whispered fiercely. "Are you insane?" Comprehension dawned. She gave Alix an exasperated look. "You didn't tell anyone, did you?"

"Well…"

"What *is it* about this guy?" Cynthia asked.

Alix scowled. "I don't know." She stood up, frustrated, and gathered her plate. "Never mind. Forget I said anything." She left Cynthia, who watched her go with puzzled worry.

As Alix took her plate to the conveyor that ferried dirty dishes into the guts of the caf, she wondered what was wrong with her. Maybe she had some kind of suicide impulse. Any sane person would report a stalker like this. 2.0 knew her name. He was after her family. He was after her. He could get past Williams & Crowe—

Alix was annoyed to find Lisa trailing her, dropping off her own plate. Her shadow, walking through the halls, and now Alix had to pee. She headed for the bathrooms with Lisa following, pushing in behind.

You can't be serious.

Alix turned as the bathroom door closed. "I don't need you to follow me in here."

"I'm sure you feel that way. But it's my job to be sure

you're safe." Lisa was walking down the line of stalls, checking inside each in turn. Then she went and started washing her hands, watching Alix in the mirror.

Alix crossed her arms. "I'm not peeing with you in here."

"Do you want me to secure the bathroom for you, then?"

The door swung open. Deb and Selena came into the bathroom. "—he's hot," Deb was saying.

They both stopped short as they ran into Alix and Lisa's standoff.

Lisa raised an eyebrow at Alix.

Fine.

Alix went into a stall. With the door locked, she could almost pretend that she had privacy. Except she didn't. Alix sat in the stall imagining ways that she might escape, listening to the water run in the sink as Lisa pretended to wash her hands some more. Trying to pee with someone standing right outside, waiting for her to do her business. It made her feel like she was about six years old.

When Alix came out, she shoved past Lisa to wash her hands and was annoyed that Lisa didn't seem offended. All Lisa said was, "This is a lot easier if you just pretend I don't exist. It calls less attention."

Deb and Selena came out of their stalls. "Is she bothering you, Alix?"

Lisa said, "No. I work for Alix."

"Will you cut it out?" Alix said to Lisa. She turned to her friends. "She doesn't work for me. She works for my dad. She's kind of a bodyguard."

"Oh." They seemed at a loss for what else could be said and bailed as quickly as they could. Alix watched longingly as they headed out.

"I know it's inconvenient, Alix," Lisa said, "but we need to keep you safe until we know what these terrorists are up to."

"They're terrorists now?" Alix asked. "I thought they were kidnappers. Or animal rights activists. And before that they were vandals."

Lisa gave her a look that said, *Don't split hairs with me, young lady.*

Alix felt a little embarrassed. The way Lisa looked at her made her feel like she was a child throwing a tantrum.

Lisa's expression said that Death Barbie knew things Alix didn't and that Alix was just a sheltered little girl. But still, Alix didn't want to back down. She was already sick of the whole bodyguard thing, and she had the feeling that if she didn't make a stand, she'd be shoved around forever.

"Who do you think these people are, really?" Alix asked. "Nobody's telling me the truth. All I get is vandals and wackos and kidnappers and activists and now terrorists. What's going on?"

Lisa sighed and leaned back against the sink. Her jacket opened, giving a glimpse of a Taser clipped to her belt and a heavy telescoping baton beside it. Lisa had shown Jonah how it extended with a flick of the wrist. A metal club with enough weight behind it to break bones.

"We don't know what they are," Lisa said finally. "All we know is that they're organized and they've targeted you and your family. And since we don't know, it means we have to be prepared for the worst. It's the only way we can prevent it.

"If you'll just help me, I can minimize the amount of disruption you experience. Or you can make it difficult. Either way, though, I'll still be here, making sure you're safe. It's your call."

"Are you going to follow me everywhere?" Alix asked. "What if I go to a party this weekend? Are you going to rat me out?"

"It's not like that, Alix. My job isn't to police you. It's to keep you safe."

"But I'm nobody important! It's not like I'm the president's daughter or something. There's no reason for anybody to care about me. It's got to be a mistake!"

"I know it's frustrating, Alix. But you're a target. I know you want to blame me, but I'm not the one who picked you out. 2.0 has explicitly targeted you. My job is to make sure that whatever they want to do doesn't work."

"Would you take a bullet for me?"

Lisa's pale blue Barbie eyes didn't blink. "Let's hope it doesn't go down that way."

Jesus, Alix thought. *She really is scary*. Walking Death Barbie, for real.

"Whatever," Alix said finally. "I'm late for class."

She pushed back out into the noise of the commons with Lisa on her heels.

Cynthia caught up to her. "Did she seriously just follow you into the bathroom?"

106

Alix shook her head. "You don't want to know."

"Does she wipe, too?"

Alix snorted laughter and glanced back at Lisa. If Lisa heard or cared, she didn't show it. "I'm in hell," Alix said.

"You know, there might be a bright side to this," Cynthia said.

"Please tell me."

"Maybe we can use her as a designated driver."

Alix laughed and shook her head, grateful that Cynthia was trying to make her feel better about the whole thing. It was all so absurd. "I wish."

They pushed into AP Chem class and found their seats. Lisa slipped in and slouched against the back wall. Alix stared out the window. Red paint still stained the glass, turning the whole chem lab a pale pink as sunlight filtered through. The custodial staff had apparently tried everything, but the paint still remained. Rumor had it that Mulroy was tearing his hair out over it. The paint would have to be sandblasted off. Which actually meant that the windows would all have to be replaced, and now the whole classroom smelled like paint remover, thanks to the failed cleaning efforts.

Alix peered through the paint residue to the world outside. Cynthia's comment about designated drivers did raise a question. *How am I supposed to go out on a Friday night with my friends if I've got adult supervision watching my every move? Talk about a crimp on life.*

It wasn't even like she had some grand plan for what she'd be doing over the weekend. It wasn't like she was some kind of wild child who was planning on getting it on at one of Brent Wall's drug-fueled pool parties, but she couldn't see going to a party on Friday night or going to the movies with her friends or catching an afternoon Starbucks with Lisa as her tagalong. She'd never needed minding in her life. Jonah was the one who needed minding. Jonah was the one who got into trouble. Alix was the good girl. Mom and Dad trusted her, and freedom was her reward.

So why didn't you tell them about stalker boy coming to visit?

Because then they'd know you have really shitty judgment.

Cynthia was right. She should have said something. Even Jonah would have been smart enough to say something. And yet here she was, lying low with the secret.

Alix gazed over at Cynthia longingly. The girl did her work, got her good grades, partied, and didn't get caught. They were a perfect pair, and it infuriated Alix that she had somehow been targeted by the universe. Cynthia was sure to be free on Friday. And Alix was sure to be trapped at home.

Alix squinted through the smeared windows as a guy in a white Animal Control suit dashed across campus holding a rat high.

2.0 had sure done a number on Seitz.

Jonah had described the details that he'd gleaned with the relish of a fanboy. It was just the kind of thing the poor kid went to bed fantasizing about. A way to get back at Seitz. But this was beyond even Jonah's fevered imagination: an elaborate network of trip wires that the SWAT people had triggered when they'd come into the school, arrays of electric pumps and toy water guns all synchronized by Wi-Fi repeaters, all of them placed just so to display 2.0's tag to the world...and then, of course, the rats. Thousands and thousands of rats.

But the most amazing thing about the prank was that there was no evidence of how it had been accomplished. None of the security cams had a bit of footage. Not a single witness. It was as if the entire elaborate setup had been teleported into the science building. Alix sighed as she stared out through the red-smeared window, watching students as they hurried across the quad to their own classes.

There was a life out there, but she couldn't quite reach it. Instead, she was stuck in here with the paint and the industrial solvents and Death Barbie, all thanks to the cleverness of 2.0.

■ ■ ■

When Alix saw Jonah after school, he looked even more miserable than Alix felt, and it almost cheered her up. He was being trailed by a mountainous guy who was twice his size, a huge steroid-infused creature whom Jonah had nicknamed Hulk but who was actually named Gunter.

"Don't be fooled by the 'roids. He's fast," Jonah groused. "I tried to ditch twice. He caught me both times."

That, Alix could at least laugh at. Other kids were coming out of school and heading for their cars or getting picked up by parents and nannies. They were all giving them weird looks. Alix with Death Barbie, Jonah with Hulk.

Sophie and Derek came over. "We're going to go get coffee...." They trailed off, looking at the security detail.

Before Alix could answer them, Lisa said, "You've got an appointment at home, Alix."

Alix glared at Lisa. "Can I check in at least? Maybe change plans? Would that be okay with you?"

"Of course, Alix."

The phone at home rang and rang. Alix tried her mom's cell, but, of course, it went to voice mail. *As usual.* Alix racked her brain as she smiled at Lisa. She pretended to dial another number and pressed the phone to her ear.

"Hi, Dad? Yeah. I was going to grab a coffee with Sophie before I come home. Is that okay?" she said to the ringing phone on the other end. "Cool! Thanks!" She ended the fake call.

"We're good," she said to Sophie. "Let's go."

Lisa was just looking at her, a small, knowing smile on her face as she shook her head. "I'm sorry, Alix—unless I can talk to your father, we're going to have to go home now." Even as she spoke, a car slid up to the curb, a black Mercedes with a driver who had undoubtedly been vetted by Williams & Crowe.

Lisa went and opened the door. She waited expectantly, her smile chilly, knowing that Alix had faked the call, not bothering to hide that she knew.

Alix sighed, defeated. "I guess I can't."

110

"Wow," Sophie said.

"Tell me about it."

Alix let herself be stuffed into the car with Jonah. She waved ironically at Sophie and Derek as the car pulled away from the curb, but Sophie had already turned away to talk to Cynthia, who was coming down the steps. All three headed off toward the student parking lot.

Alix wistfully watched them recede.

"Seat belts," Lisa said.

Alix sighed. It was like having Mom with her all the time. *I'm in hell*, she thought. *I'm in pure, living hell.*

10

JONAH STARED OUT THE CAR window, gazing longingly
at the streets of Haverport as they slid by. Alix found herself feeling sorry for him. When the doctors described Jonah,
they started with words like "active" and "impulse control"
and ended with words like ADHD and Adderall.

Jonah had been thrilled at the Adderall proposal. He'd
been planning on selling it to juniors and seniors who were
cramming for SATs and Advanced Placement tests, but then
Dad had vetoed the idea of drugging him. And it really was
hard to tell how much help the kid needed. Between his jokes,
hyperactivity, and the compulsive urge to go AWOL from
Seitz, something was clearly amiss, but it was hard to tell if it
was something wrong with the way Jonah's brain was wired
or if the real problem was that Mom and Dad were trying to
jam him into a life where he simply refused to fit. Sometimes
Alix suspected that the kid was smarter than all of them and

that his reckless persona was just an act designed to get him out of Seitz once and for all.

Jonah caught Alix looking at him. "What?"

Alix smiled. "Nothing."

He was a pain in the neck, but she liked him. Lately she'd been realizing that not everyone ended up liking their sibs. Sometimes they just weren't made to get along. Sophie hated her older sister, Simone. But Alix liked Jonah. Even if he was always one step away from turning fugitive on her.

As she settled back in the car, her phone buzzed. She dug it out of her purse.

Cynthia, texting: SAW YOU GET PICKED UP.

Alix felt secretly pleased that even when Cynthia was busy, she still was looking out for Alix.

I'M IN HELL, Alix texted back.

TOO BAD. I'M DRINKING COFFEE WITH SOPHIE AND DEREK. SHE'S TELLING ME ABOUT ALEC. TOTAL TRAINWRECK!!!!

UPDATE ME.

HE'S A WEEEEET KISSER.

EW!

"Who are you texting with?" Jonah asked.

"Cynthia."

"She's cute," Jonah said. "I saw her in a bikini at the pool."

Alix rolled her eyes at him. "Dream on. She's so out of your league."

CAN YOU COME OUT?

CAN'T. STUCK WITH DEATH BARBIE AND MY BRO.

:(WE'LL FIGURE SOMETHING OUT.

That was Cynthia. Always looking out for her friends. It was the opposite of the mean-girl garbage that some girls played at. Cynthia paid attention to people. It sometimes made Alix feel like she wasn't the best friend in the world, but Cynthia didn't seem to care. Cynthia did nice things for people and then went on and didn't worry about whether there was payback. Alix had once called her Zen nice, and Cynthia's only comment had been that Zen wasn't Chinese; it was Japanese.

Cynthia texted again, ANY MORE FROM YOUR BOYFRIEND?

???, Alix texted back.

STALKER MAN!

HA!

"What?" Jonah leaned over, trying to see, but Alix jerked her cell out of sight as she texted.

WISH I WAS THERE.

THERE'S A RAVE NEXT SATURDAY.

RUB IT IN, WHY DON'T YOU?

LOL. NOT WHAT I MEANT. WE'LL BUST YOU OUT. GIRL GOTS TO HAVE FUN.

Alix smiled secretly. The car pulled up to the curb. Hulk and Death Barbie climbed out and opened the doors for her and Jonah.

The house looked pretty much the same as it always had. The Williams & Crowe surveillance van was still parked across the street, but other than that, the security people had faded into the background. For all she knew, they had snipers in the trees. Inside the house, there were a few workmen from

114

an electronic-security firm rewiring the house for another layer of protection.

"What's all this?" Alix asked as she threw her satchel onto the counter. The activity was like an ants' nest. Her father was in the middle of it with George Saamsi. George grinned at her.

"Security through the wonders of science and technology," he said.

"Yeah?" Jonah asked, immediately interested in the way he always got interested about something militaristic.

"Motion sensors. New electronic eyes. Also, we're putting in cameras for the street and yard approaches. Just in case."

"In case of what?"

George shrugged. "Whatever 2.0 decides he's up to."

Alix watched the proceedings, feeling as if her home was being taken over by an army. George seemed to read her mind. "Don't worry, Alix. After today, they'll all be gone, and you'll be able to go back to your regular life."

"You mean my bodyguard's going, too?" Jonah asked.

George laughed. "You should look at this as an opportunity to study self-defense."

"You don't have him following you around everywhere," Jonah grumped.

"Gunter knows eight different ways to kill a person with his bare hands in less than five seconds."

"Yeah?" Jonah perked up and went off in pursuit of Hulk.

George's eyes were twinkling when he caught Alix watching the exchange. "Please don't tell your mother I said that."

"Don't worry. I've got enough problems as it is."

"I hear you've been having some adventures lately."

"I've got my own personal stalker. It's awesome."

George chuckled, and Alix was glad he was there. Somehow, it made all the disruption feel just a little more…if not normal, then at least acceptable. Alix had always thought of him as family. His official title was chief science liaison for Banks Strategy Partners, which really just meant that he was her father's best friend and that they'd always been partners. She'd grown up with George around, in and out of their lives, dropping in for dinners. A familiar face at events. Every so often he showed up for the holidays with his ninety-year-old mother in tow, a woman who went from vague and disoriented to whip-funny, depending on her medications.

Now George was urging the workmen to wrap everything up. Jonah wandered into the living room and fired up his Xbox. Pretty soon he had his sword out and was busy swinging away at some kid in Indonesia, his heavily armored avatar moving through a burning lava landscape, mirroring his movements on the Kinect.

Alix got a Diet Coke out of the fridge and went to the backyard and the pool. She thought about swimming but didn't really like the idea of getting into her bathing suit while all the security people were there. She went back inside and watched Jonah hack through enemies, envious of his ability to just do whatever he wanted without letting anyone else's watching eyes bother him.

All she wanted was privacy, but when she went up to her

bedroom, she just found more people, wiring up windows, attaching strips of security tape to everything. She wandered back downstairs, feeling like a stranger in her own house, feeling observed and self-conscious everywhere she went.

Dad came out of his office and looked surprised to see her. "What are you doing home?" he asked.

"Hello? I'm done with school."

"Oh?" He checked his watch. "Of course." He shook his head. "I lost track of time completely." Alix thought he looked exhausted, worn by work and stress.

"Dad?"

"Yes, Alix?"

"Can we talk?"

He started to check his watch again but caught himself. He smiled tiredly at Alix. "Of course. Do you want to go into the study?"

Alix eyed the ongoing work. "Could we go out somewhere instead?"

"You want to take your old man on a date?" he joked.

Alix couldn't help but feel a little better. "I'll buy you as many espressos as you can drink, if you'll bust me out of here."

Dad laughed at that, and for a second it felt like everything was normal again. "You're on."

■ ■ ■

Of course, Lisa and one of the security team named Mendoza tagged along, but they followed in a chase car, and they took

117

a table far enough away to give the illusion that they weren't with Alix and her dad. They still had a good view of the parking lot and the doors, but at least it gave the effect of leaving Alix and her dad in a bubble of privacy. It wasn't perfect, but somehow having her father with her made her feel better, and, in a way, it was nice to spend time with him without any other intrusions. He'd even turned off his cell phone.

"They can call Lisa if they need us," Dad said simply as he shut it down.

Alix was surprised once again at how different it was to have her father's whole attention. Before she'd finished kindergarten, Alix had already become skilled at discerning when her father's mind had shifted away from the moment at hand—even if his eyes were still fixed on her, and even if he was still making the appropriate yeses and nos and affirming noises of someone who was listening to what she was saying.

Mom had a story about how one day, when Alix had been about six years old, she'd been talking to Dad, and, of course, Dad hadn't been paying attention. So Alix had climbed up on his lap, grabbed his chin, and yanked his face. She'd stared into his eyes, an inch away, and said, "Your head isn't listening to me!" Which Dad found hilarious. It had become a catchphrase for the family.

Today, it was different. Dad's head was listening to her, and it was nice. It almost made ending up with a security detail worth it.

Alix chose a skinny latte, and Dad picked a double espresso. They went outside and sat on the flagstone patio

118

under the trees. It was a relief to be outside, away from routines and the frenetic activity in the house.

"All right, Alix. What's on your mind?"

Alix sipped her coffee. She felt hesitant even asking. "Oh, I don't know." She hesitated again and mentally kicked herself for it. "Why did 2.0 tell me to ask you about what this was all about?"

Dad frowned. "Ah." He sipped his espresso, then set the tiny cup down in its saucer. For a moment he paused, staring down at the cup with a furrowed brow, as if he would find enlightenment in its coffee blackness.

"I wish I had a good answer for you," he started slowly. "I keep wanting this to make some kind of sense, myself." He looked up, serious. "I wish I could say that we understand who 2.0 is, or what really motivates him, but it's all guesses."

"So…" Alix hesitated, then made herself press the issue. "What's your guess?"

"My guess?" Dad blew out his breath. "Okay, candidly, and without a whole lot to go on, my guess is that 2.0 is an activist of some kind. I'm sure you know that some of the work I do relates to politics, and the ugly truth is that any time you get involved in politics, you're going to generate strong responses." He grimaced. "We're a radicalized culture these days. It really doesn't matter whether it's the right or the left; you're going to end up with someone who's sure that you're doing the worst thing in the world. A talk radio host or some blogger decides they hate something that someone you work with does, and that's it. They whip up the witch hunts.

Mob logic." He shook his head, gazing at Lisa Price and Mendoza. "I've seen it happen to some of my clients. You see it with movie stars, too. PETA targets someone. Or Save the Whales. Or the Tea Party. It doesn't really matter. All that matters is that politics has gotten so ugly that it's hard to have a reasoned conversation about anything anymore. There's no room to disagree in a civil way. Someone always has to be cast as the Antichrist."

"But what's that got to do with us?"

Dad laughed. It was a surprisingly bitter sound. "To be honest, I didn't think this had anything to do with us. I really didn't." He reached out for Alix, his eyes pleading as he gripped her shoulder. "I am so sorry I didn't see this coming. I should have seen it. I just..." He shrugged helplessly. "I missed it. I've never considered myself to be a public figure, so it never occurred to me that we might be subjected to this kind of...abuse. Some of our clients, sure. But not us." He took another sip of his espresso and then stared down into the cup, puzzled. It was already empty.

"Do you want another?" he asked.

Alix didn't, but she said she did just to make him feel like he wasn't the only one. Mom told him to control his caffeine because he was intense enough and it would ruin his sleep, but he couldn't help the urge for just one more cup.

Alix watched him go to the counter, and he seemed like someone carrying the weight of the world on his shoulders. Once again, she thought she should tell him about 2.0 and her conversation with him. But then, she rationalized, they were already fixing the house security. And he hadn't done anything to her, after all.

Why are you protecting him?

2.0 had said their truce was over. That she was collateral damage. So why couldn't she just rat him out and be done with it?

Dad came back with the new skinny latte and more espresso for himself. "I got decaf," he said gloomily.

Alix couldn't help smiling. "Mom will be glad."

"I'm sorry about all this, Alix."

"Don't worry about it." Alix sipped her new latte, setting it next to her other, still nearly full one. "So why did 2.0 want me to ask you about all of this? Why did he think you'd know?"

Dad sighed. "We've got people going over all our files and client lists, trying to identify a reason. It might be something as simple as the fact that we have a client 2.0 hates. Or it could be that we show up on a donor list, or we were photographed at a fund-raiser. We don't know if they want to kidnap, or ransom, or terrorize."

"You said they were vandals before."

"Did I?" He nodded vaguely. "Oh. In the beginning." He rubbed his eyes and sipped his espresso. "Of course. No, this is different. These people have a history of attacking laboratories. Research facilities. We originally thought they might be associated with PETA."

"Because of the rats."

Her father smiled sardonically. "Yes. They stole a large

121

number of rats from a company that uses rats as subjects for chemical-safety testing."

Alix made a face.

"Yeah," Dad said. "I know. It's not a pretty thing sometimes to see how much our prosperity depends on things like making sure products are safe. I'd rather test on rats than people, though. Science might not be pretty, but it keeps us safe." He shrugged. "Other people see it differently."

"So..." Alix puzzled. "They're like animal rights activists?"

"When they were just attacking testing labs, the FBI thought so."

"But you don't now?"

Her father looked troubled. "We have no idea. None of it makes any sense." He leaned forward. "I know this is difficult for you, but please be patient. We're hoping they'll make a mistake or the case will break open somehow, and we'll figure out what they're about or who they are...and then we'll all be able to go back to our regular lives, and we can just forget all this."

Alix's heart broke. Dad looked so sad and lost and troubled that she realized she couldn't keep anything from him.

You have to tell him.

"Dad..." Alix lost her nerve and trailed off.

Dad looked up at her. She hesitated. *Now or never. Pull yourself together, Alix.* "I saw him again."

Dad's expression went from puzzlement to slow comprehension. "2.0?" he asked.

122

"Yeah." Alix blew out her breath, feeling relieved to finally be coming clean.

"At school?"

She shook her head. "At home. A couple nights ago. When I said I saw a shadow, maybe, in the backyard. I . . . It was more than that. I was downstairs . . . getting a drink of water. I saw him through the glass. He was looking in. . . ." She was about to continue, to tell him the rest, but Dad's expression was changing even as she talked, turning from caring attentiveness to shock and disappointment and severity. Now that the words were coming out of her mouth, they sounded horrible to her, too. She broke off, unable to keep going in the face of Dad's anger.

Dad's voice was tightly controlled. "Why didn't you say something when it happened?"

"I didn't . . . I don't know."

She felt herself wanting to cry and forced down the reaction. It was the little-kid-nailed-by-her-parents response. She never went against Mom and Dad. She'd almost never lied to them about anything. They'd always had a policy of letting her tell them everything so that she wouldn't feel the need to lie.

Once, when she'd been a sophomore, she and Denise and Sarah Landow and a bunch of guys had gotten wasted over at Sarah's house while Mr. and Mrs. Landow were in New York for the ballet. They were completely hammered, but Denise was desperate to get home, so Sarah was going to drive her. And even though it was 1:00 AM, Alix called her dad to be picked up. She just told him that Denise needed to get home and that they were all too drunk to drive. It was the first time she'd ever been so drunk, and Dad drove over, picked up Alix and Denise, dropped Denise off, and took Alix home, and all he did was tell her she needed to drink Gatorade.

In the morning, when she was sick and hung over, he just sat by her bed, amused, and suggested that maybe there was a lesson in this somewhere. He never did anything about it other than to talk with her about alcohol poisoning and addiction patterns. He thanked her for calling him, and for not getting in a car with a bunch of drunks, and that was it.

A couple of months later, when she asked him why he hadn't busted her harder, he just looked at her, puzzled. "How can we learn if we don't make mistakes?" And then he said, "I just want to make sure you don't make any mistakes that are permanent. Keep me in the loop, okay?"

Coolest dad ever.

Jonah pointed out that Dad was never like that with him. But Jonah didn't seem put out about it. After all, Jonah knew he wasn't trustworthy.

But Alix was. And yet she'd let a stalker inside her house, and as soon as she said even the first part of the truth, she realized how serious it actually was. 2.0 had been looking in their windows, she'd talked to him, and it hadn't shown up on a single security tape.

Now, seeing her father's disappointed expression, she realized that she couldn't bear to tell him the rest. That she'd actually been stupid enough to open the door. To talk to her stalker. She couldn't bear to see her father looking any more disappointed in her than he already did.

"I'm sorry," Alix whispered. "I'm so sorry."

The look on Dad's face was so shocked and horrified that it made her feel sick. She braced herself for the angry dressing down she knew she deserved.

Instead, Dad reached out to her and pulled her into a hug. "Hey. It's okay. Just tell me what happened. Don't worry, honey...."

He kept comforting her, and Alix started to cry, ashamed that he was still so forgiving, even when she didn't deserve to be forgiven.

11

"YOU IDIOT!" KOOK SHOUTED AT Moses. "You were at her *house*?"

"I was scouting," Moses replied as he dug in the fridge. "Nobody even caught a whiff of me."

"You don't know that," she said. "I can't hack every damn camera all the time. There's bound to be new spycams.... Gahh!" She grabbed her blue hair and stalked back and forth in the kitchen. Adam wandered in, huge headphones on his ears, head moving to the beat of his own internal sense of groove. He opened the fridge, oblivious to Kook's shouting at Moses a few feet away.

She grabbed his shoulder and yanked his headphones off.

"Ow!" He jerked away. "What the hell, Kook?"

Kook pointed at Moses. "You know he was over at her house?"

Adam glanced at Moses. "Seriously?"

126

"Doing some kind of Peeping Tom routine," Kook said. "He *talked* to her."

"I wanted to see what they were up to," Moses protested.

"That's what you've got *us* for! We're the anonymous ones!" Kook said. "You've got an identity. They've already got you on camera."

"All they've got is versions of me."

"You know what I mean." She scowled at him. "We shouldn't be doing this. You're in too close."

"I'm not too close."

"I'll bet you know what color bra she wore today."

Moses glared at her. "I know you're wearing a black one—so?"

Adam watched the two of them arguing. "Nobody ever asks me what color bra I wear."

Kook shot him a dirty look. Adam raised his hands defensively. "My bad." He went back to the fridge and started pulling out two-liters of Coke. He peered between the bottles and then pulled out a quarter round of the most expensive-looking cheese that Moses had ever seen.

"What's that?"

Adam at least had the grace to look guilty. Moses couldn't believe it. "Is that for the rats?" he asked.

"Just one of them." Adam opened his jacket, revealing a white rat tucked into his inner breast pocket. "He's cute, right?"

Moses stared at the ceiling. "I live in an asylum."

"This from the stalker?" Kook said.

"I am not a stalker," Moses shot back.

Tank came in carrying a load of pizza boxes and stopped abruptly. He still had on his welder's helmet, and judging from the look in his eyes, he wanted to slam the welding shield down and hide.

Adam took the pizza boxes from Tank and put them on the huge trestle table that they'd set up in the kitchen. "Come on," he said, draping his arm over Tank's shoulders. "Mom and Dad are fighting."

"Fuck you, Adam," Kook called after him.

"Not really interested, but thanks." He ushered Tank out of the room, leaving Moses and Kook to face off.

Moses said, "You want to seriously mess with Tank's mind any more than it's already been messed with?"

"Don't pull that con-man shit on me. We're only fighting because you're an idiot. The kid'll be fine as long as you don't fuck up his entire life because you're addicted to some chick."

Moses paused, trying to feel out the edges of Kook's rage. "What's getting you? Seriously. So I went and peeked in their windows. You know how good I am. You know Williams and Crowe are nothing for me."

"Sure sure sure. You come and go like the wind. You're a real genius at that shit."

"That's right. I'm a ghost. They never even know I'm there."

"Except when you screw up and punch some headmaster."

"That was one time."

"What would your uncle say if you gave him that line?"

Moses grimaced. "Well, I didn't screw up this time."

"So what about the next—" She held up a hand before Moses had a chance to respond. "No. Don't answer me. This is getting serious now. That's what I want to say," Kook said. "This is getting serious, and we can't afford a screwup."

"We knew it was going to get serious," Moses said.

"Banks pushed the panic button way sooner than we expected."

"Just because the brother pulled a disappearing act on them. It wasn't even us. They just overreacted."

"It doesn't matter why, does it? What matters is that now they're crawling with big guns. Williams and Crowe has it out for us. After the rat raid, they're off the leash."

"Those rats." Moses shook his head. "They're turning out to be a serious pain in the ass."

"Don't change the subject." Kook glared at him. "I'm telling you, don't get wrapped up in the target. We've been planning this too long for you to screw this up."

"I won't."

"You better not. I swear to God I'll pull the plug on this whole thing and let you burn if I think you're going to screw it up."

Moses looked at her. "Come on, Kook. I'm not going to screw it up. You know me."

"No, I don't. I used to think I did. But now?" Kook shook her head. "I have no idea who you are."

Moses could see how worked up Kook was. She looked positively strung out. She was pretty deep into her high, riding the weird, ragged edge of pot and caffeine that she claimed kept her inspired and that also kept her sleepless for days at a time. The high that Adam kept telling her wasn't healthy, but she didn't care. *She's exhausted.* Moses could see it in her bloodshot eyes and the dark circles under them. Even her Goth makeup couldn't hide it.

He was aware of Adam and Tank listening from the doorway. Everyone was so fragile. So damn fragile.

"Yeah, you do know me," Moses said. "You do."

"No. You're changing. Half the time I think you believe your own bullshit."

"I'll never change on you. Trust that. I will never let you down. That's what people out there do," Moses said, willing her to believe. "That's not us. We're solid. We're granite."

"You say. And then you go and sneak out and look in the target's window."

"Okay. My bad. It won't happen again."

"You promise?"

"Promise." He went over to her, bent lower, so he was looking into her wild, dilated eyes. "This is me, Kook. It's still me. Same as I always was. I'm a chameleon out there, but that's not who I am here. Not with us. We're family, right?"

"Sure we are."

"I'm serious. I won't risk us. Not ever. Not for a second."

Kook looked up at him. In her eyes, he could see the wounds she hid from the outside world. They were family all right. He had scars. She had scars. The two boys listening at the door had scars. He pulled Kook close, into a hug.

130

"We're family," he said.

Kook went rigid for a second and then hugged him back. "My big black brother."

"You know it." He laughed. "Get in here, you guys."

"Is it safe?" Adam called.

"Yeah," Moses said. "Get in here. You might as well listen where you can actually hear."

They both slunk into the kitchen. A rat ran across the floor, startled by their movement. Tank jumped and said, "Would you put that thing back in its cage?"

"I—" Adam checked his jacket. "It's not mine. I still got my little guy. You must have let that one out when we moved all the cages."

"No way. Don't blame that shit on me," Tank said. "If there's rats still around, it's because you kept letting them loose when you fed them."

"Let it go," Moses said. "Come here, you guys. Gather round. Kook's right. This is serious. No mistakes from here on out. We've got no room for mistakes."

He looked around at his crew. A ragtag bunch of kids as haunted as he was. Not a single one of them the same, and yet every one of them related, bound together by hurt and horror.

"We can still back out," he said. "We can pull back right now. Walk away. This is our last chance, though. Once we start the next stage, we're going to be up to our necks."

"Once you're halfway across the channel, you might as well keep swimming," Adam said.

"I don't even know what that means," Moses said.

"The English Channel..." Adam shook his head. "Never mind. You'd have to be a swimmer."

Tank snickered. "A prep school swimmer. We should have sent you into Seitz. Target would have loved you."

Adam wrinkled his nose with disgust. "I can't think of anything worse."

"Knock it off," Moses said. "Seriously. After we make the next play, we're committed, forever. Right now, we can still walk away, live good lives. Forget any of this even happened. But after this? We're in too deep. There's no backing out."

He looked at each of them. "I'm not much for democracy, but this one time, we need to vote. I need to hear that you're all in. I already got one vote, but I need to hear it from you three. I'm ready to go on. But if you don't want to carry this weight, I get it. You can back out now, and I'd understand. So...are you in?"

Moses found himself holding his breath, wondering if he was making a mistake of leadership doing this. He knew he could talk them into it. He could poke and prod and cajole. He was good at that. He could con a body just as well as Simon Banks. He knew which words would produce which results, and it was tempting to use them. He shook off the urge.

There's no other way. There's no way to do this. And then, on the heels of that thought, came another. *It's too much. This is too much to ask of anyone. I shouldn't be pulling them into this at all.*

Kook blew out her breath. "Yeah. I'm in. I was in before. I'm in now. All the way down the rabbit hole, if that's what it takes."

Adam gave Moses a lazy mock-salute. "You don't have to ask me. The ride's been good so far. I'm definitely around for the finale."

Tank nodded, his welding helmet wiggling. "In. Most definitely in."

Moses looked around at the group, and for a moment he couldn't speak.

"Like you say," Tank said. "We're family. Nothing's going to change that."

Moses blinked and looked away, afraid they'd see tears in his eyes.

Sometimes he felt so alone that it felt like his body was being ripped apart by the loneliness, and then, at times like this, he felt so complete that he wondered how he'd even been able to walk down the street without them, let alone breathe.

He pulled them close. "That's it, then," he said. "We're going for it."

133

12

LIFE SETTLED INTO A ROUTINE. Alix and Cynthia defaulted to going home every day and hanging out in her room or playing Xbox with Jonah in a weirdly domestic habit that got Death Barbie off their backs.

Alix got the feeling that Cynthia was taking pity on her and wanted to be elsewhere, but, still, she loyally went home with her even though it would have been more fun to spend time driving out to the ocean, or going shopping with Sophie, or teasing Derek—or doing almost anything other than staying at Alix's house.

"You think you're ever going to get your life back?" Cynthia asked as she fiddled with the Xbox and swapped out Jonah's SwordSlayer IX game.

"Ask 2.0," Alix said. "Why?"

Cynthia looked uncomfortable. "There's that rave...."

Alix got it immediately. "And nobody's going to be excited to see my security detail show up."

"It's not me," Cynthia said. "But everyone else is sure that Death Barbie is going to rat them out to their parents. Either that or call the cops."

"Thanks for the trust."

"I'm just saying."

Alix felt the gulf between her and Cynthia widening. "I get it if you want to go without me."

"You idiot," Cynthia said as she booted up Left 4 Dead. "I'm not trying to ditch you. I'm trying to figure out a way to bust you out."

Alix laughed. "My dad would kill me."

"Better to beg for forgiveness than ask for permission," Cynthia quoted.

"Is that one of those sayings from your father?"

"I think it was some admiral."

Alix sat with the idea. Her parents would lose their shit if she actually did this, but she'd been cooped up for the last week with Lisa. Even if she had started feeling bad about calling the woman Death Barbie, she was dying for some time alone.

"What am I supposed to do about 2.0? He's out there somewhere."

"Have you seen anything from him?" Cynthia asked. "Has he done anything else? Has he even shown his face since the school thing?"

"You mean other than when he was stalking and staring into my kitchen?"

Cynthia snickered. "Yeah. Other than that."

"When did you get so blasé about all this?" Alix asked. "2.0 basically said he was coming after my family."

Cynthia shot her a serious look. "Yeah. I've been reading about that."

"About what?"

"Assassinations."

"*What?????*"

"No! Sorry!" Cynthia waved her hands frantically. "Not like that! Not like someone's going to snipe you. Just about people who get targeted. What I read is that the most dangerous thing a target can do is have a routine. The routine is what makes it easy for the bad guys to get at you. If you don't have a routine, then they don't have a chance to set up on you." She glanced around the house. "It could be that the most dangerous thing you're doing is coming home every day and playing Xbox."

"I don't know."

Cynthia looked bummed. She pulled out the flyer. "Check it out."

"Where is this?"

"Some warehouse in Hartford."

"Long drive."

"It's an out-of-the-way, out-of-the-pattern long drive. It's as safe as houses."

"I thought you said my house wasn't safe," Alix cracked.

136

"You know you want to go."

Alix considered the unpalatable idea of another weekend alone in the house with bodyguards watching her swim in the pool.

"Yes," she said decisively.

Cynthia perked up, looking more like a happy puppy than a girl. "Yes?"

"Yeah." She laughed. "I definitely need it."

"Hell, girl. You deserve it!"

Alix felt a frisson of excitement. *Hell yes. I deserve it.*

And what were the risks, really? Cynthia's theory of safety pretty much matched what Lisa had been telling Alix about how Williams & Crowe thought about security. A target needed to have a pattern in order to be vulnerable. It was why Death Barbie and Hulk took a different route to school every day. They changed up their travel a lot, to make it harder for Alix to be picked out.

So it made sense that if someone was looking to mess with her, the one thing they definitely wouldn't be prepared for was the same thing that Lisa and the rest of the Williams & Crowe people wouldn't be prepared for—Alix's ditching them all unexpectedly.

"I can't make my parents worry, though."

"We'll leave a note." Cynthia's eyes glinted with mischief. "And we'll have you back before dawn. Well," she amended, "at least by late morning."

Alix laughed. "So how are we going to do this?"

"Are you kidding, girl? I've been thinking about this for

137

days." Cynthia tapped her head. "Been using my big brain to work it all out."

"So Derek's right. You never do study."

"I never study boring things, that's all. Ditching Death Barbie is actually kind of awesome."

■ ■ ■

Alix's heart was pounding as they went into the mall. Cynthia had chosen it because of the layout of the back doors. The trick was all about pulling a switch. Denise and Sophie were happy to help.

"We just need a little misdirection," Cynthia had explained. "Lisa's job is to keep an eye on you, but she isn't actually watching you. She's watching to make sure nobody grabs you. So we're going to take advantage of that...."

Denise and Sophie would be the decoys. It would take a quick switch of people in the changing rooms at Aritzia. Denise would go in earlier and wait for Alix to go in. Lisa would want to watch the dressing room door where Alix went in, but she wouldn't know that Denise was already in there.

Everything was going as planned as she shopped around, and Alix made her way to the dressing rooms. She slipped into the stall and met Denise. Silently, they swapped outfits. After a minute, Alix leaned out of her changing stall. "Lisa?"

Lisa glanced back at her. "Yes?"

"Can you get me this in a four?" She held out a camisole.

Lisa glanced around the place. There was no one in the store. Alix watched, with her heart racing.

When Lisa went away, she switched to the stall across from her and waited as Denise accepted the new camisole from Lisa over the top of the stall. "Thanks," Alix heard her sort of grunt. Alix put on a blond wig that she'd brought in her purse to further confuse and distract Lisa.

Alix waited until she heard Sophie arrive on the scene and start to chitchat with Lisa, pretending to be surprised to see her friend's bodyguard there.

Sophie's arrival was the cue. It was going to happen soon.

Alix heard the door across from her open. Denise would be wearing the wig she'd styled in an approximation of Alix's brown hair. As Sophie was chatting up Lisa, Denise would be walking away from Death Barbie, toward the racks on the opposite side. Sophie followed, calling out, "Hey, Alix, how's it going?" and walked over to her.

Three, two, one… Alix peered out of her own dressing room door now. Lisa was trailing after them, her back to Alix. *Now or never.*

She slipped out of the dressing room and walked away as quickly as she could. Walking, trying not to run…trying not to panic as her heart pounded.

Behind her she heard an exclamation—Death Barbie discovering the switch too soon. *Dammit!* Alix bolted. She hit the service entrance, labeled EMPLOYEES ONLY, and then was off and running down the back corridors of the mall.

"Alix! Stop!"

Alix spared a glance back. *Oh shit.* Lisa was scary fast. The woman was charging down the corridor like some kind of insane Olympic sprinter.

Okay, fine. Let's run, then! Alix put her head down and ran, putting everything into it, just like at track and field.... She blasted past a FedEx guy with a bunch of packages on a cart and hit the loading-entrance doors. Slammed out into bright sunshine.

Cynthia was waiting right where she said she'd be, in her Miata with the motor running.

Behind her, Lisa shouted again, *"Alix!"*

Cynthia leaned over and shoved open the passenger door as the mall doors slammed open, Death Barbie coming through them like a freight train.

"Come on!" Cynthia shouted.

Alix dove in.

Cynthia peeled out, driving so fast Alix almost fell back out the open door. "What are you doing?" she shouted as she grabbed for the dash and the seat, trying to stay inside the careering car.

"Get in, already!"

"I'm trying!" Alix dragged her legs in and yanked the door closed. She glanced back. Lisa was running full out. "She's going to catch us!"

"Not if I can help it," Cynthia said grimly. She gunned the engine. They squealed in a tight turn, heading for the mall exit. Death Barbie cut the corner, barreling toward them.

"She's still coming!" Alix warned.

"How'd she see you leaving?"

"The switch didn't go so—Car!" Alix pointed.

"I see it." Cynthia shot past the BMW. Alix glimpsed the driver staring at them in horror as they blasted past, and then they were in the exit lanes, weaving. Ahead, the traffic light turned red.

"Oh hell," Cynthia muttered, slowing for the light.

Alix glanced back. Lisa was gaining on them. "Um... Cynthia?" They were never going to get away.

"Fuck it." Cynthia gunned the engine. "Hold on."

Alix slammed back into her seat as the Miata accelerated. Cynthia slewed into the oncoming lane and ripped past all the cars stopped at the intersection.

"What are you *doing*?" Alix shouted, but it was too late. They blasted out into the intersection, tires squealing as Cynthia cranked the wheel over. Horns blared. Alix grabbed for the door handle and braced to hit the oncoming cars.

"Ahhhh!"

They were sliding, all four wheels skidding across pavement as they made the turn. Alix was staring into the face of a driver of a Tesla, who was staring back at her with equal horror, both of them realizing they were about to die.

The Miata's tires caught. They shot through the rest of the turn, with Cynthia whooping triumph. *"Goddamn*, I'm good!"

Alix was gasping with adrenaline, relief, and fear. She twisted around, checking for Lisa.

Death Barbie had finally given up. The bodyguard was bent over, hands on her knees in the middle of traffic, red-faced. Panting and exhausted, staring after them.

Alix shivered at Lisa's expression. The woman looked so pissed she could have been a demon pursuer from one of Jonah's Xbox games.

"I am so dead," Alix muttered as she slumped back into her seat.

"Buckle up," Cynthia said. "Safety first, and all that." She started to laugh.

"Safety first," Alix said as she snapped the seat belt into place. "Is that what that was?"

"We're alive, aren't we?"

"That's the bright side, I guess."

"Yeah. That was a little more excitement than I was expecting."

"Where'd you learn to drive that way?" Alix asked.

"My dad got me lessons."

"Fuckin' A, he did." Alix closed her eyes. "Please don't ever do that to me again."

Cynthia laughed. "I thought you wanted some excitement!"

"Yeah, well, I've got enough for a lifetime now. So thanks."

"What? You don't want to go back, do you?"

"No." Alix closed her eyes. Her heart was slowing, the adrenaline leaking out of her, leaving her drained and a little depressed.

It had seemed like a lot of fun to engineer this game.

142

Escape from Death Barbie—she'd thought of it in her mind, but now that it was done, she wasn't so sure of herself. A couple of weeks ago she would never have done this. Cynthia, neither, for that matter.

It was like having security everywhere—everyone minding her every move—had made her more rebellious instead of less. She was used to being trusted. And now having that trust stripped away was more than a little uncomfortable.... It wasn't *her*.

Am I untrustworthy?

Alix didn't like the thought, but the reality of ditching Death Barbie was starting to settle in. Watching Lisa running after her, full out, desperate not to lose the girl she was supposed to protect...

She's the one who would have taken a bullet for you.

Alix felt ill.

Dad would be pissed, and Mom would be disappointed, and Jonah would think it was all a joke and be impressed that she'd actually rebelled against anything at all. But Lisa...

Lisa was the one Alix actually felt bad about.

Alix closed her eyes and rubbed her forehead, trying to scrub away the feeling of guilt.

The Miata cut through weekend traffic. Cynthia drove expertly. Just like her studying, Cynthia took her driving seriously.

It was kind of funny. They were both such serious girls, and here they were, finally cutting loose with a high-speed escape.

Dad is going to kill me.

Cynthia pulled off the highway.

"Why are we stopping?" Alix asked.

Cynthia gave her a look as they pulled into a Home Depot parking lot. "You think Death Barbie didn't get my license plate? They're going to be looking for my car. We have to ditch it."

Alix laughed incredulously. "Are you serious?"

"Aren't you?" Cynthia shot back. "Your dad called the FBI when Jonah went missing for, like, three hours. You better believe they're looking for us already." Cynthia climbed out of the car. "Come on. I've got another car for us."

"Seriously? You've got a plan for this?"

"What else was I going to think about all week? School?" Cynthia snorted. "If you're going to plan an escape, you've got to do it right. It's all about the details."

"Jesus Christ, Derek's right."

"About what?"

"You *are* an overachiever."

"I am not!"

"I'm pretty sure most people aren't this OCD about going to a party," Alix said as she trailed after Cynthia.

"Most people don't have Death Barbie screwing up their social life," Cynthia shot back.

Alix pulled Cynthia to a halt. "Hey, I'm sorry. I wasn't trying to dis you. It's just…" She sighed. "It's just a lot, that's all. My parents are going to worry."

"It's a little late to be freaking out about that, don't you think?"

"Yeah, I know. It's just that I've never done anything like this before."

"You think I went over the top." Cynthia looked so crestfallen that Alix almost wanted to apologize just for criticizing her.

"Running the light might have been…" Alix tried to find words.

Cynthia groaned. "I know, I know. I just panicked. Death Barbie made me think of that old *Terminator* movie." Cynthia hesitated. "Why don't you leave that note we talked about," she suggested finally. "If they find my car before we're back, they'll still know you're fine."

Alix thought about it. "I could just text them…."

"No. Turn off your cell for sure. Leave it in the car."

"Oh, come on. You don't think they'll track that, too, do you?"

"I don't know what Williams and Crowe can do, but if you actually want to party tonight, I'd bet on paranoia."

Cynthia led her back to the Miata. They found paper and a pen, and Alix wrote:

Dear Mom and Dad, Just need to blow off some steam. I'll be back tomorrow. Love, Alix.
PS—

She hesitated. *PS??? What hell am I thinking?*

PS—Sorry?

PS—You look after Jonah for a change?

"Will you come on, girl?" Cynthia urged. "This is like the slowest getaway in history."

"I'm trying! This is hard for me. What am I supposed to say? What did you tell your parents?"

"Are you crazy?" Cynthia rolled her eyes. "I didn't tell them anything. They think I'm sleeping over at *your* house."

"Lucky you."

Finally, Alix settled on:

PS—I'm sorry. Please don't worry. I'm fine.

"Better?" Cynthia asked.

"Yeah."

"Thank God. Then dump your phone and let's go, already." Cynthia led Alix out of the parking lot to an adjacent one and another car, a beat-up orange monstrosity that looked like it had come out of the seventies.

"What the heck is this?"

"Dodge Dart." Cynthia grinned. "Total death trap. Your dad would shit if he saw you in this."

"Where'd you get it?"

"I borrowed it from a cousin."

Alix shook her head. "I can't believe how well you planned this."

146

"Okay, so maybe I am an overachiever. Perfect SATs, and perfect getaways." Cynthia sounded a little defensive. "Do you want to party, or not?"

Alix stared at the car, still hesitating. It wasn't just that she was going to be grounded for this escapade, with all kinds of "proportional" and "related" consequences that Mom and Dad loved to come up with (though ususally for Jonah); it was that it felt like, by getting into the battered Dodge Dart, she was crossing a boundary. Stepping across into some other place, becoming someone else. By blowing off everything that a sensible person would do and getting into this car, it felt like she was breaking something permanently.

It's just a damn car.

"We doing this?" Cynthia pressed.

Alix looked up at her friend.

Are we?

Alix grinned. "Definitely."

13

"ARE YOU SURE THIS IS THE right place?" Alix asked.

Cynthia was eyeing their surroundings doubtfully as
well. It was a warehouse district, nondescript buildings all
around. Old factories. Old redbrick. Cracks in the concrete.
"It's in the flyer," she said.

In the failing light, factory and warehouse shapes loomed
menacingly. The rusty Dodge bounced over railroad tracks as
they drove deeper into the industrial area.

"What's that up there?" Alix pointed.

"Car lights."

Behind them, another car's beams shone.

"It's got to be here somewhere."

They followed the lights. More cars were converging.
People flocking to the secret point of contact. Total under-
ground. Guerrilla party. Just ahead, cars were parked, people

sitting on hoods in the warm spring night. Cynthia pulled to a stop.

"I told you I had it right."

They got out and stood staring at the warehouse. More cars were pulling up. The busier it got, the more secure Alix felt about the venue. They were in the middle of industrial nowhere, but they weren't alone.

"Let's go," she said.

But now it was Cynthia's turn to hesitate. "I don't know. We don't have to do this, Alix. We could just go back."

"Seriously? After everything we went through to get here?"

"I'm just saying that it's no skin off my nose. The 'rents won't know one way or the other, for me. It's different with you. I don't..." She shrugged.

Alix laughed and waved the bottle of vodka that she'd brought along.

"I'm already busted," she said. "I'm not doing the time if I don't get to do the crime." She popped open the vodka bottle and took a swig, making a face, and then offered it to Cynthia. "Come on. I need a party."

Alix headed for the entrance. Every time the door opened, the throb of bass reverberated from deep within the warehouse. She paused, looked back, and grinned. "We can't be daddy's girls all the time."

That did it. They were nearly racing each other by the time they made it to the door. They paid some feral Latino street

149

kid who looked like he was about twelve to get in, and the kid pushed the door open for them. A deep growl of thumping bass emanated from the warehouse's maw, welcoming them.

Inside, the huge space was already thick with bodies. The bass was a deep thrum in her limbs, in her bones, rubbing out Death Barbie and all the hassles of the last two weeks. Lights strobed. Dancers, wearing kandi cuffs and masks, gyrated to the driving sounds; glow sticks dangled around necks, illuminating skin and sweat and bodies ecstatically entwined.

Alix pushed into the crowd, loving the intensity of the music. She started letting her body move to its rhythms, trying to shake off all the irritations of 2.0's interference in her life. Trying to loosen up, to feel the vodka that she'd already drunk, the freedom of the crowd and music, and the joy of being completely out from under anyone's thumb. Free. Completely free.

She swayed with the beat, enjoying the spectacle of hundreds of people filling the space, dancing up on old warehouse crates that had been illuminated with strobes, while others danced inside enormous industrial metal cages, clutching bars and writhing like they were the prisoners of some postapocalyptic dance tribe. Rusted sheet metal hung from the walls, sprayed with green glowing icons. *Radiation, Bicycle Lane, Peace, Biohazard, Migrant Worker Crossing, Chairman Mao*...a Dada procession of symbols against the industrial metal decay. At one end of the floor, Alix glimpsed a massive rusted iron wheel, like some kind of insane steroidal hamster wheel, that spun with glow lights, blurring and pulsing to the beats of the DJ.

Alix took another swig of vodka and passed it to Cynthia. They danced. Cynthia drank and handed it back, and Alix decided she'd had enough and let the bottle go, gifting it to a stranger, who mouthed thanks and then sent the bottle... wherever. It didn't matter to Alix. She threw her hands up and danced. She didn't need to be drunk. She was already glowing.

They danced, feeling the ecstasy of the beats, of movement, of being completely alive. Cynthia was grinning back at her. Her tight white T-shirt glowed blue under the black lights. The vodka burned in Alix's blood. Perfect.

Someone was handing out orange and lime glow sticks. Alix tied one around her wrist, another around her neck. The music went on and on, an ocean of sound flowing through her.

Cynthia disappeared and returned a few minutes later with a pair of pills.

"What is it?" Alix shouted.

"What do you think?" Cynthia said.

The old Alix would have worried about where it had come from and what was in it, but this Alix, this newly alive Alix, didn't care. *For once, I just want to have fun.* She didn't want to have to look over her shoulder anymore. Just for a little while.

Fuck it.

She popped the pill and danced.

Her body felt warm and delicious. She was high and

drunk, and the music rolled over her. A girl was spinning fire, arcs whirling fast and hypnotic, tracing lines and circles around her sweating body, her dreads spinning wide. Cynthia was dancing between some boys, one on each side, and she was laughing.

Alix danced until her limbs felt heavy. She let the crowd push her out toward the edges of the dance floor, looking for space, for room to breathe. She moved toward the wall, tired, slowing.

A streak of blue caught Alix's eye, down along the wall. She stopped dancing, her chest heaving.

There it was again—a blue spark slipping along the edge of the warehouse floor.

A blue rat.

Alix laughed out loud.

Whoa. Cool drugs.

She'd never seen a blue rat.

Alix laughed again. Jesus, she was high. The rat wasn't blue. It was white, turned bright and ethereal by the black lights of the rave. Alix stared at the rat, loving how it looked, how it moved. It was mesmerizing the way it dashed back and forth along the edge of the dance floor, disappearing behind crates, streaking past lovers making out, ducking behind the big industrial dance cages. Darting this way and that…

Gorgeous.

Alix couldn't help wanting it. She stumbled after it, wondering how the thing had gotten here all the way from Seitz. She could imagine it thumbing a ride up from the school.

Cute rat... *Cute little guy like you shouldn't be out like this*, she thought. *You'll get stomped.*

She followed the rat as it slipped behind the DJ's stage and racks of amps. This close to the speakers, the music wasn't something that Alix heard so much as felt. A physical envelopment pressing through every pore of her body. Mom and Dad would have been shaking their heads and reminding her that she'd be deaf by forty, but Alix couldn't be bothered to care. She felt fantastic, and she'd found the most amazing blue rat.

As she eased past the amps, she caught sight of the DJ up on his stage, looking down at her. Gorgeous blond boy, slender as a willow, his headphones held to his ear as he mixed beats. Alix smiled up at him. She waved, feeling delighted and drunk and high and fine. The beautiful boy smiled back, and the beat shifted; hammering chimes began filtering into the music, gothic, dark, and ecstatic.

The blue rat flashed across the floor again. Alix followed, winding behind the amps, stumbling over scaffolding and cords. She felt unsteady on her feet. How much vodka had she drunk? Part of her wanted to go back to the dancing and feel the throb and rush of all the other dancers around her, but she couldn't quite let the blue rat go.

The rat slipped out of the black light and became a white shadow. It disappeared through a crack in the wall. *Not a crack. A door.* Alix pulled it open. The room beyond was pitch-black. She stepped inside cautiously. The music's volume lessened, replaced by a ringing in her ears.

153

Flashes of light from the dance floor threw her shadow across bare concrete. The rat was sitting in the center of the dark room, up on its hind legs. It was sniffing the air, gazing at something.

What the—?

A wall of rats.

A whole huge wall of caged rats.

She turned in a slow circle, stunned at the sight. The cages were everywhere, she realized. They rose from floor to ceiling, disappearing into the darkness above. The smell was now so clear and obvious that she couldn't believe she hadn't noticed it immediately: the musky scent of wood shavings and urine. Thousands and thousands of rats, poking their noses through the wires of their cages, nipping at the metal, reaching through with tiny claws, staring down at her, all of them struggling to get free.

Out on the dance floor, the hammering chimes rose and blurred into an electronic wail. Alix stared up at the rats, trying to make sense of what she was seeing.

Am I going crazy?

And then suddenly it hit her. Rats. Thousands of rats. Stolen from a testing lab. 2.0. Right here. They were right here. She was inside their lair.

Cynthia. I've got to find Cynthia.

A shadow blocked the door, dimming the room. Alix spun.

A girl with blue hair and the feral kid who had taken money at the door were standing in the doorway. They were both shaking their heads and moving to block her exit. Their expressions were murderous. "Glad you could make it to the party, Alix," the girl with the blue hair said.

"Oh, no you don't," Alix said, or at least *thought* she said, because she was already charging. Their hands raked her, snagged her shirt, and dragged her back, but fear gave Alix strength. All her self-defense lessons came flooding back. *Fight like hell.* Alix punched and elbowed and bit and screamed, and abruptly broke free of their grip.

Alix plunged into the seething crowd with the pair pursuing, but the swamp and surge of bodies caught her. She couldn't move. Sweaty bodies smashed into her, pushing and shoving her and making her stumble. In the strobing light and darkness, everything was fragmentary and horrific. The great spinning iron wheel. The frenzied bodies and caged dancers.

Squeezing through the press was like fighting against the tentacles of a monster. Everyone seemed to be grabbing at her, slowing her. The music shrieked demonically, and the pulse strobe of light and darknesss increased. The dancers became blurred traceries of color and shadow and reaching, clutching hands.

Alix tried to make her mind sober, to control the horror of her high. *Find Cynthia. Just find Cynthia.*

Behind her, the feral kid and the punk girl with the blue hair had disappeared, but she knew they were out there, hunting her, just as she was hunting Cynthia.

There!

Alix clawed her way toward her friend, shouting. Cynthia was dancing with some girl and totally unaware of anything. Their faces were close, almost kissing. Alix stopped short, confused. Was Cynthia gay? She hesitated, embarrassed to be interrupting her friend, suddenly unsure if she would be welcomed.

Fear pushed her on. "Cynthia!" she shouted.

Cynthia whipped around, looking pissed. "What do you want?"

The girl was glaring at Alix, too. Alix broke off, feeling even more uncertain, embarrassed to have shattered their moment. She scanned the dancers, terrified her pursuers were about to emerge from the crowd and grab her once again.

"We've got to get out of here!" she shouted over the roar of the music. "I have to leave!"

"Why?" Cynthia shouted back. "Things are good!"

"They're here! We've got to get out of here!"

"Who's here?"

Cynthia's girl was disappearing into the crowd. Cynthia wasn't even listening to Alix now, she was craning her neck and motioning for the girl to come back. "Wait!" she shouted.

Alix gave up and just grabbed Cynthia's arm and headed for the exit.

"*Hey!*" Cynthia protested. "What are you *doing*?"

Alix ignored her, just kept dragging her drunk, high friend through the crowd. Cynthia pried at her grip.

"What the hell, Alix?"

"We're getting out!"

Finally, Alix found the door. They stumbled out into the chill, late-night air.

"What the hell is wrong with you?" Cynthia shouted. "I was having a good time!"

Alix ignored her. "Where is the car?"

Cynthia didn't say anything. She was just scowling. Alix realized she hadn't actually spoken the question.

Damn, you really are fucked up.

"Where's the car?" Alix said again, out loud this time. Her voice sounded tinny and distant against the ringing of her ears and the sudden night silence outside of the party.

"Why? What's going on?" Cynthia's distant voice replied.

"They're here," Alix said. "2.0."

"Are you crazy?"

"Where did you get that flyer? That party flyer?"

Cynthia shook her head, puzzled. "I don't know.... I just got it. They were just around. Denise, maybe? Why? Who cares?"

God, the girl was *so* slow. Put some booze and drugs in her and the IQ went right out the window. Alix realized she couldn't wait for Cynthia to get off her high. She grabbed her friend again. "Just come *on*. I'll explain later."

"Will you quit grabbing me!" Cynthia dug in her feet. "What the hell's your problem?" she asked. "Are you tripping? Are you jealous?"

"Jealous?" Alix stared at her with confusion. "Why?" She spied Cynthia's Dodge Dart and reached for her friend again. Cynthia jerked her arm away, glaring. "Quit grabbing!"

157

"I saw rats," Alix explained.

Cynthia started laughing. "*Rats?* You saw *rats*? How high are you? What else did you take in there?"

Alix ignored her and headed for the car. The doors to the Dart were locked.

"Where are your keys?" Alix kept looking over her shoulder, expecting the crazy girl with the blue hair and the little feral kid to emerge from the darkness, but they weren't anywhere around.

"I can't drive," Cynthia said, shaking her head fuzzily. "I'm totally fucked up."

"We're both going to be fucked up if you don't hurry! Give me your keys!"

Babysitting drunks was never Alix's favorite thing, and drunk Cynthia was turning into a huge, floppy pain in the neck. Cynthia wasn't taking any of this seriously. Now she was looking back toward the party.

"But I met that nice girl," she said sadly.

Alix went to dig in Cynthia's pocket herself, but the girl was laughing now and fumbled them out. "Okay, okay. Here." She offered her the keys. Alix reached for them. They fell out of Cynthia's hand and hit the ground in a jangle of metal.

"Oops!" Cynthia giggled again.

Alix wanted to scream. She got down on her knees, feeling for the keys in the darkness. Trying to spy any gleam of metal. Cynthia stood by uselessly and giggled.

"Did you see that girl I was with?" she asked as Alix searched.

"Yeah, I saw her." Alix swallowed, trying to focus on her search.

"I really liked her."

Alix's mouth was dry, and she was feeling more and more blurry. Why did she drink so much? She wasn't in any shape to drive. She could barely walk. The ground was tilting and swaying under her. She felt horribly sick and dizzy. Her hand made slow, blurred traceries when she moved it.

"She's here," Cynthia said. "Don't sweat it."

"Who's here?" Alix asked, fighting off the fog of drugs and booze. When Cynthia didn't answer, she looked up.

It was him.

Her stalker. 2.0. Standing right there, beside Cynthia.

The two of them were looking down at her, watching while she crawled around in the broken dirt and concrete and weeds, hunting for the keys.

"I thought you said one would be enough," her stalker said.

"Yeah, well, I didn't want to kill her," Cynthia answered.

The two of them became four in Alix's vision. Alix tried to stand up, but the ground didn't cooperate. It flipped out from under her. She sank back to the asphalt, groaning.

"Cynthia?" she slurred.

Cynthia smiled apologetically. "I'm sorry, Alix."

"Sorry?" Alix was having a hard time making her mouth move. It felt rubbery and thick.

Nothing was making any sense. Now the girl with blue hair was there, too. And another one, short, the feral Latino

159

kid she'd seen. He was holding something in his hands. A Taser. She recognized the device from Death Barbie's many protective toys.

Alix tried to get up again, but her legs were noodles. The ground rose and fell in waves, like when she'd taken a fishing boat tour off the coast of Thailand with her family when they'd spent two weeks in Phuket. She struggled to steady herself and almost made it upright, but the ground betrayed her again and tilted.

She collapsed against 2.0, and he grabbed her as she fell. "Whoa! Slow down there, girl."

"Wh-who?" Alix turned her head, trying to see all of them, trying to see where... She reached for Cynthia. "I thought you were my friend!"

Cynthia looked apologetic. "I know."

The dizziness was turning to blackness. Alix felt herself leaning more heavily against her stalker, and then she was sliding to the ground again, sinking into a deeper, darker blackness than any she had ever known.

The last thing she heard was Cynthia.

"See? I told you I gave her enough."

14

"GET HER INSIDE NOW," MOSES SAID. Kook and Tank scooped her up and started dragging her clumsily across the concrete.

Moses grabbed them and slowed them down. "Be careful with her, all right? She's valuable." Other ravers were sitting outside on cars, drinking, going in and out of the old warehouse. Moses watched carefully to see if anyone was paying attention to a passed-out girl being carried by a couple of her friends, but nobody seemed to care. Cynthia was watching the girl being taken away as well.

"Hey," he said, chucking Cynthia on the shoulder. "You okay?"

Cynthia shook herself. "Yeah."

She didn't sound okay. She sounded weird and uncertain. "You need to talk?" Moses asked.

Cynthia pressed her hands to her head. "I'm too drunk to

talk. I had to drink a bunch of vodka with her, and it mixed like shit."

Moses didn't buy the excuse. Cynthia looked stricken. "Hey," he said. "If there's something going on, you tell me. You were in there a long time with her. Everything I've read about deep-cover work is that it hits pretty hard. Maybe you start identifying with the people you're hanging out with. Even my uncle said he sometimes started to feel bad for people he was working. You know someone long enough, you get attached. It's natural to get overconnected."

Cynthia glared at him. "You should talk. Peeping-Tomming her house?"

Moses grimaced. "Yeah, well, nobody said any of us were perfect."

Cynthia watched Tank and Kook as they slowly hauled Alix away. "Her parents are going to freak."

"Yeah." Moses turned the fact over in his mind, remembering how he'd looked forward to this exact moment. Trying to decide how he felt about it now. It was happening, for real, finally. The moment when he hit the fish tank and it burst and water went everywhere. The moment when Simon Banks discovered he didn't have control. The slippery bastard was about to learn that his lies couldn't save him this time.

"Payback's a bitch," Moses said softly.

"Her brother..." Cynthia trailed off.

Moses felt a rush of irritation. "Oh, get off it. It's not like these people cared about any of us. You think they cared about Tank when he was in the hospital on a respirator?

For sure they didn't give a damn about my dad, or yours. Or Adam's or Kook's people. These people don't give a damn."

"I know, but..."

"Seriously, Cyn. We all wanted payback. This is what it looks like."

Cynthia looked away. "What happens if this doesn't work?"

"Rule four: Always have a Plan B. This will work. It's Plan A, or it's Plan B. And either way, we aren't going to be the ones who lose. Not this time."

"Did you see how she looked when she went down?"

Moses started to give another sharp retort, but something in Cynthia's expression made him hold back.

"Yeah, I saw it." The truth was, Alix's collapse was worse than he wanted to admit: The girl he'd watched for so long turned into nothing but a limp doll. A rag of a person going flat and vulnerable, her personality slipping away. He couldn't get rid of the memory of her frightened, dilated eyes, begging. The pretty goldfish trying to understand why she'd been busted out of the fish tank, wondering why she couldn't breathe anymore.

Let it go. This is just Stockholm syndrome–type shit. Identifying with the target. It's natural. Let it go.

The first thing to do was not to think of her as a person. She wasn't the girl who ran track like a demon possessed her. She wasn't the girl who was stuck taking care of her brother because her parents were too distracted. She wasn't the girl who had opened her door to him, against all reason.

Alix Banks was the target. They'd nailed their target. Bull's-eye. Now it was time to make the target useful.

Bull's-eye.

"Come on." Moses tugged Cynthia's arm. "We need to get out of sight. We're going to have to disappear you, too."

Cynthia didn't respond to his pressure. "It wasn't supposed to go like that," she said.

"How the hell did you think it was going to be? Did you think she'd just faint all nice and clean? I told you it was serious. You knew that."

"I knew it, but I didn't *know it*, okay? Lay off me."

Moses sighed, feeling sour. He knew, all right. He also knew that if he started expressing doubts like the ones on Cynthia's face, it would infect all of them and the plan would unravel, right here and right now. It could all fall apart, just as the stakes had been raised to an impossible level. This was Texas hold 'em just the way Kook liked to play. A game of odds and guts, and, at some point, you were all in, and all you could do was win or lose. The one thing for sure was that you couldn't walk out, because all your chips were already on the table.

"I hear a good plan lasts for about six seconds after the battle starts. Of course we were going to hit bumps."

"I don't know if I can take many more bumps like that," Cyn said. "Did you see the way she looked at me?"

I saw.

He forced down the thought. "Brace up, girl. It'll be harder before it gets better."

"That's what I'm worried about."

Moses put his arm around Cynthia's shoulders. "It's not your job to worry. That's my deal. This isn't on you. You did good. Now, let's get you inside. You deserve a break after all the work you did. Wasn't there someone you were dancing with?"

He kept on. Talking her down, talking a good line. Helping her feel okay. Leading her to safety and comfort and the certainty that even if they did something hard, they were doing the right thing.

■ ■ ■

Dawn. Moses perched atop his warehouse, looking out across the city. The sun, breaking through the jagged horizon, its rays bathing him in golden heat and light, a balm and a comfort, caressing his face, sinking into his bones. Warmth and renewal. Despite the night without sleep, he almost felt good. In this moment, with the sun warming him, and the first sounds of the city starting to grind and beep and come alive, he could almost relax. The night had been a frenzy, but now, settled in his home, his muscles were unknotting. Everything was finally arranged. And in the clean and pristine environs of Haverport, the Banks household was surely already awake.

He'd watched the feeds with Kook, enjoying the blow-by-blow of the Williams & Crowe people meeting with the frustrated parents after Alix escaped. He'd listened as Simon

165

Banks reamed out his killer dogs. Watched the man dress down Lisa Price, hammering her again and again as they stood in his living room, unaware that Moses and Kook were silently watching from behind the steady eye of Jonah's Xbox.

"How could a couple of kids fool you?" Banks shouted.

The Price woman didn't give an inch. "That's an interesting question. I was under the impression that you'd convinced your daughter of the seriousness of her situation."

"That woman freaks me out," Moses muttered to Kook.

"Death Barbie, for reals," Kook agreed. "I put some tabs on her. She basically doesn't have a life. All that woman does is work out, do target practice, and clock hours for Williams and Crowe. She's a top dog there."

"Yeah?"

"Oh yeah, Williams and Crowe sent their best for this gig."

"Good to know we're so important."

"Well, Banks and his clients are important, anyway."

Death Barbie wasn't backing down from Simon Banks. "My job was to guard your daughter, not to keep her from planning an escape."

"I hired you to protect her!"

Lisa looked at him coldly. "I'll remind you, once, that you aren't the only person who's unhappy that you've become a target. We're doing our best to locate Alix now. She should be back under our care soon."

"You wish." Kook snorted.

Moses had to restrain himself from shushing her. They were so close to the action that he instinctually worried that

Death Barbie would hear them. The technology Kook had assembled was astounding.

"Can you imagine how much easier this would have been if we just could have bugged his offices in DC?" he murmured.

Kook scowled. "You going to bring that up again?"

"That wasn't what I meant. We tried. It's no one's fault."

"Well, it definitely wasn't my fault," Kook said. "My stuff was all set. You're the one who couldn't break in."

"I wasn't expecting Fort Knox."

"Yeah, the house was way easier."

"Thanks to Cynthia."

"Access helps. She got just about every room."

Banks and his killer dogs had lapsed into wary detente. Williams & Crowe people were putting out calls for assistance with the local PD. Moses listened as they debated the seriousness of the situation. Debated whether Alix was actually in danger and how long they should wait before calling in more help.

Moses was glad to know they hadn't put all the pieces together and were continuing to fumble around. Some of them still even insisted 2.0 was a group of animal rights activists. Trying to peg the blame to PETA or some such.

"Those rats really screwed with their heads," Kook commented.

Moses couldn't help chuckling. "Who knew people were so suspicious about animal lovers?"

"One of the top domestic terrorism threats, according to the FBI."

"No wonder they latched onto that for so long."

Moses watched them, considering the possibilities. It wasn't a kidnapping yet. Not to them. It was just one willful girl, pushing back against her parents. They weren't calling the feds—yet.

He guessed they'd have at least another day before it escalated. Williams & Crowe would work the case a little longer, hoping for a local police lead. By then, they'd probably find Cynthia's car, and the note Alix had left, and that would drag the time line out a little more....

And then?

And then Simon Banks, who had looked so smart and quiet and in control in the back of the courtroom, with his shiny, ever-present iPad, would discover there were some things he couldn't control.

Moses remembered the man from the trial. Monitoring everything for his clients, smug, knowing that he had already won. He remembered watching George Saamsi getting up to testify on the science of the drugs that had killed Moses's father. Remembered the man testifying that the drug was proved safe. Remembered Banks, in the back of the courtroom, so calm and in control as he orchestrated witnesses on behalf of his client.

Now, though, Simon Banks would finally understand everything. He'd finally understand that Moses didn't give a damn about the man's clients or the testing of rats. He cared that Banks was always at the trials. The fixer. Always present: An asbestos lawsuit. At the Azicort safety hearings in DC, with handpicked witnesses all demonstrating that there was no reason to believe Azicort caused comas. At a Food and Drug Administration hearing about bisphenol A...Banks was always there. The master puppeteer, pulling all the strings.

Now we get to see how you like it when someone's pulling your strings, Moses thought. *Let's see you dance, sucker.*

The sky in the east was lightening. Moses could just make out the ocean, and the sun beyond it, rising. He closed his eyes, letting the warmth of the sun seep into him.

He was tired, but it was a good tired, the tired that told him he'd been pushing hard. Adrenaline still ticked in him from their near failure to hang on to Alix and all the final setup work they'd had to do after the grab, but now it was giving way to exhaustion. Still, he'd moved the plan forward. Taken another step closer to his goal.

Day by day, his dad used to say.

"You add up each small step and you get down the road. Little farther down the road each time...little steps. You just put your mind on those steps."

Moses remembered his father's hands, huge, as he sat with Moses, working a jigsaw puzzle. Moses remembered how much patience the man had when Moses wanted to scream with frustration at the task.

"Just keep testing the pieces. Don't worry about the whole puzzle. Just keep working these little pieces," his dad had said. *"If you work all the little pieces, one by one, well, pretty soon,*

169

all those pieces come together, and then all those pieces add up to something bigger.

"*At the end, you got yourself a masterpiece.*"

Piece by piece. Moses was working the pieces, all right.

And in tranquil, sleepy Haverport, Simon Banks was working his pieces as well. Trying to put together a puzzle he didn't understand, trying to find the shape of a world that Moses was constructing for him.

Moses closed his eyes and breathed deeply. His uncle had taught him to relax in the face of almost unbearable tension. "*Let everything go. Let all the fear and worry go. Just commit, and smile, and don't let anything rattle you. When you're right where you're at, feeling cool and comfortable in your own shoes, well then, people can't help but go along with your program. You're so friendly, so well-spoken, they got no problem with you at all. They love that they can trust you. They want to trust you. They want you to know they're open-minded....*"

Moses exhaled. *Let it all go.*

Pretty soon, there would be more work. More problems to deal with. He'd have to take care of Cynthia, make sure she got props for the work she'd done. She'd turned her own self off and become someone else for almost a year. She deserved to be rewarded for that.

When she'd started drilling for the role, no one had thought she'd be able to pull it off. And then, at some point, every time she'd spoken or turned her head or joked, she'd come off exactly like a Seitz girl. It had been creepy. They'd turned Cynthia into a chameleon. Some chick who chewed

170

gum with her mouth open and lived in the sun-drenched Los Angeles sprawl had become something else entirely.

They were so close, he could almost taste it.

All the work of forging records, hacking school databases, building an identity that was credible...and then inserting Cynthia so perfectly into the school. Moses remembered talking on the phone with the headmaster, pretending his poor English, shutting down conversation so that Cynthia became the single point of contact...a nice, rich Chinese girl from a Chinese tech dynasty who could sit beside Alix on the first day of school and shadow her from class to class, and eventually become her friend.

Moses had carved and shaped Cynthia into what he needed. From a girl who grew up in the back of a strip mall grocery store into someone who walked and talked East Coast like a natural, rolling so smoothly into Seitz that she didn't cause even a ripple. She fit where he needed her to fit.

He'd fit each member of 2.0 into the puzzle picture he was building, filing off the sharp edges of distrust and difference so that they could work together. He remembered pulling each one into the team.

It had been such a simple beginning. Just him and Cynthia sitting in the back of the courtroom. Two kids who had lost their dads to heart attacks. He remembered running across Kook by luck. The girl from his uncle's underworld, who knew how to build credit card cloners and liked to go crusading in her spare time. Kook had been the one who'd managed to tunnel through the labyrinth of industry associations and

171

research institutes to Banks's actual clients. And that had led them to more class actions and eventually to Tank. They'd flat-out rescued Tank. No way was Moses going to leave that kid in the foster system. And then came Adam, the one who had genuinely won his class action, but won too late. After the money couldn't help his aunt at all.

"Yo, Moses."

Tank, climbing up out of the trapdoor that he'd cut in the roof with a torch, after welding a ladder and catwalk to make the climb, so that they could all sit up here and see the world. The wreckage of old industrial America, the factory and its warehouses.

Tank balanced on the roof as he walked over to meet Moses.

"Hey."

Moses nodded to him. "What up?"

"Your girl's starting to move."

"She talking?"

"Not yet." Tank slapped down the visor on his welder's mask and turned to face the dawn. Moses knew the kid was staring at the sun through the shield, staring straight at the ball of fire. Moses was struck again by how young the kid was. Tank was the one Moses worried most about involving in all this. Too silent. Too weirdly broken by foster homes. Now his hands did more talking than he did. Tank coughed, a muffled sound from behind his visor—the asthma that Azicort had claimed it could fix.

"You should probably go down there," Tank said. "For when she wakes up, right?"

"Yeah," Moses sighed, feeling the weight of his responsibilities.

I didn't ask for this, he thought.

Except, the truth was, he had. He'd gone out and created it. Every bit of it. And now another piece of the puzzle needed to be fitted into place.

15

ALIX STIRRED GROGGILY. SHE HAD BEEN dreaming, dreams of music that pounded with a thudding urgency. Music that she was drowning in. Music hammering at her, swaddling her, muffling her. She was drowning in a deep blue ocean of music.

A voice called to her from the bottom of the ocean.

Alix...Alix...Alix...

Something cold pressed against her face. She turned over and banged her head against something hard.

Ow.

She rubbed her head. *Ow.* She reached out, grabbing at the hard, cold thing in her bed.

What the—?

Alix opened her eyes, squinting against a blaze of light. Bars. Cold, rough iron bars. She sat up slowly, trying to get a sense of her surroundings.

"Alix."

She turned.

Him. Her stalker. 2.0. Sitting on the other side of the bars, perched on a short stool. Watching her.

And all around her, bars. He had her in a cage, and they were both sitting inside a puddle of light cast by an electric lantern he had sitting beside him. A puddle of light that bled away into darkness.

How the—?

Cynthia.

Cynthia was one of them. She'd walked right into the trap because Cynthia was one of them.

Alix wanted to cry at the betrayal. Cynthia, who had seemed so harmless. Cynthia, who had chosen to sit right beside her on the first day of school. The good girl who turned out to like a little fun as long as it didn't screw up her college admissions. The *wonderfully mature* girl that Mom had so approved of.

Wonderfully mature.

Cynthia, who had gotten them fake IDs to get into an over-21 club, and Alix had never thought to question how she'd gotten such good ones. She'd just been impressed at the things Cynthia could pull off.

You are such a sucker.

She'd been so starved for a genuine and empathetic friend that she'd walked right into Cynthia's trap. She couldn't help but think of everything that Cynthia knew about her.

Her head was pounding. It felt as if someone were driving

a spike into her brain. Alix put her hand to her head, hating that she was showing weakness to her captor, and then not knowing why she cared. She *was* weak. Of course she was weak. She was in a fucking cage, and she'd walked right into it.

She wasn't just weak; she was *stupid*.

"Hey, Alix." 2.0 had a bottle of water in his hand. He offered it to her. "You're going to have a headache for a little while. Booze and sleeping pills, you know?"

Alix tried to speak. All that came out was a croak.

He was still holding out the bottle. It took a second for it to register with Alix. The bottle. The concern in his expression. A chance. A bare chance.

"Yeah," she croaked. She faked a wince of pain. Adrenaline began pulsing through her. She pressed her palms to her temples. "Horrible headache," she said thickly.

She reached out with a shaking hand for the water bottle. A trembling, grateful hand. "Please…" She let her arm sag a little. She was reaching, but not quite far enough to reach the bottle.

He slid the bottle between the bars.

Alix lunged and seized his wrist with both hands.

Got you!

She yanked hard.

Unbalanced, 2.0 plunged forward. His face slammed into the cage. He yowled and tried to pull away, but Alix had both of her hands tight around his wrist now, and she wasn't letting go. She knew she had only one shot, and she wasn't going to waste it.

176

She twisted his arm around. He was fighting now, reaching through with his other hand. He clawed at her. Alix jerked her face away from his reaching fingers. She fought to hang on, twisting his arm harder. *Just a little more.* In a second she could put him in real pain. Pull his arm out of its socket maybe. Force him to take the keys off his belt. Then she'd open the cage—

He yanked back hard. Alix's fingers slammed against the bars. She yelped as her fingers went numb. She gritted her teeth against the pain and held on. He yanked her against the bars again and again. It felt like her fingers were being smashed by hammers. He was terrifyingly strong.

Too strong.

With a sharp twist, he ripped free. Alix tried to recapture him but he was too fast. He jerked his hand clear. Alix lunged, jamming her arms through the bars, reaching for him. "Come here, asshole!"

He leaped back. "Jesus Christ, girl! *Goddamn!*"

Alix withdrew, glaring at him. Her body shook with adrenaline. She clenched her hands, trying to shake off the numb pain in her fingers. She watched him carefully, hoping she'd get another shot but knowing she wouldn't.

He was pacing in front of her, glaring. Massaging his wrist, then reaching up and touching his bruised face. Blood dripped from a cut on his brow, running freely, staining his eye. He pressed the heel of his hand to the wound.

"I was trying to be nice to you," he growled.

"Fuck you!"

His expression hardened. "That how you want to play it? We can play it that way."

A door opened, a searing rectangle of daylight spilling in.

Alix gasped. With the light from the door, she could see that the room she was in was huge. A vast, black, echoing tomb. She spied high beams overhead, iron trusses, and nothing else. An empty warehouse space of some kind.

Shadowy figures came dashing across the emptiness.

"What's going on!"

A girl's voice. For a second Alix's heart leaped. *Cynthia*, she thought inanely.

But no. This girl was short and vicious-looking, dressed in a black T-shirt and black jeans. She had a pierced nose and wide-bore tribal earrings and electric-blue hair. Black eyeliner, done heavy on her top and bottom eyelids, shocking against her pale skin. The Goth girl who'd helped grab her. The one from the rave. And with her the Latino boy, the feral little kid.

Blue-Haired Goth looked from 2.0 to Alix. "You okay, Moses?"

"Moses?" Alix laughed despite herself. "Your name is Moses? Like parting the Red Sea *Moses*?"

2.0 glared. "Keep it up, girl. Keep it up and see what happens."

Alix shut her mouth, suddenly aware of how vulnerable she was. For a moment she'd felt powerful. Dangerous, because she could hurt him. But now she was acutely aware that she was the one locked in a cage and that there were three of them out there and they could do anything they wanted with her.

The Goth girl was smirking, looking from her to 2.0. "What the hell did you do to her?" she asked.

"I didn't do shit! I offered her water for her headache."

The girl laughed darkly. "No good deed goes unpunished." She reached up to Moses's face, surprisingly tender. "Let me see." Moses bent to let her inspect the cut. "I need better light," she said. "Looks like you'll have a nasty bruise, for sure." She frowned. "Did she chip a tooth, too?"

Moses touched his mouth, surprised, then gave Alix a cold look. "Guess she did."

Alix could see the glint of blood on his teeth as he spoke. He touched his lip again and winced.

"Don't let her grab you, Tank," he warned.

"I won't."

The feral little kid was pacing around the perimeter of Alix's cage. For a second Alix thought he might be worried about her, and she felt a flood of warmth for him, but then she realized he was actually inspecting the bars of her cage. His eyes went from one bar to the next, studying each join carefully. Finally, he nodded with satisfaction.

"Told you I could figure out the welding," he said to the Goth. "It's way easier than rigging something to explode."

"Sure, Tank. You're the Wizard of Welding. Good for you."

The kid laughed and started to say something, but his words were lost as his breathing took on a sudden rasp. He pulled an inhaler out of his pocket and took a quick hit. It was a routine movement, fast and efficient.

"Wizard of Welding," he said on the exhale, grinning. "I do like the sound of that."

The Goth girl smiled over at him affectionately. "Don't let it go to your head, kid."

Alix didn't like how they ignored her entirely. It made her feel like she was an animal in a cage.

"Hey!" Alix said. "What is this? Why are you keeping me here?"

To Alix's frustration, they continued to ignore her. The blue-haired girl kept checking out 2.0's wound. "You'll be fine," she announced. "You really are an idiot. First you let her bite you, now this?"

2.0—Moses—examined the blood on his hands and eyed Alix. "Yeah. Girl's fierce, all right." His expression was unreadable, a blankness that made Alix feel more like an object than a person. It chilled her the way they talked around her or looked right past her but didn't bother to talk *to* her.

"Why are you doing this to me?" Alix asked again.

"Come on," the blue-haired girl said to Moses. "Let's get you checked out. I really need better light." She led Moses away. "Come on, Tank," she called back. The short kid followed. As he left, he scooped up the electric lantern, carrying it swinging with him, casting shadows as he went.

"Hey!" Alix shouted after them.

"Hey!"

They walked out the door.

180

The door closed.

The darkness was total.

"You can't just leave me here!"

Her voice echoed in the blackness.

She shouted again, *"Hey!"*

Alix kept shouting for a long time, but the cavernous darkness swallowed all her calls for help.

16

ALIX SLEPT. LATER, BY FEEL in the blackness, she found the water bottle and drank from it, gulping. Convulsive. She kept the empty bottle. She didn't know why. She wanted to think it might be useful as some kind of tool, even though she knew it wouldn't be.

Exhausted and demoralized, she slept again. When she woke, she felt groggy and had to pee, and it was still pitch-black. She had no idea how long she'd been asleep. It could have been hours, or days, or minutes.

Alix shouted for help some more, but her voice just echoed back.

"Hey! I've got to go to the bathroom!"

She began to wonder if they had left her alone in the building. Maybe they'd decided to just let her starve to death. Maybe someday people would find her: stupid Alix Banks, the girl who'd walked right into the hands of the people who killed her.

The pain in her bladder was unbearable. Alix shouted and shouted and finally gave up. She went over to one side of the cage, hiked her skirt, and peed in the darkness, relieved and horrified, hoping that her urine wouldn't run the wrong way and soak her cage.

She paced carefully to the far side of the cage. She tried to orient herself in the direction that she thought the door might be, and, leaning against the bars, she wrapped her arms around her knees and listened in the darkness.

She wasn't even really sure exactly where she was in Hartford. She'd never come to this area, and with Cynthia driving, it was hard to follow. The route had been twisty and confusing. Probably on purpose, now that she thought about it. God, she'd been stupid. Trusting Cynthia. Alix leaned her head back against the bars and kept running her situation over in her head, trying to figure it out. Trying to understand.

Ask your father.

That was what this was all about. 2.0—the one called Moses—had wanted her to ask Dad what all this was about. And Dad had said that it was probably something to do with a client, even though Moses had been adamant that it was about Dad.

Payback, he'd called it.

And I'm collateral damage.

Alix began running possibilities through her mind. Maybe they were going to try to ransom her. Or use her to extort something from Dad. Maybe if he gave them what they wanted, they'd let her go—

You've seen their faces.

Alix felt ill. Kidnappers who planned on letting you go would probably hide their faces, right? So maybe they really were just going to leave her in the cage and let her die.

Part of her wanted to panic at the thought, but mostly she was exhausted and angry at herself for walking right into a trap. Good-girl Alix, thinking she was busting loose. And Cynthia coaching her into the trap the whole way.

Alix decided she hated Cynthia.

Then she decided she hated herself. She'd been naive.

You trusted Cynthia. You trusted Dad.

He'd said it probably was just people who were confused and crazy. But these people were focused on him like laser sights. He was the target, and she was collateral damage, and she still didn't understand why.

What did you have to do to someone to make them want to destroy your entire life?

Alix got up and tried to stretch her legs. It had to be morning, she thought. By now Mom and Dad had to suspect that she hadn't just run off to a party. They'd be searching for her. Lisa would be searching for her.

Death Barbie.

If anyone was going to find her, it would be Lisa. Alix

remembered the woman's expression as she and Cynthia ditched. The fixed gaze of a single-minded hunter. That woman had almost caught a car on foot.

Alix fantasized about Lisa blasting into the factory and saving her. Homing in on Alix's phone and crashing through the door—except she'd ditched her cell, just like clever Cynthia had suggested.

Alix found herself wishing she had a hidden phone. A secret one that they could track. Something that would let Death Barbie call in a drone strike. Send in the SWAT teams...

Quit it, Alix. You're on your own.

For all she knew, she'd gotten Death Barbie fired. She'd ditched the lady, after all. Maybe Dad had canned her for being incompetent. Maybe Alix had helped get rid of the one person who had even a tiny chance of rescuing her.

Alix huddled in the darkness. She could smell her urine. This wasn't a movie. She was in a cage in a warehouse in the dark, and the reality was that they could do whatever they wanted to her.

She wondered if she'd end up as a bunch of bones that someone would find in the woods in another decade. A mystery girl identified by DNA, the way she sometimes saw a discovered body reported in the news.

Alix began to sob. She had never felt so miserable and hopeless. The darkness pressed down on her, and she sobbed.

No one came.

Nothing happened.

She was alone.

■ ■ ■

The door opened.

Alix squinted in the sudden spike of light. *Daylight?* It was daylight. And the shadow walking toward her…

Moses.

Alix tried to dry her tears on her hands. To clean her face and hide her fear.

You don't get to see me cry, you asshole. You don't get to see anything. You're not going to see me crying.

He had a paper plate in one hand and the lantern in the other. He set the lantern down and offered her the plate with a sandwich on it. She held out her hand, but he put the paper plate down just outside the bars.

"Cheese sandwich," he said.

Alix glared at him. She decided she wasn't going to eat the sandwich, just to show Moses that she didn't need him.

I'm not going to do anything you want me to.

It was a small thing, but it was what she could do.

"Suit yourself." He sat down on the stool. He wrinkled his nose. "Did you piss yourself?"

"What do you think?" Alix snapped.

He picked up the lantern and circled the cage. Held it over the wet place where her urine had run and then soaked into concrete. "I'm sorry," he said. "We'll get something for you."

"A chamber pot?" Alix challenged.

"I don't know." He sat down again. "We'll figure it out. If I could trust you, I'd just let you use the toilet." He touched his forehead. "But, you know. You're a fighter. I got a bite in my arm and a chipped tooth, and Kook says I should be glad I don't have a concussion." He touched his swollen brow, again, significantly. "Starting to think I can't really risk letting you out. So…" He shrugged. "Here we are."

"Why are you doing this to me?"

He sighed. "Your dad didn't tell you, did he?"

"You're animal rights activists or something, right? That's why you did the thing with the lab rats."

"Is that what he told you?" He laughed. "Sucker even lies to his own daughter."

"He doesn't lie to me."

"If you say so."

"You think I'm going to believe you?"

Moses grinned abruptly. The same wild smile that Alix had seen before. The one that had urged her to open the door to her own house, for God's sake.

Alix wished she could punch the smile bloody.

"Believe me?" Moses asked. "*Believe* me?" He started to laugh, shaking his head.

"What's so funny?"

"'Believe,'" he said again. "It's a funny word. 'Believe.' 'Believing.'"

He got up and started to pace back and forth in front of her cage. "Do I expect you to believe me? No, I don't.

'Believing' is for Santa Claus, right? It's for Tooth Fairies. It's for your boyfriend when he says he's never met anyone like you and wants to feel you up. That's believing. It's for little kids. Belief. You believe in God?" he asked sharply.

Alix was startled by the question. "I don't know. I guess. Sure."

"I don't. Used to, you know?" He shrugged. "Now I don't."

He paused, seeming to pick his words. "The thing about belief—" He broke off, scowling. He sighed and shook his head, working over something in his mind. His frown deepened.

Alix had the feeling that she was seeing some version of Moses that wasn't exposed often. Not cool and relaxed, but frustrated and burdened. It made him more real to her. Not a captor. Not the merry prankster. She felt as if the darkness between them was charged with electricity.

She almost had the feeling that if she could just find the right thing to say, he might even let her go. And if she said the wrong thing, not.

Uncertain outcomes everywhere.

Alix waited, watchful. Trying to get a feel for her captor. Trying to understand what made him spark.

The silence between them lengthened.

Finally, Alix prodded. "The thing about belief is…"

Moses gave her a sharp look. "Seriously? You're going to push on me?"

Alix couldn't help glaring. "Seriously? You put me in a cage. Now you want me to be *polite*?"

He seemed to like that because he smirked. "Okay, girl. I'll give you that."

Emboldened, she said, "My name is Alix."

"Okay, *Alix*. The thing about *belief* is that you can't prove it. You have to 'believe' in God because, hey, the only way you'll ever find out if you're right or wrong is after you get cancer and die, right? If the feds shoot me"—he shrugged—"then I'll *know* whether God exists. But until then? I'm just guessing.

"With God, people can tell you all kinds of things. Preacher up in the pulpit says he's real, but he doesn't know. He's never met God. So all you got is belief. You make a choice. You believe in God. Or you believe that there's no God. You believe your mom and your dad when they say they love you. Belief is what you can't prove—one way or another. Your folks maybe say they love you—but you can't get inside their heads, can you? You can't know for sure. You've got a theory about them loving you, but you can't test it."

"My parents love me."

"You believe that, huh?"

"All parents love their children," Alix said.

Moses laughed sharply. "Tell that to Tank. He's got a row of cigarette burns down his spine that says different."

Alix swallowed, horrified. "Tank's the little one, right?"

Moses's expression softened at the mention of the kid. "Yeah. That's right. The little one with the crappy lungs."

"Why's he with you?"

Moses glanced over, evaluating her. "Because sometimes,

if you see something bad, you can't let it stand. Sometimes you see something so bad you know that if you walk away, you're just as bad."

The way he said it made Alix feel weirdly uncertain. As if anything she asked after would reveal how posh her life was and how little she understood of the world. As if she was too naive to even be talking about Tank's life. Finally, she summoned her courage. "So what happened to him?"

"Ask him sometime. He'll tell you if he wants."

Whatever brief rapport she'd had with Moses was gone. His expression was back to brick wall.

"Does this mean I'm going to be with you for a while?"

"Depends on you, I guess."

"Come on. What's this all about?" Alix asked. "Just tell me. My dad will give you what you want. Is this some kind of ransom thing? You want our money? We aren't that rich, you know."

Moses laughed derisively. "Please don't be one of those one percent kids who says they're middle class."

Alix knew better to than to bite on that one. She kept silent.

Moses sat down across from her, watching her speculatively. "You really believe your dad loves you?" he asked.

Alix was about to answer, but then she hesitated. She knew what Moses was getting at, but she suspected that the question was a trap and that he'd twist her answer.

If she said yes, then he'd make her give examples of all the things that were supposed to show that someone loved you, like they gave you candy or kissed you good night or paid your tuition to Seitz... but that didn't really get to the heart of the question. It wasn't like Dad had thrown himself in front of a bus for her or anything like that.

So then Moses would force her to settle on the word that he'd already fixated on. *Believe*. Did she believe her father loved her?

"Yes."

It felt good to say it firmly, to throw it in his face. She didn't care. Dad loved her and he was out there, and he and Williams & Crowe and a hundred other people were working overtime to get her back—

Alix suddenly realized what she needed to do. She wasn't powerless. She might be stuck in a cage, but there was still one thing she could do.

Play for time.

She needed to drag this out as long as possible. She needed to give Dad and Lisa and the FBI and everyone else time. She needed to keep Moses talking.

She didn't need to win an argument or prove she was smarter than he was; she just needed to drag out the minutes on the clock. Slow Moses down, give Dad time to find her. That was the way she had to fight.

"Yes," she said again, stronger. "I know he does."

Instead of challenging her, Moses smiled. "Yeah. I think he loves you, too. And that's why I believe this is going to work."

"You believe," Alix taunted.

Moses's smile widened. "Bad choice of words, huh?"

"You're the one who's so interested in language."

"Language is how we hack other people's brains. It's how we make them see things the way we want them to see them. Your dad should have taught you that, him being so good at PR and all.

"But you're right about believing things. I don't actually believe in anything anymore. Belief is for suckers. You can believe the doctors when they say your dad is going to last longer than six months because he's got new heart medicine...." He shrugged. "I'm done with all that. I'm only interested in testing. Experimenting. You poke the rat, see what it does—"

"Is that what I am, a rat?"

He went on as if she hadn't interrupted. "—you make a hypothesis. You build a theory, and then you poke the rat and test it. Poke it again, see if you're right. Change the theory until you can predict what happens in the next experiment. Then you don't *believe* something anymore. You *know*.

"The truth is, I can't tell whether your dad really loves you, but I've got a hypothesis about what he'll do when you don't show up at home."

So do I, Alix thought. *So we're going to have a nice, friendly, long conversation, and see who's right.*

"He's going to freak," she said.

"That's what we're hoping."

"And I'm just collateral damage," Alix said. She reached through the bars for the sandwich on its paper plate.

"Yeah. Pretty much."

"At least I know it's not personal," she said as she took a bite. She looked at the sandwich, then at Moses with surprise. "This is really good cheese."

"You thought I'd feed you Velveeta or something?"

"Aged cheddar doesn't really go with the decor." She took another bite and then another. She wanted to control herself, but she couldn't stop from wolfing down the sandwich. *God, I'm starved.*

Moses watched her eat. "There's more where that came from. We've got a fridge full of gourmet cheese—Spanish, French, English, German, goat, cow, sheep...."

"Seriously?"

"It's a long story."

Alix tapped the bars of her cage meaningfully. "I'm not going anywhere."

"Let's just say that some of the people in my crew have a soft spot for rats. Enjoy the food." He made a move to get up. Alix rushed to find something more to talk about. Anything to keep him here and talking—

"Why did you come to my house?" she blurted out. "That night. Why did you come to my house? You could have been caught."

"By Williams and Crowe?" He shook his head. "No way. Not there, at least. I know how they're set up there."

"I could have gotten you caught, though. Why come to my house? Was there something that you were looking for? I saw you...." Alix swallowed, remembering how he'd looked at her through the glass, smiling....

"Truce," Moses murmured, and there was a tiny smile on his face as he remembered, too. He made the *T* with his hands.

"Truce." He shook his head, still smiling, and the way he said the word made Alix want it so badly. Some way to not be in conflict. Some way to be safe with him...some way to put down the fight for a little while.

"Truce," Alix said, and was surprised at how good the idea sounded to her. How much she wanted to find some way to get along with this stranger.

Moses's expression had softened. He was almost like a different person entirely. A kinder person. Someone who saw her not as a tool in his plans but as a human being. And with the softness of his expression, she thought she could see regret as well.

"Why did you come over?" she asked again, softly.

"Why did you open your door?"

The words could have been a challenge, but they weren't. Moses wasn't trying to act tough anymore. The swagger was gone.

"Maybe I wanted to talk to you," Alix said.

A whisper of a smile. "Maybe you wanted to go out for coffee."

"Did you?" she asked.

"Maybe."

"You're a terrible stalker."

He laughed at that, and Alix was struck at how young he seemed. He wasn't much older than she was, and she could see it in these moments. And yet, when he put on his mask of confidence, he came off as so much older. So much harsher. But now there was a kindness.

"Truce," Alix whispered. She found herself reaching through the bars. Wanting to touch him. He started to reach out for her as well; then his face hardened.

He drew back, scowling. "Nice try, girl. Real pro."

"I wasn't—"

"You really are his daughter. Clever, conniving, manipulating…" Moses got to his feet and started pacing back and forth. "You get inside my head. You make me doubt. And I didn't even see it coming. You know just how to make someone believe. It's got to be genetic. You and your damn dad."

"That's not true! I wasn't manipulating you! I—"

His voice turned mocking. "'Hold out your hand, Moses.' 'Come back for a little more, Moses.' 'Go on and trust the nice girl, Moses.'" He shook his head. "You're good. I'll give you that. You're damn good."

"What do you mean?"

"I guess I shouldn't blame you. It's what you people do. It's second nature. You lie. You manipulate. Your dad would be proud of you right now, Alix. For a minute you actually made me doubt myself."

"Why won't you trust me?"

195

"Why should I?"

"Why should I trust you? I'm the one in the damn cage!"

"That's not personal."

"It's pretty personal to me!"

Moses slammed his hand against the bars. "You know what's personal? Finding your dad dead on the bathroom floor. That's personal!" He slammed his hand against the metal again, shaking the cage. "Watching your mom have a heart attack in the grocery store. That's fucking personal!" His face was right between the bars, brimming with hate. "If I did half the things to your family that your dad did to mine, you'd be dead by now!"

Alix shrank from his sudden fury, but she forced herself to rally. "If that's true, why don't you do it? Why don't you just kill me already!"

He stopped short, glaring at her. Took a step back, fighting to master his rage. Finally, he said, "That's what you people do. You're the ones who kill. I'm better than you. I'm not going to dirty myself like you."

"What are you *talking* about? I've never killed anyone!"

"Your dad kills people. He gets paid to kill."

"That's a lie! He's never done anything to you! He doesn't even know who you are!"

"That's because to him, we're just numbers. We aren't even people to your dad. I'm surprised he didn't tell you how he makes his money. Too much of a coward, I guess."

"I don't believe you!"

Moses laughed. "You know what's nice, Alix? I don't have

to care if you believe me or not. I don't have to spin it for news cameras. I don't have to argue it in court." He paused, suddenly thoughtful. "You know how nice that is? Just for once, I don't have to convince anyone. It's just the truth. Everything good in your life comes from blood money. Your school, your house, your pool, your fancy *Architectural Digest* kitchen, all of it. You might want to deny it, but your whole family's covered in blood."

"You're lying!"

Moses laughed. "Well, someone sure is, but it isn't me." He started walking away.

"You're lying!" Alix shouted after him.

"Enjoy the cage, Alix."

17

YOUR WHOLE FAMILY'S COVERED IN blood. Your dad kills people. He gets paid to kill. To him, we're just numbers. He didn't tell you?

Alix huddled in the darkness, trying to process the claims that Moses had made. Trying to make them fit into some kind of picture that made sense. But it was insane. Dad didn't kill people. He did public relations—

"Alix!"

Suddenly the warehouse floor was flooded with light. Huge overhead hanging lamps blazed alive, making Alix blink and squint in the brutal glare. Cynthia came dashing across the concrete floor.

"What the hell have they done to you?"

Alix didn't understand why Cynthia was concerned. Cynthia had betrayed her. At least that was her memory, but here the girl was, frantically trying to unlock Alix's cage.

Alix stared up at her, squinting against the stabbing bright light.

"Cyn! Come back!" Moses and three others came pelting through the door. "We've got this under control!"

Cynthia whirled around. "You're a fucking animal!" she shouted at Moses. "This isn't what we talked about!"

Moses stopped short in the face of Cynthia's rage. The others drew back as well: the blue-haired girl and Tank and a tall white kid with bleached hair...the DJ from the rave, Alix realized.

"Give me the keys," Cynthia demanded.

"I was going to let her out earlier," Moses said defensively.

"Are you okay?" Cynthia asked Alix.

Alix didn't know what to think. With Cynthia there, and Moses back on his heels, it felt like some kind of insane prank, like a joke or game that had just gotten a little out of hand. "Well, I'm still locked up," she pointed out.

"Give me the keys," Cynthia said again to Moses, her voice turning dangerous.

"Look what she did to me!" Moses protested, pointing to his face.

"Looks like what you deserved!"

"Cyn," the girl with the blue hair said, "we all agreed." She jerked her head toward Moses and his bruised brow. "Wonderboy here got himself beat to shit—"

"Thanks," Moses said.

"—so we decided it was safer if we didn't let her out. This isn't a game. If she gets out, we're done. And she's a fighter. No telling what happens if we let her out. We've got to be smart about this. Keeping her prisoner like this, it's not simple."

"We agreed she wasn't going to get hurt!" Cyn shouted. "That was what you promised me. We weren't going to hurt her."

"You know, I'm the one with the bruises," Moses pointed out. "*Look at her!* She looks like a lab rat!"

Everyone's gaze turned to Alix, sitting on the floor in her cage with her paper plate and water bottle. Everyone's eyes went to the urine stain in one corner. They all suddenly looked abashed.

Tank went over to the cage, a key in his hand. "Do you promise not to run away if we let you out?"

Alix stared at the kid, perplexed by the question. "Sure. Yeah."

"You can't believe her!" Moses said. "She'll say anything to get out."

Cynthia glared at him. "I believe her, and I'm the one who lived with her for the last eight months." She took the key from Tank.

"I'm sorry, Alix," she said. "It wasn't supposed to be this way." She glared over her shoulder at Moses. "It wasn't supposed to have been like this *at all.*" She unlocked the door. "Come on. You can come out. No one's going to hurt you."

Hesitantly, Alix crawled out. Cynthia helped her up. Alix wasn't sure if she wanted to shove Cynthia, but her body took the decision away from her. She was so stiff and sore that she staggered. She ended up leaning against Cynthia for support.

"Thanks, I think."

Cynthia was still glaring at Moses. "You promised that you wouldn't hurt her," she said again.

"I didn't want to hurt her. I wanted to keep you safe. She's too dangerous to all of us on the loose." He shrugged. "If it's a decision between us and her, I'm going to worry about us first."

"Nice speech," Cynthia said. "Remind you of anyone?"

Alix was surprised to see Moses suddenly look stricken. The expression was so fast she almost missed it, but it was there: shock and shame and then a hardening into a blank wall.

"This is all on you," he said to Cynthia. "You're risking everyone."

For a second Cynthia hesitated, then said, "We can't do it this way. If we do, we're no better than they are."

She took Alix by the arm, and her voice was gentle. "Come on. Let's get you cleaned up."

18

CYNTHIA GUIDED ALIX THROUGH A bewildering maze of workshops, empty manufacturing lines, and old storage racks to what appeared to be a locker room where workers had once bathed and changed into uniforms of some sort. There were orange industrial lockers in long rows, and benches, and rows of sinks and showers, along with cracked white ceramic tiles on the floors and walls.

Cynthia pulled a bunch of the workmen's lockers open.

"You can use some of my clothes," she said. The opened lockers revealed neatly stacked T-shirts, carefully hung skirts, and blouses. Designer labels. Prada bags. Michael Kors skirts and jackets. Manolo high heels. Derek Lam blouses. One locker had makeshift shelves welded into it, holding makeup: NARS lip glosses, Dior eye shadows. Another locker for accessories: ECCO bags and Ray-Bans, Oakleys, Dolce

& Gabbana. Another held perfectly pressed Seitz uniforms. White blouses, pleated skirts, Seitz school emblem blazers, kneesocks. Other clothes. Juicy jeans. All-Star high-top sneakers. More and more lockers.

"You have clothes here?" Alix asked, puzzled.

"I live here," Cynthia said softly. "This is my home."

An entire girl's wardrobe jammed into scratched metal lockers. Bangles. Hair clips. All the things a girl might need, stored incongruously in the factory.

"But…" It was too surreal to take in. "But…"

"We'll get you cleaned up, then we can talk. We've got a lot to talk about."

Cynthia led Alix down the locker aisle to a row of shower stalls and pulled aside a water-stained vinyl shower curtain, revealing a dubious, fifties-era tiled stall. Old lime-green tiles, some of them cracked and shattered. Bare concrete overhead.

"Go ahead," she said when Alix hesitated. "I'll keep out the wolves."

The shower pipe was rusted, and the spray head appeared to be a scavenged fire-extinguishing nozzle of the kind that hung from the ceilings of Seitz. Alix remembered the little welder kid. *Tank.* The one who wanted her to promise not to run away. He must have done this.

"Shower's optional," Cynthia said at her hesitation. "It's up to you."

■ ■ ■

Water gushed over Alix, cleansing hot, stripping away the darkness and fear. Cynthia stood outside the bathroom, guarding it.

"I won't let them bother you," Cynthia had said, and Alix, against her best instincts, believed her. What else was she supposed to do? She didn't even know where she was inside the factory complex, let alone how to get away if she managed to break out.

Not yet anyway.

The scalding water poured over her, sluicing away grime and sweat, the hangover of the party, the pain of sleep, the stains of imprisonment.

The water was so blissfully hot that Alix thought she'd never loved a shower so much: the relief of being out of the cage, the sense that she could stop time as long as she stood under its spray, the feeling that behind this vinyl curtain she didn't have to face whatever was out there. She didn't have to confront the strange youths who lived in this warehouse, who looked at her with such calculated interest that it seemed as if they weren't even from the same planet as she, let alone that they might speak English and be part of her country.

Alix scrubbed herself and soaped up again, and still she lingered in the gushing water. Despite everything, she felt grateful for Cynthia's kindness. And then she wondered if that was some kind of mindfuck that they were gaming on her as well. Cynthia playing the good cop, and Moses playing the bad one—the one she was supposed to fear.

If she was honest, she did fear him. She didn't understand him. She didn't know what he wanted, but she suspected it was something she wouldn't want to give, no matter how much Cynthia pretended to be her friend.

And what about the rest of them? Were they really Cynthia's friends? That blue-haired, pierced gutter rat? The shaggy little brown kid with the ringlets of hair who reminded Alix more than anything of a scruffy Hobbit? The tall one, lanky and smooth, who had DJ'd the rave—what about him?

And, of course, there was Moses. Presiding over them all. He was the one they looked to. The boy who had been so seductively intriguing when he'd stood behind her and whispered in her ear as he wrecked Seitz, and who had turned out to be so monstrous when he'd put her in a cage.

"Your dad kills people."

"Your whole family's covered in blood."

It sounded ridiculously melodramatic. As if she were part of a family of assassins. As if her father were someone who went around with a sniper rifle, killing targets for cash. The whole thing was so absurd it made her want to laugh.

Except that Moses and his crew clearly believed it, and were crazy enough to kidnap her.

At least you know he's not planning on murdering you.

So what did he want from her? Why grab her at all?

It didn't matter, she decided. All she needed to do was keep playing for time. Dad was out there, and right now he'd be calling all the people he'd called when he'd thought Jonah had been taken. Right now, there were people tracking her down.

Just hang on.

"Did you drown in there?" Cynthia called through the shower curtain.

"Just a sec."

She shut off the water. Cynthia passed in a towel and Alix wrapped it around herself.

She came out, feet cold on the tile, and navigated around the drains, with Cynthia hovering as Alix went back to the lockers.

As nice as Cynthia was acting, she was standing a little too close. Keeping an eye on her still.

Alix turned on her. "I'm not going to bolt while I'm in a towel, okay?"

"Alix—"

"You aren't going to let me go, are you?"

Cynthia's lips compressed. She avoided meeting Alix's gaze. Instead, she turned and rummaged in her lockers. She pulled out a tank top and then a black hoodie. She found some painter's jeans. "These should fit. They're loose on me."

"You're just like them," Alix accused. "You just pretend to be nicer."

Cynthia's head jerked up, anger flaring, but the expression was gone as fast as it came. She took a breath. "Just listen to what we're going to tell you," she said. "That's all. Just listen."

"Listen to my kidnappers, you mean."

"We might know something you need to hear."

"That's rich, coming from someone I don't even know."

"You do know me, Alix."

"Are you even a student?"

Cynthia had the grace to look apologetic. "I graduated a year ago. I could have gone to any college I wanted. Full ride to the Ivy Leagues. I'm here instead. You should listen to us."

"So that's why you're so good at everything. You've already done it."

Cynthia didn't meet her eyes, just dug in her lockers again. "You want underwear, too?"

"No thanks." Alix didn't bother hiding her anger. "I think I'll go commando."

"Whatever."

Fully dressed in another girl's clothes, Alix let Cynthia guide her back to the factory's main floor. They walked past long empty production lines with rusting machinery sitting silent, ducking under snaking tracks of conveyor belts and rollers that seemed to go nowhere in particular. The factory was huge.

Now that she was less disoriented, Alix tried to pick out details. Anything she could use to identify the place. She noted high clerestory windows, where sunlight filtered down and laid angular shapes of yellow on the open, smooth concrete. Not far away, a pair of double doors beckoned, offering escape, but their handles were tangled in heavy links of chain.

Cynthia led her out of the production area and into what Alix thought might be warehouse space. Flat concrete stretched ahead for what felt like a quarter mile. Along one side, empty steel racks rose from the floor all the way to the fifty-foot-high ceilings. An abandoned forklift lay on its side near one of the aisles between the racks.

At the far side of the warehouse, the DJ kid and the younger kid whom Moses had called Tank were riding skateboards. They skidded along makeshift iron skate rails, which looked like they'd been refashioned from what might have been part of the factory's production lines, and rumbled up and down a couple of plywood ramps.

Tank shot upward, pulling his board out from under his feet, kicking his legs, and then tried to land. He failed spectacularly, coming down hard, and slid down the ramp on his back. Alix winced. She could practically feel the kid's skin shredding, but Tank popped right back up, unconcerned, and kicked off again, making another run at the ramp.

When the two boys caught sight of Alix and Cynthia, they slewed to a halt.

"Took you long enough," the bleached DJ said. Tank didn't say anything at all. Just stared at them. For a second Alix thought it was her they were hating on, but then she realized it was all about Cynthia. The tension between them was palpable.

"She's here now," Cynthia said. "You want to do this or not?"

"Moses is pissed," the DJ said.

"Yeah?" Cynthia shot back. "Well, so am I."

The lanky boy laughed and dropped his board to the concrete. He kicked off easily, weaving between imaginary obstacles as he rumbled across the open space. Tank rolled in his wake, leaving Cynthia and Alix following on foot. The boys popped their boards beside a door and pushed it open. When Cynthia and Alix reached them, the DJ made a mocking bow and waved them through.

"M'ladies."

"Don't be an asshole, Adam," Cynthia said as she shoved past.

"Don't be pissed at me. I didn't lock up the rich girl."

Inside, Moses and the pierced gutter girl were leaning against a steel counter, talking. They shut up as Alix entered.

The room was a large kitchen space. A big metal table dominated its center, with an assortment of folding chairs surrounding it. The rest of the kitchen was all industrial steel sinks and gleaming steel counters and big steel walk-in coolers. An impressive pile of pizza boxes was stacked in one corner, and a thick wheel of some kind of hard white cheese sat on one of the countertops. Adam and Tank sidled in behind her.

Alix felt surrounded.

Once again, Alix was struck by how different Cynthia looked from the rest of the freak parade. She was perfectly coiffed, even now. Long lustrous black hair, combed silky, carefully applied makeup. A Seitz girl, through and through.

And yet Alix had seen the lockers that Cynthia lived out of. She was one of these—*kids?*—too. Some kind of Stepford plant of a perfect daughter, used to snare her.

Moses was looking at her, smiling slightly. The confidence was back. The relaxed persona that he used when he wasn't...whatever the other version of him was. The version that looked like a real person and had feelings like a real person.

Alix realized everyone's eyes were on her. The blue-haired girl with all the piercings looked like she'd be happy to rip out Alix's lungs. More than anything, she reminded Alix of a predatory creature from the Realms of Fey, a strange, bloodthirsty urban sprite. The blond DJ was watching her, cool and amused, like he thought she was beneath him. Like he was too beautiful to be bothered with her at all.

Tank was different. His tangled, curly black hair hid his eyes almost entirely, but Alix could see them roving the room, taking stock of everyone and the situation almost as carefully as she was.

"So," Moses said slowly. "Cynthia thinks we owe you an apology."

It wasn't what Alix had expected. She'd expected him to be like he'd been when he had her in the cage. All swagger and confidence, telling her how it was, and how ignorant she was, and trying to sell the line about Dad being a killer.

Instead, he was carefully picking his words. "You should know that was my call. If you want to blame someone, blame me. I overreacted." He touched his face. "I knew you were a fighter, and then I got pissed when you fought. You made me lose my head." He smiled slightly. "Not often that happens."

"Is that your apology?" Alix asked. "You're blaming me for making you angry when you stuck me in a *cage*?"

Suddenly she was pissed. Really pissed.

"I'm not blaming—"

"Basically, you are."

"Try again, Moses," the DJ said, amused.

Moses looked like he was about to say something nasty, but he stopped and took a breath. He held up his hands, defensive. "Okay. My bad. I'm sorry. I'm sorry for how we treated you. You didn't deserve that."

"Deserve what?"

"Getting locked in there for so long."

"I didn't deserve to be locked in there at all!"

"Whoa! I'm trying to say—"

"You're trying to say you're not sorry at all!"

"He is," Cynthia sighed. "He's just an idiot."

"An idiot for sticking his hand in the cage," the blue-haired girl muttered. "Rich girl didn't suffer that much."

"Shut up, Kook," Cynthia snapped. "Just shut up."

Kook looked like she was about to snap back, but Moses held up a quelling hand. "It's done," he said. "I'm sorry. I should have thought of a better plan. I should have thought of you." He inclined his head, and now, finally, Alix had the feeling he was genuinely contrite. "I'm sorry."

"So you're like ... what? The leader or something?"

He glanced at the other kids in the room, and there was that flash of smile again. The one she'd seen when he was pulling his pranks. "Oh, I don't know. We've got shared interests, maybe. I'm just good at planning."

"Sometimes," Cynthia amended. "When you don't let your stupid run away with you."

"I already apologized," Moses reminded her.

"So what do you want with me?" Alix asked.

"Nothing, really," Cynthia said. "It's your father we're interested in."

"You keep saying that, but I don't understand why."

Moses eyed her for a moment, considering his answer. Finally, he said, "Okay. Sure. Let's do this." He grabbed a chair and dragged it to the table, sat down and leaned it back on two legs, kicking out his feet.

"Grab a seat," he said.

Alix hesitated, trying to decide if she should just make a break for the door.

Which door? a voice in her head mocked. *The one with the chains on it?*

She decided she wasn't giving up anything by sitting down. All of it was to her advantage, anyway. *Time. Just keep using their time.* She pulled out a chair. The others found perches on the counters or grabbed chairs of their own.

"How much do you know about your dad's business?" Moses asked.

Alix shrugged noncommittally. "He's in PR."

"Public relations. Sure. But you know what kind of PR he does? You know what his work actually is?"

"It's like ads and stuff."

Cynthia leaned in. "Don't sell your dad short. He's a specialist. He works mostly in product defense and crisis communications. A lot of his focus is on science-litigation strategy and legislative outreach."

"I thought you said you didn't know what my dad did?" Alix accused.

Cynthia looked away. "I wanted to know if you knew. Do you understand what all that means?"

Alix thought back to what Dad had always said. "Nothing special. Just that he helps his clients tell their side of the story. A lot of times, people want to see things in black and white, so he helps make sure that they have the whole story. Otherwise, extremists—probably people like you—end up controlling the debate." She looked pointedly at Moses. "Sometimes there are more sides to a story than some people want to accept."

"Hot damn!" Moses started to slow-clap. "You're good!"

"He should hire you," Kook said. "Little Miss America PR sweetheart. You make him sound so reasonable."

"He is reasonable," Alix shot back.

"You believe that?" Moses asked, looking suddenly interested.

Alix started to answer, then hesitated. There it was again. That word.

Believe.

It was a fetish word for Moses. The guy just kept circling back to it.

"What do you think?" Alix said instead of answering.

"I think you don't have any choice," Moses said softly. "You've got to believe him. He's your dad. Every little girl believes her daddy."

Kook snorted at that, but Moses ignored her. He laced his fingers across his stomach, watching Alix thoughtfully.

213

"What is it with you and belief?" Alix asked.

Moses smiled. "Let me tell you a story."

"Like a fairy tale?"

"Once upon a time, there was a princess..." Adam started.

Moses cut him off with a grin. "Once upon a time, there was a huge company called Marcea Pharmaceuticals. Marcea made all kinds of drugs to make people's lives better, and they made a lot of money doing it. But one day, people started saying that one of Marcea's drugs was a killer. Rumor was that a cholesterol drug called Alantia was causing heart attacks. Not a lot. Not every person to who took the drug... but more than just a few. Maybe a couple in every hundred, but still, way more than if people didn't take the drug.

"Now, this was a bad thing. Marcea had a lot of money riding on this cholesterol drug of theirs. Alantia was supposed to make people healthy, and it was killing them. And now the Food and Drug Administration was getting involved, threatening to force the drug off the market." He paused. "So... what could the company do? They'd spent hundreds of millions of dollars on research and were looking to make billions on the upside. The news that their drug was dangerous was a disaster for them.

"So Marcea made a plan. They decided that Alantia wasn't the problem. The problem was all the research reports that were claiming their drug caused heart attacks. The drug wasn't the problem. The science was the problem. The science that was getting reported to the FDA, and that the FDA was starting to believe... *that* was the problem. The FDA was starting to *believe*"—Moses smiled at the word—"that Alantia killed people."

"Marcea had to show that the health studies were biased," Cynthia said. "Otherwise, the FDA was going to shut them down."

Moses continued. "So Marcea Pharmaceuticals hired some scientists to test their drug some more. And they hired more scientists to go back and reanalyze the studies that showed Alantia was a heart attack in a pill. They needed to show that the old studies were flawed. If they could raise doubts about those studies, then they were safe. Of course, they knew if it was Marcea's own scientists doing the work, nobody was going to believe them, so they hired outside people who weren't directly connected to them to do the work. They paid university researchers. They paid private foundations—"

"So?" Alix interrupted. "It's a free country. They can study what they want. If someone was trying to kill your business, you'd fight back, too."

"Absolutely," Moses agreed. "And luckily for Marcea, it turned out that every single one of Marcea's new studies showed that their drug was safe and that the FDA was wrong to be worried. False alarm."

Cynthia said, "The news got reported everywhere, and the FDA backed off."

Kook added, "And, of course, Marcea Pharmaceuticals's stock jumped through the roof. Sales kept rolling. Execs get their bonuses. Everybody's happy."

"So?" Alix asked. "What's your point?"

"So?" Moses smiled. "You should be proud."

"About?" Alix pressed. "What's this got to do with me?"

Cynthia sighed. "Your dad came up with the science strategy and got the word out. He let everyone know that Alantia was safe. It was a textbook case of successful product defense."

"So? Then he did the right thing. If something is safe, people should know it's safe. Why should I care about this?"

Kook flipped her chair forward and leaned in, her smile as sharp as a knife. "Three years later every one of Marcea's studies was discredited."

Cynthia said, "All those studies Marcea commissioned were flawed. Bad sample sizes, altered dosages, tons of problems. Every single study they commissioned was proved to be garbage. But the press didn't see any of that. They didn't catch it. Some journal of chemistry reports a study—and it's the truth—and the news cycle rolled on. The FDA didn't regulate.

"Marcea made a billion dollars every year during those three years that they were touting their counterstudies and keeping Alantia on the market. Over a hundred thousand people had heart attacks. Half of them died. The drug finally got banned."

Moses was looking at her. "Your dad got a performance bonus for keeping the drug on the market for those extra three years. Fifty thousand extra heart attack deaths and your dad got a million-dollar bonus."

He paused.

"My dad was one of the ones who died."

19

"THAT'S A LIE!"

"The hell it is!"

They had both surged to their feet. Now Cynthia interceded, putting herself between them.

"How about we keep the shouting to a minimum?"

"Fine." Moses scowled. "You talk to her. Maybe she'll listen to you." He didn't sit down but began pacing instead.

Cynthia gently pressed Alix back into her seat and motioned Moses to still himself as well. "Listen, Alix. I know this is a lot to take in. Every one of us had a hard time when we first heard it, but Moses is telling the truth. Banks Strategy Partners was the lead product-defense consultant for Marcea. Your dad ran their strategy, from the beginning, when they needed to defend the science, to the end, when they were in court and had to defend themselves from the lawsuits."

"I saw your dad in court," Moses said, as he kept pacing. "Sitting about ten feet from me."

"A lot of us saw him in court," Adam said.

Kook and Tank and Cynthia were nodding.

Alix felt ill.

Cynthia said, "Your father's company is the gold standard for product defense. There are other companies that can do some of what he does: Exponent, Gradient, ChemRisk, the Weinberg Group, Hill and Knowlton..."

Alix started at the names of companies she recognized from her father's own work history. Cynthia continued. "A lot of firms can help a company 'tell their side of the story,' as your dad apparently likes to say, but Banks Strategy Partners is the best. Your father does the PR and George Saamsi does the science, and they've got a hundred people under them to help make their plans happen."

"They're kind of like the Williams and Crowe of product defense," Kook said. She was rocked back on two legs of her chair, watching the proceedings with a smirk on her face. "Mercenaries for hire. Top gun to the top bidder, you know?"

"You're lying."

"About what?" Adam asked. "That your dad got a million-dollar bonus, or that he's got a hundred other clients just like Marcea?"

"My dad doesn't kill people," Alix said.

"Actually, what I think you're claiming is that he doesn't *murder* people," Moses said. "I think we'd all agree with that.

We know your dad isn't a murderer, because, otherwise, he'd be locked up like all the other serial killers. That's what Texas has got death row for, right?"

"Ipso facto," Cynthia said. "If he's not in jail, he must not be a murderer."

"So, yeah," Moses said, "according to the cops and the laws, your dad isn't a murderer. And Marcea Pharmaceuticals isn't either, and none of the paid scientists who did all the screwy studies are murderers, either. They're all upstanding citizens with nice houses and nice families who go to work every day and come home and kiss their nice kids good night. They go to Little League games on the weekends and donate to their churches and volunteer at the local homeless shelter, and they probably pet their dogs every day. They're all double-plus-good people living the double-plus-good American dream."

"But people are still dead," Tank said.

Kook had stopped smirking. She rocked forward and brought her chair down so she was looking Alix in the eye from across the table. "It's kind of funny when you think about it. If you go to a school and shoot a bunch of kids, we call that murder. But if you're a CEO who keeps a cholesterol drug on the street for an extra three years and you take out fifty thousand people with heart attacks, you get a bonus and your face on the cover of *Forbes*."

Alix was feeling more and more trapped. Part of her wanted to scream at them that they were all insane, but another part wasn't sure. A cruel worm of doubt twisted inside her. How much did she really know about the work Dad did? How much did she really understand?

It doesn't matter, Alix told herself. *Just play for time. Just keep them talking. Play for time.*

She took a deep breath, trying not to show them how rattled she felt. "I don't know the CEO of Marcea," she said. "I've got no connection to these people."

"We don't care about Marcea," Moses said. "Just like we don't care about DuPont. Or General Electric. Or Bayer. Or Dow Chemical. Or Merck. Plenty of people know about them. There are whole books written about this stuff. Investigative journalism articles. *New York Times. LA Times. Chicago Tribune. 60 Minutes.* Lots of people know what these companies get up to." He looked at her seriously. "I mean, sure, I admit, at first I wanted to get back at Marcea, but then I started seeing all these crazy connections. I started seeing all these companies using the same tricks."

"I'd like to think I helped a little with that," Cynthia said drily.

"Credit where credit's due." Moses inclined his head. "It almost takes a genius to dig all this up. To see all these companies coming up with the same strategies. And at that point, you realize that Marcea isn't the problem. I mean, sure, they're evil, but they don't know how to keep their heart attack pill on the market on their own. They need your dad for that."

Cynthia said, "Everywhere we looked, Banks Strategy

220

Partners popped up. Even when another product-defense company was involved, a lot of times it turned out that they subcontracted back to BSP. Simon Banks is the best there is, and everybody in the industry knows it."

"When you absolutely, positively have to confuse the hell out of an issue," Kook said, "call Banks Strategy Partners."

Moses said, "You know what they call BSP? The people who hire them? The people who use your dad's methods?"

Alix didn't want to know. She didn't want to hear it.

"The Doubt Factory," Moses said. "It's a good name, right? Because, really, that's what your dad produces. He doesn't make products. He makes doubt.

"If you want everyone to ignore those FDA studies that say you're killing people with your drug, you go to Simon Banks and buy a little doubt. You sprinkle it all over the issue. You spread it around. Pretty soon, the Doubt Factory has people so confused that you can go on selling whatever the hell it is for just a little longer. Aspirin. Tobacco. Asbestos. Leaded gasoline. Phthalates. Bisphenol A—the list goes on."

"Azicort," Tank said with a cough.

Moses glanced over at Tank, nodding. "Azicort. For sure we're interested in Azicort."

"What's that?" Alix asked.

Kook smiled sweetly. "Oh, nothing. Just an asthma drug that causes comas and death."

"We think," Cynthia interjected.

Kook rolled her eyes. "Oh, come on. We know it. How many people were in Tank's class action? Like, fifty?"

Cynthia said to Alix, "We know Kimball-Geier Pharmaceuticals hired BSP about a year before Tank had a near-death experience, which, given your dad's track record, looks pretty suspicious."

"But I didn't do anything," Alix protested. "This isn't my fault. I wasn't involved with any of this."

"Yeah, well," Tank said with another cough, "neither were we."

20

"SO..." ALIX STARED AT ALL of them. "You want to... what? Ransom me or something?"

"Nah, girl," said Kook. "That's them. They're the ones who care about money. Money isn't shit."

"It beats starving," Alix shot back.

Moses snorted. "Adam, how much you got in your bank account?"

"I'm down now." He shrugged. "Probably still about a hundred and fifty thousand dollars."

"You are such a shit!" Cynthia said. "You've been holding out!"

Adam smiled unapologetically. "I figured we'd still have expenses. Might need to throw another party and earn some more. Why? What are you down to?"

"Forty, maybe? Seitz life was expensive."

Adam grinned. "Nice threads, though. You got to admit you dress fine these days."

"I got sixty K," Kook volunteered.

"I don't have any money," Tank said.

"That's 'cause your lawyers sucked ass," Kook said.

"You see?" Moses said to Alix. "Most of us already got money."

"You, too?" Alix challenged Moses. "How much money do you have?"

"Me?" Moses waved his hand at the factory around them. "I got mine tied up in real estate." He laughed. "It's not about money at this point. We've all got our blood money, straight from the source. Every one of us, we've all been paid. We got it from lawsuits and settlements. We got it from reparations.... The problem is that people like your dad think money matters. The people who hold your dad's leash are all about money. It's all they understand—keeping the money spigot turned on full bore. Us?" His expression turned cold. "Don't ever think this is about money. It's about a whole hell of a lot, but one thing's for sure: It's not about the goddamn money."

"If you can't buy your parents out of the morgue, money isn't worth a whole lot," Cynthia said. "None of us are in it for the money."

Slowly it dawned on Alix what they were saying. The factory was starting to make sense. The kids all living in it. The pizza boxes piled in the corner of the kitchen. She suddenly saw Cynthia in a new light. She thought of the factory's shower room, and Cynthia's lockers full of clothes. Armani. Versace. Michael Kors. All that beautiful clothing hung in those banged-up lockers.

Other things started making sense, too: Adam and Tank riding their skateboards in the cavernous, empty factory. The gutter girl, Kook, her face pierced and tatted up in ways that she'd never seen a girl her age modified. And at the center of it all, Moses.

This motley group of teens, living in this factory. Not an adult in sight. No family dinners.

No supervision. Just a bunch of kids, throwing raves and partying. Feeding gourmet cheese to their rats.

"You're orphans," Alix said slowly.

"Told you she was smart," Moses said to the others.

"You all live here, for real?" Alix asked.

"For now," Moses said. "We've got business here. Might keep us in town for a little while longer."

"My dad," Alix said.

"We like to think of him as the target," Kook said.

Alix felt light-headed. She wanted air, and there was no way to get out. The room was feeling tighter and tighter. "My dad didn't kill your families!"

"Nobody's saying he did," Cynthia soothed.

"We're not?" Kook raised her eyebrows. "I thought that was exactly what we were saying."

Alix felt nauseated. They were all orphans. "My dad didn't kill your families," she said again.

Moses said, "Well, me and Cynthia, our parents were

Alantia heart attacks. Adam's aunt was asbestosis. Kook's parents were a cancer cluster. Tank didn't have parents, but Azicort did his sister, and then did a pretty good number on him before the doctors figured out what was happening."

"I—" Alix started, but her throat caught. The room felt smaller and smaller. She couldn't breathe.

"If you really want to split hairs, I guess your dad didn't kill our parents directly," Moses was saying, "but he sure helped the people who did. Every time someone needed protecting, he was there to give them good, profitable advice. Every time. He's at the center of it. He's the connection to all of them. He's the one who helps them get away with it."

Alix was beginning to feel as if she wasn't in her body. Everything felt surreally distant. Blackness pinched the edges of her vision.

Breathe. Just breathe.

She gripped the table, trying to anchor herself. Her father was…what? A criminal? *A killer?*

She stood abruptly. Swayed. Grabbed a chair for support. Everyone leaped up, ready to block her from escaping.

"I need air," Alix gasped. "I need…" She started for the kitchen door.

Adam blocked her. "We aren't done talking."

Alix looked around desperately. Found Moses. "Please," she begged. "I won't run away. I just…I just…bathroom."

Cynthia came to her rescue and shoved Adam aside. "Cut it out, Adam. Let her go."

Adam said something in retort, but Alix wasn't paying

attention. She was already stumbling out into the wide factory expanse. The building loomed around her, huge and empty. She realized she was lost.

"Bathrooms are back over there," Cynthia said, pointing.

She barely made it. She dashed to the row of sinks and threw up. Cheese sandwich and bile. She gagged again, but nothing else came up except ropes of spit. Alix stared down at the sink, at the contents of her emptied stomach. She ran water, trying to make it go away, trying not to think about the kids in the kitchen. All of them looking at her accusingly. All of them without parents. All of them alone.

Her stomach twisted and she puked again.

When she was finally done, she carefully washed her bile down the sink. She felt numb to the world. Everything still felt distant, as if someone else was performing the task of cleaning up.

Small things. Just focus on small things.

Alix found herself staring into the cracked mirror over the sink. A washed-out face stared back at her. The girl's hair was tangled from a shower, unbrushed. Deep circles of exhaustion bruised the skin around her eyes. She didn't recognize herself.

A cold thought circled in her mind:

If everything you know about yourself isn't true, how do you know who you are?

How do you know what truth is?

How do you know if someone is lying to you?

And then another, colder thought:

What if everyone is lying to you?

Alix remembered Dad sitting with her, watching TV, making jokes about CEOs who were lighting themselves on fire. Remembered his sneaking another cup of coffee when Mom wasn't watching. Remembered his bringing her home drunk from a party and never busting her. Just telling her to stay safe, because he loved her and didn't want her to ever make a permanent mistake.

Who are you if you can't trust anyone at all?

Alix felt like she was going insane. She couldn't peel the truth away from the lies. Who could she trust? Moses? Dad? Cynthia?

Cynthia had lied to her for the last eight months. She'd sat beside her in AP Chem, pretending to really care about her. Alix's eyes narrowed at the thought. That betrayal was something she could hold on to. That was real, at least: Cynthia had been lying to her for the last eight months.

Alix stared at her reflection and watched herself nod deliberately, an acknowledgment of that single fact. She'd been a fool, and Cynthia had used her.

And that led to another thought, an anchor she could hold tight to: *You can't trust any of them. They're using you.*

That thought was followed by another realization. She was alone. Cynthia had followed her across the factory, but had let Alix be alone.

Alix quickly scanned the locker room, looking for an escape. She spied a few windows, high up above the lockers.

As quietly as she could, she dragged a bench over to a

window and climbed up. The glass was smudged with grime and dust. She wiped it with the sleeve of Cynthia's hoodie and peered out.

Bars on the outside. Alix was disappointed, but not surprised. She couldn't see anyone outside, anyway. She wondered if she broke the window and started shouting if someone might hear her. A last option, she decided. If she started screaming, Cynthia would hear, and everyone else would come running. But still, she needed some way to alert anyone who might be outside.

A note?

Alix craned her neck, trying to see where the factory was. Hunting for landmarks. The factory area had been deserted when they'd arrived at night, and from the lack of sound outside, she didn't feel particularly hopeful that someone would conveniently wander by to help her out, but still, maybe a note dropped from the window…

But too much time had passed already. Cynthia was sure to check on her any second. Rescue notes and screaming would have to wait. Alix climbed down and carefully dragged the bench back into place. She returned to the sink, drank a little water, and swished her mouth.

It was then that Alix realized each sink had its own toothbrush on the sill. Six basins in a row, five toothbrushes beside the basins. Even Sophie didn't have that many sinks in her bathroom.

Alix smirked. They were just people. Just kids. Just crazy

kids. They weren't superhuman. The mundane thought of the whole 2.0 crew brushing their teeth at their individual sinks gave her a kind of strength.

She stared again at herself in the mirror.

They want something from you. They wouldn't be talking to you if they didn't want something from you. That means you're in control.

She wanted to laugh at the idea that she had any control at all, but still, it was something to hold on to. They might have her trapped, but she had something they needed.

So all she needed was to fool them. To make them believe that she was a reasonable person. They wanted someone to listen to their story.

So let them talk.

She'd listen. She'd let them talk. She'd let them use as much time as they wanted, talking.

And then...?

Alix stared at herself in the mirror. She hardened her expression.

You're a fighter, she told herself. *So fight.*

21

WHEN ALIX CAME OUT OF the bathroom, she found Cynthia waiting for her.

"You okay?" Cynthia asked, looking concerned.

It's all an act, Alix reminded herself. *She doesn't care about you at all. She's just someone who wants to use you.*

Alix made herself smile wanly. "It's a lot to take in."

The 2.0 crew were all out of the kitchen. Kook was riding a skateboard, showing Tank how he could really kill himself. Adam was sitting on the floor with one of their rats, dropping a nugget trail of what looked like deeply veined blue cheese in front of it, encouraging it to follow where he led. Moses was standing a little ways off, keeping one eye on his crew, and one on Cynthia and Alix's approach.

Kook shot up the skate ramp, caught its edge one-handed and kicked her feet over her head. She held the stand, one-handed, frozen, graceful, then let herself drop and come

231

swooping down. As she shot past, she had the most intense expression Alix had ever seen on anyone's face. She looked like some kind of pierced demon.

Tank tried the same move and crashed.

Despite the fact that the kid had apparently welded her cage, Alix couldn't help wincing. The crash looked brutal.

"So," Alix said, trying to find her way into conversation with Moses. "Why don't you just blow up my dad if you hate him so much?"

"That's not what we're about," Moses said.

"You don't want to kill my dad. You don't want to ransom me. So what do you want?" Alix asked for what felt like the hundredth time.

Cynthia cleared her throat. "Your father trusts you."

"And?" Alix prompted.

"We want to get access to his main office network. We can't get into his offices in DC. But if you get us on his laptop in his home office, we think we can get inside."

"You've got to be kidding. He doesn't tell me things like that."

"It's not that difficult," Moses said. "Kook's good with computers. We just need a little of your help. Your dad trusts you. All you need to do is install a little bit of software, and we'll do the rest."

"I've seen his computer," Alix said. "It's password-protected. He's not going to tell me his password. I've never even been on that computer."

"You don't need to worry about that. We just need you to

232

be able to get physical access to his laptop while he's logged in. Just need you to do something like spill a little coffee on him in his study, and while he's gone, plug in a special something we've got rigged up. We think we can do the rest."

"Stuxnet, baby!" Kook called from where she was making another run at the ramp. "It's a worm. DoD-certified badass wormtastic. I modified it. You just plug it in the USB drive. As long as it gets plugged in while he's logged in, I can do the rest." She shot up the ramp, did another handstand, and came whooshing down again.

"What's that going to accomplish?" Alix asked.

"We want the Doubt Factory's client files. All of them. Your dad's clients spend a lot of time denying that their products are dangerous. We know they're lying, but that's almost impossible to prove. If we can get those files, it would show exactly what they know, and exactly what they're trying to protect themselves against."

"And then..."

"And then we'll put the news up all over the Net. We'll send the juicy bits to every newspaper and website that still knows how to report a story. We think there are enough smoking guns in your dad's files to indict a couple dozen CEOs. It would open the door to civil suits, wrongful-death suits, class actions, government investigations...."

"And destroy my family in the process," Alix pointed out.

"Karma is a bitch," Adam observed from his place on the floor where he was feeding his rat.

"Screw you," Alix shot back.

"Sorry, don't swing that way. Moses is into you, though."

"Shut up, Adam," Moses and Cynthia said at the same time. They both said it so quickly and automatically that Alix had to laugh. Moses glanced over, looking embarrassed.

"What?"

"Nothing," Alix said. But it was sort of funny, how automatic they'd sounded. As if everyone was in the habit of telling Adam to shut up.

Then she realized what Adam had said, about Moses being "into" her, and she felt herself blush suddenly. *Why are you blushing?* She looked away, concentrating on Kook and Tank, watching them skate, and avoiding meeting Moses's eyes.

Cynthia must have sensed Alix's discomfort because she said, "Come on. We can watch them skate from over here. You can sit down."

She led Alix to an old storage rack and climbed up onto the first level of shelving. Alix followed, and soon they were both perched five feet off the ground. Alix let her legs dangle off the edge as she watched the activity below.

Kook finished her run and kicked the skateboard to Adam. He passed the rat into Kook's arms. A second later he was rolling away. Neither of them said anything during the exchange. It was like they knew each other so well they didn't have to say anything at all. Perfectly intertwined, and yet Adam and Kook were completely mismatched compatriots. The sleek boy who seemed so concerned about his every pose and the pale gutter-punk girl who seemed bent mostly on putting as much hardware into her face as was humanly possible. And yet they traded skateboard and rat without friction or comment.

All of them were like that. It was as if Moses had gone around recruiting the most bizarre group of misfits he could possibly find. If Adam and Kook looked like an odd pairing, what about Tank, the frail Latino-looking kid who reminded her of a Hobbit? And Cynthia, the perfect Seitz student? Not a single one belonged with the others. Like glassware at the thrift store. A mug next to a martini glass, next to a chunky wineglass, next to a shot glass, and only hopeful arrangement made them seem as if they belonged together. And yet this strange crew of kids still somehow managed to fit.

Alix snuck a glance at Moses. He was watching Tank, and she was surprised to see the affection on his face.

Tank crashed again. Moses flinched and leaned forward, as if he were about to rush to the boy, then caught himself and leaned back against the storage racks, pretending to be nonchalant about the whole thing.

Alix couldn't help smiling. The hard version of Moses was gone again, replaced by the ... what?

The decent version?

She realized that Moses was now looking over at her, somehow aware of her eyes on him. Alix looked away.

Why do you even care?

But apparently she did.

My world is insane.

235

Moses took her look as an invitation to join her. He climbed up to where she and Cynthia had found their perch.

"So," Alix said, "have you changed your mind and decided to let me go?"

"Don't know. Have you decided to help us?"

Alix knew the smart thing would be to say yes.

"No."

"Then I guess not."

"Why would you trust me, anyway?" she snapped. "I could just lie and tell you whatever you wanted to hear."

"So why don't you?" Moses asked.

"Because—" She broke off. *Why don't you just lie?* It made sense. Just tell him whatever he wanted to hear and then run like hell. And yet here she was, stupidly saying the wrong thing.

"Maybe I'm stubborn," she said.

"You want to know what I think?" Moses asked.

Alix snorted. "Yeah. Sure. Give me your theory of Alix."

He laughed. "'Theory of Alix.' I like that." He paused, smiling. "Okay, here's my theory of Alix."

"Constructed from long hours of observation," she added.

"Indeed." Abruptly, Moses's smile disappeared. "From many long hours." And his expression became so intense that Alix felt a sudden chill of self-consciousness.

She realized she didn't want to hear whatever he had to say.

He was looking at her too seriously, as if he were carving her up into tiny pieces and inspecting each part. It was

236

so intense and invasive that she felt as if she were naked. She was surprised to find that she felt an almost overwhelming shame.

She didn't want him to say anything. He was peeling away all the layers of who she was, and she knew before he opened his mouth what he would say.

He would look at her vacations to Saint Barts and her parties in the Hamptons and all her stupid obsessed conversations about boys with Cynthia and all her worrying about SATs and whether she should go to Harvard or Dartmouth or Bryn Mawr, and he would see her as a joke.

She suddenly could see herself in his eyes, and she hated what he saw.

"Never mi—"

"You're ethical."

"What?" Alix looked at him, confused.

"You're ethical."

Alix wasn't sure she liked that assessment any more than the one she'd been expecting.

"You make me sound like some kind of Goody Two-Shoes."

He laughed at that. "I didn't say you were obedient. I said you were ethical. They're different. It's why you're stuck now. You know we're right about your dad—"

"I didn't say that."

"—and you also know you love him. So you're stuck in a lose-lose situation, and you keep trying to find some way out."

"The way out would be to lie to you."

"So why haven't you?" He was smiling as he answered his own question. "Because you're ethical."

Alix rolled her eyes. "Because I'm stupid."

The truth was, she had no idea why she hadn't just told him what he wanted to hear. Was she actually starting to believe his crazy conspiracy theories? Was she having some kind of Stockholm syndrome moment? All she knew was that each time she considered lying to him, she felt queasy.

"I know you, Alix," Moses said. "I really have been watching you for a long time."

"Yay," Alix said bitterly. "Me and my shadow."

"You can try to make a joke out of it, but I see you. I've seen you with your brother, trying to take care of him. I saw you take Cynthia in."

Alix glanced sidelong at the girl sitting beside her. "She manipulated me."

"No. You helped her. She asked for help, and you helped her. The first day of school, she said she was lost at Seitz, and you took her in."

"That just says I'm a sucker."

"No." Cynthia shook her head. "It says you're kind."

"Oh, look, I'm kind and ethical. Nominate me for sainthood."

"There are worse things to be," Cynthia observed, and before Alix had a chance to reply, she jumped down from their perch, leaving Alix sitting alone with Moses.

"Cyn's right, you know," Moses said.

"So why am I not feeling like I won the lottery?"

"No one said being ethical was easy," Moses said. "But that's why you won't lie to me now about whether you're going to help us." He shrugged. "It's one of the things I always liked about you. You don't take the easy way."

"I could still lie to you."

"You won't."

"I might."

"You won't."

It was irritating to have him sit there, looking smug and psychoanalyzing her. She gave him a sour look. "Okay, so if you're so smart, why kidnap me? Why not just try talking to me instead? I mean, Christ, I've seen college recruiters who do a better job of selling than you do." She laughed. "Most people, when they want to change your mind, they don't resort to kidnapping."

"We tried, actually."

"That's funny. I didn't notice."

"You're right," Moses said with a laugh. "You didn't. We put Cyn right next to you for eight months. She had all kinds of questions for you about your dad. But it was like you were asleep. Everything went right past you. You were too cozy. So I decided to shake you awake."

"And now I get to spend the rest of my life in a factory."

"It's not about you."

"Right. It's about my dad. I get it."

"No." Moses jerked his chin toward Tank, who was still making runs at the ramp on his skateboard. "It's about him.

239

Kids like him." He waved his hand toward the rest of the 2.0 crew. "Kids like them."

"They don't really qualify as kids."

"We were all kids when this started. I was Tank's age when my dad had his heart attack."

Alix felt awkward at the mention of Moses's loss. "I'm sorry. I forgot—"

"Don't be. You didn't do it. Like you said, it's not your fault. You weren't involved."

"Still…"

"It's not on you," he said shortly. "You want to know what *is* on you, though? Whatever happens next. The next kid who sucks on Azicort like Tank's sister did—that's on you.

"She died because of Azicort. Tank barely made it. Doctors stuck him with so much adrenaline that the kid should still be bouncing off the walls. And there are going to be more kids like him, because your dad's working overtime to make sure Azicort doesn't get blamed."

"I think someone would notice if an asthma drug was killing people."

"Oh, sure, they notice. And then your dad and his good buddy George Saamsi get to work. They blame other medications. They blame genetic defects. They say patients didn't use the correct dose. They say it wasn't used as directed—that's what they said about Tank. I watched good old Santa Claus George get up in front of the FDA and show them studies that proved Azicort is as safe as houses."

"But you know better," Alix said drily.

"Damn straight."

"Because you're so much smarter than anyone else in the whole world."

"No. Because I'm paying attention."

Alix could feel her annoyance rising again. "Not every company is evil, you know. Just because someone sues McDonald's for having hot coffee, it doesn't mean the company was bad. It just means people are idiots. I know you like your big conspiracy theory and all, but maybe it was something else that made Tank sick."

"You sound like your dad."

"Go to hell."

"You know what's keeping Azicort on the market?"

"Is there any way I can keep you from telling me?"

"Doubt. As long as people are still in doubt about how dangerous Azicort is, it means no one has to do anything. Kimball-Geier gets to make another couple hundred million for the year, your dad gets a bonus, and everyone waits until next year to decide. As long as there's doubt, we can always wait until next year."

"Maybe there's legitimate doubt, though! Just because you want someone to blame doesn't mean you're right."

"I told myself that for a little while." Moses laughed. "But people like your dad have been doing this for the last hundred years. If you dig back, you can see the playbook getting built. First, it's DuPont and some chemical dye that's killing workers in the nineteen thirties. Then it's Big Tobacco fighting to keep their cigarettes from being blamed for lung cancer, and you've got asbestos fighting to keep themselves from being blamed for asbestosis, and then it's the lead industry, trying to keep lead in paint from being blamed for screwing with kids' brains. There's a whole kitchen cabinet full of household drugs that are using the same tricks. You know the aspirin industry tried to stop aspirin from being labeled for Reye's syndrome? Hell, even Tylenol used some of these plays. And then there's the chemicals. Look up diacetyl sometime. It makes microwave popcorn taste like butter, and it literally obliterates people's lungs when they breathe it."

"I don't understand—" Alix tried to interrupt, but Moses was rolling now. He held up his hand and didn't stop talking.

"At first, you think all these things are different, but then you start to see a pattern. The same scientific experts show up on different witness stands. The same tactics get used in different industries. At first, you think you're just obsessed because you're pissed about losing your mom and dad, and this is looking like a conspiracy. But you're a sane person, so you know conspiracies don't really exist, and, anyway, conspiracies are for crazy people, right? And you definitely don't want to think you're going crazy, because that means not only did you lose your parents, but you're also developing paranoid delusions.

"But still, it's right there in front of you like a neon sign. Every time a company gets in trouble, that company hires someone like Simon Banks, of Banks Strategy Partners. And you finally see it. It's not a conspiracy. It's just business. As long as they can keep the people confused, they can keep selling. Doesn't matter what it is. Microwave popcorn, Azicort, aspirin to little kids…"

"You really do sound like a conspiracy theorist."

"Theory, hell. It's just basic product defense. ExxonMobil spent a lot of money to try to make people doubt whether global warming was real. That's documented. It's not an accident people in the U.S. still can't make up their minds about whether it exists or not. An oil company mounted a straight-up propaganda campaign to keep them confused. They gave six hundred thousand dollars to the Heartland Institute and two million dollars to the Competitive Enterprise Institute, and if you're a regular person, that sounds like a lot of money. But if you're ExxonMobil, you make between fifteen and forty-five *billion* dollars in profit every year, so keeping people confused about global warming was actually dirt cheap to them."

He gave her a speculative look. "What would you be willing to do if you could make another forty-five billion in just one year? This is just an accounting problem for them." He shrugged. "Anyway, you don't need to believe me. It's just the truth."

"The truth."

"There actually is such a thing as unimpeachable truth, Alix. Not 'he said, she said.' Not 'in my opinion.' Just facts. Documented facts."

"Documented on the Internet, you mean. Mostly by crazies."

"No. Real truth. Unimpeachable truth. I like to think of it as Information 2.0."

"Is that what your 2.0 symbol is all about?"

"Sure. Right now, all we have is Information 1.0, right? And it makes it easy to obscure the truth about things. It makes it easy for your dad to make a living. But maybe there's a way to make information more solid. Make it more trust-worthy, you know? A way to cut through the lies to some-thing so solid and true and real that people like your dad can't undermine it. Real truth. Information 2.0. If you had that, it would change everything. You'd have a world where you could actually trust what people say."

"Sounds utopian."

"No. It's not utopian. Truth exists, Alix. We just have to hunt for it more right now. Some of it's sitting right in front of us. If you really believe your dad's clients are so innocent, then you just have to help us crack the Doubt Factory to con-firm it." Moses jerked his head toward where Tank was sitting on his skateboard, resting. "Let's take a peek at Kimball-Geier Pharmaceuticals. Let's see if they really think Azicort is as safe as they say it is."

Alix stared down at the floor.

Moses touched her arm gently. "My dad's death isn't on you. The next kid who goes into a coma from Azicort, though?" He nodded down at Tank, who was taking a hit off his inhaler. "The next one who dies? That *is* on you. Because now you know something is wrong, and you're not doing any-thing about it."

Alix swallowed. *Don't believe him. He's manipulating you. He's just screwing with your mind.*

"This is my family," she said. "You're asking me to hurt my family."

"It was my family, too," Moses said. "And Cyn's and Adam's and Kook's and Tank's, and lots more besides."

"What if there's nothing in those files?" Alix asked. "What then?"

Moses grinned abruptly. "Well, then you're off the hook, aren't you? That's the beauty of the truth, right? Then we're just a bunch of crazy kids with our heads full of conspiracy theories." He looked at her seriously. "There really is truth, Alix. We don't have to guess. If we can see those files, we'll know. We'll know the truth. And that's all we want. Truth."

Truth. He was saying there was truth, but all Alix could feel was that she was surrounded by lies. *How can you know who to trust? How can you know who's trustworthy?* Alix felt sick. "Okay," she said. "Fine. I'll do it."

Moses straightened, looking surprised. "Really?"

Alix closed her eyes, feeling wretched. "Don't look so shocked. Yeah. Really. Tell me what I need to do. I'll do it."

"Look at me and say that again," Moses said. "Tell me you're okay doing this."

Alix looked him in the eye and told him what he wanted to hear. It was easy to do.

He'd made a good case.

22

MOSES WAS STRUCK BY HOW vulnerable Alix looked. Standing before him in her borrowed clothes, just at the edge of the warehouse, she looked isolated and adrift, and he was surprised at how much pity he felt for her—for the situation that he'd put her in, for the fact that her world was going to be forever different... for everything, really.

Beyond the factory doors, Adam was waiting in the Dodge Dart, the engine already running. Moses held up the USB stick. It was tiny. Little more than the metal USB plug itself along with the barest bump of extra plastic. Kook and Tank had constructed it so that a person would hardly notice that something had been plugged into the computer. When it was inserted, it would hardly stick out at all.

"All you need to do is put this in his work computer," Moses said. "Just get this into his laptop, and you're done."

"Nothing else?" She looked doubtful.

"That's all. It's a lot, actually. The software on the stick will do the rest. Kook modified it. As long as it gets plugged in while he's already logged in, it should be able to do the rest. All you need to do his get him away from his computer for two seconds. Spill some soda on him, get him to change his shirt. That's it. Simple. It just takes a couple seconds for the software to run."

"And it won't...you won't point all this at him?"

Moses looked at her sadly. "If we find what we think we're going to find, people are going to be so busy suing Fortune 100 companies that no one's going to be worrying about you or your family. People will go after the money; all the money is in the companies. Banks Strategy Partners is tiny in comparison to the whales they'll be hunting."

He placed the USB stick in her hand.

She looked crushed and overwhelmed. But then, everyone did, when they first got the download. He remembered how he'd felt when he and Cynthia had started piecing it together years ago. Then Kook and Tank and Adam. Each one of them with his or her own story of loss, and all of them connected. All of them with their memories of sitting in courtrooms, too late to do anything except sue. No eye for an eye. No pound of flesh. Nothing except a check from some class action, with the lawyers walking away rich and everyone else putting a dollar amount on the bodies that they'd put in the ground.

Each time Moses had laid out the reality of their situation, they'd been shell-shocked at first, but they'd understood. But then, they'd all been predisposed to believe. They'd all felt the pain that Banks Strategy Partners dealt out to the world. It made them more than willing to step up.

Alix, though?

All she'd ever felt were the benefits of her father's work. While other people were watching their moms die of cancer or their dads on dialysis machines, Alix was flying down to Saint Barts. How much harder would it be for a girl like that to take in this kind of information?

What must it be like to find out that your father was involved in the dark business of zero-sum, balancing shareholder profits and executive bonuses against the ruin that they visited upon the people of the world?

Moses had watched Simon Banks long enough to think the man looked like a pretty decent dad. Distracted, sure, but he might actually be a better parent than either of Moses's own had been. For sure he was better than Tank's. The man was good people—to the people who were his.

But now Alix knew that her father was something more. The smiling facade hid dark bargains of power and influence and money.

A part of Moses longed to comfort her.

It's not your fault you got born into the wrong family, he thought. She wasn't responsible; her father was. She'd been born into the wrong place at the right time, and so now she was in her father's evil up to her neck.

Moses was surprised at how much empathy he felt for her, seeing her looking so wrecked.

But he sure as hell wasn't going to comfort her. That

wasn't his role. Cynthia was the one who was there to give Alix comfort. His job was to push the puzzle piece into place, just as he'd pushed every other puzzle piece into place, building a picture of the world that would finally make sense, that would finally let all his losses make sense.

Cynthia rattled the doors suggestively. "We doing this?"

Moses took out a strip of cloth. "Sorry," he said. "We've got to do this."

Alix looked surprised.

"Blindfold," Moses said apologetically. "We don't really want you leading people back here."

"You don't trust me," she accused.

"We're careful," Moses said. "Stakes are high."

"But I already saw the warehouse when we drove here," she protested.

"That was night, this is day." He shrugged. "Humor us. Cyn took you the long way last time. You're going direct now. We need to get you back to your old man before he calls in the feds. It's better if you don't know exactly how to get back."

Alix looked like she was about to protest again, but Cyn said, "It's safer for everyone like this."

Hesitantly, she nodded.

Moses took the cloth and wrapped it around her head, aware of the wisps of her brown hair, seeing her breathing tighten as she lost her sight. He stepped closer, smelling Cyn's shampoo in Alix's hair, so different from when he had stood behind her at Seitz when they'd started the cascade of events that had led to this moment.

Standing this close to her was surprisingly electric. He felt his own breathing quicken. Even disheveled and dressed in Cyn's clothes, Alix did something for him. Even with her veneer of upper-crust Connecticut stripped away, she made his pulse pound.

Or maybe it was because all that garbage had been stripped away.

In this moment, Alix seemed so much more real and normal, separated from the posturing of her wealthy suburbs. He remembered her in the cage. The way she'd seized on his wrist and yanked him into the bars. Surprisingly strong. So determined that he'd barely gotten away. As hard-core as Kook, as smart as Cynthia, as smooth as Adam. Moses liked her. Despite himself, he liked her.

It worried him.

"You keeping your eye on the target?" Kook had asked a few nights before. "You getting distracted?"

"Hell if I know," Moses muttered.

"What's that?" Alix asked, turning blindly toward him, reaching out.

"Nothing," Moses covered. "I wasn't saying anything."

"You going to take all day?" Cyn asked pointedly. Her gaze was knowing. Moses glared at her and finished the knots, making them tighter than necessary, showing that he didn't care. Proving to Cyn that Alix Banks wasn't anything other than a puzzle piece for him.

"All done," he said. He stepped back and was instantly sorry for the distance.

250

Cynthia took Alix's hand. She pulled aside the sliding warehouse door and led her out into bright sunshine. Moses and Kook followed, watching as Cyn guided her into the back of the car. Cyn climbed in with her, keeping her company, making her feel safe, and also making sure she didn't take off the blindfold.

They slammed the door. The little orange car pulled out.

"Here we go," Kook said.

"Yeah," Moses muttered. "Here we go."

"Think she'll do the right thing?"

Moses gazed up at the sun. There wasn't much to say. They'd made their choices. Moses was surprised to find the sun had moved so far across the sky. They'd been talking all day.

"We're betting a lot on this girl," Kook pressed.

"You're telling me."

"If this goes sidewise, we're all screwed," Kook said. "High stakes now."

"It was always high stakes. We're just finally seeing it."

"I'm just saying."

"She's the one," Moses said finally. "The plan's good. And she's the right one."

Tank came up behind them, rolling fast across the smooth concrete. He came to a halt, popped his skateboard. "She's the only one," he said.

"Well, then it's pretty much the same thing, isn't it?" Moses said.

Kook gave a snort of disgust. "You better be sure you know what you're doing."

Am I?

How could he be sure? It suddenly felt as if his careful puzzle had become jigsaw pieces flung into the air, with him counting on them all falling into place perfectly.

It was a gamble. No way around it. But he couldn't admit that to Kook. He couldn't admit that to anyone. He had to be strong. There was no way they'd follow if he showed how weak he was. He'd dragged them into this. It had been his plan.

You got them this far.

Against all the odds, he'd gotten them this far.

So now he was just going to have to get them out at the other end. He was going to step up, just the way his uncle had stepped up when the Nevada state investigators came down and wanted him to testify. Uncle Ty had made sure his gang was safe, even if the cops were going to throw the book at him, and Moses was going to do the same. *I'm going to get them through.*

"Just got to have faith," Moses murmured.

Kook snorted. "That sounds a lot like 'belief' to me."

Moses didn't answer the barb. It sounded a lot like belief to him, too. And it scared the hell out of him.

Can I trust you, Alix Banks?

He wanted to.

Don't trust. Test.

And yet, despite himself, he desperately wanted to trust her. He wanted to believe in her, and it scared him more than all his enemies combined.

23

ALIX'S HOUSE WAS MOBBED WITH people. Haverport PD cars clogged the drive, along with a half dozen of the low-slung armored SUVs that Williams & Crowe favored. An entire ants' nest of activity, all frantically trying to find her.

As Alix walked up the steps, she felt more and more like she wanted to turn in the other direction and flee. Cynthia and Adam had dropped her off a few blocks away, but as she made her way home, her pace slowed. Each step became more hesitant as she anticipated the storm she was about to face.

She braced herself, took a breath, and opened the door.

The startled shouts began before she was even halfway inside. People were looking up, surprised. Mom and Jonah and Dad, all looking shocked.

"Alix!" Dad's face broke wide with relief. He lunged for her with a glad cry and sob, and bundled her into his arms. Alix let herself sag against him and found herself crying as well, relieved that he didn't hate her for running off. Desperately grateful that she was home, and then Mom and Jonah were there, too, babbling and crying and hugging, and they were all together again. All of them together, and all of them safe. Alix wished she could stay inside their embrace forever.

Of course, Jonah broke the mood. He smacked her upside the head and said, "I'm the one who's supposed to do the running away!"

Alix would have smacked him back if he hadn't been crying as he said it.

■ ■ ■

Once everything had calmed down, people started asking her questions. Dad assured the police that they didn't need to file any other missing person's report, but Williams & Crowe stayed, and from their looks, she suspected they wouldn't be going away.

The interrogation started in earnest, beginning with Mom's haranguing her about ditching Lisa.

"You can't just run off and do things like this!"

Dad laid a quelling hand on Mom's arm. "It's all right. I think we can save the lecture for another time."

"What were you thinking?" Mom pressed. "You can't just run off with your friends to party! What are you wearing?"

"Leigh," Dad said. "It's all right." His eyes were serious. "I think Alix already knows the lesson."

Alix smiled gratefully at him.

"Why don't you tell us what happened," he said.

"I was—"

Alix started to say, *I was kidnapped. Cynthia was a plant. There are a bunch of kids who want to destroy you.*

She stopped short. It sounded insane. The second she tried to say the words, it made her feel like she was some kind of hysterical conspiracy theorist.

Alix felt in her pocket. The USB stick they'd given her was still there.

It was real. It was all real.

"I was—"

Kidnapped by a Stepford Student?

She remembered Cynthia. The girl who had pretended to be her friend but who had also stood up for her against all the rest of them when she'd been trapped in Moses's cage. She thought of the stories they'd told her. Their crazy, lunatic theories. Their ridiculous claims.

The man in front of her was supposed to be evil. Every day, Dad helped companies kill people, if 2.0 was to be believed.

It didn't make any sense. Even saying any of it made her feel like she was crazy. The USB key burned in her hand.

She found she couldn't say anything at all. She couldn't tell them about the kidnapping. She couldn't…"Dad?"

He saw her distress. "Is there something you need to talk about? Did something happen?"

"Can we talk in private?"

"In *private*?" Jonah complained. "But I want to see her get busted!"

255

"No one's getting busted," Dad said.

"She isn't?" Mom asked, surprised.

They exchanged one of their parental talk-about-it-later-not-in-front-of-the-kids looks, and Mom subsided. Alix wondered who would win out in the end and how bad her grounding would be.

"Please, Dad. I just want to talk in private."

He smiled gently. "Let's go into my office."

As they entered, Alix caught a glimpse of his laptop, sitting open on his desk. She felt guilty just seeing it. All it would take was a little misdirection. She could plug in the little USB stick and walk away, and forget about it. Moses and his crew could do whatever they did.

Dad was looking at her, puzzled. "Are you all right?"

Alix felt ill again. All the things Moses and Cynthia and everyone had been saying came rushing back. All the accusations. All the companies.

He's your dad.

Alix pulled the USB stick out of her pocket and offered it to him. She couldn't meet his eyes.

"What's this?"

"It's a USB...." She trailed off.

Never mind. It's nothing. Just a funny thing I got at a rave. Kind of embarrassing, actually. Can I have it back?

"I think it's a virus."

It felt as if a dam were breaking. Suddenly she could breathe. "I think it's a virus. I didn't run away. I was kidnapped. It was 2.0. You're right. They were trying to come after me. They were coming after us. And they said horrible things about you, and I didn't want to believe them, but they sounded so real...."

The words kept pouring out of her. More and more, a river of all the fears and worries she had been keeping back while she'd been trapped. She could feel tears welling up. And before she knew it, she was crying again as she told him everything, purging all her guilt for doubting him, all her horror and fear, all her powerlessness.

Dad pulled her close as she kept talking, and for the first time since the kidnapping, she felt safe.

■ ■ ■

A little while later, he called Lisa into the room, and she had Alix go over everything again, slower, with details that she took down in a notebook. She questioned Alix seriously and without comment.

When Alix apologized for being an idiot, Lisa just shook her head and said that she knew what it was like to be seventeen, and Alix had felt a gush of relief at the forgiveness.

"You mean these are all kids?" Lisa asked finally. She looked shocked.

"Yeah. I mean, they're my age. High school, you know? Except for the little one, Tank. He's younger. He's like twelve or thirteen, I think."

"Kids," Dad said, shaking his head.

Lisa was scribbling in her notebook. "Were there any adults involved?"

"You mean, like, over-eighteen adults?" Alix shook her head. "I don't think so. They were all young."

"A bunch of kids," Dad muttered again. "Just a bunch of crazy kids."

Lisa was waving in another Williams & Crowe agent to review the details again with Alix. Lisa dug into Alix's story with an intensity of focus that made it feel more like an interrogation, but Alix didn't complain. After all the trouble she'd created for everyone, and Lisa in particular, she had the feeling she owed Death Barbie some meek obedience.

She showed Lisa the USB drive. The woman took it with two fingers, regarding it with a revulsion that Alix would normally have reserved for a cockroach found deep-fried in a plate of french fries. "We'll have it analyzed," she said.

"Did they hurt you?" Dad asked.

"Not really. Just when I yanked Moses against the cage. But I hurt him a lot more than he hurt me. I think I chipped his tooth." As she said it, she realized that it might sound like she was bragging, but Lisa and Dad and the other agent were all smiling. Alix smiled, too. *Screw him. He deserved it.*

"And they kept you in a cage for how long?" Lisa asked, still writing furiously.

"I don't know. I slept." Alix realized she didn't even know what day it was.

"A cage," Dad fumed. He was looking angrier and angrier. Alix didn't think she'd ever seen him so mad.

"What are you going to do?" she asked.

Her father exchanged a look with Lisa. "You say it was in a warehouse?" he said.

"Yeah. On the south side of Hartford. Where all the warehouses and the trains run."

"Do you think you can lead us back there?" Lisa asked.

Alix nodded. "Yeah. I remember from when Cynthia drove me. It was getting dark, but I know exactly where it is. They didn't let me see it when we were coming back. But I remember the exits. I'm pretty sure I can find it."

Lisa's smile was almost sharklike. Alix hesitated, suddenly uncertain. "What will happen to them?"

Lisa looked impatient. "Well, they've been breaking a lot of laws, Alix. There's conspiracy. There's fraud. There's kidnapping. Probably other things, depending on how aggressively the DA goes after them."

"Aggressively," Dad declared. "She'll go after them aggressively."

Lisa nodded. "There you go. They'll be brought up on charges. The ones who are minors will probably be treated differently, but it sounds like the ringleaders may be over eighteen. We'll press to try them all as adults, though. This is serious. It's not a game. And the things they're doing have escalated way beyond pranks."

Alix swallowed. "We can't just, I don't know…give

them...some kind of warning...I mean..." She trailed off. "I mean, I think they're just really confused. They're just kids," she said again.

"Harris and Klebold were just kids," Lisa said. "Give a kid a TEC-9, and you've got a killer. Today, they're trying their hand at kidnapping; tomorrow, who knows how many bodies we're sorting."

Still Alix hesitated.

Lisa knelt down in front of her. "Time's passing, Alix. If they suspect their plan isn't working, they'll pack up and run. They've been doing this for a little while already. And every time they do something, they escalate. They're learning, Alix. Every time they succeed, they learn. You're the only person who can stop them before someone gets hurt."

Alix swallowed, wishing there was some clear answer. She thought of Cynthia, playing as her friend. Moses, so hot and cold. Kook and Adam and Tank.

"They're orphans," she said. "I mean, they're alone. Maybe they're just hurt and confused."

Lisa looked at her kindly. "They're escalating, Alix. It started with tagging. But now it's gone beyond that. They raided a lab and stole a semitruck full of rats. Then they assaulted your school's headmaster. Then they drugged you, and put you in a cage. They're out of control. We can't guess what they'll do next. And when they find out this little virus trick has failed, they'll escalate again."

What was right, and what was wrong? It was so impossible to tell. "Okay," Alix said finally. "I'll show you. But only if you let me go with you all the way. I want to see them."

"Alix…"

"I have to see them. I have to go back."

■ ■ ■

Lisa made Alix wear a bulletproof vest.

"They don't even have guns," Alix protested.

"Do you remember the last time we had a conversation about safety?" Lisa asked. "I think that time, you ended up spending a night in a cage in a factory while we all tore our hair out looking for you."

Alix subsided into abashed submission, and Lisa fitted her with the vest.

Now Alix sat in the SUV, watching with interest as Lisa pulled on her own body armor, along with the rest of the Williams & Crowe team. Dad sat beside her, his expression hard. He'd tried several times to persuade her to wait at home, to just show them on Google Maps where they needed to go, but she had remained adamant. In the end, he'd come along, too, as if he were going to be more protection than the professionals from Williams & Crowe. She was glad to have a familiar and comforting presence there, though, as they got closer and closer to the factory.

Alix had expected the police or FBI to be with them, but it was only five SUVs full of Williams & Crowe people who navigated slowly between the warehouses, letting Alix zero in on the one where she'd been kept.

"You're sure they don't have weapons?" Lisa asked as she loaded rounds into her tear gas gun. It had a drum for the tear gas canisters and a short, fat muzzle so wide that Alix thought she could almost slide her hand inside.

"I don't think so," Alix said.

"You don't think so? Or you know?"

"I didn't see anyone with guns."

"We need to be sure," Lisa said. "Did you see any evidence that they had any weapons?"

"Well, the one kid talked about making things explode. The little one, Tank, said that. But he just said something like that once. He was like some kind of tinkerer or something."

"A bomb?" Lisa prompted. "Was he making a bomb?"

"I don't know. He didn't say that, exactly."

Alix had the uncomfortable feeling that her words meant different things to her than they did to Lisa, because her bodyguard was already nodding significantly to her compatriots and radioing to the other vehicles. "We're going in hot. Possible explosive ordnance."

"What's 'going in hot' mean?" Alix asked.

Lisa glanced back. "It means we aren't going to give them a chance to blow us up."

"I didn't say they had a bomb rigged," Alix protested.

"Better safe than sorry," Lisa said. She slammed a bullet-proof helmet over her head. Beefy guys were climbing out of the other vehicles. They, too, had blunt guns with tear gas rounds, but they also had what looked like assault rifles slung on their shoulders.

Alix reached over the backseat and grabbed Lisa before she could exit. "The one kid, Tank. He has asthma. Will the tear gas hurt him?"

"If it does, we'll revive him after."

"You'll *what*?"

But Alix didn't have a chance to say anything else because Lisa's radio squawked to say the rest of her people were in place. "Stay here," she ordered. "If things go sidewise, we can't have you in the cross fire."

She pushed the door of the SUV closed and stole toward the warehouse. More black armored forms were scampering for the building. Alix saw them holding automatic rifles at the ready. More and more Williams & Crowe people in SWAT-type gear preparing to go in.

"They're just kids," she whispered, suddenly horrified at all the firepower that was being brought to bear. "Dad, they're just kids."

"It's not the time, Alix," her father said.

"But they weren't like—"

She didn't get a chance to finish. Events were unfolding already. One thing cascading into the next, into the next.

Alix watched with her heart in her throat.

A couple of guys with a heavy iron battering ram dashed to the warehouse and pinned themselves at either side of the entrance doors. They waved hand signals to the rest of their team. There were soldiers at every door now, locking down the entrances.

At a signal from Lisa, the tear gas gunners stood back and aimed their weapons at the upper clerestory windows.

Oh, God, what have I done?

But it was too late to stop what was already in motion.

Tear gas and pepper canisters boomed from the guns. They arced toward the factory's windows, trailing yellow smoke.

Shshshshshshshshs...

They hit.

24

SSSSHSHSHSHSHSS...

Tank's longboard shot across the ancient concrete of the factory floor, weaving easily past cracks where subsidence and age had broken the smooth, open space. The kid was fluid, Moses thought. Whenever that boy was on a skateboard, he looked perfectly self-possessed. Without doubt or fear. Just a perfectly tuned object, speeding toward his goal.

Even if he sometimes crashed.

Moses briefly envied Tank's silent self-possession. The kid was like a hermetically sealed person. Whatever went on inside his head almost never came out as words. There was Tank, rolling around on his board. There was Tank, building his latest Rube Goldberg contraption, and that was all there was. The rest of him was silent depths so deep they might as well have been the Mariana Trench.

Tank never seemed impatient. Tank never seemed worried.

Moses checked his watch again. Alix was late, and he had no idea why. Right after they'd sent Alix off with Cyn and Adam, he'd been frustrated to discover that the Banks household had gone dark to their surveillance. Sometime while they'd been convincing Alix to go along with their plan, the place had fuzzed out, and now Kook couldn't pull a single image, either inside, or outside the house.

"Either they put up new electronic countermeasures, or Alix disappearing made them do another sweep and Williams and Crowe found our bugs."

"Which is it?"

"No way of knowing, unless you want to go over and ask."

He didn't. But after being almost godlike in his knowledge of what was happening, it was frustrating to suddenly be blind again.

Am I being too trusting?

Maybe Alix was just grounded, and they'd have to wait longer. Or maybe she'd lost the USB key. Or maybe...Moses grimaced. *Why am I sweating it?* Nobody else was sweating it. Just him.

How come I'm the only one who's nervous?

He schooled himself to be still. *Maybe they're all pretending to be calm. Just like me.*

He took another tour of the factory, trying to act relaxed. Kook was deep in another coding session. A sweet haze of marijuana smoke hung about her, and green cans of her latest energy drink were stacked around her in a tower that Tank had carefully built as she worked, with her so buried in her code that she hadn't seen him doing it. A whole fortress of AdrenaPUMP.

"Anything from the Trojan horse yet?" Moses asked.

Kook gave him a sour look. "You asked me fifty times already. Go bother someone else. You'll know if your girlfriend gets it online."

"She's not my girlfriend."

"Go bullshit someone who will believe you," Kook said, and went back to her coding.

Moses made a face and wandered back to the main factory floor.

Adam and Cynthia were kicking the hell out of a heavy bag. Taking turns practicing elbow strikes.

"Pivot!" Adam was saying. "You want your hips in it! Whole body, girl! Whole body."

WHAM!

Cynthia hit again, and the bag swayed.

"Yeah! That's what we're looking for! Do it again!"

BAM!

Cynthia was hitting the hell out of it. They were both sweating. "Okay, now try your shin kicks," Adam said.

For Adam, it had started out as a bit of a joke. He hadn't really thought Cynthia would learn. Didn't have the killer instinct, he said. She didn't have the rage—

THWOCK.

Cynthia's shin hit the bag and it swayed. "Good!" Adam

said. "Give me a combo punch. One, two, hook! *Good!* Keep going!" Adam turned and ambled over to Moses. "Any word from our girl?"

Moses shook his head. "Nah."

"She still seemed pretty pissed in the car."

"We rattled her cage pretty hard."

Kook gave a shout from her workstation. "Hey guys! Come here! You got to see this!"

They all ran for Kook. She was staring at one of her screens, her pierced eyebrows knitted with concentration. She expanded the security cam windows, filling up her monitors with surveillance views of the outside of the factory.

SWAT-type people were just outside. Tons of security goons, blocking all the entrances.

Moses swore.

"I do believe that's Williams and Crowe," Adam said mildly.

"I told you we couldn't trust her," Kook said.

Moses didn't have a chance to retort. Tear gas boomed toward the factory, trailing yellow smoke.

Glass shattered.

More tear gas rounds followed, a rain of toxic smoke, pouring in.

■ ■ ■

Alix watched as the Williams & Crowe teams smashed the doors open. It took a couple of swings, but they tore the metal doors off their hinges. The doors fell inward, and tear gas billowed out. More smoke was pouring out from the broken windows above, yellow smoke that made Alix's throat seize in silent empathy for Tank.

Security teams with gas masks charged through the doors, M-16s held ready.

It was like hitting a fly with a sledgehammer, Alix thought.

Dad seemed to sense her anxiety. "Williams and Crowe recruits from special forces for their security work. They'll be fine."

I wasn't worried about them. Alix had a sudden sickening image in her mind of Cynthia lying in a pool of blood, shot dead by some armored guy with an M-16. Or Tank. And Moses? What about him?

A gun went off and then another.

Alix startled at the sound. *Oh God, I didn't want them dead! I wanted...*

More smoke was pouring out of the building, billowing clouds of it.

"Is something on fire?" Alix asked.

Their driver turned on his radio. There was a lot of shouting coming over the channels.

Someone took over the channel—Lisa's voice. "Hold fire! Hold fire!" Her voice was almost frantic. Alix listened, her throat tight with tension.

The driver shut off the radio again. "They'll be cuffing them now," he said, pointing to the doors. "They should be coming out right there."

Dad glanced over. "Are you sure you want to see this?"

Alix wasn't sure. "I—" she started, and broke off. "Is that normal?" she asked, pointing.

Massive billowing clouds were rising into the sunny sky. Not the yellow clouds of tear gas, but obscenely bright colors, white and red and blue gushing into a vast, towering plume of brilliantly stained smoke. Faster and faster, thicker and thicker.

The guard turned the radio back on. Squawks of confusion crackled from its speaker.

"Goddammit! I can't see!"

"Bars—"

"Fall back! Fall—"

"—cage—"

"—back!"

"—shot—"

"Help with Jennings!"

All the Williams & Crowe people were still inside. Not a single one had emerged.

Alix leaned forward, staring. Realizing what was happening.

In the distance, sirens wailed.

"Oh no," she whispered.

■ ■ ■

"Check it out!"

Tank was pointing to one of their distance cams. It gave

a wide view of the factory, and now a tricolored cloud was rising fast and huge from it, a billowing stream that kept on roiling.

Moses stared at the rising plume. "Damn! That's really big."

"It should be," Tank said with satisfaction. "Half the factory is a smoke bomb. It was like ten tons of saltpeter."

Cynthia came up beside him, toweling the workout sweat from her face and neck. "Wow. It's pretty."

Moses smiled sadly. "Yeah. It is."

"Here comes the rest," Kook said. She pointed at another monitor where more people were carefully approaching the smoking factory. "There's your girlfriend," she said.

"My, my." Adam laughed. "She does look pissed."

She sure did. Moses watched as Alix approached the building. She was fighting to get close, being held back by her father and some Williams & Crowe goon. Alix looked shocked as she stared up at the smoking building. He thought he could read every emotion on her face. The surprise at all the smoke pouring out. The confusion of trying to figure out what had happened. Smart rich girl trying to figure out why everything had gone sidewise for her.

She looked shocked and pissed, for sure, but he thought he could make out another expression there, too—a glint of tight-lipped admiration as she put the pieces together. Realizing that she'd been played.

Now you see it, now you don't. Like a magician whipping aside a cloth to reveal the white rabbit where the snowy dove should have been. Moses's uncle had loved magic almost as much as he'd loved graft. The delight of the switch, the gasp of amazement as someone realized that they'd been fooled, as the world tilted off its rails and did something that was simply impossible—

"I should have called Guinness Book of World Records!" Tank said. "I'd be famous!"

"You'd be famous in jail," Kook said fondly.

"How long before the newspeople arrive?" Cynthia asked as she clipped her hair up off her sweaty neck.

"Can't be long now," Adam said.

"Hell of a lot better than a press release."

Kook said, "I still wish we could have gotten into Banks's computers. Would have loved to see what's going on behind BSP's firewall."

"Take the win," Cynthia advised. "With that much smoke and everything we rigged inside, we're on the five o'clock news, for sure."

"Still…"

"Oh, stop it. We agreed that whichever way things went, it was a win. This isn't hacking some Russian mafia credit card ring. We're probably already on the NSA's radar as it is. As soon as the news crews get there, let's get this thing triggered and call it a day."

Smoke continued to rise, a tower of color so big it looked like the city of Hartford was going up. Moses watched the monitor that had Alix in it. She was still staring at the scene that she had helped trigger.

Sorry, girl, he thought. *You can't believe in anything, and you sure can't trust.*

The only thing you could do was test.

Cynthia touched his shoulder. "I'm sorry about Alix," she said softly. "I sort of thought she'd..." She trailed off.

Moses remembered being brought up to trust. To think that people would do the right thing. His dad had always believed that people would do the right thing and play straight with you if you asked them to. It was another thing his uncle had always scoffed at about his dad.

You know who you can trust? his uncle had once said. *Nobody. En-Oh-Body. You trust yourself, and you watch your back, and everything else, you test.*

"I saw her coming a mile away," Moses lied.

25

THEY FOUND THE WILLIAMS & CROWE team in cages.

Every door that the security teams had charged through had turned out to be elaborately booby-trapped. As the last men ran in, the cages clanged down and locked with huge heavy iron latches.

There was no mechanism to open them.

Alix had to stifle her amusement at all the security teams sitting in their cages, sweaty and demoralized. About a million fire and police department people were standing around the cages, scratching their heads and trying to figure out what tools they'd need to get the cages open.

Alix remembered Tank standing outside her own cage, inspecting it and saying, "Told you I could figure out the welding!"

You sure did, kid, she thought. *You sure did.*

They'd all known what they were doing. All the way. And

274

she'd helped them pull it off. Moses had played her. Right from the start.

If she thought back, she should have seen it coming: Moses's comments that he didn't believe in things, he only tested. Saying that he'd poked her dad enough that he thought he knew what he'd do when Moses grabbed his daughter. She'd thought Dad would move heaven and hell to get her back. Moses had banked on his using Williams & Crowe for revenge.

Moses had played her.

Or did you try to play him and lose? a voice snarked in her head. She'd said she'd help him, and then she'd changed her mind. What would Moses have done if she'd followed through with her promise? What would that have meant to him? What would it have meant to her?

The whole factory smelled like caramel. A byproduct of the burning sugar that the 2.0 crew had used to construct their massive smoke bomb. Alix could construct the chemical reactions in her mind. The sugar, the saltpeter, all of it going up through elaborate, perforated iron tubes that Tank had likely constructed and were still baking with the heat of that massive smoke bomb burn.

Alix caught sight of her father talking to Lisa through the bars. Death Barbie glanced over at Alix, and Alix thought she could detect her disappointment.

It wasn't my fault.

Of course, no one was going to come straight out and blame her. It wasn't like there weren't screwups galore to go around. Williams & Crowe had completely underestimated 2.0 again. Fire trucks and police cars and hazmat vehicles filled the parking area outside, all of them called to the scene by the insane plume of smoke that had risen over the city.

Lisa was looking pissed, talking into her radio, and listening to whatever was coming back from her bosses as she paced back and forth in her cage. Her squad sat glumly around her, staring out from the bars like gorillas at a zoo exhibit.

Homo securitus, Alix thought. Or maybe, if you were feeling really snarky...

Homo suckerus.

All of a sudden Lisa was hurrying to the bars and calling to the cops, agitated. A second later Alix saw why. News vans had started pulling up, and camera people were climbing out to survey the scene. Channel 3 already had a crew panning the factory. Blow-dried talking heads started touching up makeup and setting up for shots.

"Alix," Dad called out to her. "Come inside. I don't want you on the news."

Like that will change anything.

Alix kept watching as Lisa begged the cops to bar access, but the locals didn't care. Some of them were grinning and shaking their heads at the newspeople's arrival, and Alix had the feeling that whatever clout Lisa had had, it had evaporated in the face of failing to notify them of her raid.

A fire chief laughed and waved the cameras inside while Lisa shouted at him to stop. The camera guys didn't wait for a second round of permission. They scrambled for the doors, jostling for the first shots of the building's interior, before some other authority changed its mind and dragged them out.

Alix watched, bleakly amused. Nobody seemed to know what was going on or who was supposed to be in charge. More Williams & Crowe personnel were arriving now, trying to get through the clots of emergency vehicles.

The newspeople were cracking up as they filmed the Williams & Crowe assault team.

"This is proprietary!" Lisa kept saying to them from behind bars. "You can't film faces without permission!"

The cameras ignored her. One of the talking heads got down on her knees, trying to get some of the trapped Williams & Crowe people to give her a quote.

"What were you doing in here?" she kept asking, as all the security people turned away.

■ ■ ■

"This about enough mayhem for you?" Kook asked Moses.

Moses had been watching Alix, and it took him a moment to realize that Kook was talking to him. "What? Oh, yeah. Go ahead."

"Let's blow this shit up," Adam with a laugh.

Kook popped open a terminal window and sent a series of encrypted commands to a server on the other side of the world.

That server would communicate with another server, and then another, as bots and zombied computers that she'd picked up over years of hacking chained the signal together.

She'd explained it all to Moses once. She never did anything directly. One encrypted signal embedded in noise and other communications bounced from place to place until, at last, a burst of commands launched itself from Estonia and landed—boom—on a local wireless network that bounced the instructions to the factory's private network and...

"Here we go," Kook muttered.

Bang.

■ ■ ■

The explosions were so loud that everyone hit the floor. A whole carpet of people diving for cover in instinctive reaction to the booming that came from all sides of the factory.

Alix hit the floor with them.

They're shooting?

But no, instead of violence and gunfire it was...

Canvases unfurling, canvas after canvas all around the warehouse. Images and info-graphics, spilling down the walls showing—

Dad?

Simon Banks's face cascaded into view, done in the stylized form of old communist propaganda. Beside him, another canvas unfurled, revealing George Saamsi, and between them, a stylized logo of a factory, generating question marks that puffed up and up and up, and below the image, the words:

WELCOME TO THE DOUBT FACTORY

More canvases spilled open. Banks Strategy Partners, with links to the names of different organizations and companies. Americans for Innovation. The Institute for Competition and Prosperity. Oil companies. Petroleum associations. Household products associations. Dozens and dozens of companies and organizations, and each one of those connected to more info-graphics with a variety of headings.

LEGAL: A spiderweb of doctors' and scientists' photos with numbers beside them representing how much money they had taken from the associations for their research, and how many court cases they had testified in on behalf of companies.

GOVERNMENT: Lists of company-paid people who also worked at government agencies. USDA. FDA. Atomic Energy Commission. EPA. Department of Agriculture. Minerals Management Service. Bureau of Land Management. Federal Communications Commission. Office of Management and Budget. And that was followed by long lists of laws and regulations that they'd consulted on.

SCIENCE: Lists of scientists and research paid, with a web of lines linking back to the companies and associations—and all those lines made more connections back to her father and George Saamsi.

CHEMICALS: diacetyl, Azicort, phthalates...

It went on and on. Alix stared at the dizzying web of interconnections. In a way, it reminded her of Moses's own breathless description of how he had dug into her father's work, the wide-eyed sincerity with which he had described all the evils he claimed her father was involved in. So certain. So sincere.

The canvases read like the work of the insane.

The camera people were laughing and filming them.

■ ■ ■

Kook whooped. They all crowded around the screens, watching as their work unfurled. All the ideas that they'd laid out.

Moses watched Alix's eyes widen as her father's face unfurled on the banner and the newspeople started to film. The live Mr. Banks's own expression was stony, taking in all the information they'd compiled about him.

"That's right," Moses muttered. "We got you all figured out."

The man was staring up at what Moses considered to be the key banner.

DOUBT FACTORY PLAYBOOK

COUNSEL AGAINST A RUSH TO JUDGMENT.
ATTACK THE SCIENCE.
BUY CONTRARIAN SCIENTIFIC RESULTS.
PUBLICIZE BOUGHT SCIENCE.

EMPHASIZE QUESTIONS RATHER THAN ANSWERS.
TEACH THE CONTROVERSY.
ACCUSE OPPONENTS OF PRACTICING
    JUNK SCIENCE.
KEEP THE PUBLIC CONFUSED.
CONFUSION = DELAY = $$$$

Mr. Banks was frowning as he stared up at all the writings, his daughter not far off, staring up at the Doubt Factory laid bare.

Moses watched Alix's expression change as she read.

■ ■ ■

"Dad? Dad?"

Dad turned to her. "They're lunatics," he said. He started to smile. "They're just lunatics, that's all. Conspiracy theorists." He walked over to the news cameras. "You wanted a quote?"

He talked happily into the camera, and by the time he returned to Alix, he was smiling more broadly still. "We should go," he said. "It will take a little while for all this to sort out. I'll get a car for us."

"But..." Alix waved at the banners and their web of connections and accusations. "What is all this?"

"I have no idea. Performance art, I guess you could call it." He gave a little chuckle. "You have to give the deranged credit—they may not have a grip on reality, but they're certainly industrious." He shook his head sadly. "For their sake, I hope someone gets them help. There are medications that can help control this kind of mental instability."

"So what is all this?"

"It's nothing, Alix," he said. "It's just the rantings of a bunch of very passionate, very unstable Occupy Wall Street types. Corporations buy the government! These kinds of radical theories..." He laughed. "It's what children and conspiracy buffs think. It's a bit like the 9/11 truthers or the people who think the moon landing never happened."

Moses watched Alix's expression change as she...

■ ■ ■

"Why is he laughing?" Cynthia asked.

"Hell if I know," Kook said.

"It doesn't matter," Adam said. "Look. The cameras are all over the banners. He's the story now. Banks is out of the shadows. They're totally sucking up the information."

"No." Moses felt his blood draining from him as he realized what he'd been too impassioned to see before. "We screwed up."

"Bullshit. It went perfect," Kook said.

"No." Moses pressed his hands against his forehead in frustration. The scope of his failure was too horrifying to accept. "We did it wrong."

Simon Banks was guiding his daughter out of the factory. He was laughing. He was smiling at his daughter, and laughing, and completely unfazed by the event that they'd engineered. Another of Kook's spy eyes picked them up outside the factory, tracking the pair as they climbed into a Williams & Crowe SUV. The last glimpse Moses got of Simon Banks was of the man looking smugly self-satisfied as he stared back at the still-smoking building, right before he closed the door and let Williams & Crowe whisk him away.

"We screwed up. We completely screwed up."

"But look at all the coverage we're getting," Tank protested.

"But that's just the thing: Banks isn't the story," Moses said, tapping the screen. "We are. The crazy kids who do crazy things."

"Crazy cool things," Kook said.

"No. Just crazy. We look bugnuts crazy." He stared at all the banners, finally seeing what he'd been blind to. He'd walked right into the same playbook the Doubt Factory used every day. *Sincerity always loses. You can't shake up the status quo.*

His uncle used to say there was a fine line between clever and stupid. Whatever scam you created needed to be bulletproof.

To that, Moses silently added another dictum: *There's a fine line between clever and crazy.*

"We look like we're straight out of *One Flew Over the Cuckoo's Nest* or something. We might as well be that old guy who lived in the cabin in Montana and wrote those goofy manifestos."

"Ted Kaczynski. The Unabomber," Cynthia said.

"Yeah, him. All they have to do is associate us with his manifesto or about a thousand Earth Firster things. The Radical Environmental Agenda or some shit. Occupy Wall Street loony tunes."

Cynthia groaned as she got it. "They'll frame the story around us. Talk about how sad it is that we don't have a mental health system. Like the Sandy Hook shootings. NRA used that tactic."

"Yeah, we screwed up. We just became the story, instead of the Doubt Factory. Now Simon Banks is just an innocent victim, and we're a bunch of crazy-ass lunatics."

Moses watched Alix and her father driving away. The memory of Simon Banks smiling as he climbed into the SUV burned in Moses's brain.

"We blew it," Moses said. "We totally blew it."

PART 2

26

ALIX SAT IN AP CHEM, staring out at the sunshine. Another hot spring day, with everyone wilting and complaining that for a rich school, Seitz ought to be able to figure out how to get its AC right. All of them sticky and bored in the heat, and all of them stuck in neutral, waiting for the clock to run out and for real life to start.

Sophie texted her under the table. GOING OUT. YOU WANT TO?

Sure.

Whatever.

Cynthia was gone.

Moses hadn't been seen again.

2.0 had disappeared entirely, like they'd evaporated into the sunshine. Poof, gone. A strange hallucination that left everyone shaken but fundamentally unchanged.

Alix thought about the whole thing often. She couldn't

287

stop thinking about the moment when she'd handed the USB stick over to Lisa and to her father. The moment when she'd been on the verge of doing something dangerous and against the grain, and then stopped short. The moment when she decided not to go play in the traffic.

Safe, because she loved her family.

Safe.

She couldn't help wondering what might have happened. If there were an alternate-reality version of Alix Banks who'd plugged that USB stick into her father's computer and unleashed the fury of the universe.

Maybe that Alix had ended up as a smashed hood ornament on the front of a Lexus, but this one was fine.

Shaken, but fine.

Shaken, until after a little while, she shook the fear off. And then what did she have? An odd little story that she was starting to doubt more and more as time passed. There wasn't even anything she could point to, to say that her near miss with the mysterious-dangerous-whatever had even been real. 2.0 was gone.

Not a trace.

Poof! Gone!

A magic trick.

Now you see it, now you don't.

It pissed the FBI off royally.

Not only had Williams & Crowe failed to notify them that they were about to go after a target of FBI interest, but it had lost them entirely. Terrorist cells weren't supposed to just evaporate into thin air, and yet 2.0 had managed the impossible. Pictures of Moses and Cynthia circulated. A few blurry photos from the rave had been recovered, showing Adam, the beautiful blond DJ. And then...nothing. Every lead was a dead end.

Cynthia turned out to be a ghost: stolen SSN, false history, a PO box for an address.

Moses showed up on a couple of surveillance tapes from when he'd punched the headmaster, but even then he always seemed to know which way to turn his back so that it was impossible to get a clear look at his face.

Moses was a phantom. Cynthia was the most solid lead they had, and she petered out. Maybe her father really had worked in tech and done data mining. Or maybe it was all lies, because no one could dig up a likeness. And the rest of them?

A kid whose aunt worked with asbestos? No good records.

Some gutter-punk girl? You could find them on every street in every city in America.

Some Latino foster kid with an asthma problem? Nobody even bothered to keep track.

Of course, the FBI went over the factory with a fine-tooth forensic comb, but it had been full of human detritus from the huge rave that 2.0 had thrown. If there was decent physical evidence of anything at all, it was hopelessly obscured. What they did come up with were a lot of banners and a whole host of surveillance cameras that seemed to observe every angle of the factory.

The FBI tech who had studied them reported that they'd been sending encrypted signals to…nothing at all. Some kind of nearby local network that no longer existed. Still, they'd managed to match a pattern and connect it to another local network that led onto another—link after link in an anonymous chain that eventually dead-ended in Estonia. Investigators were left pulling their hair in frustration. They had nothing.

Well, rats. They had a lot of rats. 2.0 had left the rats with a sign that said FREE TO GOOD HOME. Those were the rats that Alix had seen at the rave. It turned out that they'd been heisted from the same testing facility as the ones 2.0 had used in the school. A private lab that had been involved in evaluating Tank's asthma drug, the one that supposedly caused comas.

Williams & Crowe had confiscated the rats as corporate property, along with several vats of Azicort, the bronchial dilator, and a long screed from 2.0 about pharmaceutical companies doing suspect testing. According to the banners, the rats in question were being used by George Saamsi and Kimball-Geier to prove Azicort was a safe substance suitable for use on chronic asthma.

It looked as though the rats had been meant to be released in another massive wave, reminiscent of the prank at Seitz, but by the time the cages had opened, most of the rats had already died of a different kind of respiratory failure—choking to death on pepper spray and tear gas.

Everyone admitted it was a lot of dead rats.

In the end, after hours and hours of investigations, the FBI came up with nothing. 2.0 was gone. Disappeared into the wind, leaving behind a fading memory of their oddball pranks and little else.

If the misfits of 2.0 were still out there, they had probably moved on. At least, that's what the FBI said. They'd resurface. And in the meantime the FBI was patient. It had other investigations and other emergencies that were more pressing. Alix's father was given the name of an agent in charge of their case, and the FBI packed up and moved out.

A few weeks later Williams & Crowe left, too, taking Lisa and their armored SUVs with them.

Alix was hugely relieved to see Death Barbie go, not least because she couldn't help but get the feeling that Lisa blamed her for getting the Williams & Crowe security people locked in the cages. It had taken hours to get them all out. They'd eventually resorted to using cutting torches.

After that, Lisa had trailed her everywhere, and Alix had meekly submitted to her guard. Neither of them suggested that Alix deserved to have time to herself or that Death Barbie had been overly protective—one of those irritating moments when the adults had read the situation better than Alix had and subsequently let her know that she was now on thin ice and had to earn her way back into their good graces.

But now, finally, Death Barbie was gone, and Alix was left feeling....

Lonely?

God, Alix, you are so lame.

She didn't have a bodyguard and a spy living with her 24-7. She should have been grateful for that much at least. Sophie and Denise were still here, and boys like James kept asking her out. And Derek was always good for a laugh, even if he didn't have Cynthia to try to compete against anymore. Derek was ridiculously relieved to find out that Cynthia had actually been a graduated senior.

"I was having major inadequacy issues," he admitted. "I was studying all the time."

Days slipped by. Alix went to the occasional Mom-and-Dad-sanctioned party. She rolled toward finals, and everything was fine, in theory.

Except... what?

She'd gotten her SAT results, and they were great, but her first thought was that she should tell Cynthia, who had helped prep her. And then she realized once again that Cynthia was gone.

That girl was like getting your braces off. The smooth, slippery feeling of nothingness, where there should have been something.

Alix looked at her SAT scores and wondered why she didn't care at all. It all felt so fake. Like she was one of those lab rats that they ran chemical tests on. You took the tests, you ran through the maze, you got the score.... Then they chopped out your brain to check for tumors.

The sound of books being gathered startled Alix. Even more startling was that it was last period, and she'd somehow managed to drift all the way through the last half of school without taking much notice of anything at all.

Jonah was standing outside her classroom door, waiting for her. He started jabbering about how Mr. Ambrose was a Nazi for docking him a grade.

"Who gives a damn how I format my bio notebook?" he kept saying as they climbed into Alix's cherry-red MINI. "I should have gotten a perfect score."

"Yeah. He screwed me with that, too," Alix said absently.

Cynthia had gotten a perfect score on her SATs, Alix remembered. She knew how the SATs were built, top to bottom, and had happily tutored Alix.

It was just a test, she'd said.

"You can make the mistake of thinking test scores say something about you," she'd said when Alix had expressed awe at Cynthia's numbers. *"But they don't. They're just something they use to put you in a box."*

At the time, Alix had taken her words for false humility and as a sop to Alix in case she royally screwed the test. But now Alix knew that not only had Cynthia gotten a perfect score, but she'd also walked away from it all to run with 2.0, a surreal gang of OCD crazypants kids dedicated to some other game entirely.

Different rats, running a different kind of maze.

Cynthia, good girl gone bad; a different rat in a different maze, passing a different kind of test.

Tests.

Alix remembered Moses handing her the USB stick.

There were all kinds of tests, and Alix couldn't decide if she'd failed or passed hers. She'd gotten away from 2.0. She'd warned her father. She'd protected her family—

"Are you even listening to me?" Jonah asked.

Alix realized she'd been sitting in the car with the engine running.

"Sure," Alix said as she put the MINI in reverse. "Why? What did you say?"

"Fuckin' A, you're getting as bad as Dad," Jonah said. "You never pay attention anymore."

"I do, too, pay attention." Alix pulled out of the school parking lot, heading for home.

"Ever since that whole thing with 2.0, you've been acting weird."

"No, I haven't."

"Yeah, you have."

"My freak-show brother is telling me that I've been weird?"

"You know what I think?" Jonah said. "I think you miss being caged up by 2.0."

Alix glared at him. "Take that back."

Jonah grinned, completely unrepentant. "Oh, come on. I bet it was way more interesting being all caged up like that. Kidnapped, by the mysteriously hot leader of the outlaw gang 2.0..." He trailed off suggestively.

"You are one screwed-up—" Alix glimpsed movement on

the sidewalk and slammed on her brakes. There was a familiar figure cutting between the cars along the street.

Oh my God.

Black guy in a bomber jacket.

Moses.

Her heart lurched. The guy turned his head. The world righted itself. Not Moses at all. Just some random guy. He didn't even look like Moses. He had a goatee, and it was graying. He was just some old guy.

Ick.

Alix watched the man unlock his BMW and climb in.

Jonah smirked knowingly as she got the MINI going again. "That wasn't 2.0," he said.

"Fuck off," she said.

"Bet you're disappointed," Jonah goaded.

"Seriously, Jonah. Fuck off. If you keep this up, I swear I'll make you walk home."

Her brother snorted, but at least he shut up.

Alix's heart was still hammering from that first glimpse of the man. Something about the way he'd moved or his style had triggered the response. Adrenaline and fear and surprise...and...what? Something else that she didn't really want to look at, and didn't like Jonah poking at.

PTSD was what her shrink was calling it.

And not just about Moses. The 2.0 crew all tended to trigger her. Sometimes it was Moses. Other times, Cynthia. Blue hair immediately reminded her of the hacker girl, Kook.

Willowy blond boys could make her see Adam. Alix had even hallucinated that she'd spied Tank once, a skate rat barreling down the sidewalk.

Alix's shrink warned that there might be depression after all of Alix's stress incidents and recommended medication to combat the lethargy and forgetfulness that Alix had started exhibiting. After all, Alix had stopped getting out of bed on time. She'd forgotten Jonah at school twice. She'd started skipping track-and-field practice because she just couldn't muster the will to care whether she remained on the team. As far as Mom and Dr. Ballantine were concerned, these were hanging offenses.

"It's just running on a track," Alix had protested. "It's not like I'm failing school, Mom."

"It's just not like you," Mom replied. "You never lay around the house like this. You never watch TV like this. Or play that game all the time…"

"Skyrim."

"It's not like you. Sophie called again, you know."

Sophie, wanting to go out and do…something. Shop for lipstick or try to find a dress that would make her size 6 look like a size 2 or…whatever. Alix couldn't be bothered. She had dragons to kill—on the Xbox that it turned out 2.0 had bugged, right inside her own house.

When Alix had told them that Cynthia was a double agent, Williams & Crowe had been delighted because it helped explain the listening devices they'd started discovering all around the Banks' property.

Cynthia had been good at what she did, that was for sure. Everything about that girl had been a lie.

So Alix had ended up at Dr. Ballantine's office, listening to the woman drone on about kidnapping and stress and trigger this and trigger that.

Dr. Ballantine had an abstract oil-smear painting on one wall. Alix would stare at the browns and reds, and fantasize about smashing it on Dr. Ballantine's head, and then she ended up wondering if that was a sign that she really was somehow going crazy.

She could almost hear Mom saying, *"Violence isn't like you, Alix."*

Alix wasn't like Alix.

If she'd been smarter about hiding how she was feeling, she'd have been able to avoid the couch sessions, but instead, she'd ended up talking to Dr. Ballantine while the shrink made notes.

"Were you scared?" Dr. Ballantine had asked.

"Of course I was scared. But I'm fine now. I mean, I got out all right."

"Are you scared now?"

Alix shrugged. "No."

Yes.

No?

Yes?

Not really.

Alix didn't know how she felt.

"Are you still skipping track and field?"

297

"I dropped it."

"Why?"

"Because it's not a real thing. Who cares if you win or lose?"

"Some people care."

Alix rolled her eyes. "Well, I don't."

"Why not?"

Because it's all bullshit, Alix wanted to say, but that would just start up another line of questioning about why she felt that running was bullshit. The only answer was that she couldn't help but think that every time she went onto the track to run around and around the damn oval, Moses would be sitting up there in the crowd. He'd be watching from behind his reflective aviator lenses and laughing at the goofy things rich kids did with their spare time while he and his crew were busy hacking together another crazed attack on "the man."

Moses and the 2.0 crew had played a different game. The games of high school seemed silly and small after that.

Alix realized that Jonah was looking at her worriedly. Again.

"I'm fine," she said.

"Sure you are," he said. "Are you taking that Xanax or whatever Dr. Ballantine says you should take?"

"Why?"

"'Cause I wouldn't," Jonah said. "They'll make you fuzzy. Fuzzier," he amended, looking at her critically.

"How would you know?"

298

Jonah gave her an exasperated look that reminded Alix of Mom when she was trying to get Jonah to pay attention to her, and that made her realize how differently he was acting generally. He hadn't been running off. He was always where he was supposed to be after school. Hell, he was practically always around, just like he'd been waiting outside her classroom when she came out. He was bitching about his grades, she realized with a start.

He's keeping an eye on you. And then she almost laughed out loud at the sudden surge of affection she felt for her ADHD, caretaking little pain-in-the-ass brother.

"Do you want to go get coffee?" she asked abruptly.

"Seriously? You think I need to be more wired?"

Alix laughed and pulled into the Starbucks. The girl at the counter looked like Cynthia. Alix stifled shock/nostalgia/fear/camaraderie as she handed over her credit card. PTSD. *It will keep happening, but less and less*, Dr. Ballantine claimed. For now, though, every time Alix saw a girl with long lustrous black hair, she was sure it was Cynthia.

And, of course, it was always some other Asian girl, and then Alix would hear Cynthia say contemptuously, *"Her? She's not even Chinese. She's Vietnamese. We're not all the same, you know...."*

As Alix and Jonah made their way back to the car, Alix deliberately made herself look at every single person in the parking lot, proving to herself that she wasn't seeing any more Cynthias or Adams or Kooks or Tanks or Moseses. None of them were here. They were all gone.

Alix put the car in drive and got them back out on the road while Jonah prattled on about whatever Jonah prattled on about now.

The FBI and Williams & Crowe had assured her that 2.0 had moved on, probably dedicated to wreaking havoc elsewhere. No one was stalking her. No one was peering in through the windows of her house. No one was watching over her.

Jonah punched her shoulder. "Are you even listening to me?" he demanded.

"What?"

"You just ran that stop sign!"

"I did?"

"Yeah. And you stopped at the crossing before, where there wasn't one."

"I guess I'm distracted."

Jonah groaned. "You are so going to get me killed."

"Do you ever wonder about the kind of work Dad does?"

Jonah gave her a surprised look. "Are you still thinking about all that 2.0 stuff?"

"I don't know. Maybe. Kind of."

Someone honked behind her.

Alix stepped on the gas and then, in a split-second decision, swerved for the turnpike entrance.

"Where are we going?" Jonah yelped as he grabbed for a door handle.

"Who cares? I don't want to go home right now."

"Is this a kidnapping?" Jonah asked.

"I just want to drive. I'm sick of people looking at me and asking me if I'm okay."

"Welcome to my world." Jonah snorted.

Alix gunned the MINI. They shot up the on-ramp to merge with turnpike traffic, rolling north toward Hartford. Alix rolled down her window, trying to enjoy the rush of noise.

"As long as we're driving…" Jonah hooked his phone into the stereo, and pretty soon they were arguing about whether he was really going to try to play reggaeton in her car while she was driving. Wind whipped Alix's hair. Jonah turned up the music, full of swagger and Spanish and innuendo.

It felt good to drive.

You could just keep on driving. Just keep going. Don't stop. See how far you can go. Just fuck it and bail.

Alix wondered if this was what it had been like for Cynthia when she walked away from a full-ride college education to join up with 2.0.

It was an insane choice. Like a train jumping its track and then deciding it was supposed to be a lear jet instead. Girls like Cynthia didn't belong in gangs of pranking, political crazies. And yet she'd joined Moses and the rest of the crew. Cynthia had done everything perfectly. She'd gotten the perfect scores. Gotten the perfect acceptance letters. She'd shown herself she could do it, and then she'd walked away.

Alix thought of all the students at Seitz, every one of them Ivy League crazy. Like horses with their jockeys whipping them forward from their starting gates, trained to gallop, to clear their hurdles… And then there was Cynthia, who, after being given the winner's cup, had thrown it down and walked away.

And for what?

Moses. The crazy prophet, leading his crazy crew right off the crazy cliff on the way to crazy town.

And because her father was dead, a voice reminded her.

So she said, Alix reminded herself. Cynthia's father was dead from Marcea's heart attack drug—*if* she could be believed.

"We're all like that," Cynthia had said.

Well, fuck you, Cynthia. Oh, and fuck you, too, Moses.

"What?" Jonah asked.

Alix realized that she'd been speaking out loud.

"Are you keeping an eye on me?" she asked Jonah suddenly. "Is that why you're being so good all the time now? Did Mom and Dad put you up to this?"

Jonah looked offended. "Of course not!"

"Then how come you stopped running away?"

"I don't know." He made an uncomfortable shrug. "It was kid stuff."

"You *are* a kid."

He glanced over at her. "You seriously want to know?"

"I'm asking, aren't I?"

Jonah glanced away, looking out the window at the bright green leaves of the birch trees along the curves of the turnpike.

"You didn't see what it was like when you went missing,"

he said. "You didn't feel what it was like at home. Mom and Dad about went catatonic when you didn't come home the next morning. They didn't say it, but they were expecting to find your body. You took off, and then you just disappeared off the map. We were all just waiting for you to show up dead. Some rag-doll girl dead in a Dumpster. Probably all chopped up." He looked over at her, then stared back out the window. "That was some sobering shit."

"But I'm fine," Alix pointed out. "Nothing happened to me."

"Only because 2.0 wasn't homicidal. They could have done anything with you. They just made you disappear. If they'd been different, the cops would have found you floating in the river or dumped out in the woods somewhere." He swallowed.

"But they weren't like that. They were never like that."

"Maybe. Or maybe they're still nerving up to do something really crazy. Who knows what nutball activists will do? PETA? Occupy Wall Street? The Unabomber? They're all pretty much nuts."

"No…"

Alix remembered Cynthia pulling her out of the cage. That had been real. Cynthia cared about her.

Unless it was staged, a cynical voice reminded her.

Alix slammed the steering wheel with her palm, frustrated. "How the hell would I know?"

"What?"

"Nothing."

Had it just been some kind of good cop, bad cop routine? Moses acting all scary, and then Cynthia coming in to save her? How was she supposed to tell what was real? All the things 2.0 had said about her father? Or what her father said about 2.0? Truth. Lies. It was just a muddle of stories that exactly contradicted each other.

Either 2.0 was a crew of lunatic kids, or Dad was some kind of überevil wizard, throwing dream dust into the eyes of the world, making sure that it stayed asleep while companies pillaged and maimed and killed.

It sounded absurd no matter how she sliced it.

Truth? Lies? Madness? Sanity? How the hell could she tell?

The news coverage sure hadn't taken any of it seriously. The entire prank had become one of those thirty-second oddities at the end of the newscast. Activists Create Human-Sized Rat Cage. They'd really dug on the giant exercise wheel. There'd been a quick pan of the hanging murals, and that was all. Hilarious. Done in less than thirty seconds. Judging from the news, the only sane thing a watcher could conclude was, *"Gosh, Diane, kids sure do wacky things these days! And now in Sports..."*

2.0 had shot its wad, and the world had yawned. But still, Alix would sit at dinner and look across at her father and wonder.

According to Moses, he wasn't just bad, he was practically the devil. Doing evil things for evil amounts of money and knowing it and loving doing it. Laughing while he danced on graves.

It made no sense. This was the man who forgot to eat dinner because he was texting. The husband who was cut off from caffeine because it raised his blood pressure and he couldn't sleep at night and then would stay up in the kitchen eating ice cream out of the carton. The dad who had picked up her and Denise and driven them home in the middle of the night and never busted either of them for being drunk and stoned.

Seriously?

"He's not a monster," Alix muttered.

"Who?" Jonah asked.

"Nothing." Alix shook her head. "Something 2.0 said about Dad. That he was doing bad things."

Jonah glanced over at her. "Why would you even listen to them after all the stuff they did to you?"

"I don't know. Some of the things they said..." She glanced over at her younger brother. "What if they're true?"

"This is that Stockholm syndrome thing, right?"

"No, jerkwad, it's not."

"It kind of is. Seriously, sis. Don't go all Patty Hearst on me. I've read up on her. She totally joined up with the people who kidnapped her. Went all crazypants, robbing banks and shit." He suddenly looked interested. "But if you wanted to rob a bank, I'd totally help. I've got an idea about how—"

"Will you shut up and listen to me for once?"

"Okay, okay, I'm just saying."

Alix gave him a dirty look. "You're the one who called in the bomb threat last fall, aren't you?"

Jonah looked at her, surprised. "Duh."

"I knew it!"

Jonah didn't even look embarrassed. "I needed to break into the admin office. I couldn't clear people out otherwise. I was going to fail English and Trig and World Civ."

"I don't want to know." Alix tried to collect her thoughts. "Look, I'm just asking, but what if some of the things they said about Dad are true?"

Jonah looked at her, confused. "Like what? He's an ax murderer or something?"

"No. Like he gets paid to..."

To what? To make people confused about some company's report about some drug? To take over the government?

It all sounded so silly. The cartoons of her dad on the factory walls...

Alix heard her father's voice. *"Sometimes people need to make someone into an enemy just so they can make themselves feel important."*

Alix thought of conspiracy theorists like the 9/11 truthers. Or the people who still thought NASA hadn't put a man on the moon. It was like they needed to know something that was special. Needed to be unique somehow, by being smarter and more clued-in to the secrets of the universe.

"They kept telling me that Dad was the worst thing in the world, basically. And all these companies, they talked like all the companies were practically satanic. Like they'd do anything for money. People we know, even. Like everyone was just a bunch of moneygrubbing psychopaths."

Jonah laughed. "I thought everybody was moneygrubbing. Rich people just do it better."

"My little cynic brother."

"I'm just saying." Jonah spread his hands, laughing still. "Anyway, whatever those people say, it's only one side of a story. These crazies always want to make it sound like some company's completely evil. You've got to talk to both sides—"

Alix picked up the quote. "—and you shouldn't rush to judgment, because that's how you end up being wrong...."

Alix broke off.

Son of a bitch.

She could practically see Moses laughing at her, wagging a finger as she quoted her father encouraging her to see both sides to every story.

But what if it wasn't about sides, or perspectives, or radicals? What if it was just about *truth*?

How did you find truth when everyone was talking about sides?

Moses was grinning at her. Alix could practically see the self-satisfied smirk as he whispered in her ear. *"Makes it kind of difficult, doesn't it?"*

Screw you, Moses, Alix thought.

"Would you quit talking to yourself?" Jonah said. "It's driving me crazy."

27

ADAM SAID, "THEY KILLED THE rats, Moses."

"I know they killed the rats! I was there, too. I'm just saying that we shouldn't give up just because we had one setback."

"You call rat murder a setback?"

"Christ, Adam," Kook said. "You sound like PETA." She lit a joint and inhaled, blowing sweet smoke at the ceiling.

"Leather kills, Goth girl."

Kook regarded him with dilated pupils. "I'd eat those rats if it would make you shut up."

"Cut it out," Cynthia said. "Adam's right. We didn't see them coming in like that." She looked seriously at Moses. "We didn't plan on being gassed like that. We had a lot right, but we missed the tear gas."

Moses looked from one face to the next and didn't like what he was seeing. A lot of fear and uncertainty. Before, he'd always been able to coax and cajole them to believe, but now? Now it was serious.

"We all saw those dead rats," Tank said. "Stakes are high is all they're sayin'."

"Stakes have always been high," Moses pointed out, but he could tell he was losing them. "So, what? We quit now? We walk away?"

"Quit while we're ahead," Adam said.

"And just let everything they've done...what? Just go? Like it didn't count or something?"

"It counted," Cynthia soothed. "Of course it counted. But getting ourselves gassed to death doesn't do anyone any good."

"Maybe at least then someone would notice!" Moses shot back. "News loves bodies."

He wished he hadn't said it as soon as the words were out of his mouth. Wrong words. Wrong tone. Everything was wrong. He'd always been good with words. He could hack people with his words as easily as Kook hacked servers in Eastern Europe. But these were the wrong words, and he knew it as soon as he said them.

"Dude." Kook exhaled smoke. "I so didn't sign up for a suicide pact."

"If you're dead, there's sure as hell no party," Adam added.

"When the hell did either of you agree on anything?"

"Around the time you started talking crazy," Kook said.

Tank didn't say anything.

"Look." Moses tried again. "I'm not saying we should suicide-pact or anything—"

"Big relief," Adam interjected.

"—I'm just saying that we're finally seeing what these guys are capable of. We finally see how they act. What they do, how they roll...and now we're walking away? We knew they were bad, right from the start. Of course they were going to use all that tear gas—"

"If that had been Tank, he would have been dead, for sure," Cynthia said. "His asthma would have wasted him."

Tank looked at Moses mournfully.

"I know!" Moses retorted. "I get it. I'm not blind!"

"So why do we want to keep stirring these people up? They're coming for us. We poked them too many times, and now they're getting serious. The next time this happens, one of us ends up dead."

"So you're okay with what they did to your family now? Because I'm not okay with what they did to mine, I'll tell you that. They're still in business, and they're still making money. I'm not stopping until I figure out how to make them pay."

"Here comes the Don Quixote shit again," Kook muttered.

"Shove it, Kook. They're out there right now, making money while people die. They're making money, and they're laughing all the way to the bank because no one stops them."

Cynthia sighed. "It's just that no one cares, Moses."

"They only don't care because they don't *know*."

"Sure they do," Cynthia said. "Everybody knows. People say it all the time. 'Corporations control politicians.' 'Money controls politics.' 'Lobbyists control Congress.' 'Corporations write the laws.' 'The politicians are all corrupt.' 'The little guy doesn't matter.'"

The others were nodding at her words.

"Everybody already knows, Moses. Everybody says those things. It's probably the one thing you can get a bunch of Republicans and Democrats to agree on: The system's rigged. We all know it. The truth is that people just don't care. We're just starting to think that it's not worth dying for something that no one cares about anyway."

Moses wanted to tear out his hair. "I thought we were trying to *make* people care!"

"Maybe it can't be done!" Cynthia shot back. "Even the Doubt Factory doesn't take money to make people care. *They take money to do the opposite*. Status quo is easy to sell. People like to be nice and consistent. They like to be told to just stay in their seats, and don't worry about the theater burning. So what are we selling? Revolution?" Cynthia laughed sadly. "Who wants to buy that?"

"It happened in the Middle East."

"We've kind of got it better than they do," Kook observed.

"So . . . what? We just sit here and let them go because they aren't screwing over enough people? Just a few? Just us? Just our families?"

Cynthia stood up. "Be serious, Moses. It's dangerous. We've got the FBI on us for sure now."

Kook was nodding. "Definitely got Williams and Crowe's attention. Those fuckers are playing for keeps now. I've got trackers all over them, and they're like a bunch of stirred-up hornets. They got clients who are shitting about us, wondering who's next. You know it wasn't an accident they used gas like that. They don't want us just caught, they want us dead."

"I don't know about you all, but I'm playing for keeps, too."

Tank finally spoke. Small voice, small kid looking up at him. "We all saw the rats, Moses. We all saw them. If we'd been inside, what would have happened? If we hadn't set everything up perfect…"

"But we did!"

"No way, boss," Kook interjected. "That was not perfect. We barely got on the news. Nobody gives a shit. And if we keep going like this, we're going to be just like those rats. Just a pile of dead kids. We'll be on the news, all right, but it will be one of those 'What's Wrong With Teens These Days' stories, right up there with the chicks on Girls Gone Wild."

"So we can make them—"

"Moses," Cynthia interrupted. "What's the first rule of your uncle's cons?"

"Trust…"

"No. It's to make sure that you're the one who's running the con. Not the one who's being conned. Don't trick yourself into thinking people are different than they are. We've already been doing this a long time. Nothing changes people. Nothing."

She looked sad. "I'm sorry, Moses. Maybe it's time to grow up. We can't fix things that people don't want fixed. You can't con someone who doesn't want to be conned, and you can't wake up someone who doesn't want to wake up."

"I just don't want to end up like the rats," Tank said.

28

IT STARTED AS AN EXPERIMENT. A quick test to see what would come back. Even though it felt disloyal to her father, Alix couldn't shake off the need to test if any of it was real.

She started with aspirin. Moses had mentioned it in passing, during one of his screeds against the evils of industry.

It was just an experiment. A quick search on Google. *Let's see how crazypants 2.0 is.* She typed:

> Aspirin, Reye's syndrome.

She almost immediately arrived at the Aspirin Foundation's page—which had a clear link to a page about Reye's syndrome.

Alix read over the page of material, scanning for something to hook onto. At the bottom of the page, it concluded:

> There is a lack of convincing evidence that aspirin causes Reye syndrome: it may be one of many possible factors but many cases currently reported are probably due to inborn

313

errors of metabolism. It is unclear whether restricting aspirin use by children has a favourable risk/benefit ratio.

So much for that conspiracy theory, she thought.

She was about to close her laptop, but she could practically see Moses laughing at her.

"That's it? That's what Seitz research is? I thought they at least taught you rich kids how to work."

"Oh, just shut up, why don't you?" she muttered. But she could remember him in the warehouse, watching Tank skateboard. Him shaking his head and saying, *"Whenever I think I'm cynical, I find out I'm nowhere near cynical enough."*

So what would a cynic do? Alix wondered. She immediately abbreviated the question to WWCD.

WWCD?

A cynic wouldn't trust anyone. She went back to the top of the page and scanned for information on the Aspirin Foundation.

About the Foundation led to supporters, which led to:

Bayer HealthCare AG

When she clicked through, Bayer's tagline said, "Science for a Better Life."

Alix's eyes narrowed. *Bayer, huh?* She could feel her inner cynic suddenly engaging, despite herself.

Leaving her first window open, she opened a new tab and searched again:

Aspirin, Reye's syndrome

She hesitated, remembering Moses saying, *"You know what they call your dad's company? The Doubt Factory."*

With a hiss of anxiety, she added the word that the 2.0 crew were so obsessed with:

Doubt

Almost immediately a link to defendingscience.org popped up. It wasn't as slick as the Aspirin Foundation's site, but it was interesting. It seemed to be electronic excerpts from a book called *Doubt Is Their Product*, which some guy had written for Oxford University Press.

Its opening pages began:

> Since 1986 every bottle of aspirin sold in the United States has included a label advising parents that consumption by children with viral illnesses greatly increases their risk of developing Reye's syndrome....

Alix kept reading, and as she did, she found herself becoming more and more appalled.

In the early 1980s, scientists discovered that aspirin was causing Reye's syndrome in children. Immediately, the Centers for Disease Control notified doctors that children were in danger from the deadly illness that affected the brain and liver and appeared to be connected with taking aspirin when they had a viral infection like the flu or chicken pox.

So far, so good.

Then the government tried to notify the public. The Food and Drug Administration wanted to put a warning label on aspirin bottles. Even though doctors had been warned, aspirin was an over-the-counter medicine; it made sense that moms and dads should be warned that aspirin was a no-no for their little kids. Parents were the people buying the stuff, after all. There wasn't a doctor standing in the supermarket aisle to warn them. A warning label made sense.

But then the aspirin industry got involved. They threw up barriers to labeling. They said that the government was being overly activist and that the science wasn't settled. They fought—and the Food and Drug Administration backed down.

For two more years the government and doctors knew that an over-the-counter medicine millions of parents were buying for their kids was dangerous, but the parents weren't being informed. It finally took a lawsuit by Public Citizen's Health Research Group to force the FDA to act.

Eventually—finally—aspirin was labeled.

So who was this guy, this David Michaels, who had written the book? His bio said he was a professor at the George Washington University School of Public Health—and it seemed that someone liked him, because he'd not only served in the government under President Clinton but was also now serving as the assistant secretary of labor for the Occupational Safety and Health Administration under the current liberal president.

Half of Alix's friends would have called Michaels a liberal, socialist traitor for that...but she also noticed in his biography on OSHA's website that the Senate had unanimously confirmed him. *Unanimously?* Alix was a little surprised at that. She couldn't remember the last time Republicans and Democrats had agreed on anything. Either they were all asleep at his confirmation hearing, or someone actually thought Michaels knew something.

Regardless, a few things seemed fairly undeniable.

1. Reye's syndrome cases had started dropping from a high of more than five hundred cases a year as soon as the Centers for Disease Control started howling about how dangerous aspirin was for little kids.

2. After aspirin got its warning label, Reye's syndrome cases collapsed to around thirty a year.

And, of course, there was one last thing:

3. The aspirin industry had fought against warning labels, tooth and nail. They'd used legal threats and obfuscation and political leverage to delay the process as long as possible.

Alix searched around some more and came up with a 1982 *New York Times* article. It was fascinating to see into the history of the fight. Right there, on the page, the aspirin

317

industry was vowing to fight the labeling initiative. The Aspirin Foundation of America was quoted:

> Dr. Joseph White, the foundation's president, said studies purporting to link the syndrome and aspirin are "wholly inconclusive." The foundation also released a statement in Washington saying that the Department of Health and Human Services "acted hastily and without scientific basis" in calling for the warning label. Dr. White has asked for the chance to present the industry's views before the Food and Drug Administration takes further action.

It was fascinating to see the language White had used. The accusations of rushed judgment, the claims that the decision lacked scientific basis—it was exactly the playbook that Moses and the rest of the 2.0 crew had described.

Fascinating. And then, a little chilling, because the Aspirin Foundation of America had apparently succeeded. They'd kept a warning label off aspirin bottles for four years.

How much extra money did four extra years without a warning label get them?

Enough to justify killing a fair number of kids, apparently.

Alix did some quick math, based on the numbers she'd been reading. If 30 percent of the Reye's syndrome cases typically ended in death, that meant that more than a hundred and fifty kids had died each year that aspirin labeling was delayed.

Four times one-fifty, conservatively. Six hundred bodies so aspirin could make a little extra cash.

"Whenever I think I'm cynical, I find out I'm nowhere near cynical enough."

"No shit," Alix muttered.

She closed the computer, feeling unclean.

Aspirin. It seemed like such an innocuous thing.

Alix thought of her mom taking aspirin. She went down the hall to her parents' bedroom. In the master bath, she found the aspirin right inside the medicine cabinet, along with Tylenol and Advil. Alix looked darkly at the two other painkillers. "I don't have time for you, too."

She plucked out the Bayer aspirin. She sat on the edge of the marble tub and turned the bottle over to study the warning label.

WARNINGS—REYE'S SYNDROME

A simple box warning right in there with all the rest of the standard drug info. All it said was not to give it to children and teenagers if they had symptoms from flu or chicken pox. Such a small thing. And yet it had apparently sent executives at aspirin companies into a panic. Their product was under attack. They needed a defender.

And someone like her father had probably provided the product-defense playbook: the science wasn't sound, don't rush to judgment...

Delay = $$$

Alix sat on the edge of her parents' whirlpool tub with the bottle of aspirin in her hand, thinking of her father, feeling more and more unclean.

29

"HOW MUCH LONGER TILL EVERYONE'S done packing?" Moses asked Cynthia. They were loading gear into a van that Kook had rented. Her hair was now red and she'd changed her earrings and piercings. Cyn's hair was bobbed short, and she was wearing her makeup differently. Moses was amazed at how a few bits of blush or toner or eye shadow could totally change the impression of a person's face.

Cynthia had bemoaned the loss of her lustrous hair, but she'd donated it to some wig maker that helped cancer victims, so she figured it wasn't a total loss. Someone would like all that hair. Adam had shifted from hipster with his porkpie hat to all-American athlete, as if he'd never left the fine Mormon confines of Utah. And Moses, well, he'd turned himself into a young Wall Street turk, full suit, leather briefcase. A suit and a briefcase carried so much authority in America that the only thing better was a police uniform.

Tank hadn't bothered changing anything.

Skate rat's a skate rat, was all he said. *Nobody notices skate rats.*

Cyn looked up from her packing. "This is almost everything. We're totally cleared out." She stared around the empty space. "I'm going to miss this place."

"Yeah, well." Moses shrugged. "What's the point?"

All their work had come to nothing. All the money, all the planning, all the time. And it had disappeared so quickly.

Right back where we started.

Right back down in the hole with all the lunatic activists, everyone from the antiwar protesters to the 9/11 conspiracists, to PETA, to the antivaccine weenies. Relegated to the nutjob end of the spectrum. Just one more bunch of radicals in a frothy soup of radicals.

"You okay with this?" Adam asked as he loaded more boxes.

"Yeah," Moses said. "You're right. It's over. No way we're going to win against these assholes."

"Sorry your girl didn't work out."

Moses laughed and shook his head. "Yeah, well, I got too wrapped up in that, didn't I?"

"I never did see what you saw in her."

"Ass," Cyn said, as she went to gather more of their gear. "She had a nice ass."

Moses ignored her. "You going to be okay?" he asked Adam.

"Oh, sure." Adam grinned. "I'm heading for Florida. There's a guy down there, wants me to DJ at his club."

"A good-looking Cuban boy," Kook added. "Biceps like this." She mimed the muscles. "Sexy as hell."

Adam shot her a glare. "Would you please stay out of my e-mail?"

Kook batted her black lashes. "You'll miss me when I'm not looking over your shoulder all the time. I'm the only one who will kick sense into you."

Adam shook his head and grabbed his gym bag. "I'm going to be so glad to have privacy."

"Just you and the NSA," Kook quipped.

Moses held out a hand to Adam. "Take care of yourself."

Adam looked at him strangely, but he took the offered hand in a strong grip, and then pulled Moses into a hug. "Don't do anything crazy," he said, as he let Moses go.

"Crazy?" Moses shook his head. "Nah. I still got some money left. Maybe I'll go around the world on a trip or something. Kick it on a beach somewhere. Watch the world burn down with a piña colada, you know?"

"And then?"

"Can't be bothered to worry about that. Maybe back out to Vegas. I hear there's a guy out there knows how to pick pockets in public. Makes a show out of it. I always wanted to learn that."

"Shit, I'll bet you end up teaching him."

"Maybe." Moses laughed. "Maybe."

Cyn came out hauling two more suitcases. Adam and Moses went and grabbed them from her. Moses grunted at the weight. "You got rocks in here?"

"They're nice clothes," Cyn defended herself. "I'm not wasting them."

"You'll blend right in at the Ivy Leagues," Kook said.

"It's going to be weird to sit in classes that are actually new to me."

They slung the suitcases into the back of the van. Cyn and Adam pulled out, waving. Tank came out of the warehouse, hauling grocery bags full of hard drives to Kook's car. Moses helped carry out the flatscreens and slide them into the back of the station wagon, buffered by blankets.

When Kook finished and closed the hatch on the station wagon, she said, "Sorry it didn't work out."

Moses shrugged. "Shit happens."

She handed him a USB stick. "This is for you."

"What is it?"

"Her. Video. Her greatest hits. Case you want to relive the fun. A lot of shots of her eating cereal."

Moses took the USB stick.

"It was a good run," Kook said. She slapped him on the shoulder.

"Yeah. Too bad the world didn't give a fuck."

"The world's give-a-fuck was broken a long time before any of us came along. Not your fault." She turned. "Come on, Tank!"

"Where you headed?"

"I got an aunt in Colorado. Crazy hippie lady. Figure we'll lie low with her. Let Tank get his driver's license or something." She turned and shouted toward the warehouse. *"Tank!"*

"I'm right here," he said quietly. He'd been on the other side of the car.

"Would you quit lurking like that?" Kook waved him into the car. "Come on. Let's get going."

"Be there in a second."

"Sure. Say good-bye." She climbed into the car and started the engine. Tank sidled over to Moses.

"When are you heading out?" Tank asked.

"Soon."

Tank was looking down at his shoes. "You never really said where you were going."

The thing about Tank was, the kid paid attention. Most people, they were so busy chattering back and forth that they missed most of what was going on. And then there was Tank—always around, always paying attention, and so quiet that you forgot all about him.

"Hell. I don't know. Probably going on the road," Moses said finally. "Vegas or something, eventually." Even to himself, it sounded like he was talking a line.

Tank peered up from under his tangled black hair. "Uh-huh."

Moses had the uncomfortable feeling that the kid could see right through him. His uncle had been like that. *You can't con a con*, his uncle liked to say whenever Moses was trying to be sneaky. Moses found himself avoiding Tank's eyes. He made himself meet the boy's gaze. "You don't need to worry about me," he said. "I'll be fine."

"Just don't do anything stupid," Tank said.

"Stupid?" Moses gave the kid his best thousand-watt, trust-me smile. "Nah. I always make the smart move, don't you know?" He waved toward the car. "Go on. Kook's waiting."

Tank looked like he was going to argue. "You could come with us, you know."

"Crunchy-granola aunts aren't my thing."

"It's near Boulder, I guess. The place is crazy white." Tank sounded bummed.

"Better than juvie. Couple years, and you're living wherever you want." Moses nodded at the car. "Kook's good people. No bullshit. Be glad she's practicing mother hen on your ass."

Tank smiled self-consciously. "Yeah." He turned away, then stopped and looked back. "Thanks, Moses. Seriously."

"Nothing to thank. I thought…" Moses blew out his breath. "Thought I'd make some kind of difference. Crazy, right?"

"Made a difference for me," Tank said. He gave a little wave. "See you around."

"Yeah. For sure."

And then they were driving away, and Moses was alone. His throat felt tight as he watched them go.

He turned back to study the factory.

Have to get the lawyers to see if you can even unload this heap of junk.

And then?

He didn't have any answers.

Inside, the factory gleamed with the scrub-down they'd

done on it. No sign that they'd ever been there. Like they'd never existed. History hadn't happened. No fights and no jokes and no scream of Sawzalls cutting iron, spitting sparks. No big bass beats while they tested paint squirt guns and control software. No coffee- and energy-drink-fueled plotting on how to bust into a testing lab and steal a whole eighteen-wheeler full of rats along with vats and vats of Azicort. No more rats. It was all scrubbed clean.

They'd done so much, and they'd done nothing.

Just like rats on an exercise wheel. You could sure look busy, but you didn't get anywhere. You didn't accomplish shit. All you did was sweat awhile.

Moses's throat felt tight.

"I tried," he said to the empty space. He didn't like how his voice echoed. He sat cross-legged in the middle of the warehouse, hard concrete against his ass. His chest constricted and his eyes burned.

He put his head in his hands. "I tried," he said again, and, finally, with everyone gone and him alone with no one to watch or judge or give a damn if he showed how weak he felt, he let go of his control and cried.

I tried.

He went to where he'd collected his own belongings. He didn't even want what was there. Just couldn't muster the need to care.

I tried.

And what did you get? You didn't manage shit. Not in the end. Didn't put together a single thing.

It had been a fantasy—and fun for a while. A way to push back against the horror of being alone, to push back against the terror that had enveloped him ever since his parents had died. A kid game, playing pretend. Pretending he mattered. Pretending he could change things. Pretending he could do something people three times his age had never managed.

The machine was just too damn big.

Time to go. Way past time.

"It was a nice idea," he muttered.

The machine was too damn big.

30

IT BECAME A SECRET VICE. Every night, after everyone went to bed, Alix would boot up her laptop and dig deeper into her father's world. She wondered if Dad and Mom caught her whether this would qualify as "Anything Inappropriate." Would they rather catch her doing research like this, or would they be happier if they just caught her flashing someone on a live cam?

She kept digging, and the deeper she dug, the more dirt she found. At some point, she stopped feeling like she was digging and started feeling like she was slipping.

And then, at some point, she was falling.

Down the rabbit hole.

She hadn't felt it coming until it was too late.

She'd plummeted into a strange land where everything she'd known and understood was now strange and distorted, as though she'd been sucking on the hookah of the caterpillar among the toadstools in *Alice in Wonderland*. Everyday labels and brands she readily recognized now all started feeling like rocks with worms and centipedes and rot underneath.

A day after her trip down memory lane with the product defense of aspirin, she went spelunking again into painkillers, this time with Tylenol.

Tylenol had its own warning label. Overdoses from that one could kill you, apparently. Not just hurt you, but kill you dead.

Oops, too much acetaminophen.

Dead.

That was what NPR said, though the label on Tylenol only warned of severe liver damage if you took over three thousand milligrams—which seemed like a little bit of an understatement, in comparison with THIS PRODUCT WILL KILL YOUR ASS IF YOU TAKE TOO MUCH. Apparently even the version of the label she was reading was relatively new. Before then, it had been even more vague. Tylenol had managed to avoid putting an explicit warning about death on the label for over thirty years.

Alix couldn't help wondering if Dad had helped out with that. Moses said he was the best. Keeping a product from being labeled as a potential killer for thirty years would be a pretty good trick.

You're being paranoid, Alix thought. *Not everything is a plot.*

Except, it was sort of starting to seem like everything really *was* a plot.

Everywhere she looked she found more household brands and more respected companies, and everywhere she looked, she found more disturbing things.

It was like in a horror movie when the pretty guy suddenly pulled off his rubber mask and revealed a rotten corpse. She started out on the computer and then started making notes because she couldn't keep all the files straight. She wanted to see the scope of what she was discovering.

There was Merck and Vioxx, the painkiller that turned out to cause heart attacks.

There was Philip Morris, fighting to claim that tobacco wasn't all that bad, with the help of Hill & Knowlton and The Weinberg Group.

There was BASF and Dow Chemical and a chemical called bisphenol A, which seemed to act like estrogen and had all kinds of interesting side effects. It was in everything from tin cans to the ink on newsprint.

There was DuPont and 3M and a chemical compound called perfluorooctanoic acid, i.e., PFOA, i.e., C8. Also known as a key ingredient needed to manufacture Teflon.

That one kind of bummed her out. Alix liked 3M. It made sticky notes.

"How ironic," she muttered as she noted down the information on PFOA on her own sticky notes.

How could the maker of sticky notes also have been involved in manufacturing a chemical that screwed up the liver and caused birth defects and cancer? Apparently, 3M had gotten out of the game after pressure from the Environmental Protection Agency, but DuPont had stuck with it, so to speak, to make its Teflon products.

Her lists just kept growing.

Every night Alix stayed up late, searching deeper and deeper. She found books in the library that helped jumpstart new lines of questioning for her. It started with books like *Doubt Is Their Product* and *Merchants of Doubt*, but it quickly expanded to old newspaper articles and long-ago magazine exposés.

Once she stayed up all night reading what she came to think of as the tobacco files, a massive public archive of tobacco-industry documents kept by the University of California, San Francisco. It documented how Big Tobacco had managed to keep on selling its cancer sticks despite decades of challenges. She stopped reading only when the sun started poking through her windows to tell her it was morning.

■ ■ ■

As her research deepened, Alix started finding more and more connections. But often she wasn't sure if it was from her own work or things 2.0 had told her.

Deep in the middle of the night, Alix found herself working through the thick sheaves of notes that she had compiled, hunting for a connection that was just at the edge of her conscious brain. Something about one of the doubt companies, as she was coming to think of these PR specialists. Something important…Exponent, maybe? Or was it The

Weinberg Group again? Some connection to her father? Or maybe to George?

Alix couldn't help thinking of Moses and 2.0 as she laid out another row of stickies on the floor.

"I should have taken some photos of those banners," she muttered. "I'm reinventing the whole frigging wheel, just to catch up to everything they already know." She frowned at her collected information. If only she had access to what 2.0 had already researched...

Maybe the TV crews had the footage. Could she get that?

She sat back, surveying the arrayed notes. Something important was here; she just couldn't quite pick it out....

"Um, Alix?"

Jonah was standing in the doorway in his sweats with tousled hair, squinting in the light. "Do you know it's, like, three AM?" he asked blearily.

"Why, am I making too much noise?" she asked.

Jonah shook his head, started to leave, then came into the room instead. He was still blinking in the light but seemed to be waking up. He sat down on the floor with her and surveyed her work. "Are you doing okay?"

"Sure," Alix snapped. She wished he'd leave so that she could get back to the puzzle, but Jonah wasn't leaving. He picked up a sticky note on beryllium. "So...what are you up to?"

"Oh, nothing...just...you know...research."

But now, as she looked at her work spread out across the floor, her laptop open, printed website articles and news clippings with sticky notes attached to them, long lists of chemicals, companies, and product-defense firms (all in different color pens so she could keep track of where the pieces fit— pink, blue, green, red)... Alix swallowed, suddenly seeing her work through Jonah's eyes.

Wow. You really are nuts, she realized. *You have completely lost it.*

Jonah was watching her warily. "You're kind of acting strange, Alix."

"I'm fine." But even as Alix said it, she herself wasn't completely convinced. "I mean," she amended, "I'm crazy, but I'm starting to figure some things out."

"This is about 2.0, isn't it? They got in your head somehow."

Alix frowned, looking around at the sweep of papers and sticky notes and documents, along with some plates that she'd brought up from the kitchen and a surprising number of venti-sized coffee cups that had accumulated in the room.

"Does Dad know?" she asked.

"Well, you're not exactly acting normal. We're all kind of talking about it. Mom and Dad keep asking about you." He lowered his voice to a serious, parental-caring tone. " 'How is Alix doing?' " He made a face. "That kind of thing."

"Shit. I have to hide this stuff." She'd been so involved in the search that she hadn't realized what it would look like if Dad saw it. "Help me clean up."

"Um. Okay. Now?"

"Yes, now! I shouldn't have all this out."

"Okay..." He started stacking the papers.

"No!" Alix stopped him. "Those are product-defense companies. They're coded red. These ones"—she took the papers out of Jonah's hands—"are client companies. They're green. Put all the green inks together."

Jonah looked at her quizzically. "You're really getting into this." He picked up another note and started reading a list of acronyms that Alix had collected. "OMB. FDA. EPA. OSHA. NIOSH. CIAR. OMFG. STFU."

"Cut it out. Those are serious." She took the list back.

Jonah let her take it, frowning thoughtfully. "You know how you're always telling me there's a fine line between clever and stupid?"

Alix eyed him warily. "Yeah. Why? Are you going to tell me that I've crossed that line?"

"Actually, I was just thinking there might be another line: the fine line between brilliant and crazy."

"I know I'm crazy," she said as she continued sweeping her papers and notes into piles. "You don't need to rub it in."

"I was actually leaning toward brilliant."

Alix glanced up at her brother, surprised.

"I mean, don't get me wrong," Jonah rushed on, "you're acting weird as hell, but this is actually kind of brilliant."

Alix flushed and looked down. "I'm not, really." For some reason, she felt embarrassed at the compliment. She stared at the papers spread around her. "I mean, it's just research. You start doing it, and you get all this information. Mostly, it's just about focusing and doing the work. Anyone could do it."

"Yeah, but most people don't. Most people don't worry about what"—he picked up the sticky note of acronyms again—"CIAR is."

"Center for Indoor Air Research," Alix said promptly. "That was a front group for Big Tobacco. There are a ton of front groups." She cast about, irritated that all her files weren't spread out for easy searching. "I've got a list just of front organizations somewhere...." She started hunting again.

"Front organizations?"

"Sure. It works better if someone like CIAR funds research that says secondhand smoke is safe. And then it looks even better if they can get some legitimate news organization or scientific journal to report their results. It makes it look like there are more perspectives on the debate, and it keeps your brand out of the fight. So you make up some kind of neutral-sounding nonprofit like CIAR or the Advancement of Sound Science Coalition, and you have them do the dirty work...."

She trailed off as she realized Jonah was still looking at her.

"What now?"

"Just remember the line, Alix. Brilliant or crazy. It's a superfine line."

But he was smiling as he said it.

They started gathering up the rest of her papers and putting them in stacks, with Jonah being surprisingly good about taking her directions as they cleaned up. Alix yawned. 3:30 AM. She really was tired.

Jonah paused on his way out the door.

"Are you okay? I mean otherwise?"

"Yeah. I'm fine." She made herself nod definitively. "I'm good." She hesitated. "Don't tell Dad, though, okay?"

"Are you kidding? He'd lose it. Just don't go running off to join the resistance without telling me, okay?"

She rolled her eyes. "I'm not that brilliant."

"Well, at least stick around until tomorrow night."

"Why? What's happening?"

Jonah gave her an annoyed look. "The party? The stupid company party Dad's making us go to? The Kimball-Geier shindig? The one on the ginormous boat that Mom's been talking about for the last week, about how I have to be on good behavior and not do anything inappropriate that would embarrass Dad? Any of this ringing a bell?"

Alix looked at him blankly. "I don't remember...."

"Gah!" Jonah threw up his hands. "You really are as bad as Dad now. You act like you're listening, but you aren't. Everyone hassles me about all this—*Jonah do this, Jonah don't do that*—but at least I listen to people when I'm looking right at them...."

Alix stopped listening. *Kimball-Geier.* Why did that name ring a bell? She started digging back through her notes. *Kimball-Geier*...

"Are you even listening to me?"

"Sure, I'm listening." She lifted up a venti Starbucks cup. *No. Not there.* She lifted a plate. *God, I really do need to clean up—Ha! There you are!*

"Kimball-Geier!" She shook crumbs off the sticky note and held it up to Jonah, grinning triumphantly. "I knew I had something!" It had a coffee ring on it, but the ink was still legible. "Kimball-Geier Pharmaceuticals," she read, feeling pleased. "They make Azicort, the asthma drug. They're one of Dad's clients. Dad and George work with Kimball-Geier." She frowned. "They actually do a lot of work with Kimball-Geier."

"I take it back," Jonah said. "You are nuts."

■ ■ ■

"Alix! Are you ready?" Mom called from downstairs. "Alix!"

"Coming!"

Kimball-Geier Pharmaceuticals was throwing a party with the CEO, board of directors, major shareholders, and other important colleagues and their families, and Alix's parents expected her and Jonah to attend. She stood in front of her closet, trying to choose a dress and not think about the skate rat, Tank. Funny name for such a little kid...

They were going to be on the ocean. She chose a Rag & Bone flared dress, letting it slip over her shoulders. Fun Jimmy Choo heels. A Michael Kors shrug, because the ocean air would probably be cool.

She turned sideways in the mirror, smoothing the dress over her hips. *Well, at least the outside is nicely packaged.*

Inside, though? Her mind was a tangle of chemicals and products and government acronyms. EPA, C8, FDA, PCB, BPA... her brain wouldn't stop working.

Alix started applying her lipstick. NARS. She looked down at the tube and was struck by the purple bruise color she'd been about to apply. Who lobbied for lipstick? Was there a Cosmetic Beauty Lobby? Probably. Only they wouldn't call themselves a lobby. They'd probably call themselves the Consumer Beauty Resource Council. Or the Cosmetic Color Association, or something equally friendly and neutral. For sure, some group ensured that they could keep selling lipstick and that nobody looked too closely at where their colors came from or how they kept lipstick from melting.

Alix rummaged through the rest of her beauty products, the blushes and the sparkling washes and the glycerine soap with the fragrance of green tea and rose. She dug into her medicine cabinet, looking at the ingredients. Potassium this, sodium lauryl sulphate, propylene glycol that—she couldn't really parse most of the chemical names, even with her AP Chem knowledge.

What the hell was in it? Who tested it? How did they test it? Had her father helped—Alix looked at the label of the small soap packet she was holding—had her father helped Tiptree & Little put some balding guy on an advisory panel somewhere to make sure that soap wasn't tested too much and didn't have too many warning labels on it?

She put the soap down, feeling a little like she'd put down a snake. *It's just soap. Get a grip.* She picked up her lipstick again and considered her half-done lips in the mirror. She studied the lipstick once more.

So? Is this stuff safe or not?

There was no way of knowing. She had a creepy feeling that if she even started to research this new topic, it would take her places she wouldn't like.

"Alix!" Mom called up again. "We're going to be late!"

Alix gripped the bathroom sink, staring at herself in the mirror.

"Alix!"

She picked up the lipstick again and deliberately finished the job. Smearing color onto her lips. Marking herself with whatever NARS decided to stick in its cosmetics. She dropped the lipstick tube into her clutch. Turned her head this way and that, admiring herself in the mirror.

Perfect.

Not a single sign that something was rotten inside her.

31

THE LIMO SWEPT SOUTH AND EAST toward the water, carrying Alix and her family toward the Kimball-Geier party. She sat next to Jonah and peered out through the tinted windows as darkness fell. Taillights and traffic, office buildings standing out against the blush of sunset sky. Manhattan rising as they got closer to the water.

"I don't even see why we have to do this," Jonah complained.

"Because Mr. Geier is your father's client."

"But he's not *my* client," Jonah groused. "It's not like I'm in business with him."

"Maybe you should be," Alix said. "I hear they're making a drug for impulse control."

Dad glanced over at Alix, his expression surprised and pleased. "I didn't know you paid that much attention."

"You mean they're going to turn me into a zombie," Jonah said.

"It's actually for appetite suppression," Alix said, "so you're safe for now."

Dad was looking so approvingly at Alix that she felt ill. She couldn't look at Dad without experiencing double vision. It felt like she was riding in an alternate, decayed version of the limo, while everyone else lived in the regular world.

For Jonah and Mom, Dad was still Dad.

For Alix, he was a sticky note that had become an index card that had become a computer file and then a folder.

Simon Banks. Born 1962. Graduated from Princeton. Majored in economics and government. Went to work with Hill & Knowlton in the mid-eighties, where it seemed he'd come in contact with its client Philip Morris, the tobacco giant. He moved from Hill & Knowlton to The Weinberg Group and continued to work with Philip Morris. From there, Simon Banks departed Weinberg for a brief and unhappy stint at ChemRisk, another product-defense company. And then, in 2002, he'd started Banks Strategy Partners, with him as the PR lead and George Saamsi as the chief science liaison.

Alix hazily remembered that period of time. Dad worked more hours, and sometime after that, they'd moved into a newer, bigger house.

From there, BSP became the story. Banks Strategy Partners. They didn't list their clients publicly, but they did list industries. Genetically modified crops. Pesticides and herbicides. Pharmaceuticals. Consumer products. Energy and petroleum.

Dad was on his cell, texting someone, as Jonah continued to complain about the event.

"It's on a yacht, Jonah."

"I've been on yachts."

Dad smiled knowingly. "Not one like this, you haven't."

"Who else is going?" Alix asked, staring out the window. She was still thinking about all the things she'd been reading. She couldn't look at her father. He appeared the same as before: same tall man, same hair receding just a little bit, a tiny bit of gray—but not like George, who had gone round and bald. Dad was vital from CrossFit, tanned from sailing. Alix had his eyes, people said.

"Your friends should be there. I know Tim and Maya are coming, so Denise should be there. The Patels should be there. I know you like Ritika and Mona."

"Sounds like half of Seitz is going to be there," Jonah groaned.

"Oh, stop it," Mom said. "I don't think you hate the school nearly as much as you say. I even heard from your biology teacher that you're doing well all of a sudden."

Jonah smiled. "We're cutting open cow hearts."

Mom made a face. "Then why not say you're enjoying it? It's okay to enjoy things once in a while, Jonah."

The coastline came into view, and then the marina. "Wow," Alix said, surprised. "That's a big boat."

Jonah crowded beside her, peering out. "What is that thing?"

"State of the art," Dad said. "It's the new design from Merseir Group."

"That thing is insane!"

Alix couldn't help but feel a little surprised at how beautiful it looked. The yacht was huge and sleek, and with party lights strung on it, it looked festive and welcoming.

"Are those sails?" she asked.

Her father nodded. "Fixed wing sails. She's a hybrid. Very efficient. She can sail, or she can run on three Rolls-Royce gas turbines and two MAN diesel engines. She's green when she wants to be, and she's one of the fastest things on the ocean when she decides she wants that. The only other person who has one is a prince in Dubai." He had his own face pressed to the glass, looking almost as wonderstruck as Jonah. "I spoke with Mr. Geier. He said he'll have the captain give you a tour, Jonah."

For once, Jonah was completely silent. Looking at the two of them, staring out at the boat, Alix was struck at how similar they were. Two kids delighted by the sight of a high-tech toy.

The limo dropped them off, and they joined the line of people being checked against security lists as they boarded the ship.

Alix spied Sophie and Kala waving at her from the starboard rail.

Mr. and Mrs. Geier were welcoming people aboard. Alix smiled on cue and shook their hands while her hijacked brain tagged Geier with all the information she'd dug up before she went to the party.

Kimball-Geier Pharmaceuticals, trading publicly on the NYSE, stock price around 20…

Kimball-Geier's last blockbuster drug had been Ventipren, another asthma medication. Azicort was the follow-up, a slight chemical variation that passed through FDA approvals without comment and replaced Ventipren after clinical trials showed it worked better. Kimball-Geier was a survivor. It had had one class action about Ventipren settled and sealed. But Kimball-Geier outright won another lawsuit related to its plant emissions' impact on a neighboring town. Yet another lawsuit had been thrown out by a lower court for lack of scientific evidence. That was the one Tank had apparently been part of. The one that claimed Azicort caused comas and sometimes death, depending on the dosage.

But that case got thrown out.

She realized Mr. Geier had said something to her. Alix smiled and nodded.

"I love it," she gushed, and walked off, wondering what he'd been talking to her about.

She made her way to the upper deck, snagging a glass of champagne from the tray of a passing waiter. She leaned against the rail, taking in the view of the city. Below her, she glimpsed Mr. Geier and her father and Jonah walking away from the main group, gesturing and laughing and pointing at features on the boat. They looked so comfortable and normal that Alix felt uncharitable for entertaining doubts about them.

Sophie interrupted her thoughts. "You've been scarce." She jostled Alix affectionately as she leaned against the rail. She had a glass of champagne of her own.

"Yeah. It's been busy."

They both sipped their champagne. Sophie tried again. "You've been a little off, ever since..." She trailed off uncomfortably.

"Since Cynthia?" Alix supplied.

"Yeah. And that whole kidnapping thing." She shook her head. "You're lucky they didn't murder you or something."

"Or something," Alix agreed.

Sophie's father was a partner in a big law firm. Galen & Tate. Alix tried to remember if the firm was one that had shown up in her research. The name sounded familiar, but it was probably a coincidence. *They can't all be rotten*, she thought. *Sometimes a law firm is a just a law firm.*

"So how come you're here?" Sophie asked.

"Kimball-Geier is my dad's client."

"Same here," Sophie said.

"Oh."

Alix suddenly remembered where she'd seen the name. Galen & Tate was the law firm that had gotten the Azicort class action suit thrown out for lack of scientific evidence. Alix's skin crawled.

Maybe there really wasn't any evidence.

The yacht cast off, easing away from the dock. The skyline of Manhattan slowly revealed itself as they slipped toward open ocean. It was warmer than she'd expected, considering the season. As the yacht picked up speed and pulled away from shore, she leaned into the wind. It was beautiful.

345

She looked down on the lower deck, where most of the adults were gathered. Her father was still talking to Mr. Geier. *What are you two talking about?* Alix felt dirty and uncharitable, thinking it, but she couldn't scrub the question out of her head.

She didn't fit here. Everyone was drinking and laughing and having a good time, and yet to her, it all felt somehow claustrophobic. As if her world had become an impossibly tight straitjacket. She couldn't escape, she couldn't breathe, and the more she watched the party, the worse it got. Alix forced herself to grip the rail and sip her champagne and exchange small talk with Sophie.

This is what normal people do. Why can't you just be normal?

A couple of men Alix didn't recognize joined her dad and Mr. Geier, and they all shook hands. Dad talked a moment longer, and then he was on the move, working his way through the crowd. Shaking hands with men, giving women hugs, clapping the occasional close friend on the back, exchanging words with lawyers and CEOs, inheritors of old corporate money.

Alix was surrounded by the cream of her society, living the good life with a champagne glass and a phenomenal view of the Manhattan skyline, and yet all she wanted to do was unzip the straitjacket of her unclean skin and leap off the yacht into the water. Anything to get away from this feeling.

George Saamsi was working his way through the crowd, making his own rounds of handshakes and back slaps.

George Saamsi. BA in chemistry from the University of California, Berkeley. PhD in organic chemistry from the University of Chicago. Hired by the tobacco company Philip Morris, eventually rising to the title of senior researcher. She'd read an actual transcript of George being deposed on the topic of secondhand smoke, where she'd first seen the term "environmental tobacco smoke" used.

It had been interesting to read George's deposition transcripts because he was always careful to never make any conclusions. He only spoke of unknowns and uncertainties that needed more study. He'd spent time researching how people felt about their smoking habits and how that might skew data when they reported whether or not they had been harmed by secondhand smoke. He spent time trying to decide how much secondhand smoke affected SIDS deaths versus how much smoking during pregnancy affected it. Even back in the nineties, he'd been focused on always finding as many questions as possible, while avoiding coming up with answers. Anything that might lead to more doubt, more research, more delay.

Alix assumed that the secondhand smoke work was where her father and George had met. There were overlaps with Philip Morris and The Weinberg Group around that subject, so it made sense. In the years following, George left Philip Morris but kept up the doubt work. He showed up in a lot of testimony at a lot of trials. He showed up in cases related to asbestos and beryllium. He testified regarding a chemical called diacetyl, which had been used in butter flavoring for microwave popcorn until it turned out it was destroying workers' lungs and was phased out, at least from popcorn, around 2007. And as 2.0 had said, he showed up testifying for Kimball-Geier Pharmaceuticals, saying that no definitive study had concluded that Azicort could be traced to any instance of sudden coma. According to George, a number of other factors were likely to blame and required additional study.

In George's work outside the courtroom, he showed up as a science advisor on the board of the Household Products Safety Advisory Board, an organization that appeared to get its funding from companies that manufactured cleaning supplies. He made regular appearances in Congress, testifying on the dangers of overzealous regulation. He was senior research fellow at the Center for Study of Indoor Air Quality.

The chief science liaison at Banks Strategy Partners was everywhere. Nice, Santa-like Uncle George seemed to pop up whenever a new chemical or substance needed defending. As Alix watched him work the crowd, she wondered if he could really be as amoral as the circumstantial evidence indicated. He looked way too nice to actually be that awful.

She remembered how badly Moses and his crew wanted to see what files Banks Strategy Partners held.

Alix remembered the USB stick that Kook had given her with the virus.

"Stuxnet, baby. DoD-certified, badass wormtastic. You just plug it in, and I'll do the rest."

Alix suddenly wished she had it now.

Is that really what I'm thinking about doing? Hacking my own dad's company?

But it was a fantasy. She didn't have the virus. Williams & Crowe had taken the thing away, and she'd never seen it again.

She did have one thing, though, and it made Alix feel traitorous to realize that she might take advantage of it.

She had her father's complete trust.

You're the good girl. The responsible girl. The levelheaded girl.

The levelheaded girl knocked back her champagne glass and headed down to the lower deck. She wove through the press of cocktail dresses and suits, zeroing in on George Saamsi, snagging another champagne on the way.

"George!"

BSP's chief science liaison turned at her call, looking surprised, but when he saw it was Alix, he smiled warmly. "Alix! I wasn't sure you'd come." He looked around. "Where are your friends?"

"Oh, they're around."

How to change the topic?

Alix tried to look troubled and let her smile slip a little. She leaned forward and lowered her voice. "It's not…" She hesitated. "It's not the same hanging out with them… since…" She made a show of searching for words. "You know. Since the 2.0 thing."

George's expression immediately became concerned and sympathetic. "I'm so sorry to hear that. It must have been horrible."

Alix tried to look like someone who was bravely hiding her pain. "The doctor says I'll get over it, eventually. It's like PTSD, I guess. Iraq and Afghanistan soldiers mostly get over it, too. And they had it so much worse than I did. 2.0 didn't do anything to me...." She shook her head. "But still, it bothers me. I know it's a small thing, but I hate it. That cage—" She broke off.

"Don't minimize it, Alix. You went through something terrible. They took away your freedom. They made you feel powerless. That's not easy for anyone to take. Just because you weren't physically hurt doesn't mean there wasn't trauma."

Alix took a long hard swig from her champagne and peered at George from over the rim of the glass, making sure he saw her doing it.

He bit, just like she knew he would. Good old Uncle George, keeping an eye out for his best friend's child.

"That's..." He paused. "That's a lot of alcohol, Alix."

Alix drained the glass and handed the empty off to a waiter. "What? This?" She snagged another fresh glass before the waiter could escape. "Chill, Uncle George. It's just to relax." It was some kind of sparkling rosé that looked gross and tasted worse when she lifted it to her lips.

George gripped her arm, stopping her from taking another drink. "Alix. Seriously. I think you've had enough."

Alix yanked her arm away and raised her voice. "Why? Because I'm such a good girl?" A couple of people glanced over at them now. *Perfect. A scene.* Except she really was getting drunk.

George held up his hands, soothing. "What's going on, Alix? What do you want me to say?"

"Nothing," Alix snapped. "I don't want you to say anything. Some kind of crazy terrorists put me in a cage because of your business, and you and Dad don't have anything to say."

"We didn't do that to you, Alix."

"You know I hurt him?" Alix said sharply.

"Your father?"

"No. The jackass who grabbed me." *Moses.* "He stuck his hand into my cage, and I grabbed him. I almost broke his arm."

"That was incredibly brave."

"No. I was pissed. He was saying all kinds of things about you and Dad."

"Ah."

"Yeah." She took another swig of rosé. "You wouldn't believe all the things he was saying. All about you and Dad killing families and fooling people into taking drugs and s-selling lies." Her words were slurring now, but she kept her eyes on George's expression. "He wanted me to write things. To say you were doing those things. He wanted me to write down everything that they were saying and put my name on it."

"I'm sorry you had to go through that. The Chinese in Korea did something similar with American GIs. It's a form of brainwashing—"

Brainwashing? Alix felt sick with the new thought, and she didn't think it was the liquor. *Am I brainwashed? Is that why I'm taking all this so seriously now? Because 2.0 got inside my head and brainwashed me?*

George was still talking. "You should talk to your therapist about it. Anything that you felt or did while they had you locked up." He gripped her shoulder, hard, looking her in the eye. "It wasn't your fault, Alix. Remember that."

Alix struggled to get back into her role. "It—it was all insane. They were saying they were going to do something to expose Dad."

"Their stunt with the warehouse." George nodded knowingly.

"Nooo…" Alix didn't even have to pretend to be drunk anymore. She was flying. The champagne and rosé had made it through her blood and straight into her head. "It was something else. It sounded big. About asthma medicine or something. Some drug killing kids or something." She tossed back the rest of the rosé and stared around drunkenly. "I've got to tell Dad. I don't know why I didn't think of it before. It was when 2.0 had me in the cage. 2.0 said he was going to make some company pay." She scanned the crowds again. "I can't believe I forgot. Dad needs to know they're still planning something!"

She lurched off, pretending to seek her father. George caught her before she toppled off her Jimmy Choos. "It's all right, Alix. I'll speak with him," he said soothingly. "I'll let him know. Now probably isn't the time."

"Do you think it's true?" she asked, making her eyes go wide and drunk and Bambi innocent. "About the asthma drug? Do you think it could be killing people?"

George laughed and shook his head kindly. "No, Alix. It

couldn't. People will say almost anything if it will win them a lawsuit. They'll try to spread a lie that a certain medicine kills just to make a buck off the jury award. It doesn't matter how many studies show something is safe, because if you can force a jury into a hysterical conclusion, instead of taking a measured approach and letting sound science dictate what's true, a trial lawyer can get a huge payday from a class action lawsuit." He snorted. "People will say or do all kinds of horrible things for money, unfortunately."

Alix forced herself to smile. "That's what I told them."

As quickly as she could, she separated from him and went to the rail. The feeling of being surrounded by unclean things was almost overwhelming. Talking to George, she felt as if he was using a part of the Doubt Factory playbook on her. Around the time he'd said "sound science" she'd started suspecting that he knew exactly what he was doing.

How much was a breakthrough asthma drug worth?

Alix leaned against the rail, sweating and hating the feeling of the alcohol that she'd drunk for George's benefit. Knocking back those glasses to make herself appear harmless to him had seemed like a good idea at the time. But now she felt blearily drunk and wanted it to stop, and now she'd just have to wait it out.

Except she still had more to do. She still had to see if the seed she'd planted...

George was cutting through the crowds toward her father and Mr. Geier.

Alix took a deep breath and pushed off from the rail. *Stay sober.* Which was a total laugh because she was feeling more and more hammered by the minute.

Suck it up, Alix. You're not getting another shot at this.

She stumbled after the trio of men, keeping her eye on them. They ducked through a door into the boat's interior cabins. Alix pressed through the crowd, hurrying to catch up. It couldn't be a coincidence. She'd poked them, and they'd reacted.

Alix slipped through the door. She found herself in the yacht's media center, the walls lined with flatscreen TVs, eight feet across. She slipped off her heels and stole across the parquet floors. She padded down a hallway, pausing at each door to listen.

At last, she found them in what Alix decided was a library. At least, the room had a ton of books on the wall, from what she could glimpse through the decorative porthole in the door. She wondered if Geier had read any of them at all. Maybe his wife read. Or maybe the books were just for guests.

The men's voices filtered dimly through the door. Alix leaned against the oak, trying to hear, then, holding her breath, she eased the sliding panel slightly wider, blessing the Dutch for their silent precision. Not a click, not a slide, just voices wafting louder out into the corridor.

"Where else could they hit you?" George was asking Geier. "They like getting on the news. Are you planning any press events?"

Geier's voice sounded puzzled as he went through possibilities. "We've got our quarterly call with investors. The FDA came back with a ruling that Azicort doesn't require a second look. Would it be that?"

"No, 2.0 likes public events," her father said. "They'll go after something big and public. Something they can prank. Something that will cause embarrassment."

"This party is about as public as Kimball-Geier is going to be for a while."

"You don't think they're on the yacht?" George asked.

"They're kids, not miracle workers," Dad said.

"Did you hear what Williams and Crowe said about that virus Alix brought back? That would have been a serious problem if it had gotten into our servers."

"It didn't," Dad said sharply. There was a pause, and then he said, "So where else are we vulnerable? Public events. Think about public places that will attract news attention."

"We've got depositions scheduled for the Romano class action down in Louisiana. We've got a presser...."

"No. They're not like that. What if they went after Sammons?"

"The man's solid. He won't say anything. He knows he's got a job waiting for him as soon as he steps down from the FDA."

"What about our science witnesses for the appeal? Would they go after them?" George asked. "2.0 spends an awful lot of time worrying about science testimony. You saw what they had up on the walls with that last stunt."

"I just don't see it. We've got Renner. I mean, sure, he's a hack, but he's happy to say whatever we want. And I think with Hsu, we've got someone a jury will like. His credentials look good, given all his papers that we've published."

"Would they go after our respiratory journal?"

"They can't do anything more to us than what opposing counsel will already try. It won't affect the trial. We got most of the credentialing issues excluded by the judge. It won't be a problem until they try another appeal, and that will be years...."

Delay = $$$

Alix didn't want to listen anymore. She padded away, as quietly as her drunken state would allow, and made her way back into the fresh sea air. She leaned against the rail, trying to force herself to breathe.

Just breathe. Don't think about it.

She wasn't sure how long she stood at the rail, staring out at the city lights reflecting on the waters, but it must have been for a long time because the next thing she was aware of was Dad joining her.

"Alix?"

Not him. Anyone but him. Alix couldn't bring herself to meet his eyes. She made herself smile, but it felt fake, and yet it was all she could muster. *At least you're drunk.*

"Hi, Dad."

"George told me you were drinking?"

"Yeah." She looked out at the city lights again. Now that he was leaning on the rail, too, she didn't have to look straight at him. She could just act like the view was the most amazing thing she'd ever seen.

"I don't mind if you have a glass," Dad said. "You're very nearly an adult. But getting drunk, Alix?"

"Yeah." She made herself laugh. "That was stupid, I know."

"I'm worried about you."

I'm starting to think I might hate you.

She couldn't look at him. She was terrified that he'd be able to see what she was thinking. "I know," she said finally. She kept her eyes on the skyline. "I'm sorry. I didn't mean to. I mean, I've been thinking a lot. Everything that happened before, it really got to me for a while. But I think it's actually going to be okay now."

"It doesn't look like things are okay."

Alix shrugged. "I think it's like AA."

"Do you think you're an alcoholic?" Dad sounded so worried that Alix almost laughed.

"No!" She paused. "I didn't mean it like that. I mean that first you have to admit you've got a problem. After that, it's a lot easier to decide what you need to do." She shrugged again. "I just couldn't admit how much the whole kidnapping thing got to me." She made herself smile at him, feeling like a bitch for lying and doing it anyway. "You were right. I was burying it."

Dad wrapped an arm around her shoulders. Alix's skin crawled as he gave her a comforting hug, but she forced herself not to draw away.

"It would be hard for anyone," Dad said. "I'm sorry you had to go through it."

"It's okay. I'm fine. I mean, I will be. I'll be fine." She made herself smile, and suddenly it was real for her. She could lie to him because she wasn't lying at all. Suddenly she could smile radiantly. "I have a feeling it's going to get better from now on."

"Oh?"

"I realized that I was having a hard time because they were trying to fuck with my mind. I mean, sorry. I mean..."

Dad was too cool to worry about the language. He just nodded.

Alix plunged on. "Anyway, that's what it was. They were trying to make me believe in their crazy world instead of me believing in my own...." She trailed off. "But I'm not an idiot. I can trust myself. Just because I get fooled once by someone, it doesn't mean I'm always going to be fooled by them."

"We only learn from our mistakes."

"Yeah." Alix nodded. "In a weird way, if it hadn't been for 2.0, I would never have figured out how important it is to have honest people around you."

"I'm glad, Alix."

"Yeah, well." She shrugged. "Being surrounded by liars will do that to you."

32

SURROUNDED BY LIARS, ALIX FOUND herself becoming one. She forced herself to smile, made herself be the good girl that Mom and Dad wanted her to be, and at night she did more and more research. After Jonah's intruding on her and her scattered notes, she became more careful about her research.

She created new filing systems and password-protected her laptop, she bought a little key safe at the mall and stuck it under her bed to keep her papers in, and she laid a few of her hairs on top just to make sure that no one messed with it without her knowing.

She regarded the two strands of hair that she'd carefully laid across the locking case. "Nice, Alix. You're a real super-spy," she muttered to herself. It felt silly, but it still felt better to her than doing nothing.

Eventually, though, the research dead-ended. There was

all the information that was out there in the public view, and then there was whatever was tucked away inside the Doubt Factory. It was possible to speculate endlessly about what Dad and Uncle George were up to, but without being able to see their client files, that's all it was: speculation.

No wonder 2.0 had wanted her to help them. They'd run into the same brick wall that she had.

She sighed and shoved her research case back under her bed. "I am so sick of liars."

So go find some people who aren't.

Unbidden, a memory of Moses and his crew popped into her head. All of them doing whatever they wanted, skating or programming or feeding rats or talking politics. Looking back on it, it felt amazingly free to her. Just thinking about it banished some of the claustrophobic constriction that she'd been feeling for the last few weeks.

So go find them, a voice in her mind suggested again.

Yeah, right. Like you could. The FBI couldn't find them. Neither could Williams & Crowe. What makes you think you're so special?

You were there.

Alix paused, considering. She'd been there. She'd been right there. She'd seen that whole factory. She just hadn't seen enough of the outside. But she'd been there. She'd been at the rave factory, with it's giant hamster wheel and many dance cages that had become Williams & Crowe cages, but then there had been the other factory, call it the bat cave, the place where 2.0 laired and lived. She'd lived in their bat cave.

Alix grabbed her keys. Jonah saw her heading out the door.

"Where you headed?"

Alix scowled at him. "Nowhere."

"Great! I'll come, too."

"Are you still spying on me?" she asked him pointedly.

"Spying?" Jonah looked hurt, but Alix didn't really buy it.

"Screw it," she said, giving up. "Come on."

"Where are we going?"

"Memory lane."

■ ■ ■

The rave factory looked pretty much the way she'd seen it the last time, except that someone had cleaned up all the dead rats and taken down 2.0's banners.

"So is this some kind of getting-over-trauma assignment or something?" Jonah asked.

Alix was sort of regretting bringing Jonah with her, given how little he could take anything seriously. But she'd decided he was more likely to protect her privacy if he was included than if she shut him out, so now he was wandering around the empty building like a tourist at a freak exhibit.

"Check out the smoke stains!" Jonah called, pointing at the ceiling of the factory, smeared with vibrant soot residue of burning saltpeter and sugar and whatever chemicals 2.0 had used to create the colors.

"Yep," Alix sighed. "Those are smoke stains."

"They pretty much snowed you, didn't they?"

"Pretty much." Alix went outside to survey the empty warehouse. She'd wanted to believe that the place would tell her something, give her a clue about where she'd been taken next, but the truth was they'd drugged the hell out of her, and then she'd woken up…wherever. In the bat cave.

Lisa had exhaustively debriefed Alix after the kidnapping, dragging out every single detail Alix could recall. *What kind of sinks had been in the factory?* Old porcelain. Two faucets, with silver rubbing off, showing what might be brass underneath. Four little spokes coming off the water faucet's handles, old-style. Restoration Hardware, like that. *What kind of lockers?* Orange. With little vents at the top and bottom. *How many lockers?* Hundreds. At least a couple of hundred. A big changing room. *What kind of windows? How many panes? How high were they from the floor? How high were you from the ground outside? How big was the building? How long did it take you to walk across it?*

Again and again and again.

Alix had described it perfectly, and yet no one could find it, and as much as she wanted this factory to lead to that factory, it felt like a dead end.

"Are you seriously trying to find 2.0?" Jonah asked. "Is it because of Dad?"

"He's not all sweetness and light, you know."

"So what? Who is?" Jonah asked. His voice sounded so knowing and cynical that it brought Alix up short.

She wanted to have some answer to that, but it sort of

mirrored her own sentiments. The more she'd researched the shenanigans of the companies that made their living by manufacturing doubt, the more depressed and hopeless she'd felt.

However cynical you think you are, you're never cynical enough. That was Moses's perspective.

Except he hadn't been cynical. None of the 2.0 crew had been. They'd been cynical about other people. But when it came to themselves, they were practically starry-eyed idealists. They'd actually thought they could change the world.

Alix thought of Cynthia. She'd apparently walked away from a pretty good future to run with 2.0. That was some crazy idealism right there. It was almost comic-book idealism. Fighting the good fight against an overwhelming evil.

She thought of Cynthia's clothes in those industrial lockers in the bat cave. And all those toothbrushes, lined up at the sinks. She could practically play the theme music in her head, imagining everyone getting up in the morning, brushing their teeth, and heading off to battle.

She laughed.

"What's so funny?" Jonah asked.

"Idealists." Alix took a last look around the empty warehouse. "Let's get out of here."

"You're done?"

"Yeah. No one ever lived here. It was silly to come."

They hadn't lived here. They hadn't brushed their teeth here or kept their clothes here. They hadn't slept here or gotten ready for school here, or woken to the smell of...

Alix stopped short. "Fresh bread."

363

Jonah looked at her like she was nuts. Alix was starting to get used to that expression.

■ ■ ■

Fresh bread. Bread manufacture. Bread baking.

Cynthia said she had been sick of smelling bread because her parents lived near a bakery. She'd made the comment in the lunchroom. The smell was like being smothered in yeast, she'd said. And in the morning, Cynthia had smelled bread when the wind was wrong. She hated bread, and she always wrinkled her nose at the smell.

Bread factories, bread production

As soon as Alix got home, she started doing map searches for bakeries on her computer, but all she came up with were custom cake shops and coffeehouses, which would have been really helpful if she'd wanted a nice chocolate Grenache tart and a sip of espresso.

Bread distribution, bread warehouse

"Is there such a thing as a bread warehouse?" Alix wondered aloud. It didn't seem to matter. She still wasn't finding what she wanted.

She gave up on map searches and started doing news searches instead. Looking for stories about bread factories...

"Well, well, well..."

There was an old news story about a Hostess factory going out of business and selling its building to another company, Maple Confections. One of Maple's big products was Harvest Health Bread. The story was all about how a bunch of baking jobs were going to still stay in the area....

Alix searched *Maple Confections*. She got a hit in northern New Jersey.

Jersey?

She measured the distances and was surprised to discover that Haverport was as close to northern New Jersey as it was to Hartford. They were in opposite directions, but the distances matched almost perfectly.

Could that really be?

Alix switched to satellite view and started looking over the entire area where Maple Confections was housed. All she could see were a lot of huge buildings that all looked alike from above.

She tried Google Street View and was surprised to find that the area was documented. With the street view, she could roam back and forth between each of the huge buildings, as if she were walking. But it felt wrong to her. This wasn't an industrial area. It seemed to be mostly foods that were produced here. There were a lot of abandoned food-storage and grain elevators.

She stopped and scrolled back.

Gotcha.

One building in particular had the style of windows that she remembered from 2.0's locker room, and for sure the building was huge.

On the outside it said NEW JERSEY CANNING SYSTEMS in letters so faint she could barely make them out.

■ ■ ■

It was strange to drive to the place where she had been held captive. Was she insane to be seeking out the people who had kidnapped her? Was she crazy to be tracking down Moses?

He put you in a cage.

And yet here she was, crossing into Jersey.

She'd left a note to her family not to expect her for dinner, that she was going out with Sophie, and now she was crossing state lines.

Alix wondered if she should have done something to protect herself. Set up some kind of fail-safe, maybe. 2.0 had let her go the last time, but that had been part of the plan. What would happen when she showed up on the doorstep?

She found her exit and followed an eighteen-wheeler that was also exiting into the warehouse district. She wound between the factories and warehouses, following the blue arrow on her phone's GPS. More eighteen-wheelers were parked at loading docks, and big rigs were on all the roads, driving in and out of the area, looming over her tiny car.

She bumped over train tracks, making her way into quieter and more abandoned areas. As she got closer to her target, her heart began to thud, and she noticed that her palms were slick on the steering wheel. Nervous energy ticked under her skin.

"You're okay," she reminded herself, and then hated that she had to say it out loud. "You're stalking *them* this time."

There.

She pulled to a stop in the shadow of a wrecked warehouse and shut off the car, staring up at the building. *New Jersey Canning Systems.* They'd fooled a lot of people, but this was it. This was the real factory. She was sure of it. This was the place she'd first met the rebellious tribe that had shaken her world.

You can still turn around. Go home and call the FBI…

"Who are you kidding?" Alix muttered. She wanted to see them again. She wanted them to know that she'd tracked them down. To show them that even though they were smart, she was smarter.

Hell yes, she wanted this confrontation.

Alix grabbed her purse and climbed out of the car. In case things went badly, she kept her phone in hand. They wouldn't catch her off guard this time. She'd see them coming. She made her way to the factory.

Weeds grew green between cracks in the pavement. Not far off, the Maple Confections factory puffed steam, but the winds weren't blowing her way today. She hadn't smelled bread when she'd been held captive, but there was the evidence. With the winds coming in the right direction, she could imagine the factory blanketed with the scent of baking bread.

367

This is the place. This is really the place. You did it. You found them.

Slowly, Alix circled the huge building, wary for signs of movement.

Nothing seemed to be happening. No cars were parked nearby. She crept up to a door and rattled it. Locked.

She went around the corner, feeling exposed and out of place in the industrial zone. Half of her expected some workman to yell at her to get out of where she didn't belong. Her little red MINI stood out like a sore thumb where she'd parked it in the weeds. It looked cute and small and vulnerable among the looming factory buildings.

The next door Alix came to was also locked. She kept working her way around the building and, finally, came to a pair of wide double-bay doors. She yanked, expecting them to be locked as well, but, to her surprise, they opened immediately, sliding aside easily on well-oiled tracks.

The factory was empty.

■ ■ ■

At first, she thought she had the wrong building.

How could it be empty?

She walked through the echoing factory, trying to match the layout to her memories. Her shoes clicked loudly on the concrete, the only sound in the cavernous space.

It felt bigger now, without anyone in it, and lonely. She remembered Tank skating across the concrete expanse.

She remembered a heavy bag for some kind of training. She remembered weights. It was all gone. She opened doors and found old hunks of machinery that might have once been stamps or presses, stored in silent rows.

She paused, listening. *Were those footsteps?*

"Hello?"

No response.

Was she even in the right place, she wondered? If she was, 2.0 had left it completely pristine. There was no history here except her own memories, and as she walked through the cavernous rooms, she even began to doubt those. It was too clean. She pushed open another door and found a kitchen and felt a surge of relief and recognition.

It was definitely the same place. The steel table was still in the center of the room. The steel counters had the right layout. She'd definitely been here. She walked around the table, running her hand across its surface, and pulled out a chair.

This is where they made me sit. Cynthia there. Tank there. Adam there. Kook on that counter over there.

And Moses, of course, the one they all looked to and trusted, right there across from her. *Right there.*

But they were gone, just like their pizza boxes and rounds of gourmet cheese.

She left the kitchen and strode out across the open space, her shoes clicking and echoing. The map felt right now. With the kitchen to orient her, it all felt exactly right. Here were the floor-to-ceiling storage racks, and there were the conveyor lines. It was all here.

She was walking faster and faster, recognizing all of it now. In the locker room, she found all six sinks, still in a line. Of course the toothbrushes were gone, and the lockers were scoured clean, without even a cashmere thread to indicate that Cynthia had installed an entire high-end wardrobe there.

"I was here." Just knowing that the place existed felt like a giant Alix-has-not-in-fact-lost-her-shit kind of affirmation. 2.0 had lived here. They'd showered here. They'd skated here. They'd plotted here.

And now, even though she remembered being frightened and angry and lost and alone when she'd been trapped, Alix was suddenly struck by how disappointed she was that they were gone. Suddenly, absurdly, intensely, Alix wished that 2.0 had never released her.

When Alix had returned to Seitz after the kidnapping, Sophie had asked her what would have happened if 2.0 had kept her; Alix knew she was really asking, *Would you have ended up chopped into a million little pieces?* But now Alix wondered if the real danger was being trapped at Seitz.

Stifling her disappointment, Alix headed back to the open factory floor and scanned it one last time.

Of course they were gone. It made perfect sense. She'd just been so wrapped up in the puzzle of it all that she hadn't thought that 2.0 might have lives and plans and agendas of their own.

The world doesn't revolve around you, Alix.

Moses had even said they were in town for only a little while. So of course they were gone. Their business was finished here. They'd humiliated her and her father, and they'd made fools of Williams & Crowe. Now they were off on some other Don Quixote mission. They were probably terrorizing some CEO in California by now. Filling the guy's Santa Barbara mansion with ocean water and turning it into a giant aquarium or something.

She turned in a circle one last time, trying to take it in. It was getting dark now, making the building gloomy.

Whatever she'd been hoping to find was gone. Closure? Some kind of conversation? People to hang out with who didn't feel morally bankrupt?

Moses. She'd at least wanted to find Moses. She'd wanted to look him in the eye and say that she understood. She'd put all the pieces together. She'd figured it all out. And to top it off, she'd tracked him down. Which meant she'd beaten him. For once, she'd beaten him. For once, she'd surprised him, instead of the other way around.

Why do you even care? What do you have to prove to him?

She remembered chasing him after his first prank. With rats running everywhere, and more mayhem to come, she'd grabbed his sleeve and called for him to wait. And he'd whirled on her, and, in that moment, she'd seen herself in the lenses of his glasses, her Seitz schoolgirl uniform and her tidy French braid, and she'd felt painfully naive.

God, she'd hated that feeling.

She wasn't used to anyone looking down on her, and there he was, looking smug, because he knew more than she did. She'd wanted to be strong in that moment, to be able to stand up to him.

"You don't need him," Alix said to herself. She took a deep breath. "You don't need any of them anymore. You answered all the questions yourself. You figured it all out on your own."

So what now?

And she found, to her surprise, that she had an answer for that as well.

The Doubt Factory.

Alix started to smile. She didn't need Moses to answer questions, and she didn't need 2.0 to give her a direction. She'd already chosen her direction. Sometime between reading about aspirin and listening to her father's plotting, she'd chosen a direction on her own. This was just a sentimental detour on the way to her actual destination.

With a new spring in her step, she strode out of the factory's bay doors and slid them closed.

Full dark was coming on. She could see the lights of New York City far in the distance, a glowing skyline. Much closer, a neon MAPLE CONFECTIONS sign illuminated the bread factory, glazing the area in reddish light. Already Alix's mind was at work, trying to solve the puzzle of how she could crack the Doubt Factory.

Her father made his living helping companies tell their side of the story, and yet every time he did, he kept a portion of their stories to himself. But somewhere deep inside Banks Strategy Partners, the rest of those stories were hidden.

She just needed to find a way to pry them out.

Alix made her way across the weedy lot to her car, listening to the distant rumblings and beeps and groans of shipping and manufacturing, the music of things being made and moved. Her MINI sat like a toy amid the warehouses. All of it was so big. Bigger than any one person.

Out on the water, she could see a container ship, its lights glowing, giant freight cranes crouching over it, starting to unload.

It's all so big, she thought, and for a second she felt overwhelmed and small. But then she banished the feeling. *Sometimes big things fall hard.*

She liked that thought better.

Smiling, Alix climbed into the MINI and revved its engine.

As she put the car in drive, a hand wrapped around her neck and jerked her back against her seat. Alix gasped and tried to break free, but she was pinned.

A voice murmured in her ear, "Didn't expect to see you again."

33

"MOSES." ALIX SWALLOWED AT THE pressure on her throat.
Her heart was pounding as adrenaline ripped through her.

Stay calm.

She had one hand on the wheel, one on the gear shift.
She swallowed again. "I can drive us straight into a wall if
you don't let go of my neck, Moses. All I have to do is step on
the gas."

The pressure eased off a little. "That probably wouldn't go
well for either of us, would it?" His voice was so familiar. So
confident. He was always so damn confident.

"I've got a seat belt," Alix pointed out. "A crash will work
out better for me than you."

"Maybe. Maybe not," Moses said. "I'll take my chances.
This just feels safer, you know." He gave her throat a squeeze.
"I'd rather have some leverage."

"Leverage for what?"

"Good behavior."

"Good behavior?" Alix laughed out loud. "After what you did to me?" She knew she was hideously vulnerable, but she couldn't help firing back. "You're the one who drugged me and stuck me in a cage! I should probably drive you into the wall just on principle!"

"Well, there you go—just another reason not to trust you."

"The feeling's mutual, then," Alix replied.

"Seriously?" Moses sounded almost hurt.

"What do you think?"

The sense of play faded from Moses's voice, replaced by a surprising earnestness. "If I wanted to hurt you, Alix, you'd already be hurt. It would've been easy with you snooping around my place."

"So why didn't you? If you don't trust me so much, why didn't you just do something?"

There was a long pause. He seemed caught off guard at the question. "Maybe I wanted to know what your game was," he said finally.

"I don't play games," Alix retorted. "That's what you do, remember?"

Moses laughed harshly. "Don't sell yourself short. You played me. When I let you go, I was so sure you were telling the truth. You made me believe, Alix, and it's not often that I get played like that. I mean, I really believed. Hasn't happened in a long time. But I got to hand it to you, you played me perfectly."

"Would you please let me go? Your hand is starting to make me uncomfortable."

"Yeah, sorry, but no. I don't trust you."

Alix let the engine rev slightly. The MINI was begging to lunge forward. "Let me go, Moses. Or I put us both into the wall, and then I scrape you off the windshield."

"You think I'm afraid of dying?" he asked. "Try again, Alix."

Alix clenched her jaw with irritation. "Just so you know, I didn't play you."

"So Williams and Crowe just happened to show up on my doorstep? That was a strange coincidence. I let you go, and then Williams and Crowe came knocking with tear gas."

"That wasn't really your doorstep."

"Bet you were disappointed to find out I was one step ahead of you."

Alix remembered the tear gas rounds crashing through the upper windows, believing that everyone inside was going to be choking and collapsing.

"No," she said. "I didn't want that." She could still feel the horror of that moment. Seeing what she had set in motion and knowing she was powerless to stop it. She swallowed. "I didn't know they'd do that."

"If I didn't have a backup plan, Tank would be dead by now," Moses said quietly. "We'd all be in jail, and Tank would be dead."

At first, Alix thought he was accusing her, but the way

he said it, it felt more like he was barely even talking to her. Almost as if he were reminding himself of something.

He feels guilty, she realized, surprised.

"I didn't know they'd be like that," she said again. "It wasn't what I wanted. For what it's worth, I'm sorry about that."

Moses was quiet in the car's darkness. Finally, he said, "Yeah, well, I guess we did drug you and put you in a cage. I hear that annoys people."

"Payback is a bitch," Alix agreed.

They both laughed darkly at that. An oddly companionable silence settled between them. Two people, each holding a threat over the other. Neither one quite with the upper hand. The MINI idled smoothly. Moses's hand was warm on her neck.

"Truce?" Alix suggested hopefully.

"Truce?" Alix could hear the smile in his voice. "I like you, Alix. But I don't trust you."

"You like me?" she asked. "And this is how you show it?"

"What's not to like?"

"Didn't I chip a tooth of yours?"

"That just made me respect you."

"So what would make you trust me? A punch in the nose?"

Moses blew out his breath. "We're past trusting, Alix. We've got too much water under the bridge for that."

"You mean because of what I did to you," Alix said. "Because of Williams and Crowe."

"Or maybe because of what *I* did to *you*. We've got history now, that's all."

"What if I said I forgave you?"

"I'd say that sounds real nice."

"But you still wouldn't trust me."

"Fool me once, shame on you," Moses said. "Fool me twice…" He trailed off. Alix saw his shape shrug in her rearview mirror. "I thought I knew what was going on inside your head, but I was wrong. I don't need to go down that road again."

"What about when you came to my house?" she asked. "You trusted me then. I could have called Williams and Crowe, but I didn't. Why did you risk that?"

"Maybe I wanted to trust you."

"Well, maybe I wanted to trust you, too."

There was a pregnant pause. Alix could almost hear Moses considering the angles.

Come on, she thought. *Just let me go. Just let us talk. Why can't we just talk?*

"No," he said finally. "That wasn't real. You could make up any story you wanted about me in your head, and maybe that made you open your door to a stranger. And I could make up any story I wanted about you and think you could be all kinds of things you weren't. But that wasn't real. I could pretend you were different from those other Seitz girls. I could pretend that you were just asleep. I could pretend that if you woke up, you'd be…" He trailed off again. "Anyway, that was just me making things up."

"I'd be what?" Alix pressed. "Snow White or something?"

He laughed. "Actually, I thought you'd be dangerous."

"Maybe I am."

"I don't have any doubt about that now."

Doubt. He had no doubt that she was dangerous. But he didn't believe she could be trusted. Alix remembered a long-ago conversation with him. Moses describing his world:

I don't believe in anything, he said. *I test.*

He's testing you, she realized. *He might not even know it, but he's testing you.*

Alix took a deep breath and turned the key off in the ignition. The MINI went silent.

"What are you doing?" Moses asked. He almost sounded alarmed.

Alix didn't answer, just pulled the keys out of the ignition and held them up for him. They dangled in the darkness, glinting.

"Trust me," she said. "I already trust you."

379

34

"YOU *ARE* CRAZY."

"Are you going to take my keys or not?"

"You don't have any reason to trust me!"

Alix laughed. "I thought we were worried about you trusting me, not the other way around."

"This isn't a game, Alix."

"I know." She let the keys drop into the passenger seat. "There they are, if you want them."

"Alix, don't do this."

"Don't trust you?" Alix asked. "Why not? Why wouldn't I trust the guy who goes off and rescues kids from evil foster homes? Why wouldn't I trust a guy who spends his time trying to stop bad people from doing bad things in the world? Why wouldn't I trust a guy who seems to have the trust and respect of probably the smartest girl I ever met? Why wouldn't I trust the—"

"—the guy who stalked you and put you in a cage," Moses interrupted vehemently.

Alix reached up and touched his hand where it rested on her throat. She could feel him shaking. Could feel his whole body shaking. She swallowed. "Yeah. That. Why wouldn't I trust that guy?" She felt him start to draw away, but she tightened her hand around his, holding him there. She pressed his hand against her throat. "Why wouldn't I trust that guy, too?"

"Alix..." On his lips, her name sounded so soft and full of regret that Alix almost wanted to cry. Instead, she pressed his hand against her throat. "I trust you," she said. "I'm not afraid of you anymore. I know you."

"That's not true."

"No," Alix said. "It is true." She lifted his hand from her throat and twined her fingers in his. "I didn't know you before. Now I do. And you know me. And neither of us is the same as we were before." She squeezed his hand gently. "Neither of us is the same."

"Alix..." he said again, his voice ragged with emotion.

"I trust you," she said, and his hand tightened on hers.

She was fascinated by their hands. Two people, interlocked. Tightening their connection to each other.

"How do you know?" he whispered. "How do you know you can trust?"

"You can't know," she said. "That's what trust is."

Slowly, she drew him forward, so that she could finally see him. Their faces were inches apart. *He's beautiful*, she thought. *He has beautiful eyes.* She reached up to touch his

381

cheek, wanting him. Wanting to see herself in those eyes, hoping that he saw something beautiful in turn.

"You're shaking," he said.

"So are you."

"Do you want me to let you go?" he asked.

"No."

"That's good," he said seriously. "I don't want to let you go."

And then they were kissing, and all Alix could think was that she was home.

■ ■ ■

"Truce?"

"Truce."

They lay together in his bed, entangled and comfortable. Alix rolled over and looked at Moses. God, he was beautiful. She ran her hand down his chest, amazed at his skin, at his body, at his muscles. It felt so surreal. She kept trying to figure out how it had happened, if it was a dream. She wondered if he was going to suddenly realize that he'd made a mistake.

He was looking at her, amused.

"What?" she asked.

"Nothing. I was going to ask you the same thing. What's going on inside that big brain of yours?"

"Nothing."

He nodded, but he didn't look away or let her off the hook. He just waited. She laughed and rolled away, feeling self-conscious.

"Nothing. I was just thinking you're like some kind of weird black Batman."

As soon as she said it, she was afraid she'd offended him, but he just laughed.

"That is so not what I was expecting you to say," he said, still chuckling.

"What did you think I'd say?"

He looked serious. "That you wanted to go home."

"No."

As soon as she said it, she realized it was true. She didn't want to go home. She wanted to lie here in his arms forever. For a million years. She wanted time to stop. She didn't feel like she was wearing some other skin with Moses. She was who she was. Some rich girl from Seitz who didn't quite fit there. But fit just fine right here.

"Black Batman, huh?" He nudged her.

"Well, sure." She snuggled into his body, lying close as she ticked off points on her fingers. "Dubious morality? Check. Comes and goes like the wind? Check. Lives in a bat cave? Check."

"It used to be a rat cave," he said, pinching her hip.

"Shut up." She slapped his hand away. "You're distracting me."

"Is that bad?" His hand ran up her skin. Alix laughed and pretended to be trying to squirm away, before letting him capture her and kiss her.

When they came up for air, she said, "The only thing that isn't like Batman is that you actually have friends."

He froze at that. He stopped tickling her and let her go.

"What?" She turned to see his face, suddenly worried. "What did I say?"

His expression had turned serious. "Nothing," he said. "I'm on my own, that's all."

"On your own..." She sat up, looking at him. "You mean you're not doing anything now? I thought you all had left to go do some other...thing."

He shook his head. "That was just kid stuff. It was bullshit."

"No." She shook him. "It was good. It was cool."

"It didn't make any difference. None of it does. I finally wised up about it."

"And everyone else left?"

"It's dangerous, Alix. If I wasn't right on my game, Tank would have died. It wasn't fair to keep them around here, taking risks for no reason."

"So you just...gave up?" Alix stared at him. "But I came all this way."

"Why do you care? It didn't make any difference. We brought all those news cameras in, and you know what people focused on? SWAT guys in cages. You couldn't even see all the banners. It was all there, laid out. Williams and Crowe. The Doubt Factory. All of them right there, and the cameras didn't even care. It was just another freaky thing protesters do. Occupy Wall Street shit. The freaks getting covered 'cause they're freaky."

"But…"

"We took big risks on you. Game-changing risks. Some of us are over eighteen. Shit gets serious then. And the bad guys, they're good. We can't stay encrypted all the time. You can't stay off every single surveillance camera. Not every time. I know the FBI's got an angle on my face. They've got Cyn, too, from Seitz records we had to match." He shook his head. "We were gambling that they were dumb and divided and weren't paying attention, but that lasts only so long. Eventually, your luck runs out. We hit that research lab for the rats. That was a huge heist. Kook had tabs on a bunch of animal rights groups, and the FBI was all over them right after we pulled it."

He paused, smiling slightly. "That was actually kind of funny. Watching the FBI come down on PETA and the Animal Liberation Front, and come up with nothing." He looked at Alix. "Sobering, too, though. Seriously sobering. When they rain down on someone, they don't screw around."

"But they didn't get you," Alix said. "You did it right."

"Sure. But then we did your school. And then we grabbed you. And then the bait-and-switch with the cages. Our luck was already too good. That last one…" He shook his head. "We were a little too clear about who we were, that time. Some dude in a cubicle probably is spending every waking minute trying to match up every single person the Doubt Factory has ever screwed. Every company they've worked for. Cyn…" He shook his head again. "They'll be trying to pattern match her for sure."

"And you...?"

"I'm a dead trail. Have been for years. I'm a ghost." He looked at her pointedly. "But it can't last forever. If the feds weren't so busy looking under rocks for the next al-Qaida, they'd probably have bagged us already."

"Maybe you're just that good."

Moses grinned, a flash of ego. "Maybe I am." He sobered. "Even really smart people get nailed eventually. My uncle was the best, and he's in prison doing fifteen years. And that man was seriously good. Eventually, you make a mistake." He gestured at her. "I mean, hell, you figured it out. You found the bat cave, right? FBI's probably right behind you."

"Bread," Alix said. "Cynthia said she smelled bread a lot at home."

Moses grimaced. "There you go. Bread. One wrong question from the feds and you would have led them right to us. I don't really care, for myself. No one's going to mind one more black kid in prison. Nobody gives a shit about me—"

"I care!" Alix interjected angrily.

"Okay, but aside from you."

"What's that supposed to mean? What am I? Just, like, chopped liver?"

"That's not what I'm saying."

"Well, then listen to what I'm saying. I care." She gave him a hard look, driving it home.

Moses smiled. "Okay. Okay. Point taken. But Cyn? She's a serious genius, and she's up to her neck in this. Probably going to start the next Google if she doesn't end up in jail.

And Tank? That boy would never survive in juvie. It would eat that little freak alive. Adam? Kook?" He shook his head. "Nah. I couldn't keep risking them. Not to get nothing."

Alix looked up sharply. "But you didn't get nothing. You got me. I'm here. I want to help."

"You want to help."

"Actually, I want you to help me." She smiled. "I'm thinking about hitting the Doubt Factory."

35

SO THIS IS WHAT IT'S like to have a secret, Alix thought.

She'd been such a good girl, and she'd kept so little from her parents, that it felt like she was a completely new person. As if she'd dragged all the cloying membranes of childhood off her body and she'd emerged.

There was Old Alix, the Alix who had gone from home to school and back again. Who'd done her good homework and gotten her good grades and been such a good girl that she'd always known she could call Mom and Dad for help if she strayed a little.

And now there was New Alix.

New Alix had secrets. New Alix slipped away in the afternoons and met Moses on walking trails in various state parks that Moses selected at random to keep their patterns broken up. New Alix persuaded Sophie to cover for her on the week-

388

ends while she slipped down to Jersey and slept with Moses in his empty factory.

But more than that, New Alix saw the world differently. She did all the same things she'd always done, and yet nothing was the same. Every morning she put on her school uniform: white blouse, plaid skirt, white kneesocks, black shoes...and even though all the movements were the same, she was different.

New Alix watched the things that Old Alix had done, and laughed.

So this is what it's like to have a secret.

Alix shrugged into her Seitz blazer and checked herself in the mirror. Smirked. Cocked her head. Raised an eyebrow.

No sign of a secret. Not even a hint that at night she rifled through the filing cabinets of her father's study, hunting for names and details that she and Moses could use to create a clearer picture of what the Doubt Factory did. No sign that she took photos on her camera phone of everything from Christmas cards from Doubt Factory clients to the tiny doodles that her father put on sticky pads and then stuffed into file folders that he always forgot to sort out later.

The filing cabinets had been easy: the key was on Dad's key ring, right there on the kitchen island the first night Alix had crept down the stairs to snoop. It was almost ridiculously easy to go through her father's papers.

The computer was another matter. She'd suggested putting a keystroke logger on the computer, to maybe grab Dad's password, but Moses had vetoed the idea.

"No. I don't want you getting nailed. He might see the USB key, and when he does, there aren't enough other people to blame. You'd get caught for sure."

"I would not."

"Well, I don't want to risk it."

"You were willing to risk me before."

Moses had the grace to look embarrassed. "Yeah, well, now I'm not," he said. "So don't do anything stupid. I don't want to risk you. I like you too much to lose you."

"You like me?" she goaded. "You *like* me?"

Moses rewarded her with an even more embarrassed smile. "Quit hassling me. I'm a guy. Guys don't talk about this stuff."

"I think that's just dudebros. Real men talk about their feelings."

Moses shook his head and blushed. "Just don't do anything stupid, okay?"

He likes me, Alix thought as she stared at herself in the mirror.

Downstairs, she found Jonah complaining to Mom about how his trig teacher hated him. Alix found a nonfat yogurt in the fridge, watching with amused distance as Mom and Jonah went back and forth.

"Jonah," Mom said finally, "it would be a lot easier for me to take you seriously if Ms. Scheibler didn't like you as much as she does."

"That woman *hates* me."

"Nah." Alix dipped her spoon into the yogurt. "She's a sucker for bad boys like Jonah."

"I'm a bad boy?" Jonah perked up at that.

Mom gave Alix an exasperated glance. "Please don't encourage him." She paused, studying Alix more closely.

"What are you smiling about?"

"Who? Me?"

"Who? *Me?*" Mom mimicked.

Bad boys, Alix thought. *I was thinking about bad boys. Bad boys like Moses Cruz—*

"Batman," Alix said. She rinsed out the empty yogurt container in the sink. "I was thinking about Batman."

36

"I WISH YOU'D QUIT CALLING me that," Moses said.

"Batman? Why?"

"I'm not a superhero."

"I don't know." Alix laughed. "You are kind of unbeliev-able."

They were on a walking trail by the river. They'd met on the turnpike and then driven into the Connecticut greenery to find a walking trail. It was far enough away from Alix's normal haunts that she felt safe from anyone she knew seeing her, and it was still close enough that she could pick up Jonah at Sirius Comix within an hour.

"I'm serious," Moses said. "My uncle could pull off amazing things, too. And then he teamed up with the wrong person, and it all went sidewise so fast he didn't even see it coming."

"You were with him a long time?"

"Since I was eleven," Moses said. "I've been orphaned

twice. Once after my parents died, then after Uncle Ty got himself arrested." Moses kicked a rock ahead of him. "Maybe that's why I've gotten so lucky recently. Universe is trying to balance me out."

Alix didn't know how to answer. There was a hole of loss there that she didn't really know how to fill. "I've got more files from my dad," she said, fishing in her purse and handing over an SD card. "It's a good one."

"Yeah?"

"His latest idea is to create a cheap news-syndication service. He actually wants to sell slanted news, instead of worrying about trying to make journalists take his quotes. I took some pictures of the mock-ups he had in his briefcase."

"Alix—"

"There's one other thing in there, too. He's got a whole notebook with a hiring plan to put a bunch of sock puppets out to monitor news articles for keywords. It's like a whole professional trolling operation to get the first comment on online news articles—he's calling it BSP Lightning Response Services. The whole pitch is that the first comment gets almost as much reader impact as the news article itself."

"So you just piggyback on the news story and refute from comments." Moses was nodding.

"And it doesn't even look like a PR company's doing it," Alix added. "Just Bernard Henderson from Indianapolis."

Moses stopped walking. Alix had already taken a few steps before she realized he'd stopped. She turned back to him. "What's wrong?"

Moses had the memory card in his hand but didn't pocket it. "You know you don't need to bring me this stuff, right? That's not why I'm with you."

"I know that. It was my idea to do it in the first place."

"Still, it's not your fight."

"This from the guy who told me it was on me if another kid died from Azicort?" Alix looked at him incredulously. "Of course it's my fight."

"When I said that before, I was just trying to manipulate you."

"Yeah, I know.... But still, you were right." Alix went back over to him and looped her arm through his. Frustratingly, he was looking away from her, and she couldn't get a read on his face. When she could see his eyes, she had a better sense of what Moses was thinking. "So... what are you trying to do now?"

Finally Moses met her gaze. Alix was surprised at the emotion she saw there. "I'm trying to make sure you don't do something stupid and get yourself caught," he said.

The words were so genuine that Alix felt her heart warm. She reached up and patted his cheek affectionately.

"You're worried about me?"

"This is serious stuff, Alix."

Alix laughed. "I think I can snoop on my dad without getting caught."

A guy with six dogs on leashes came down the path. The guy was sweating, running after the panting pack. Alix and Moses got out of the way of the stampede.

"That's not what I'm saying. You've got a good life. Your parents..." Moses trailed off. "They're good to you."

"But bad to everyone else, right?"

Moses shook his head, his brow furrowed with frustration. "How did we end up on opposite sides of this argument? I'm the one who's supposed to be all crazy, and you're supposed to be the one who doesn't want to make waves."

"Relax, Batman." Alix grinned. "Just enjoy it."

"Seriously, Alix. Cut out the superhero stuff. That's the kind of thinking that gets people nailed. Don't get cocky."

Alix sobered and reached out to him. "I get it." She held his gaze, trying to let him know that she wasn't crazy, that she wasn't reckless. "I'm careful. I'm really careful. You can trust me on that."

"I just don't want to lose you."

They started walking again, their arms interlinked. Alix leaned against him, enjoying the stolen time together. Moses still didn't seem totally relaxed, though. Alix glanced up at him again. "You're not going to lose me," she said. "Okay?"

He blew out his breath. "I know."

"But you don't believe me."

"Sometimes things get under your skin. You watch two parents die. You see your uncle locked up...." He trailed off, looking troubled.

"Moses?"

"Yeah?"

Alix swallowed, unsure of how to ask the question. "What were your parents like?"

"You really want to know?"

She slipped her hand into his and squeezed tightly. "I just want to know whatever you feel like telling me."

As she said it, she was surprised how true it felt. She just liked being with him. She liked the way it felt to have Moses holding her hand, and she liked the easy way he gave her room to stand aside when a jogger zipped past them. Everything she did with him felt right. She didn't even have to think about it.

When she'd dated Brad Summers in her sophomore year, she'd always felt self-conscious, trying to figure out even the simple mechanics of holding hands, let alone kissing. Let alone anything more. It had all been something she had to think about. She worried what Brad would think when she held his hand, or when she didn't. When they kissed, she worried about what he was thinking when she let her tongue slip into his mouth.... It had all been so much *work*. Watching herself from the outside, and trying to do everything *right*.

With Moses, Alix didn't think about any of that. She just was. She walked beside him because she liked it, held his hand because she wanted to, kissed him how she liked, and liked what he did to her in turn.

Alix caught him looking at her. "What?"

"Beats me. You were the one smiling."

Alix felt herself blush. She looked away. *Okay. Maybe still a little self-conscious.*

Out on the river, a man was sculling downstream. Strong strokes, silent and smooth. They stepped off the trail to watch.

"Watch out for the poison ivy," Alix warned.

"Which one's that?"

"Seriously? There's something you don't know?" Alix asked. "I thought you knew everything." She pointed out the shiny leaves. "Those ones. Three-leaf clusters."

Moses frowned, staring at the plant for a serious moment, seeming to lock it into his mind. "Never needed to learn about plants. I'm a city boy."

"And what city was that?"

"Chicago. Then Vegas. After I started living with my uncle."

"Chicago?" she prompted.

"You're the inquisition today, aren't you?"

Alix felt a little annoyed at the implication. "You know, you stalked me for like eight months and did background checks on all my friends and family. I'm still catching up here. Help me out, will you?"

Moses laughed. "All right. I hear you. I'm not used to talking about this stuff. My uncle always said it was smarter not to tell too much real stuff. It's better to separate...different parts of your life."

"Like targets and friends."

Moses blew out his breath. "Yeah. So, with my family... I don't know. It was a long time ago. My dad worked for the city. He was an engineer. Built overpasses and stuff. My mom

397

was an actress before they got married. She was in plays, little parts, though. Nothing big. Later on, she was an office manager for a company. Middle-class life, all that."

"Were they nice?"

"I know I liked being with them. I liked my dad when he came home from work, and we'd do these puzzles together when I was real little...." He shrugged. "I don't know. They didn't really get a chance to screw me up much. My uncle did all that."

"They sound nice." Alix tried to remember what she'd been like when she was that age. Wondering what her life would feel like if it were suddenly snapped into pieces the way Moses's had been. She mostly remembered Zoe Van Nuys and Kala Whitmore starting a rumor that she stuffed her bra.

Alix cast her mind back, trying to pin down more details from that time. Birthday parties, sure. Her ninth she remembered because it had been a German chocolate cake with five layers, and Dad kept saying that the slice he was giving her was as big as her head.... She remembered Mom and Dad's anniversary—their twentieth?—the two of them going out dressed in black while Alix and annoying baby Jonah were stuck at home with a sitter Alix nicknamed Milkface. That was before they'd moved to Connecticut and gotten the bigger house. Before Seitz. Right around the time Dad had started Banks Strategy Partners. Alix was disturbed to find that her memories were so fragmented.

The rower passed out of sight, and they started walking again, arm in arm. "My mom and dad took me to Disney World," Moses said. "I remember that. My dad let me go on whatever ride I wanted. I went to SeaWorld, too. Saw Shamu. My dad got me a stuffed Shamu, even though Mom said it was expensive. He got me one that was so big...." Moses stretched out his arms.

Alix was struck by how soft Moses's expression became when he let down his guard. "I remember carrying this big orca around, and it was about as long as I was. Shamu's tail kept dragging on the ground." He was smiling at the memory, and his words were coming faster. "And I remember there was a hot dog stand outside Dad's office building. Sometimes, if I was off school, he'd take me to work. I had to stay in his cubicle and stay quiet and color or read, but at lunch, we'd go out and have hot dogs...." He trailed off. The softness left his face and his expression closed up again. "It's all stupid stuff. I don't know why I remember the things I remember."

Alix swallowed and looked away, trying not to show him how much it affected her, but the sadness she felt was almost overwhelming. Listening to him hunt for memories of something good, and knowing how much he'd been robbed of.

"It sounds nice," she said, and was glad her voice sounded almost unaffected. "They sound nice."

Moses said, "I can't remember their faces unless I look at a photo, you know? It's weird. But I remember my dad had calluses on his hands because he'd lift weights in the basement. Sometimes I try to remember more, but mostly I remember finding Dad in the bathroom on the floor. Him trying to get up and not being able to. And then Mom—" He broke off.

"And you ended up in Las Vegas."

"Yeah." Moses's voice hardened. "Uncle Ty. Tyrone Cruz. He always said Ty was short for Typhoon. Man was in the Army and got kicked out. That man..." He shook his head. "My Uncle Ty knew how to smile. That man could smile himself out of anything. Smile himself into anything, too." Abruptly, Moses deepened his voice, mimicking, becoming someone else entirely. " 'We don't do the nine-to-five, Mo. We too good for that ant work. We be grasshoppers. Smaaaart grasshoppers. Let the ants do all the work.' " He shrugged. "I didn't figure out until a lot later that there was a name for his racket."

"He was a con man, wasn't he?"

"Taught me everything I know. Taught me the long con and short con. Taught me to pick the marks and rope them. Taught me how to talk just the way you knew the mark wanted to hear. Taught me body language. How to read people. How to keep my fingers fast. Taught me how to fool the eye. Taught me how to slip a watch off a man's wrist and chase after him and get a reward. Simple shit like that. But he taught me to fool the person behind the eye, too. Taught me how wearing a uniform will make someone trust you. Put on hotel livery, you ain't just some stranger anymore. Wear a suit with a conference badge on it, and people think they know you, even when they don't. How to talk, how to look, how to be. He taught me all that. Hacking is what he called it. Just like Kook does on computers, but I hacked people. I hacked conversations. Mostly, though, I did a lot of roping people into rigged poker games." He shook his head.

"Was that good money?"

"When Uncle Ty wanted to work, it was. We'd make a big score and live for weeks on it." He glanced over at Alix. "I mean, this is small money in comparison with Seitz life, but plenty to pay rent and eat steaks and for Uncle Ty to go out with his ladies."

"Sounds surreal."

"Looking back, I think it was. But I was young. It was just different. At first I thought it was strange, but then I just got used to it. Uncle Ty taught me different scams, we'd make a score, and he'd go out and party. And I'd read books in his apartment until he came back. It was life."

"Did you go to school?"

Moses smirked. "Homeschool."

"I'm serious."

"Sometimes. Mostly it just turned out that I could always do whatever they wanted me to do, but I could do it faster alone. Uncle Ty didn't really care." Moses deepened his voice again. "'Long as you can read and do numbers, you're good, son.'" Moses laughed. "Mostly by that he meant he wanted to make sure I could count cards and figure odds. The rest of it was all just grind and rules for sheep. Uncle Ty always thought my dad was a fool, the way he went to college and got a job with the city and all that. 'Working for the man,' he called it. My dad believed in rules: Play by the rules, work

401

hard, get ahead, American dream, all that. Uncle Ty wanted to play only if he could rig the rules. If he couldn't rig the game, he wouldn't play. He said all that rules and obedience and college crap was for sheep."

"Do you think I'm a sheep, too?"

"What?" Moses looked over, surprised.

"I mean, my whole life, it's been rules. Get good grades. Stay in school. Don't be late for class. Get an SAT tutor. Have at least three extracurriculars. Keep your GPA above 3.9. Volunteer for two charities. Get into an Ivy League school. Get a job that people can brag about, maybe in an investment bank. Then get a husband who's even richer than you so you can get a baby and then quit your job, or maybe become a supermom and do it all and rule the universe...."

She trailed off, thinking of all the obedient Seitz boys and girls streaming across the quad in their school uniforms, heads down, cramming hard for the next round of exams, sweating hard for their 4.0.

"So, like I said, do you think I'm a sheep, too?"

"That was my uncle. Not me."

"But that's what I do. I go to school. I get good grades."

"So? My dad built bridges. You don't do that without going to college. I don't think you're some kind of Seitz robot girl."

Alix wasn't sure what kind of assurance she was looking for, but that wasn't exactly it.

"Gee, thanks," she said drily.

"Alix." Moses stopped walking. "Seriously. Neither of us has to be whatever our people were. Maybe we're outliers, right? Data scatter. Maybe we don't show up as normal at all. You don't end up in an investment bank, and I don't end up in jail with my dumb uncle. You're not like those other Seitz girls."

"But I kind of am," Alix pushed back. "That's where I come from, right? Rich. White. All that."

Moses laughed. "Well, you're definitely white and you're definitely rich. But no, you're not the same. First time I saw you, I could tell."

"What did you think you saw?"

"Something was just real screwy with you."

Alix slugged him in the arm. Moses fended her off, laughing as she came after him again. He finally trapped her hands in his, leaving them both staring at each other, breathing hard.

"I'm serious," he said. "As soon as I started watching you, I had a feeling about you. All the other girls you ran with... they were like perfect little dolls. Heads down, doing their little tests, going to their little parties, buying their little cars. Kook called you all cogs, but it was more than that. It was like you were the shiniest, prettiest, most expensive, high-tech cogs you've ever seen. I mean, you were all perfect, right?"

"And I wasn't?"

Moses started walking again. "You know what I mean. It just looked like all the rest of your friends were going to find

403

a nice, expensive slot to fit into...and you weren't. I just kept looking at you and thinking your shape was wrong. Like if we bumped you right, you'd pop out. And then you'd be seriously dangerous."

"You said that before, about my being dangerous. But I'm not."

"Quit it," Moses said.

"Quit what?"

"Quit it with the thing where you cut yourself down. You're going to one of the best private schools in the country. You're dangerous already. And that's before you're...you."

"And I am...?"

"Okay." Moses stopped. "How long did it take for you to put all the connections together about the Doubt Factory?"

"I don't know. A couple of weeks."

"It took me years."

"But you told me where to start. It was easy with a jump start."

"How late did you stay up doing all your research?"

"Late, I guess. I had classes, too."

"Three AM? Four AM?"

"Sure. When else was I going to do it?"

Moses laughed. "You know a lot of your friends who spend their spare time rooting around in government acronyms? Trying to keep NIOSH and OSHA separate?"

"No, but—"

"What's the Donors Capital Fund?"

Alix cast her mind back to her research, recalling her notes. "It's a money anonymizer. There's also Donors Trust, which is pretty much the same. Same address, anyway. Companies funnel money through it, and then Donors Capital Fund passes it on. Donors Fund spends a lot on climate doubt, but you can't tell who's giving the money to them. They're funneling millions these days."

"You see?" Moses was smiling at her. "You're interested in the world, Alix. You might not know that, but it's kind of rare. Someone throws a puzzle at you, and you start working it, and you start putting all these interesting pieces together while you work it. And, boy, do you work it. Next thing I know, I've got this Seitz girl wandering around in my factory, uninvited."

"Well..."

"Seitz preps people to take a test, or go to college, or get a job, but it doesn't want them to do anything important or new or risky or dangerous," he said. "You're not like them. You don't want to be on a shelf."

"So you think I was just waiting for you to come along?"

"I think there are some people who want to bite into something and just chew it to pieces. Not just take a little bite, but just mash the whole thing up and keep chewing. If I didn't come along, you'd have stayed on track, for a while, and then, at some point, I think you would have jumped. I don't think you were ever going to end up as an investment banker. You were never going to be a sheep."

"I might have ended up working at BSP."

"No." He shook his head. "Definitely not."

"No?"

"You would have ended up running BSP. You would have ended up turning BSP into a global company with offices in sixteen countries, but you wouldn't have ended up just working there. Don't sell yourself short, Alix. You're dangerous."

"I feel nauseated and complimented at the same time."

"Just saying you're not a sheep."

"My boyfriend's full of compliments today."

Moses looked at her seriously. "Is that what I am? Your boyfriend?"

"What, you think I sleep with just anyone?"

"I didn't say that."

"Of course you're my boyfriend...." Alix faltered, suddenly feeling presumptuous and unsure of what Moses really felt for her. "I mean, if you want..."

Maybe he doesn't like you that way.

"I mean," Alix stumbled, "if you think I'm your girlfriend...." She felt like she'd stepped off a cliff and found open air under her feet. She threw up her hands. "Will you help me out here? I'm dying! What do *you* think we are?" She could feel herself blushing horribly.

Moses burst out laughing and pulled her close. "I think you're cute when you're blushing," he said.

"You're a jerk," she said, her words muffled against his chest.

"Good thing you like me, then." He pulled her in tighter.

"So this is serious, right?"

"Boyfriend, girlfriend, going steady, whatever you want to call it, I'm good with it."

It felt almost criminal how much she liked being wrapped inside his arms.

37

BY THE TIME SHE PICKED up Jonah at Sirius Comix, Alix was sweaty and happy, enjoying the fact of her secret life with Moses. She looked at her little brother affectionately. Life was good, the brother was good, all was good—

"You're late," Jonah complained.

"Sorry." Alix grinned unrepentantly. "I got held up. You could have called."

"I left my phone in your car," he groused. He reached around on the floor and came up with it. He gave her another glare. "You used to be on time."

Alix nodded absently and pulled out into traffic. "I said I was sorry already."

"It's okay." He was fiddling with the phone, staring at it. "I know why you're late. I get it."

Alix glanced over at him, feeling a twinge of worry. She

suppressed it. First rule of getting away with things was to deny deny deny. "Get what?"

"I know where you're going," Jonah said. "I know what you're hiding from Mom and Dad."

Deny deny deny. "I don't know what you're talking about."

"Sure you do." Jonah held up his phone and grinned. "I tracked you."

"You... what?" Alix spluttered.

"I put a tracker app on my phone. See?" He showed her the screen. "It wasn't even hard. Just left my phone in your car a couple times." He started fiddling with the screen, tapping.

"At first, it was weird because you kept going to the river, and that didn't make any sense because you never used to do that, but then I got you on the weekend, and I had you in Jersey."

He held up the screen again for her, an aerial view of industrial buildings, train tracks, and roads. "It's your factory, right? The one where 2.0 put you in that cage."

Alix almost drove off the road. "No! That's not what that is!"

"Watch the road, will you?" Jonah braced himself as Alix got the car straightened out.

"Get out of my private life!" She was trying not to panic, but she could feel herself starting to hyperventilate.

I need to warn Moses.

She tried to force herself to be calm. "That's not what you think—"

"Oh, come on, Alix! I know what you're doing. You're not going over to Sophie's every weekend, and you're not doing college-application prep or whatever the heck it is that you tell Mom and Dad you're doing after school."

"You don't know anything."

"This is me we're talking about! I've been recording you. I'll bet if I go through this last track a little, I'll have you and your boyfriend sucking face." He started fiddling with the screen. "Here, let's try this...."

Moses's voice crackled from the phone's speaker. "—here, just lean the seat back—"

"Who's this talking, Alix? Sure doesn't sound like Sophie."

Alix stared straight ahead, keeping her eyes on the road, trying to keep her voice steady. "This isn't any of your business."

"Not even when the guy you're hooking up with is wanted by the FBI?"

Alix tried not to show her panic, but inside, she was furiously working the angles, trying to figure out how she could warn Moses. Trying to figure out how quickly she could pack.

"It's more complicated than that, Jonah."

I'm leaving, she suddenly realized.

Alix was surprised at how certain she felt. Moses was going to have to leave, and she was going to run with him. There wasn't any question.

Jonah intruded on her thoughts. "How is being wanted by the FBI complicated, exactly? I'm just trying to get this straight in my head."

Alix glared at him. "They only want him because he kidnapped me."

"Whoa." Jonah shook his head pityingly. "You don't make it sound any better when you admit you're hooking up with your kidnapper."

"You know what, Jonah? My love life isn't your business. And he's not my kidnapper. I stalked him this last time. "

"Aaaand still sounding crazypants."

"This doesn't have anything to do with you!"

"What about when you get arrested?"

Alix tried to keep her voice controlled. "Who did you tell about him?"

"I just don't get it. What is it with this guy? He was totally stalking you, and then he kidnapped you, and now... what? You just decide you've got to hook up with him?"

"Who did you tell?" Alix pressed. Her heart was pounding with fear. "This is important."

"I'm just saying you never used to lie. Now you do. All the time—"

"Who knows about this, Jonah?"

Jonah continued prattling, undeterred. "Not that you're any good at it. You're a total amateur. Actually, amateur's too kind. I mean, it's like, how can such a smart girl be such a dumb liar?"

"What's that supposed to mean?"

Jonah gave her a self-satisfied smile. "Mom and Dad would've already caught you if I hadn't been covering for you."

Alix almost slammed on the brakes. "*What?*"

411

"I told you. You're an amateur. They've been asking where you were, what you were up to. I promised I'd keep an eye on you. They were worried you were doing some kind of PTSD thing," he said. "I've been covering for you for weeks. They still think you're their good girl." He looked over at her. "I'm not a rat."

Alix didn't know whether to laugh or cry. She was so relieved to hear that Jonah had kept the information to himself that she felt like she'd been given a death-sentence reprieve.

She pulled over to the curb and turned off the car, giving Jonah her full attention. He was smiling at her, like he knew just how much leverage he had. "Okay," she said. "You got me. So why are you pushing on me now?"

Jonah's smile disappeared. "I want to know what you're doing."

"And I already told you it's none of your business what I do with my boyfriend."

"Not that!" Jonah waved a hand dismissively. "I've got, like, hours of audio already."

"You little—"

"I want to know about the other stuff. You're giving him something. I heard it on my recordings."

"No." Alix shook her head. "Just. No. This isn't up for discussion."

"You think you can Mom-voice me?" Jonah laughed. "I could call Williams and Crowe, you know. Your friend Death Barbie would be inside that factory of your boyfriend's like

412

that." He snapped his fingers. "Williams and Crowe SWAT goons looked superbadass the last time. I bet they'd do a whole lot better if they were hitting the right place."

"You wouldn't."

Jonah shrugged. "Maybe I would, maybe I wouldn't. I want to know. It's something to do with all that stuff you were obsessed about before, isn't it? All the work Dad does. That's what this is about, isn't it?"

Alix cast about, trying to find another solution, *any* other solution than trusting Jonah. "You really want to know?"

"I already said I did."

So much for secrets.

"Okay," Alix relented, "but not now. Tonight. After Mom and Dad go to sleep, we'll talk."

■ ■ ■

By the time Alix finished explaining everything that she'd been researching, and describing her hunt for Moses, Jonah was staring at her, wide-eyed.

"This is so nuts."

They were both sitting on his bed. Jonah's iPod clock read 2:00 AM. Alix's mouth was dry and sticky, and her throat was hoarse. "It's the truth. Real truth. Not the back-and-forth smoke and mirrors Dad does. Facts."

"Yeah, but…" Jonah shook his head, frowning. "Alix…" He shook his head again. "I covered for you because I thought it was kind of hilarious that you were rebelling. But this is

413

serious. You can't just go mess everything up for Dad. This is our life. You can't mess all that up."

"Not even if we're getting our money from hurting other people? Killing them, even?"

"That's an exaggeration."

Alix climbed off the bed. "Come on, then, I'll show you."

"Show me what?"

"You want proof, don't you?"

She peeked out Jonah's bedroom door and motioned him to follow. "Come on, daredevil. And be quiet. I don't want us caught."

To Alix, Jonah sounded horribly noisy as they stole down the stairs to Dad's study. Even his breathing was loud.

"Would you be quiet?" she whispered fiercely.

"I am!" Jonah whispered back. "When did you become such an expert at sneaking around?"

The question gave Alix pause. When did that happen, exactly? At some point, she'd become a spy in her own family's house. Some kind of screwed-up mole, planted in deep cover. Alix couldn't help but be reminded of Cynthia—the perfect friend whom Moses had planted right beside her. She remembered how betrayed she'd felt when she found out.

And now you're doing the same thing to Dad.

It hadn't felt so clear-cut as that before. But with Jonah trailing right behind her as she found Dad's keys on the kitchen island and then began opening his filing cabinets in his study, she suddenly felt weirdly exposed. With Jonah

414

watching her do this, it wasn't just a game anymore. It was real.

Alix forced down her rising anxiety. "Here. Check this out. This is a whole file on how Dad has a rapid-response group for negative articles about his clients on the Internet. They've got searches that help them catch bad news, and then they pay people to swarm the comments using sock-puppet names." She rifled through more files. "This one is all about a plan to put news releases into small-town newspapers. Ones that don't have good editorial controls. Cost estimates. Number of readers."

"Yeah, but this isn't evil, Alix."

"Read it," Alix said. "Wait till you get to the part where he and George are practically salivating over the weak fact-checking. They keep saying it. It's a pitch they're putting together for their clients. Weak fact-checking is a *plus* for them."

"Still…"

Alix kept rifling through the familiar files. She'd been through all of them before. "These are just some of the things they work on. I've done searches on client names—" She broke off, frowning.

"Kimball-Geier…"

She pulled the sheet. It was a legal opinion. She went back into the files looking for more, but all she had was the single sheet. She checked the date. It was recent, but there wasn't anything else.

"See if you can find any more sheets like this," she whispered to Jonah, then she went and checked Dad's briefcase as well. Nothing. She went back and studied the paper again.

"What is it?" Jonah asked.

"Azicort. It's an asthma drug. I heard Dad and George and Mr. Geier talking about it on that yacht a while back."

"You were spying on Dad all the way back then? You're like that Russian spy.... What's her name? The superhot one who grew up pretending to be an American and then got caught?"

"I just got tired of people lying to me, okay?"

Jonah held up his hands. "I'm not judging."

Alix went back to the memo. "It looks like they're going to settle another lawsuit. They've got this asthma drug, Azicort. Moses told me it was killing people.... The kid ... Tank. It puts people into comas. Sometimes it kills them if a doctor doesn't figure it out fast enough." She read over the letter again.

"Dad wants them to settle this case...." She frowned. "The people who were suing are giving up." She remembered the members of 2.0 comparing monetary settlements.

"Geier was the guy with the fancy yacht, right?"

"The CEO," Alix said absently, as she read more. The papers were dense with legal jargon. "It looks like they're talking about studies they did on rats, and that they knew there were dangers. Coma. Death. Dosages." She shuffled through her dad's files, frustrated. "There should be more, but I'm not finding it. I think Dad's advising them to settle because

416

there's a new, more definitive study about to come out, and it's bad for Azicort. He thinks it's better for them to settle and then get the FDA to reapprove them for a different respiratory use. They've gotten friendly hearings at the FDA...." She looked up from the paper, frowning. "I wish I could see what he keeps on his computer. If I could get on his client files, this would be clear."

"You don't already know?" Jonah snarked.

"We don't have the girl, Kook. The hacker," Alix explained. "She wrote a program to break Dad's laptop open. If we could get on that..."

"You wouldn't get anything at all," Jonah said.

"How would you know?"

Jonah smirked. "Because I happen to know that Dad doesn't keep anything valuable on it. All his important files are stored on servers at his offices down in DC. They've got it completely hived off from the Internet for security. Even his laptop doesn't connect to that other network."

"Bullshit."

"I'm serious! Lisa was making Dad and George game out different ways that 2.0 might try to hurt them and their clients. I was right there. I heard them talking."

"So how do you know about Dad's laptop?"

"Lisa got worried once they figured out that 2.0 had hackers working for them, and she started asking about data theft. Dad and George said they keep all their sensitive client data off the Internet, so it can't be accessed by anyone who doesn't work inside the actual BSP offices. Maybe they've got a couple files with them on their laptops, but mostly it's at BSP, and there's all kinds of check-in, check-out trackers. Dad and George kept saying you'd have to be inside the actual offices to get anything."

"What happened then?"

"Not much. Lisa got paranoid that 2.0 would try to hold you hostage, maybe make Dad release his client files that way. She was real uptight about the client files."

"What did Dad say?"

"Beats me. They closed the door on me when they started talking about"—Jonah lowered his voice to a conspiratorial whisper—"*hostage scenarios.*" He made a face. "Lisa was freaking about that idea, though. She didn't want any of Dad's clients getting exposed."

"I'll bet she didn't." Alix stared at the legal memo, thinking about the strange crew that Moses had once assembled. "The kid's name was Tank," she said. "The one who took Azicort."

"You told me that already."

"Yeah. I know. It's just…" Alix trailed off. "It was kind of a joke name, right? Like the kid was big and tough, even though he wasn't. I think Azicort maybe did something to him. I never got a chance to ask, though." She frowned, tapping the file on the table thoughtfully. "Moses would know." She snapped a pic of the memo with her phone and then carefully put the paper back where she'd found it. "I'll bet the lawyers in this class action would give a lot to know what's in Dad's files."

"You'd seriously sabotage Dad like that?" Jonah asked.

Alix didn't know how to respond.

Jonah looked pained. "Come on. You can't be serious."

"What would you do if you were walking past someone on the sidewalk who was bleeding and you were the only person in the world with a bandage? Would you let them bleed out?"

"What kind of a screwed-up question is that?"

Abruptly, Alix realized she'd said too much. *Don't get him more involved. Get him out. Make him forget about all this.* She made herself smile. "It's nothing. I was just thinking."

"Oh, no you don't. You're planning something, aren't you?"

"I think we're done for the night. It's three AM."

"I'm your brother."

"You're my little brother." She patted him on the shoulder. "Seriously. Let it go, Jonah."

"I could still tell Dad," he threatened.

"You could," she admitted. "But you won't."

"How do you know?"

Alix smiled. "Because if you do, I'll let everyone know that you're the one who called in the bomb threat last fall."

"That's not fair!"

"Shhhh." She put her fingers to her lips. "I've got some things I need to do, that's all. It's probably better if you don't know what they are. It's no big deal. I promise. Just be good for a while, until I get back."

Jonah was frowning, his brow knitted. "You're going down to DC," he said. "You're going down to DC, and you're not going to take me."

38

A WEEK LATER ALIX WAS on the Acela with Moses, cruising south. The Acela ran smooth and fast, down through Connecticut countryside before plunging into the heart of New York City. Minutes later the train emerged, rushing for Philadelphia, Baltimore, and, as Jonah had guessed, Washington, DC.

"Are you sure Jonah isn't going to rat us out?"

"Will you calm down about that? I know him. He's mostly just pissed I'm not bringing him along."

"How did you persuade him to stay?"

"I told him that if he kept his mouth shut, I wouldn't turn him in for his bomb-threat prank on Seitz last fall."

Moses warned, "You know this is just a scouting trip, right? We aren't going to try anything this time."

"I know."

"It probably won't work," Moses said. "A lot of these things, they're just about trying different approaches. Learning about the people involved. Learning how their systems work."

"I know."

"We tried this before, you know. We never got past the front desks."

Alix smiled. "I know."

"You act like you're listening to me, but I don't think a word I've said has actually stuck inside that head of yours."

Alix leaned back in her seat, watching the greenery and buildings rush past. "I heard you."

"What did I say?"

"The program you've got isn't as good as the one Kook wanted to use before. This is only a keystroke logger. We need to get it installed on Dad's computer, which is basically impossible, because it's inside all these layers of security that you can't get past without someone like Kook doing the hacking, and even if she was she wouldn't have access to their main servers, and blah blah blah..."

"I'm serious, Alix."

Alix patted his hand reassuringly. "I know you are. But we've got Dad's swipe card already, and I've got the key to his corner office. I think that counts for something."

"Yeah, well, just because you can grab his wallet off the kitchen counter—"

"And clone his key card. I did that, too."

"Only because I gave you the machine to do it! Don't get cocky, Alix. Sneaking around and snooping through your dad's stuff at home isn't the same as this. This is real. We're talking about real—" He broke off, leaned close, and lowered his voice to a whisper. "We're talking about real *breaking and entering.*"

She leaned over and kissed him. "You're cute when you worry."

"Why are you so calm about this? When Kook and Cyn and Adam and Tank and I were doing this, we never figured out how to crack the Doubt Factory. Never. We figured out how we might have gotten inside, but after that Kook needed some way to get on the network, and for that we needed security keys. . . . It was a mess."

"But we're already further along than that," Alix pointed out. "Anyway, I'm sure we'll work it out. Dad knows I'm coming down to DC for vacation with Denise and Sophie, seeing the nation's center of political gridlock and all that, and letting Denise check out Georgetown for the millionth time. He's not going to even see this coming."

Moses scowled. "You know what the problem with amateurs is?"

"Too much confidence?" Alix asked brightly.

"That's right. Too much confidence."

"You told me that last week." She kissed him again. "I think you're forgetting something, though."

"Oh, yeah? What's that?"

"This time, you've got me." She smiled so dazzlingly that Moses was almost fooled into believing their scheme would work.

∎ ∎ ∎

"Mr. Banks? Your daughter is here to see you."

Alix waited at the front reception, tapping her fingers on stainless steel. In her head, Moses's instructions kept repeating themselves.

"Look at the tags for the security people. Pay attention to their uniforms. Watch how they make your visitor pass."

The man smiled at her and said, "Elevator four."

She went in and the doors closed. She'd never thought about how infuriating it was to have no buttons on the elevator, but right now it felt like a serious crimp. She could only swipe a building pass and then get on an assigned elevator and finally ride up to the preprogrammed floor.

So the first hurdle was to get inside the building, which was owned by some other company. Then to get access to the elevators, then to ride up to where Banks Strategy Partners was located on the tenth floor. Alix had grabbed Dad's swipe card and office key at home, but they had no way of grabbing his computer password. Hence the keystroke logger.

"I can get us into the main office building, but after that it's all on you. You're the one who has to get passes for the elevators and keys for your dad's offices," Moses had said.

"How, exactly, do you break into an office building where you aren't invited?"

"Don't worry about it. I just need to bump into the right worker."

"How is it that easy?"

Moses had laughed and held up her keys. Somehow, he'd gotten them out of her purse, while it was on her shoulder....

"That's amazing!"

"Here, let me see your bra...."

That had led to a pleasant distraction.

Focus, Alix.

She rose up through the levels, fighting a feeling of claustrophobia in the button-less elevator.

This can work. This isn't crazy. This can work.

She had the USB key in her pocket, loaded with the little virus. A simple keystroke logger. Nothing fancy. Not like the Stuxnet-modified worm that Kook had created before and taken with her when she left. Just something simple that most anyone could use with a little training. All Alix needed to do was get the logger onto the computer. Just a few mouse clicks on the right computer and she'd be done.

"Will it set off an alarm?"

"Kook wrote it before she left. It's not something that's out in the wild, so it's got a good chance of sliding past their alarms."

"How good is a 'good chance'?"

"You don't have to do this if you don't want."

"I'm just asking."

"It doesn't report to anywhere else. It doesn't try to get access to networks. It just wants to sit and listen right on the computer. It's pretty innocuous, as far as viruses go. It's the best chance we've got."

"It just wants to listen," Alix muttered to herself, trying to master the jittery energy that was popping just beneath her skin. "No one will notice."

The elevator door slid aside and Dad came out to greet her, pushing through BSP's emblazoned doors.

"Alix! Great to see you!"

He won't see it coming from me. He won't even know it's happening.

Alix went into his arms and let him hug her while she checked for where the swipe cards unlocked the main office doors.

Hug him back, idiot.

Alix made her arms tighten around him, remembering how it had used to feel to be hugged by him, how safe and happy she'd felt. Now it felt more like being hugged by rose thorns. It was all she could do not to show how her skin crawled.

I know what you do.

She smiled brightly at him. "I thought I'd surprise you. You want to go out for lunch?"

"I'd love to! Just let me finish up an e-mail."

He sounded so pleased and happy that Alix felt herself faltering, even as she followed him past reception and down

425

the hall, past conference rooms and offices to his own corner office, looking out across DC toward the Washington Monument. She couldn't really do this, could she?

The next kid like Tank is on you, she reminded herself.

She steeled herself for the next step.

"Oh, Dad, I almost forgot! Denise needed to print out some essays for her Georgetown interview. I told her I could print them here and get them to her. Is that okay? It's just a PDF."

"Sure, Alix."

Alix hugged him and gushed. "Oh my God, you're a lifesaver! Denise is going to love you forever."

She fished the USB key out of her pocket. Smiled innocently. "Can you just print it?"

He didn't even blink. He took the key and popped it into his computer.

Of course he did. He trusted her.

The file opened up.

Political Innovations in Cluny, France.

"Looks dry," Dad commented.

Alix's mouth sure felt dry. "Yeah. That's the one." She suddenly felt horribly and completely transparent, standing next to him, staring at the computer's screen, wondering if Kook's virus would work.

"Just one copy?" he asked.

"Um...I think she wanted two."

Alix was sure he could hear her heart drumming out warnings of betrayal. She stared at the screen, trying not to look suspicious and feeling flagrantly so.

Nothing telltale happened. Which was good, Alix hoped. The virus was supposed to be stealthy. While they were looking at medieval European power in the church, Kook's program was slicing through Dad's computer defenses and setting up shop.

As least, that was the idea.

Either that or it was all a fantasy, and Kook wasn't the hacker who had successfully rewritten a Stuxnet virus, and she wasn't the girl who spent her late-night hours hacking Chase Manhattan for Eastern European credit card thieves. Maybe she was just a crazy girl in over her head, with a boy who wasn't all he was cracked up to be, and Alix was about to set off every single alarm in the whole damn building.

Alix licked her lips, waiting for alarms and red flags. Sirens. Security guards. German shepherds. SWAT.

The printer began spitting out paper.

"I'll just print out one more," Dad said. "Just in case Denise spills coffee or anything."

Alix looked up at her father, her heart thudding with wonder as everything went exactly as planned.

"You're the best, Dad. Thanks."

■ ■ ■

When she came out of her father's building after lunch, she saw Moses. He was in jogging clothes with an ostentatious Bluetooth headset on his ear, and he was stalking back and forth on the far side of the street, doing stretches and pretending to be one of those pretentious people who liked to believe that everyone wanted a sampling of their oh-so-important conversation.

Alix crossed the street. He looked different. He'd done something with makeup to make himself look older. Small lines. A bit of gray at his close-cropped temples. It was amazing how makeup reshaped a person. It was a trick Adam had known how to do, Moses had said. That boy could make anyone look like anything. Give him a wig, a uniform, a little greasepaint, and a little foundation, and people's faces changed.

And that was without even adding any latex. None of the real makeup craft of the theater. Adam had made Moses look legitimate enough as a driver of an eighteen-wheeler that they'd been able to hijack an entire shipment of rats, and drive it right out of a testing facility without raising alarms.

And now Moses was using Adam's tricks again. Moses looked almost distinguished, except that he'd pulled his socks up on his calves, making himself look intentionally dorky. And that headband. Alix shook her head. Nothing like the Secret Service–style agent of cool who had whispered in her ear outside of Widener Hall when they'd first met. Nothing like the boy she was falling in love with.

Slow down, girl.

Moses turned away from her as she passed, ignoring her entirely, saying something into his headset—"don't care who you have to get on the wheat-subsidies study group"—and then she was past him.

Amazing. His whole body language was different.

Alix kept walking. Moses would stay a little longer, making sure she wasn't being followed. She'd protested that it wasn't necessary, but Moses had just given her a bored look. "How about you trust the experts on this, huh?" And she'd subsided.

If everything went well, he'd be joining her soon. She abruptly turned around and flagged a cab. Another thing Moses had told her to do. Do something surprising, see if anyone gets startled.

A few minutes later she was sipping a skinny latte on the steps of the Library of Congress, looking across at the arrogant rise of the Capitol. The white dome stood against the blue sky. It was hot. She kept an eye out to see if anyone seemed to care about her, but, of course, no one did.

A half hour later, Moses ambled down the street and joined her. Relaxed in a suit jacket, no tie, looking like any one of a million other government workers.

"Well?" He leaned against the concrete wall. "How did it go? Did you figure out which computers we'll need to install this on?"

Alix grinned and tossed him the USB key. Moses grabbed for it and barely caught it.

"It's already done," she said.

She couldn't help laughing as Moses gaped in surprise.

"I told you. I'm your secret weapon."

429

39

IN THE HEART OF THE DOUBT FACTORY, a series of alerts began popping up on the company's central servers.

One by one, notifications appeared on cell phones and workstations in a variety of offices around DC, and people whose job it was to pay attention began paying attention.

■ ■ ■

At Williams & Crowe's regional office, a nondescript building in Arlington, Lisa Price checked her phone as a message arrived.

Five minutes later she was pushing through glass doors emblazoned with the words Data Integrity Monitoring. A Williams & Crowe computer-security technician was staring at a slew of warnings and alarm messages.

"What do we have?"

"Not sure yet. Something running on the servers at BSP. Cerberus flagged it and sent the alert."

"Do we know who did it?"

"Cerberus diagnostics says it came from…a Mr. Simon Banks's workstation. It's also under his login." He pointed as a new window opened up. "Now Portcullis just flagged it, too."

"Call and get me a rundown of everyone who's in the building."

The technician picked up his phone and started making calls as Lisa scrutinized the rest of the diagnostic information their security alert had sent.

"This is a pretty sleek virus," Lisa said.

The tech hung up from his calls. "Sneaky as hell, for sure. We're running pattern matching now. It looks a little like code that was used to go after online commerce sites a couple years ago. Estonian, we think."

"What did we ever do to Estonia?"

The tech smirked. "Decided not to use the chip-and-pin system?" He popped open another screen. "And here we go.… Beltway Properties is sending us their K Street building's access data now. Let's see who went up to Banks Strategy Partners…tenth floor."

They both scanned the names. Lisa frowned. Under VISITORS…

"Oh, Alix," Lisa murmured. "What have you gotten yourself involved in?"

"Do you want me to shut this down?"

"Yeah. Kill it."

The tech nodded. "We don't have remote access—all we're getting is the radio SOS from the system. I'll have to send a team to go over everything."

"No! Wait!" Lisa gripped his shoulder. "Don't do anything yet. Let it run. Send someone over to pull a copy, but let it run for now. There's no way Alix is working on her own. Maybe there's a way we can use this to our advantage."

"What about BSP?"

"Get a team to analyze just how bad this is. After that, I'll talk to Banks myself. With his daughter involved, he'll need some convincing." She grimaced. "But call George Saamsi. He'll understand the client situation. Bring him up to speed on everything. After that, I'll decide how to talk to Banks."

Lisa wasn't looking forward to the conversation. Banks would have to be notified that he had a serious breach and that his daughter was the source. And that there were more interests involved than just his personal family issues. He'd be in denial.

Why couldn't you just leave well enough alone, Alix? Lisa thought. *You had such a bright future.*

"You're sure we should let this run?" the tech asked.

"The system's cut off from the outside, right?"

He nodded reluctantly.

"Then it's harmless as is. I want to talk to people higher up first. Until we have a strategy to protect our clients permanently, I don't want to frighten off our little secret mole. Let her think she's succeeding. If we play this right, we have a chance to wrap up 2.0 once and for all."

Tonight, she'd need to talk to Mr. Banks and explain to him the situation with his daughter. Maybe Saamsi could help him understand the gravity of the situation.

Lisa paused. Or was it Banks himself? Could he be compromised as well? She considered the possibility because she was trained to follow paranoia down to the worst possible outcomes, but she decided it was unlikely.

Banks wouldn't need a sneaky little Estonian program to grab anything he wanted. The man could do whatever he liked and cover his tracks easily. No, it was his daughter who was the security threat. And behind her...

"Hello, 2.0," Lisa murmured. "This time, I'm not going to miss."

40

"JUST FOLLOW MY LEAD," MOSES murmured as they rode the elevator from the parking garage level.

"Are you sure this is going to work?" Alix asked as she tried to keep her mop and yellow bucket from banging against the elevator doors. They were both dressed in good approximations of the gray jumpsuit uniforms that Beltway Properties cleaning staff wore, purchased at a supply store in the city that afternoon. "This feels risky."

Moses smiled conspiratorially and for a second the seriousness that he'd been carrying lightened. "Trust a uniform, Alix. People love to trust uniforms."

"Then they shouldn't make buying them so easy."

Moses lifted the security badge that he'd pickpocketed off another custodian in the parking garage. "They also trust badges."

"Well, they better not look too closely, or someone's

434

going to notice you're not the same black dude as the one on the tag."

"They won't look," Moses said. "They'll know they can trust me."

"I hope you're right."

The elevator doors opened, revealing the polished lobby of 609 K Street. Across the lobby, a security guy was sitting behind the central desk pulling his own night shift.

They pushed their mops and buckets across the open lobby, ignoring the guy. Alix suppressed an urge to whistle innocently.

Just two custodians pushing their mop buckets, just two people getting their job done and heading home. No need to think about us. No need to worry.

As they got close to the elevators, Alix had a horrible urge to look over at the security guy.

Moses seemed to read her mind. "Try looking sleepy and bored and like you wish you weren't here. And keep your head low. You don't want the cameras to see your face," he advised quietly.

"I know," Alix whispered back. "I'm the one who told you where the cameras are."

"My girlfriend thinks she knows about surveillance."

"Your girlfriend knows how to study up."

She realized what he'd done as they reached the elevators. He'd completely distracted her as they made their way across the lobby. Forcing her to forget the audaciousness of what they were doing.

She swiped her father's key card in the elevator, and the doors opened. "Floor ten," she breathed. "Going up."

■ ■ ■

To Moses, it felt claustrophobic, standing in the elevator without any buttons or controls. Just polished stainless steel, a little prison box like the one his uncle had ended up in. Their reflections were distorted, both of them looking bloated and alien in their uniforms, with their yellow plastic mop buckets. He reached to hold Alix's hand and felt a jolt of comfort from the contact. He stared at their polished steel reflections, trying to calm himself and stay focused on the job.

As the elevator rose, carrying them to the place that had become his obsession, Moses wondered if he was making a mistake by risking Alix in this way.

Is that where this ends? Moses wondered. *Am I going to jail?*

Even if it worked, what was supposed to happen next? Another heist? Was he supposed to go all WikiLeaks and end up as a hunted whistle-blower? The FBI already wanted him. How long before the wrong people decided to devote real energy to finding him?

Or maybe he was just going to end up in a box, six feet under. Another number in all the statistics of black men that his father had warned him about and that his mother had feared. *Don't end up like your cousin. Don't end up like so-and-so's nephew—*

Don't end up in a coffin.

He remembered each of his parents in their coffins, each of their smooth faces beyond pain, even though when they'd died he'd seen the terror in their eyes.

He remembered those funerals. First Dad, with Mom to stand beside him. Then Mom, and only Uncle Ty to take care of him. He remembered standing there, not knowing how to cry and not knowing how to let go, with his stiff-faced uncle holding his hand. *Don't worry, boy. I got you. Your uncle Ty's got you.*

The elevator opened, revealing an antechamber with locked glass doors. Beyond the doors, BANKS STRATEGY PARTNERS gleamed on a wall over the reception area.

"Welcome to the Doubt Factory," Alix said.

Moses found he couldn't move.

"You okay?" Alix asked.

Alix tugged him, and he let himself be pulled off the elevator. Moses swallowed. "I've spent the last three years wanting to get into here. Cruising by outside, looking for some way…" He trailed off. This was where all his pain had come from.

His father lying on the bathroom floor, gasping. Trying to get up and failing. And then his mother, a year later, collapsing under the stress of loss. Tumbling to the floor of the grocery store, cans rolling, bottles shattering, lettuce spilling out onto the linoleum tiles while everyone turned and stared. And him standing there, stupid with shock. Seeing the thing he'd feared the most, happening right in front of him. He remembered trying to make his body move, to run to her, and instead finding himself frozen and unable to do anything at all.

It had all started here.

All those years living with his uncle, the man not knowing how to do anything except teach a young boy about the con...

And now, at last, Moses had come full circle. A business office, just like all the other polished business offices. It was infuriating that the place looked so *normal*.

"It feels like..." He hesitated. "It should be bigger. I don't know. More..."

"Like Mordor?"

He nodded. "Maybe. Yeah. This is the place that did it to us. Me. Adam. Cynthia. Kook. Tank. All of us. Someone inside here came up with a plan and made sure that we all ended up where we did."

"Are you going to be okay?"

It should have been filled with bats, Moses thought. Bats and the sulfurous stink of evil. Instead, it was sterile AC air and a tenth-floor view of other buildings that were just the same size. Modern evil. It didn't look like anything except another office building.

If you wanted to look at evil, it was just a bunch of suits and ties, a bunch of cubicles and computers, the quiet whirring of commerce. Evil wasn't anything. It was just business as usual.

"Moses?" Alix asked. Her tone was worried. "Are you okay?"

He turned to her. The girl who had risked everything to join him on this Don Quixote quest, standing there in her custodial uniform, looking concerned.

438

You're not alone, anymore, he realized. *She's with you. She cares about you.*

The Doubt Factory had stolen so much from him, and yet it had also given him Alix. The thing that had destroyed his past had given him the girl who made him want a future. He wanted a future with her.

So let's put the Doubt Factory in the past.

Suddenly Moses felt a weight lifting off him.

It was all going to work. He'd finally made it here. And thanks to Alix, he was going to make it through to the other side.

"I'm good," he said, and couldn't help smiling. "Let's go dig up some secrets."

■ ■ ■

Alix booted up her father's computer. Her face lit blue as the screen glowed alive with its security challenges.

"Okay," she said. "This is where we see if Kook's programs are as good as she thought."

"Oh, they're good all right."

Moses plugged his slate into the computer's USB drive and held his breath. A second later the retrieval program kicked back the answer they were looking for. The password was as long and as bad as a software-license code.

"Damn. Your dad's serious about security." He started reading off numbers and letters, letting Alix type, with her confirming each letter and number out loud as he worked through the sequence.

Alix hit Enter.

Authenticating ...

They held their breaths.

The computer continued with its boot sequence and opened to a familiar desktop layout.

"I'll be damned," Alix whispered.

Moses couldn't help grinning. "I told you Kook was good!"

"Yeah, she's a genius. What do you want to get?"

"Let's see if we can look at some client files."

It took a little bit of rooting around in the server's file structure, but eventually Alix found what she was looking for and popped open a database search window. One of the fields said *Company*.

Alix typed * in the window and hit Enter.

Corporate names started spooling:

Dow Chemical
Monsanto
ConocoPhillips
Philip Morris
Kimball-Geier Pharmaceuticals
Lukoil
Merck & Co
Pfizer Inc
Marcea Pharmaceuticals
Apple Inc

Hewlett-Packard
American Petroleum Institute
Google
Intel
National Rifle Association
Amgen Inc
Household Product Association
Eli Lilly & Co
American Fuel & Petrochemical Manufacturers
Oxbow Corp
Microsoft Corp
Hill + Knowlton
Oracle Corp
Novartis AG
Bayer AG
AstraZeneca PLC
ExxonMobil
Koch Industries
Facebook Inc
Amazon.com
National Association of Manufacturers
3M
Royal Dutch Shell
Chevron Corp
BP
Edelman
Procter & Gamble
Association of Equipment Manufacturers

Unilever
Personal Care Products Council
Pharmaceutical Research & Manufacturers of America
Archer Daniels Midland
CropLife America
Syngenta AG

The list just kept going.

And going and going...

"This can't be right," Moses said. "It's like every major company in the world. BSP can't have done doubt work for all of them. I mean, BSP is good, but they're not this big."

Alix frowned and started opening files, checking the contents under individual company names.

"Some of this looks like standard PR," she said. "Totally legit work. Crisis communications, that kind of thing. Some of it looks like it's more like ad campaign stuff...just general image polishing."

Fighting a feeling of disappointment, Alix went back to the main search screen and started checking pull-down menus. "The database is broken down by industry type, but it's obviously not organized by 'unethical business work' or anything like that."

"Okay, that makes sense. So what do we have?"

"I don't know. There's a ton of stuff in here. Some of this looks like they're consulting with other PR firms. Some of it's just letters and stuff. Just really basic correspondence." She popped open a file. "This one's just a pitch letter. I don't think Google hired BSP, but I guess Dad thought they had an image problem that he could help with."

Alix popped open another file, trying to get a feel for what she was seeing. She laughed out loud. "This is interesting. Some of the company names are connected to potential campaigns that Dad's got ready to roll, just in case....Like BSP expects something bad to happen and wants to be able to pitch as soon as it does. They've got a whole section here for environmental disasters: chemical-plant explosions, toxic leaks, pipeline breaks, drilling platforms exploding..."

Moses leaned close. "Did they do the BP oil spill?"

"I don't think so," Alix said. "My dad was making jokes about them when the Gulf thing happened. I think he was pissed that they hired someone else instead of him."

She looked up at Moses. "This is too big. It's like the tobacco files. There's millions and millions of documents, but a lot of them look totally legit. It'll take time for us to comb through it all. Is there someplace you want to start? Some way you want me to sort all of this? Start alphabetically? Go after Big Oil? Big Pharma? Big Ag?"

"Let's start with Kimball-Geier. What's up with Azicort?"

■ ■ ■

"Well?" Lisa said, leaning back from her laptop and turning to Mr. Banks. "I told you they'd try something like this."

They were in Williams & Crowe's Data Integrity Monitoring

Center, watching red flags pop up as the kids started accessing files.

"Well?"

Mr. Banks's jaw was clenched, holding back an ocean of roiling emotions as he watched the pair poking around in the BSP central file servers.

Lisa waited patiently for the man to come to the conclusion that was inevitable.

Frustratingly, he seemed unable to make the call. A minute ticked by.

Lisa pressed gently. "We're going to need to shut them down. You have clients who are at risk. Williams and Crowe has clients at risk...."

"I want him gone," Banks said through clenched teeth. "I want him away from my daughter."

Lisa nodded, pleased. "Once we have them, we can arrange for him to disappear."

"I don't care how you handle it. I just don't want him near my daughter ever again. Make it happen."

Lisa hesitated, then pressed again. "We'll need to address your daughter at some point as well."

"I'll deal with her."

"We have clients who will need assurance...."

He gave her a cold stare. "I'll take care of Alix."

You're in denial, Lisa thought, but all she said was, "Of course."

Lisa pulled out her encrypted phone and dialed through to the response team. "Timmons? We're on. Targets are in the

444

building. Tenth floor. Mr. Banks's private office. No. You don't need to be that careful. We just want the girl. It doesn't matter what happens to the other one, but nothing can happen to the girl. The other one...we don't want to hear from him again. And we don't want news. Just silence, understood?"

She waited, listening for the response. She turned back to Banks, who was still staring, transfixed, watching as his daughter and the boy who had turned her against him rummaged through his files one by one.

"We're up and running," Lisa said.

"How long?"

"Not long. Our people are very good. We'll secure the building, then lock down the tenth floor. Then we'll move in."

Banks nodded sharply. "And it will be quiet?"

"By the time they're done, there won't be a trace of him. It will be like he never existed. None of this will have happened at all."

"Don't do anything to the boy in front of Alix."

"The team understands." She stood up. "We have a car waiting. You can be near the offices in fifteen minutes. You'll want to be there when they bring out Alix."

41

MOSES WHISTLED. **"I NEED ANOTHER** hard drive," he said.

Alix handed him another terabyte drive. Moses swapped out the one that he'd just filled, and Alix dumped it into the duffel bag. It was more than she'd expected. Huge amounts of information, and they were still going.

"I think we ought to be going soon," she said. "We've already been here for half an hour."

Moses shook his head. "We've still got a lot here. You wouldn't believe the stuff they have just on Azicort. Kimball-Geier has reams of studies that say Azicort causes comas if body-weight dosage goes off by much. And sometimes it happens anyway, and they still can't figure out why. They've even got transcripts of emergency room interviews that they had investigators do. They know that this is happening. This is how Tank ended up in the hospital! They've known there were problems for years. They've been putting out studies blaming other drugs and patient diets—"

Alix interrupted. "We don't have time for this, Moses. Just get all the info."

"This isn't just the smoking gun," Moses protested. "It's the whole smoking arsenal! Just the Azicort information is worth millions—maybe even billions—in class action lawsuits. I mean, you should see the nondisclosure agreements on this stuff. It's amazing. Tank's alive, but his sister died because they were hiding this...."

Moses went on, scanning documents. "It's worse than I thought," he kept murmuring. "They're insane. When we broke into the safety-testing labs and stole Kimball-Geier's rats, the thing we should have stolen was their test data. Azicort's just a straight-up coma drug. That is, if it doesn't just stop your heart completely..."

"That's great, Moses, but let's get this done and get out."

"What's wrong with you?"

"I don't know." Alix rubbed her arms. "I just don't like being here. I thought we were going to get in and get out. Fifteen minutes, a half hour, tops. Time's up."

She went to the window and looked down, hoping that no one could see what was going on. That no one would think the glow of a computer screen was suspicious at 3 AM.

You're being paranoid, she told herself. *Lots of people work late in DC.*

"Just hurry up," she said to Moses.

"Okay, okay, but there's terabytes here. BSP went full

digital. All their old files are scanned. Everything. It's a paper trail that goes back to tobacco." He popped open a file. "Check this out. It's like a treasure trove. I've got CEOs signing off on things that they've denied for years. It's Eldorado. People could go to prison. There's a ton of stuff on Marcea in here. With this, I might be able to file a civil suit. Wrongful death or something, and go after a CEO. I might be able to go after the actual people!"

"Not if we get busted trying to get it out," Alix said. "So hurry it up, will you?"

Moses looked back at the computer. "This just takes time. I'd hook up more drives, but they've got only two USB ports on this computer. If I had Kook, maybe we could rig something faster...."

Alix wasn't really listening as Moses rambled on about what Kook and the rest of the crew would have been able to do. She stared down at the street.

Were those shadows moving?

She squinted, trying to tell if she was seeing human forms down in the darkness, moving along the edges of the building. They didn't look like regular pedestrians. She blinked and stared more closely. Maybe she was imagining them.

Or maybe not?

"Seriously," she said, turning back to Moses. "We need to get the hell out of here."

"Why are you so jittery all of a sudden?"

"I've got a bad feeling."

Moses popped another hard drive in. "We're good."

Alix peered out the windows again, trying to see. The hair on her arms was standing up.

"I don't like this," she murmured. "I don't like this at all." She made a snap decision. "Okay, we're wrapping up. It's time. We're going."

"But I've only got half of it!"

"Better than none," Alix said grimly. She yanked the hard drive out of the computer.

"Alix!"

"We're going."

She tossed the hard drive into the duffel. Moses looked like he was still going to protest, so she yanked the power plug out of the wall, too.

The computer's screen went black.

"What are you *doing*?"

"Making sure we get out in one piece." She zipped up the duffel and grabbed Moses's arm. "Come on!"

"Why are you so paranoid all of a sudden?"

"Like I said, I've got a bad feeling," she said as she dragged him out of her dad's office.

"You've got a bad *feeling*? You know how long it's taken me to get here, and now you want to leave just because you've got a bad *feeling*?" His voice was rising, even as he followed her down the hall to the reception area.

Alix didn't answer. All she could think was that something was terribly wrong. They'd done it wrong. They'd set it up wrong. Something…

By the time she shoved out through BSP's main doors,

she was practically running. She hit the Down button on the elevator. "Come on," she whispered. "Come on, come on."

Nothing happened.

Frowning, she hit the Down button again, then stared up at the glowing floor numbers.

L stayed stubbornly lit.

Alix pushed the button again.

Nothing changed.

Moses stood beside her, staring up at the unchanging floor number. "What was that you were saying about a bad feeling?"

■ ■ ■

From Alix's perch by the windows, she could see shadows converging. Moses joined her, watching as more stealthy forms filtered toward the building. The elevators weren't working anymore, and to their dismay, they'd found that the building's fire stairwells were also locked down. They'd hammered on the doors, at first thinking they were stuck, and dashed around the entire floor of the building, hoping there might be some other escape, but now the reality of the situation was sinking in, and Alix found herself filled with an almost unnatural calm.

"Williams and Crowe, for sure," Moses said.

"Yeah." Alix wondered if Lisa was down there somewhere. Death Barbie incarnate. Coming for them.

"I must say I hate those guys," Moses said with a sigh.

"Well, we might as well make it a big event." He picked up the office phone and dialed.

"What are you doing?"

"You remember how Williams and Crowe came in for me the last time? The only thing that keeps us safe right now is if this turns into something public." He turned his attention back to the phone.

"911? This is Simon Banks. I'm at Banks Strategy Partners on K Street, and I'm seeing what look like gangbangers on the street."

"What are you doing?" Alix hissed.

Moses shrugged. "Confusing the issue." He went back to talking into the phone. "They've got…it looks like they've got automatic weapons of some kind. I don't know who they are or what they're doing, but we need the cops here, right now! Send SWAT! Hurry! It looks like they're trying to break in!"

Alix peered out the window. Vehicles were converging around the building now. Moses rolled his chair over and peered down. "Looks like Williams and Crowe isn't worried about us noticing them now."

"Yeah."

"We'll need to watch out for snipers," Moses said. His voice was oddly flat as he pointed at the buildings across the street from them. "Once they get set up, they'll be looking to shoot inside for sure."

"They aren't actually going to *shoot* us! Who would authorize that?"

451

Moses gave her a look. "Williams and Crowe would probably do anything to get a clean shot at me."

He peered out the window again. "Sure wish the cops would get here."

Alix didn't like how calm he sounded. No, not calm—*resigned*.

Alix pulled out her phone.

"What are you doing?"

"I'm going to try to buy us some more time."

The phone started ringing. "Pick up," Alix whispered. "Go on. Pick up. You always have your phone."

She peered down at the increasing activity as Williams & Crowe set themselves up around the building. "This is real, isn't it?"

Moses glanced down at the lights as well. "Getting more and more that way." He glanced over at her. "Not like the last time we threw a shindig like this."

Alix swallowed. "No. The bad guys have the right address this time."

The phone picked up.

"Alix?"

Dad's voice.

■ ■ ■

"Alix?"

Lisa turned. Mr. Banks had his cell pressed to his ear.

"Mr. Banks?"

He cupped his palm over the phone's receiver. "It's Alix!"

Lisa held out her hand. "Let me speak to her."

Banks ignored her and turned away. "Are you okay, honey? What are you doing?" Lisa pressed close, listening in. When he tried to shake her off, she glared at him. Finally, he relented and let her listen.

"I'm fine, Dad."

"You're in my office, aren't you?"

"Yeah."

"Alix. I don't know what that boy's been telling you—"

"How could you, Dad?"

"How could I what?"

"You killed people, Dad."

"That's not true."

"It's true, Dad. I'm looking at the files. All the companies you've worked for have been letting innocent people die. The drug companies and the asbestos companies. The lead companies. The chemical companies. It's like every big name is here."

"Alix—"

"They knew people would be dying, Dad. Kimball-Geier knew. You knew. You helped them with their strategy. People are dead because you helped them!"

"It's not like that, Alix."

"Dad, if Williams and Crowe tries to come in here, I'm going to make sure this goes on the news. I can send things out that only you would believe. You know what I'm looking at."

Banks waved at Lisa. "You need to back off! She's threatening to release client files!"

Lisa tried to get her hand on the phone. "Let me talk to her."

Banks shook her off again. "I'll handle this!' he whispered fiercely. "You just figure out how to get her out of there."

Lisa didn't back down. "Your phone isn't secure. You don't know who else is listening. We have clients—"

Banks brushed her off. "I know my business. Take care of yours. Get Alix out now. We don't want to be the story here."

Lisa spun away, scowling. George Saamsi joined her as she strode across the lawn to her teams.

"Do we have a problem?" he murmured.

"Banks's daughter is up to her neck in this. She's not a kidnap victim this time. She's the one who's driving this."

Saamsi's gaze went from Banks to Lisa, then to the response team.

"She's threatening to release client files," Lisa said.

In the distance, sirens wailed. Saamsi swore. "They're going to try to turn this into a media circus. This is exactly what they love to do. In about ten minutes we're going to be front-page news."

"Banks is trying to talk to her, but…" Lisa made a gesture of frustration. "I think we've got ten minutes before everything goes wrong. Our best bet is to hit them now. The longer we wait—"

Saamsi cut her off. "I understand. It's time to cut our losses."

"And that means?"

Saamsi looked at her fiercely. "Protect our clients."

The sirens were growing louder.

"And Alix?"

"You can't save someone who doesn't want to be saved. Just make sure our clients stay out of the news. I don't want a single whisper of our clients leaking out."

The first police department squad cars were arriving, along with ambulances.

"This is going to turn into a jurisdictional nightmare in about two minutes," Lisa warned.

"So get it done." Saamsi turned and started striding toward the police and rescue vehicles, holding up his hands with authority. "I'll handle the cops," he called back. "You just handle those kids."

Lisa was already jogging toward her team, thinking about how it needed to happen. She crouched down with Timmons, her strike leader. "What's our situation?"

Timmons said, "We've got all exits blocked. Elevator locked. Stairwells locked. We've got them bottled."

"I want you to go in."

"I've got thirty split in three go-teams—"

"No." She pulled Timmons closer. "This has to be quiet. Quick and fast and quiet."

Timmons frowned. "There are risks."

"There are more risks if you've got a lot of witnesses."

Timmons's eyes widened. He hesitated. "These people armed?"

Lisa gave him a hard look. "That's the assumption. We're proceeding under the assumption that these are unstable terrorists with knowledge of explosives, and we need to stop them, fast. We're sure a fast resolution will save lives."

"A *fast* resolution," Timmons repeated.

"You understand?"

He nodded sharply. "Elam and Mint and me, then. We can do it."

"Quietly."

He gave her a look of irritation. "I know my job." He glanced over at Simon Banks. "The boss okay with this?"

Lisa glanced back to where Banks was still on the phone, pleading with his daughter. Still under the impression that he could use all his persuasive skills to get her to undo decisions that had already been made.

"He's not the most important consideration anymore," Lisa said. "As far as we're concerned, we've got two armed intruders on BSP property who intend domestic terrorism. For all we know, they could have a suicide device. The next time I see them, I want body bags."

■ ■ ■

Two seconds after Alix hung up with her dad, the lights went out. Williams & Crowe had cut the electricity, and they were in the dark now, illuminated only by emergency battery lights that apparently even Williams & Crowe couldn't get access to.

"We need to hide!" Alix said.

Moses looked up at her, his expression somber. "Oh yeah? Where?"

"In…" Alix thought furiously, trying to come up with a way to escape.

Moses smiled tightly at her lack of an answer. "I don't have any more tricks up my sleeve, Alix. I should have had a backup plan for this, but I let myself rush. I screwed this up."

"No. It was my fault. I pushed too fast."

There had to be some way to hide, or sneak past, to get down from the tenth floor…. Alix's mind kept racing, but a more rational part of her knew that Moses was right. She was still just trying to believe. Making up fantasies that weren't real. A little kid fantasy that kept her hoping, even though there was no hope left. The fantasy that if you were doing something for good, you were supposed to be rewarded for it.

"It's over," Moses said. He seemed to be speaking more to himself than to her. "It's over." He looked up, his expression firming. "This doesn't have to be you," he said. "I can give myself up."

"No!"

"Just hear me out! We can hide the drives." He held up the duffel. "I can give myself up. I can tell them it was me who dragged you into this. I can convince them that you didn't have anything to do with it."

"I won't do that, Moses."

"Why not? You could even come back later and get the drives. We can hide the drives, we can save the data—"

"I'm not leaving you!"

Moses glared at her with frustration. "Why not? You know they're going to gas us! Maybe even shoot me if they get a chance. You need to get as far away from me as possible." He put the bag down and started striding back toward the elevators, waving at her not to follow. "You stay back. Once they get me—"

Alix stormed after him. "The hell I will!"

"You don't need to do this!" Moses said. "It's not your fight! You can say I forced you. Say I brainwashed you! It's me they want. So let me take the heat." He reached the elevators and turned to face her. "Try to keep one of the drives and put it out later, maybe." His voice turned pleading. Cajoling. "I can take the heat. We can't hide, but you can hide the drives. You can maybe come back later and get one. You don't have to go down for this."

Alix swallowed. It was so tempting. Just run away. Pretend it hadn't happened...

"No."

"But it's not your fight!"

"The hell it isn't! If they're taking you, they're taking me, too. I'm not leaving you, and I'm not saying it was your idea. I got us into this. This was my fault. I got us into this."

"But—"

"And it is my fight!" Alix fought back tears. "Don't you dare ever say that it isn't my fight!"

Moses paused, taken aback at her outburst. All the argument went out of him. He wrapped her in his arms and pulled her close. "I'm sorry. I didn't mean it that way."

"It is my fight," she said with her face muffled in his chest. "We're together."

"I know. I get it."

The number indicator on the elevator began changing.

L...1...2...

Alix dried her tears on the back of her hand. "Here they come."

3...

4...

Moses was staring into her eyes. "I..."

Alix could feel her heart starting to pound. Williams & Crowe was coming, and all she cared about was Moses's gaze. She pulled him down to kiss her. Kissed him again.

6...

"I'm sorry I got you into this."

"No, I'm sorry I got you into this."

He smiled at that.

7...

They both took an instinctive step back from the elevator.

"Get ready," Moses said.

Alix felt him gripping her hand hard as she watched their fate count upward. She wanted to run. She wanted to believe there was an escape, even though she knew there wasn't.

"We need to get back," she whispered. "We're too close."

His hand was holding hers so hard it felt like it was going to break.

9...

Moses looked over at her one last time, and his eyes were filled with sadness and wonder and regret.

10...

"I love you," he whispered.

The elevator chimed.

They were still holding hands as smoke enveloped them.

42

GUNFIRE RATCHETED FROM THE UPPER stories, distant pop-gun sounds. Glass shattered and spilled from a window, crashing to the street below. The gunfire cracked louder. Smoke began billowing out. Confused shouts echoed from the fire team in Lisa's radio.

"What's our status?" Lisa demanded. "What's our status? Did we get them?"

More gunfire. A confused flurry of shouts.

"Smoke bomb!...A-squad?...A-squad? Timmons? Door's jammed! Ram it!"

"What's going on?" Lisa demanded.

The squad com crackled alive with someone coughing. "No worries. We've got it under control. Our friends had a little surprise for us. We've got a couple people down. We sucked something nasty. We'll need paramedics."

"What about our targets?"

A small hesitation. "Looks like they're going to need medics, too."

"*What?*" Lisa demanded. "They're still alive? I'm going to have your ass—" She glanced over her shoulder at the street. FBI units were rolling up now. Nothing happened in DC without their taking interest.

Worse and worse.

She spun away and cupped her mouth to her com. "What the hell did I tell you?" she whispered fiercely.

"Come on," Timmons protested. "We got them already. They're just kids."

Simon Banks was striding over, his face white.

Lisa snagged George Saamsi. "They're still alive," she hissed.

Saamsi's eyes went from her to Banks. "Finish it," he growled as he went to intercept his partner.

"Clean up the mess," Lisa murmured into her radio. "Do you understand? Clean it up."

News trucks were showing up now. The situation was turning into a goddamn media bloodbath. Worse, the FBI's badges had gotten past her people's blockades. Cops and FBI were swarming toward the building.

"Cops are coming your way," she said. "Finalize this."

"Is that an order?"

"Yes, it's a goddamn order, Timmons! Get rid of those kids!"

Lisa waited, holding her breath. *Come on, Timmons. Get it together.*

Gunfire cracked in her earpiece.

Once. Twice.

On the streets, everyone panicked and scattered for cover, but Lisa sagged with relief.

Her com crackled alive again.

"It's done."

"Good," she snapped. "Now clean up the scene and get the hell out of there."

All around her, the crime scene was crumbling into disarray. Cops and FBI and EMS and Williams & Crowe personnel all sorting through the confusion. Lisa watched with satisfaction as her people made themselves helpfully obstructionistic.

Just a few more minutes.

Med-tech people went in, but her strike teams managed to bog down the cops who had been trying to go in with them. Lisa suppressed a smile. There wouldn't be much left for the cops to reconstruct by the time her people got done in there. It would pass. Timmons's people knew how to clean up a crime scene.

Lisa grabbed Saamsi. "It's done. We're clear." She jerked her head toward the cops and FBI agents. "We're going to need some political cover. Let our clients know. We need this to be forgotten."

"It's clean?"

"Just a couple of crazy activists with guns," Lisa said.

George got on his cell and started working through his contacts. Soon, phones would be ringing all over the city.

Congressional offices, DC police headquarters, and the FBI would all be hearing from patrons and friends. The investigation would die. Someone in George's contact list would take control of the investigation.

And really, what was there to investigate? Tragedies happened all the time. This was just one more example of the radicalization of America. Some lunatic fringe who had drunk the Kool-Aid of Occupy Wall Street rhetoric and gone astray.

An ambulance worker emerged from the building pushing a body bag on a stretcher. Another body followed. The cops started freaking about bodies being moved, which started a larger argument between Williams & Crowe, the cops, and the FBI. Simon Banks saw the body bags and gave a howl of anguish. He fought through the crowd. "Is that my daughter? Is that my daughter?"

He lunged for a body bag, fumbling at the zipper.

"Sir! Sir! Don't!"

Lisa reached the crowd just as Banks got the bag open. He collapsed, sobbing. Alix Banks lay disheveled and blood-soaked inside the black body bag. Pale and gone. An empty husk. Lisa felt a moment of regret.

Sorry, kid. It didn't have to be this way.

Banks was clawing at his daughter's body.

"Alix!"

His hands scrabbled in his daughter's blood. He clutched at her corpse, trying to hold her to him. Lisa was afraid he was going to knock over the stretcher with his crazed grief. She tried to restrain him, but he shook her off with a wild strength. It took her and George Saamsi to finally pull him away.

"Simon! Simon! Let them do their work," George soothed.

News cameras were snapping pictures. *We don't need to be the story.* Lisa waved frantically for the EMS people to keep going.

"I'm sorry. Mr. Banks?" She tugged at his shoulder. "There are news cameras. This is starting to turn into an even bigger problem."

Banks wheeled on her. *"What did you do to my daughter?"* He took a wild swing, and Lisa leaped back. She could practically feel the flashes of the photojournalists as they caught the scene.

George managed to drag him back. "Alix had a gun, Simon!" His voice was urgent. "It's a terrible, terrible tragedy, I know. I'm so sorry about your daughter, but there's nothing Lisa—or anyone—could do." His voice turned soothing again. "What were they supposed to do? She was with a wanted terrorist, and they were armed…." And then, following up, using the words a fellow PR man would understand. "There are cameras running, Simon. We can't become the story here. We need to be going. You need to grieve in private."

Lisa had to hand it to him—George Saamsi was good. She left him to deal with the shattered father and went to see what else she could do to cover up the damage.

The FBI agent in charge snagged her. "What the hell happened here?" the man asked. "Why can't anyone get access to a crime scene?"

Lisa shook her head. "Call your boss. I heard it's a national-security thing. We're supposed to keep things clear until we get an okay from higher up."

"Goddamn private armies," the man muttered, but he got on the phone.

Not a bad operation, overall, Lisa decided. The bodies were disappearing into ambulances, and the crime scene was becoming more and more muddied. In just a little while, all the events that had happened here would be gone. Swept away and forgotten. A small, personal family tragedy among the many larger tragedies that pummeled the nation every day. Not news at all. Maybe a few lines in the Metro section, and then gone for good.

She watched as Saamsi finally managed to get Simon Banks stuffed into a black town car and sent away.

That's right. Nothing to see here. Move along, folks.

Saamsi was coming back across the lawn to her. He was frowning.

"Lisa?"

"Yeah."

"Why is that man standing in the lobby in his underwear?"

"What?" Lisa whirled.

Timmons was stumbling out of the building, stripped down to his tighty-whities.

"What the…?"

"Gas." He choked.

"What gas?" Lisa asked.

He knelt down and retched. "Didn't…get up to the tenth."

466

"What do you mean you didn't make it up to the tenth? You were there. I talked to you!" She grabbed him and pulled him close. "You said you took care of it!"

"Not me." He put his hands on his knees and gagged.

"What's going on here?" George asked.

A cold finger of fear skittered up Lisa's spine as pieces started clicking into place. "Where's the ambulance?" she shouted, casting about wildly.

"What ambulance?"

"The one with the goddamn bodies in it! The one with the goddamn bodies!" She started pushing through the crowd. *There!*

The ambulance was driving slowly toward the curb. Lisa shouted, but in the confusion, no one was listening.

Lisa put her head down and ran.

For a second she thought she'd catch up. The ambulance slowed as it bumped down off the curb and into the street, and Lisa put on a burst of speed. The ambulance made a clumsy turn into its lane and Lisa caught a glimpse of the driver.

A kid?

It was a goddamn kid, barely tall enough to see over the steering wheel. An unruly mop of black curly hair puffed out from beneath the blue uniform cap of an EMT.

He was *grinning* at her.

"Stop that ambulance!" Lisa shouted, but it was no use. The kid flicked on the lights and sirens, and her words were drowned in a flood of emergency noise.

467

43

"HEADS UP, PEOPLE! DEATH BARBIE'S onto us," Tank shouted into the back of the ambulance.

Cynthia cursed. "Already?" She was unzipping her EMS jacket, revealing a flak jacket that read SWAT. "Get them out of their bags," Cynthia said to Kook.

"Kinda of busy saving our asses here," Kook murmured. She was still in her own EMS gear with her laptop propped on her bloody knees. Her fingers left slick dark stains on the keys as she typed.

Cynthia cursed again. Everything was happening too fast. She went to unzip the pair of body bags, revealing the bloody visages of Alix and Moses.

"Romeo and fucking Juliet." She scowled.

Kook shot her a dirty look. "Let's have a little optimism here, all right? I'm trying to work."

"Yeah. Optimism. Got it." She started digging in her raid kit for syringes.

Optimism optimism optimism.

The ambulance was slowing. The front door opened, and Adam piled into the cab, still wearing his Williams & Crowe SWAT gear, and hauling a duffel bag. The ambulance accelerated again. Adam grabbed for support, nearly falling over as Tank gunned the engine.

"We've got Shortstuff driving?" he complained.

"I've got my license," Tank shot back. "Quit whining."

"Only because Kook hacked the DMV," Adam muttered as he stumbled into the back of the ambulance. They bounced over another curb, and everyone grabbed for handholds.

"Watch it!" Cynthia shouted. "I'm trying to work back here!'

"Sorry!" Tank called back.

"What's the rush?" Adam asked. "I thought you or Kook was going to be driving."

"Death Barbie's sending her troops after us any second," Cynthia said.

"Already?"

"Can't expect everything to go perfectly," Kook muttered.

Optimism optimism optimism.

Moses's zipper was jammed. Cynthia swore. "I don't have time for this! Adam, get this open." She turned and went back to rummaging in her raid kit while Adam fumbled and fought with the zipper. "Jeez, he looks terrible."

"Just get him out of the bag more. I need a shoulder." She finally found her syringe and uncapped it. Squirted clear fluid into the air. She took a deep breath.

You can do this.

"Are you sure this is going to work?" Adam asked.

Cynthia paused with the needle in her hand. "You're asking now?"

"I'm just the muscle here. You're the one who read all the drug studies."

The ambulance squealed around another corner, and they all scrambled for support.

"Sorry!" Tank called before they had a chance to complain. "We're almost to the Beltway!"

"Is it going to work?" Adam asked again.

"Just hold Moses still," Cynthia ordered. "I don't want him bouncing around while I stick him."

Adam gripped Moses's bloody shoulders. "Your hands are shaking," he observed.

Cynthia shot him a glare. "No," she said. "They're not."

She slid the syringe into Moses's arm. *Nice and easy.* She pressed the plunger, and fluid flowed out of the syringe.

"How long is it going to take?" Adam asked.

"I don't know. Probably a couple of minutes."

"You don't know? I thought you were the doctor here."

"I'm pre-med, asshole. Anyway, no one would know. It's all in the drug interactions and dose." She was already fumbling for another syringe and popping the cap.

"Get Alix ready."

Adam unzipped Alix's body bag the rest of the way and got a shoulder exposed.

Cynthia paused, on the verge of sticking her. It was horrifying to see Alix inert and smeared with blood this way. Nothing like the girl she'd known at Seitz. She looked like some kind of corpse bride. So pale.

"Snow White," Adam murmured.

"Cyn was thinking more Romeo and Juliet," Kook said.

"Talk about pessimistic."

"That's what I said."

Optimistic optimistic optimistic.

"Okay," Cynthia said. "Let's see if we can make Snow White wake up." She buried the needle into Alix's flesh and shot her full of drugs. She knelt back, waiting. In Cynthia's mind, all she could see were long biochemical chains interacting. *It should work*, she thought.

Nothing happened. She checked Moses. No change. She pressed her fingers to his cheek.

Did he feel colder?

"Give them another shot," Adam said.

"I don't have any other shots."

They waited, staring at the two inert and bloody bodies peeled out of black bags.

Two more casualties they could lay at the feet of the Doubt Factory.

44

ALIX CAME AWAKE RETCHING. She rolled over and nearly fell off the stretcher and then retched again. She blinked in the light. She was swaying. No, *everything* was swaying.

And *swerving*.

She was dimly aware of someone else gagging and coughing. The sound made her retch again. She blinked in the light and found Cynthia and Adam peering over her.

"What the—?" Alix recoiled.

Cynthia straightened, smiling. "Welcome back from the dead, girlfriend."

"What are you doing here?"

"We thought we'd kidnap you again," Adam said. "You know, for old time's sake."

A sudden terror made her lurch upright. "Moses! Where's Moses?"

"Here," a voice croaked.

Alix whirled to find Moses lying beside her on a stretcher, looking wasted and covered with blood.

"Oh my God, what happened to you?" Alix ran her hands frantically over his body. "Where are you hurt?"

"It's fake blood," Cynthia said.

"For effect," Adam added helpfully. "Needed to make you look good and dead."

"But…but…"

Alix tried to take it all in. She was in an ambulance, half-zipped into a body bag, and she was covered with sticky blood. Her hands, her arms. Her hair was matted with it.

She stared around herself, trying to put everything together. Cynthia and Adam and Kook, everyone wearing SWAT and EMS gear. Makeup that made them look older.

Cynthia and Adam and Kook cracked up. "You should see your face," Kook said.

"What am I missing?" someone called from up front. *Tank?*

"Nothing. We're all good," Moses called forward.

Alix whirled on Moses. "Is this another one of your damn pranks? Did you set me up again?"

"Whoa! Not me. Not this time." Moses was slowly dragging himself out of his body bag. Unzipping it and then crawling unsteadily onto the ambulance's bench. "This wasn't my gig."

"It was mostly Tank," Kook said from where she was perched with her laptop and a pair of DJ headphones around her neck. "He was worried that Wonderboy here was going to do something stupid." She looked up briefly from her laptop, frowning. "None of us expected you to be the stupid one, though. You about got the two of you killed."

"You were following us?"

"What am I, an amateur?" Kook made a scornful face. "We bugged the factory before we left. Just had to listen in every once in a while. Sure enough, the stupid came up, just like Tank thought it would."

"You were listening to us?"

"You and your sexytime." Kook glanced up from her keyboard. "It would have saved me a lot of late nights if you would have just gotten to the talking instead of all that grunting and groaning."

Alix could feel herself blushing. Moses looked uncomfortable as well.

Adam clapped her on the shoulder. "Don't worry. I mostly made them fast-forward through the embarrassing parts. Straight people getting it on…" He made a face. "I mean, I guess it's fine. If you're into that kind of thing. But it would have made our lives a lot easier if you'd actually talked more about your plans while you were at the factory. We couldn't get all the details we needed. We didn't have time."

"So… how did you know we'd be here now?"

They all exchanged glances. "Your brother."

"Jonah?"

"We heard you saying to Moses that he knew about you both. We got the rest of the details we needed out of him."

"But...he wouldn't have..."

"Oh, he was a pain in the ass about it. He wouldn't help unless he could come along."

"He's *here*?"

"God, no. Waiting in the van, as soon as we switch vehicles. He's too useful to let anyone see him. As soon as we wrap this up, he's going right back home to keep an eye on your dad and George Saamsi for us. That kid is a piece of work."

Alix leaned back, stunned. Jonah. Of course. She should have known that he would never stay put. "I can't believe..."

"Believe it, girl." Cynthia was smiling. She gave Adam a shove and said, "Go up and drive before Tank gets us killed."

Adam went forward. A second later the ambulance swayed as he took the wheel. Tank came back to join them.

The boy's expression turned solemn when he saw their condition. "You made it," he said to Moses.

"Thanks to you, I hear."

Alix looked uncertainly from Moses to the small boy. They weren't anything alike, and yet some part of them seemed almost as if they were twins. Older and younger versions of an experience she knew she would never fully understand.

Two orphans who had lost everything.

Tank scuffed the floor with a shoe. "Knew you were going to try something stupid."

"I thought you were done with me."

"Still family," Tank said. He looked up. "You're the only family I got." His face looked stony solemn, and then, abruptly, the facade cracked and he lunged into Moses's arms, wracked with terrified sobs. "I can't lose any more family," Tank said. "I can't."

Moses was taken aback. He wrapped his arms about the boy, feeling Tank's shaking. "Hey, bro, I'm sorry," he whispered. "I'm sorry, bro. Didn't mean to scare you. Didn't mean to scare you at all."

Tank wiped his eyes. "Can't lose any more, you know?"

"I know," Moses said solemnly. "I get it. I won't do anything stupid. I'm not going anywhere."

"I still don't get it," Alix said. "How did you get us here? The elevator opened and—"

"We gassed you," Cynthia said apologetically. "We gassed the Williams and Crowe guys who were coming up to get you, and then Adam took their place, and we came up and gassed you, too. After that, it was just about staging and calling up the reinforcements."

"I got to shoot off some sweet guns, too," Adam called back. "Don't forget that!"

Cynthia pressed on. "By the time everyone else had gotten up there, you were dead, and they were focusing on cleaning up the scene. The only tense moment was when Adam had to meet up with the rest of the Williams and Crowe people who were stuck hiking up the stairwells. We were afraid someone would make him take off his SWAT helmet and get a good look at him before we could get your bodies out. But everyone was so freaked out by the other guys that we gassed that it was just a matter of wrapping you in body bags and pretending to be the friendly neighborhood ambulance association wheeling you out."

"That was actually nerve-racking," Kook said. "I wasn't expecting your dad to be right at the doors when we came out with you. Lucky he was so focused on you. I thought he'd recognize Cynthia, even with medical glasses."

"My dad was there?"

Cynthia nodded. "Yeah. I was just glad you looked as dead as you did. He was all over you. You never could have faked through that."

"Was he mad?"

Cynthia looked at her incredulously. "He thought you were *dead*, Alix. He was a wreck. Crying and yelling at George Saamsi and Death Barbie. It was a mess."

Alix swallowed, trying to decide how she felt about the news. Her father was stricken with grief that she'd died. Some part of her felt for his distress, but she couldn't quite make herself feel sorry. He'd helped kill so many people, and he felt bad only now? Simon Banks cared only when the person dying was his own child. He didn't feel bad about Moses's parents or Tank and Azicort. Dad only felt bad when it was personal to him. Alix was interested to discover that she didn't have much sympathy for him. Mostly, it felt right to her. *Maybe now you understand*, she thought.

"Where did you get the gas?" Moses was asking.

Kook smirked. "It's Azicort."

Cynthia was nodding. "When you absolutely, positively want to give someone a near-fatal coma, most doctors choose

477

Azicort. We had a whole vat of the stuff from the rat raid. Tank rigged a blower. The only real problem was not knowing how much we were dosing you with." She peered closely at them. "You seem okay, though."

"The more I hear, the less I want to know," Moses groaned.

A new fear gripped Alix. "What about the files? We left the files!"

"No! I got them!" Adam called from up front. "You can thank Williams and Crowe for that. I would have missed the bag, but it turned up while we were waiting for the bodies to get cleaned out. And seeing as I was so helpful, I volunteered to take it down to Death Barbie."

Alix slumped back, relieved. "It worked then. We did it."

"I wouldn't be so sure of that," Kook said. She had her headphones pinched between ear and shoulder, and she was typing madly on her blood-smeared laptop. "Our friends just put our description out on the police bands."

Cynthia hurried over to listen in. "Hell." Her face turned hard. "I didn't think Williams and Crowe would risk involving outsiders."

Kook motioned for Alix. "You got your phone on you?"

"I don't…" She felt her pockets. "Yeah. Here."

"You want to call Death Barbie?"

Alix's skin crawled. "Why?"

"I've got an idea." Kook's eyes were positively glowing. "And it'll be way better if she gets a call from the dead."

"Okay." Alix dialed.

Lisa picked up almost instantly. "Who is this?" Her voice was breathless.

"You don't recognize my voice?"

"Alix?"

Her words were suddenly hesitant.

"Tell her to call off the goons or you go public," Cynthia whispered. She and Kook were messing with the laptop.

"Go public with what?"

"Just tell her!"

When Alix relayed the message, Lisa laughed contemptuously. "You're just kids."

"Now play this," Kook said, and held up her laptop.

"Hang on. I've got something for you," Alix said.

Kook pressed Play. Alix heard a voice that sounded a lot like Adam's issuing from the speakers.

A conversation back and forth.

"Come on. They're just kids!"

And then Lisa's clipped tones.

"Finish it. Clean up the mess."

A pair of gunshots echoed.

Alix flinched involuntarily.

"It's done."

"Good. Now clean up the scene and get the hell out of there."

Alix felt a sudden, cold rage.

She took the phone back. "Call off your dogs, Lisa, or I'll send this to every single cop and every single news organization in the city. You might know how to bury some things, but I can make this go viral. If you keep messing with us, I guarantee I can make you famous, at least until someone who's more important than you decides you need to disappear. It sounds like you people know a lot about making sure lips stay sealed. Your choice. Either you back off or I make you the top of the news cycle."

She hung up without waiting for an answer.

"How long to our car switch?" Cynthia called up to Adam.

"Van's waiting in a parking garage at the next exit."

They all waited in tense silence. Kook was listening to her headphones. Abruptly she broke into a wide smile.

"False alarm. They're sending out a new description. The emergency vehicle is a false alarm."

A spontaneous cheer erupted in the back of the ambulance. Alix slumped against Moses, relieved.

"Nice," he murmured. "You sounded downright dangerous."

"That's because I am."

Moses laughed and wrapped an arm around her and pulled her close. Their blood stuck together.

"Yuck," Cynthia said. "You two really are a mess."

She was right. Blood soaked their clothes, smeared their skin, and matted their hair. But as Alix let her head rest on Moses's sticky, bloody shoulder, she thought that she had never felt so clean.

EPILOGUE

Dear Dad,

By the time you read this, our lives will have changed so much that we may not even be the same people anymore.

I'm sure you think I'm crazy for doing this, and I know you feel like I've betrayed you, but I finally understood that even though you were always willing to talk to me, you weren't actually willing to listen.

I know you'll say that there's no law against the kind of work you do and that everyone deserves a voice, and, for sure, I can't think of any way to stop companies like yours from existing, and I definitely can't think of any way to make companies like yours just shut up.

I mean, free speech is free speech, right?

Anybody can get up and say anything. Anybody can get up and twist and lie and exaggerate and obfuscate. And for money, people like you and George will. But if that's what you're willing to do, then you should be famous for it. If that's your job, you should be proud of it.

You're the Doubt Factory.

You're the place where big companies go when they need the truth confused. You're the place companies go when they need science to say what's profitable, instead of what's true. You're the place companies go when they need to convince people that up is down, and blue is red, and night is day, and wrong is right.

And I can't change that.

But it's funny how you also don't want people to know about you or know what you do. You never want people to see you. I mean, if you've got free speech, it seems like you should be standing right by it, saying it loud and proud, with your name and your clients' names attached. Not some front organization. Not some fake science journal. Not some fake research group.

You.

I realize that there's nothing I can do to change who you are, and probably can't change what you do, but I can change whether people see you.

I'm uploading your client files today, and even though your clients are going to make the first headlines, I think you're going to turn out to be the story.

Congratulations. The Doubt Factory is going to be famous.

Love,
Alix

PS—Tell Mom I'm sorry for making her worry, and tell Jonah that I miss him and that the Xbox is still bugged.

Alix folded the letter and stuck it in the envelope and put a stamp on it. She'd drop it in a mailbox in some no-name town. Some nice place without any surveillance cameras on its streetlights. The letter would eventually find its way to him, long after she'd moved on.

She tucked her black-dyed hair into a ball cap and stepped out of the motel.

Moses was leaning against the rail, waiting. "All set?"

"Yeah."

Down in the parking lot, Kook honked the van's horn impatiently.

"Next stop, Gulf of Mexico!" Adam called, waving up at them. "All aboard!"

"A beach vacation." Alix sighed theatrically. "Just what I've always wanted."

Moses laughed. "Well...just until the heat dies down."

Alix glanced over. "Does that mean we're going to go after the money anonymizers? The ones I told you about?"

"Well, like you said, there's an awful lot of cash flowing through them. American Petroleum Institute...Donors Trust...A lot of money funding a lot of doubt...and no one knows where that money's coming from."

"I don't like anonymous money."

"Yeah. I think it would be worth shining some light and seeing who's paying for doubt these days."

"You think Kook can get us in?"

"She says she can."

"I don't want this one to be like the last time. We get in and we get out and we have a real backup plan—"

"It'll be fine." He was looking down at the parking lot, where the rest of the crew was out of the van: Tank and Cyn and Adam and Kook, all of them waving their arms impatiently. "We aren't alone this time."

Kook leaned on the horn again.

"Family's getting restless," Moses observed, smiling.

"Are we going or not?" Cyn shouted.

"Are we?" Moses asked, holding out his hand.

"Yeah," Alix said, sliding her hand into his. "We're going."

ACKNOWLEDGMENTS

I'd like to thank a number of people who inspired me, supported me, and kicked me to make this a better book.

Holly Black, Malinda Lo, Sarah Rees Brennan, Cassandra Clare, and Cristi Jacques helped me brainstorm the heart of this book while on retreat in Mexico, and sparked the creation of many of the characters who populate this story. I don't think I've ever had so much fun planning a novel. Other people who provided support, problem solving, and detail fixing along the way include Tobias Buckell, Rob Ziegler, Charlie Finlay, and Ken Liu. Diane Budy read early drafts and cheerfully acted as a reading lab rat. My wife, Anjula, took time out of her own busy schedule to read through a draft of the manuscript and provide responses, and she was immensely encouraging and supportive as this book crashed toward deadline. I owe her more than I can say, and I'm grateful for every day I have with her.

I am particularly grateful to the many people at Little, Brown Books for Young Readers who believed that a book about public relations was worth supporting, and I'd especially like to thank my editor, Andrea Spooner, and assistant editor, Deirdre Jones, whose help and wisdom and candid assessments gave me better insight into this book, and whose dedication and willingness to work too many long hours helped me push this book through to completion. As in all things, details matter, so I owe a tip of the hat to my fact-checker, Christoph Berendes, for saving me from a number of embarrassing gaffes, but most especially for making sure that I didn't confuse livers and kidneys. If there are remaining errors in this book, they are my errors solely.

Much gratefulness also goes to my friend Michelle Nijhuis, whose article for *Pacific Standard*, "The Doubt Makers," jump-started my interest in this topic many years ago, and whose guidance and research suggestions for this book were invaluable. I'd also like to thank Dr. Theo Colborn and Dr. Frederick vom Saal for a long-ago conversation in which they shared their experiences as science researchers who had to battle the product-defense professionals. On a personal note, I'd also like to thank the many scientists, journalists, and public servants who continue to drag the ever-evolving tactics of the doubt industry into the light.

Finally, I'd like to thank my much-neglected son, Arjun. I swear, now that this book is done, we'll have more time to read together.